E.R. PUNSHON
BROUGHT TO LIGHT

ERNEST ROBERTSON PUNSHON was born in London in 1872.

At the age of fourteen he started life in an office. His employers soon informed him that he would never make a really satisfactory clerk, and he, agreeing, spent the next few years wandering about Canada and the United States, endeavouring without great success to earn a living in any occupation that offered. Returning home by way of working a passage on a cattle boat, he began to write. He contributed to many magazines and periodicals, wrote plays, and published nearly fifty novels, among which his detective stories proved the most popular and enduring.

He died in 1956.

The Bobby Owen Mysteries

1. Information Received
2. Death among the Sunbathers
3. Crossword Mystery
4. Mystery Villa
5. Death of a Beauty Queen
6. Death Comes to Cambers
7. The Bath Mysteries
8. Mystery of Mr. Jessop
9. The Dusky Hour
10. Dictator's Way
11. Comes a Stranger
12. Suspects – Nine
13. Murder Abroad
14. Four Strange Women
15. Ten Star Clues
16. The Dark Garden
17. Diabolic Candelabra
18. The Conqueror Inn
19. Night's Cloak
20. Secrets Can't be Kept
21. There's a Reason for Everything
22. It Might Lead Anywhere
23. Helen Passes By
24. Music Tells All
25. The House of Godwinsson
26. So Many Doors
27. Everybody Always Tells
28. The Secret Search
29. The Golden Dagger
30. The Attending Truth
31. Strange Ending
32. Brought to Light
33. Dark is the Clue
34. Triple Quest
35. Six Were Present

E.R. PUNSHON

BROUGHT TO LIGHT

With an introduction
by Curtis Evans

DEAN STREET PRESS

Published by Dean Street Press 2017

Copyright © 1950, 1954 E.R. Punshon

Introduction copyright © 2017 Curtis Evans

All Rights Reserved

Published by licence, issued under the
UK Orphan Works Licensing Scheme.

First published in 1954 by Victor Gollancz

Cover by DSP

ISBN 978 1 911579 07 6

www.deanstreetpress.co.uk

Detective Stories, the Detection Club and Death:
The Final Years of E. R. Punshon

> ... but, they dead,
> Death has so many doors to let out life,
> I will not long survive them.
>
> *The Custom of the Country* (c. 1619-23; 1647)
> JOHN FLETCHER AND PHILLIP MASSINGER

WHEN IN 1949 E.R. Punshon published *So Many Doors*, his twenty-sixth Bobby Owen detective novel, the Englishman was seventy-seven years old, with nearly a half-century of published novels behind him and a comparatively scant seven years of life and letters remaining before him. 1901, the year of the appearance of Punshon's first novel, *Earth's Great Lord*, saw the death of Queen Victoria, the long reigning granddaughter of King George III for whom a regal age of European global dominion has been named; while 1949, a year during which a convalescent Europe was still bleakly recovering from a world war that had reduced much of its civilization to ashes and rubble, saw the testing by the USSR of its first atomic bomb and the proclamation of the formation of the People's Republic of China. The world was changing with a fearsome fleetness that not merely old men who had first glimpsed light in the Victorian era were finding hard to follow.

Rapidly changing too was the craft of crime and mystery fiction that E.R. Punshon had long practiced (this admittedly a minor thing compared to unsettling phenomena like armed revolution and atom splitting). Like the once seemingly imperishable British Empire, the hegemony of the between-the-wars "Golden Age" clue-puzzle detective novel was breaking asunder, under pressure from increasingly popular rival forms of mystery fiction, such as hard-boiled, noir, psychological suspense and espionage. Already stalked by Raymond Chandler's famous gumshoe, Philip Marlowe, as well as ill-humored and hard-drinking would-be Marlowe doppelgangers like Mickey Spillane's brutish Mike Hammer, Punshon's well-born English policeman Bobby Owen, along with other of his surviving gentlemanly detective colleagues from the era of classic crime fiction, soon found himself in the sights of no less deadly a professional killer than James Bond. Agent 007's creator, Ian Fleming, who cited as his literary influences Raymond Chandler, Dashiell Hammett, Eric Ambler and Graham Greene, published his first Bond spy novel, *Casino Royale*, in the United Kingdom in 1953, where it enjoyed immediate popular and critical success. In the United States, where the novel appeared in 1954, the same year as Raymond Chandler's much-lauded *The Long Goodbye*, *Time* magazine wryly declared that "Bond . . . might well be [Philip] Marlowe's younger brother, except that he never takes coffee for a bracer, just one large martini laced with vodka."

Upon the publication of *So Many Doors* in the UK and the US (in the latter country it would prove the last Punshon mystery published during the author's lifetime), crime fiction reviewers deemed the novel and its author representatives of a vanished era. "The twenties were the plotter's heyday (consider Freeman Wills Crofts, J.J. Connington, Dorothy L. Sayers)," observed the Democratic-Socialist *London Tribune* in its review of the "well-plotted" and "studiously told" *So Many Doors*, "and to the twenties, in spirit at least, belongs Mr. Punshon." In the United States, Anthony Boucher, dean of American mystery critics, allowed in the *New York Times Book Review* that the narration of *So Many Doors* was "leisurely"; yet, after noting the seventeenth-century English stage derivation of the novel's title, he approvingly added that there "is something Elizabethan, even Jacobean, about the obscure destinies that drive [Punshon's] obsessed and tormented characters, and about the frightful violence that concludes the story." Punshon, it seemed, still had something to say in the harried and hectic atomic age, when crime fiction reviewers and readers alike seemed increasingly to believe that brevity was the soul of death.

* * * * *

To his death in 1956 E.R. Punshon maintained a loyal following in the United Kingdom among readers who staunchly adhered to the strict standard of fair play puzzle plotting associated with Golden Age detective fiction. During the Fifties the aging but seemingly indefatigable author, who still lived quietly with his wife Sarah at their house at 23 Nimrod Road, Streatham, produced, through the medium of his prestigious longtime publisher Victor Gollancz, nine new mystery titles-- *Everybody Always Tells* (1950), *The Secret Search* (1951), The Golden Dagger (1951), *The Attending Truth* (1952), *Strange Ending* (1953), *Brought to Light* (1954), *Dark Is the Clue* (1955), *Triple Quest* (1955) and *Six Were Present* (1956)— that detailed the final criminal investigations of his longtime series police detective, Bobby Owen, now risen to the august rank of Commander (unattached), Metropolitan Police. Additionally Punshon continued to remain active in his cherished Detection Club, a London-based social organization of distinguished detective novelists, in which the author had been inducted, along with Anthony Gilbert and Gladys Mitchell, in 1933, three years after the Club's founding, joining such luminaries from the crime writing world as G.K. Chesterton, Dorothy L. Sayers, Agatha Christie, E.C. Bentley, Anthony Berkeley, R. Austin Freeman and Freeman Wills Crofts.

Like other British institutions the Detection Club from 1939 to 1945 bore the bitter burdens of war, including the devastating Nazi air raids known collectively as "the Blitz." When the Club revived its meetings and annual dinners in 1946, it became immediately apparent that time had wrought cruel changes with its membership. On seeing his brother and sister detective novelists again at the Club premises after the long interval of war years, John Dickson Carr, a comparative stripling at the age of forty, recalled that he had been "shocked" by their appearance, which he had found decidedly "greyer and more worn."

By 1946 eight of the original twenty-eight Detection Club members, including G.K. Chesterton, R. Austin Freeman and Helen Simpson, had passed away and many other members were now elderly and inactive. Several more members would expire over the next few years. Even the formerly quite engaged Freeman Wills Crofts and John Rhode (Cecil John Charles Street), now in their sixties and living in the country, became markedly less involved with Club affairs, as did an increasingly infirm Henry Wade (the landed baronet Henry Lancelot Aubrey-Fletcher). For his part, John Dickson Carr, deeming British life under postwar conditions and the governance of the Labour party intolerable, would in 1948 depart for his native United States. Besides Punshon, only Christie, John Rhode and Henry Wade, among original members, and Anthony Gilbert, Gladys Mitchell, Margery Allingham, John Dickson Carr, Nicholas Blake, Christopher Bush and E.C.R. Lorac, among the smaller number of Thirties inductees, remained substantially active as crime writers into the 1950s. Of these Lorac and Wade, like Punshon, would not survive the decade, and another, John Rhode, would barely outlast it.

Clearly some new blood was badly needed. During Punshon's remaining span of life the aged and ailing Detection Club received transfusions, so to speak, from seventeen new members. Although with the deaths of Baroness Emma Orczy and A.E.W. Mason (in 1947 and 1948 respectively), Punshon became the oldest surviving member of the Detection Club, the author, who served as Club treasurer between 1946 and 1949, during the postwar years remained extensively involved in Club affairs, actively participating in hearty debates concerning prospective new members, like Christianna Brand, Michael Innes, Michael Gilbert, Elizabeth Ferrars and Julian Symons, as to whether or not they practiced fair play and sufficiently respected the King's (later Queen's) English, the Club's chief requirements for induction. (These debates are chronicled in detail in my CADS booklet *Was Corinne's Murder Clued? The Detection Club and Fair Play, 1930-1953*.)

In 1949 Punshon found himself at odds over the matter of new enrollments with the man who unquestionably was the Club's crankiest and most cantankerous member: Anthony Berkeley, famed author of *The Poisoned Chocolates Case* (1928) and, under the pseudonym Francis Iles, of *Malice Aforethought* (1931) and *Before the Fact* (1932), three of the best regarded British crime novels from the Golden Age. In April Berkeley wrote a provocative letter to Punshon in which he claimed that as the Club's "First Freeman" he possessed blanket veto power over prospective members, despite the fact that he no longer served on the membership committee. During the early days of the Detection Club, Berkeley had observed at a meeting that the Club had two "Freemans" as members (R. Austin Freeman and Freeman Wills Crofts), and he pronounced that as the person who had originally suggested forming the Club he would be its "First Freeman." To this suggestion everyone else had laughingly assented, taking the office as a joke; yet now, nearly two decades later, it seemed that Berkeley had not been joking.

Incensed by Berkeley's gambit and the rude language in which he had couched it, Punshon wrote Sayers, enclosing his antagonist's "offensive" letter (which evidently has not survived) and warning that "[Berkeley] intends to make some sort of fuss." Punshon speculated that "possibly it is better to take no notice [of the letter], except perhaps as regards the absurd claim of his to hold some special position as what he calls 'First Freeman.' I have a vague idea that once before he put forward a claim to be a permanent member of the [membership] committee on the same ground." He noted dryly that while he had forborne responding to the specifics of Berkeley's letter, he had sent the notoriously tightfisted "First Freeman" a reminder that his annual membership fee was due, to which he had received no reply.

"Bother AB!" responded Sayers in a letter to Punshon that she composed the day after receiving his missive. "I do wish he was not so rude and silly." She entirely concurred with Punshon's recollection of the once comical but now rather annoying office of First Freeman and added resignedly: "If he tries to make a fuss at the meeting, the committee will have to cope; but I hope he will have more sense. I am sorry he should have written to you so impertinently."

By the summer of 1949 the First Freeman's irksome machinations had been checked--but only, Punshon feared, for the moment. With considerable skepticism Punshon wrote Sayers, "I gather the reconciliation with Anthony Berkeley is now complete and the hatchet well and truly buried. Until dug up again." Sayers, who soon would succeed E.C. Bentley as President of the Detection Club, advised members to tread carefully around Berkeley's tender sensibilities. "Let a (more or less) sleeping Berkeley lie," she urged. Nevertheless Sayers agreed with Punshon that the Club members would have to keep Berkeley off the membership committee, because were he to be on it the Club would "never get any new member . . . he turns them all down on sight." She lamented that "Berkeley is a difficult man to work with."

Sayers found working with Punshon, whose detective fiction she had enthusiastically promoted as a book reviewer for the *Sunday Times* between 1933 and 1935, to be an altogether more pleasant experience. Surviving correspondence between the two authors suggests that Punshon was, along with Anthony Gilbert (Lucy Beatrice Malleson), the Detection Club member with whom Sayers got along most amicably at this time. The two communicated fairly frequently during the postwar years, chatting not only about Detection Club matters, but more personal affairs as well.

As treasurer of the Detection Club, Punshon gave his attention to matters large--such as any taxes the Club might have to pay to a revenue-hungry British government ("we have to remember that we may be dropped on by the Income tax people")—and matters small. As an example of the latter, Punshon advised Sayers in December 1948 that the Club should give a "small Christmas present" to Mrs. Buchanan, caretaker of the Club premises at 12 Kingly Street, Soho. ("A room and loo in a clergy house," Christianna Brand bluntly recalled of the locale.) Although payment for services was included with the rent, Punshon pointed out that "services included are very often badly neglected and so far as I have noticed in this case they have been quite well carried out and the room always seemed neat and tidy." "[E]ven in this sordid age," he reflected with characteristic gentle irony, "a few thanks and expressions of satisfaction . . . often please as much as gifts—at any rate if accompanied by a gift." A few days later Sayers gave Mrs. Buchanan a £1 Christmas tip (about £32 today).

Sadly, Punshon suffered a serious setback to his health in August 1949, not long after a busy summer that saw the English publication of *So Many Doors*, his nettlesome skirmish with Anthony Berkeley and the annual Detection Club dinner at the

Hotel Café Royal, Piccadilly. (Recorded treasurer Punshon of the latter event: "L87/9/9—Miss Gilbert paid L6/9/4 for after dinner drinks. I gave the head waiter L1. Total 95/9/1. Great success.") After writing Freeman Wills Crofts and John Rhode to inform them about the Berkeley brouhaha, Punshon went into hospital for an operation. In September Sayers wrote Punshon that she was pleased to hear from his wife that he was "making a really good convalescence," adding: "We will miss you greatly at the October meeting, but of course you must have a good long holiday and get quite fit."

By early November Punshon, recuperating at Christopher Bush's house, Little Horsepen, near Rye in East Sussex, was able to report that he was "very much better," though the same month he resigned as Detection Club treasurer. (Christopher Bush succeeded him to the office.) Later that month Punshon wrote Sayers from Bournemouth, where he was taking a "long rest." He wished her good fortune with the recently published Penguin paperback edition of her translation of Dante's *Inferno*, remarking, "I don't know any translation of Dante except the old one [1805] by [Henry Francis] Cary, and that was a fairly pedestrian performance." He also heaped praise on Penguin's ambitious paperback publishing scheme, deeming it a "very praiseworthy attempt to turn us into a nation of book buyers instead of borrowers. A Real Revolution—if they can bring it off." Punshon had particular reason to applaud Penguin's effort, as the previous year the company had issued a pair of 1930s Bobby Owen mystery titles as paperbacks. (Three more titles would follow in the next half-dozen years.)

Punshon remained active in Detection Club affairs in 1950, though he urged that Michael Gilbert be tapped to replace him on the membership committee. "Would [Anthony Berkeley] take the suggestion as an insult," he sarcastically queried Sayers, obviously still smarting over the events of the previous year. Punshon also participated in evaluations of the work of proposed new member Julian Symons (1912-1994), one of Britain's new wave of consciously self-styled "crime writers." Of Symons's recent *Bland Beginning* (1949), a novel based, as was Punshon's own *Comes a Stranger* (1938), on the Thomas J. Wise literary forgery scandal, Punshon wrote Sayers, "On the whole I should be inclined to say 'yes,' even though I think the character drawing deplorable and the construction and final explanation a bit shaky. But he does manage to produce a readable story and it is certainly an intelligent and clever book."

By 1952, Punshon's health had declined to the point where he felt unable to attend the Detection Club's annual dinner. "[A]s they used to say in the war, the situation on the (health) front has deteriorated," he mordantly wrote Sayers, adding ominously that he had scheduled an "appointment with a specialist." The next year, however, both he and his wife, now octogenarians, managed to make it to the dinner, much to the pleasure of Sayers, who promised, "you shan't be bothered with the [initiation] ceremony at all—there will be plenty of people to carry candles." Sayers promised the Punshons good seats at the High Table to hear philosopher Bertrand Russell speak, and in a contemporary letter Christianna Brand somewhat cattily reported observing Mrs. Punshon sitting "terribly close to the speakers so as not to miss a word, and sound asleep."

Sometime in the 1950s an increasingly fragile Punshon took a dreadful tumble down the landing steps at the Detection Club premises at Kingly Street, an event Christianna Brand vividly recollected many years later in 1979, with what seems rather callous amusement on her part:

My last memory, or the most abiding one, of the club room in the clergy house, was of an evening when two members were initiated there instead of at the annual dinner [possibly Glyn Carr and Roy Vickers, 1955 initiates]. As they left, they stepped over the body of an elderly gentleman lying with his head in a pool of blood, just outside the door. . . . dear old Mr. Punshon, E.R. Punshon, tottering up the stone stair steps upon his private business, had fallen all the way down again and severely lacerated his scalp. My [physician] husband, groaning, dealt with all but the gore, which remained in a slowly congealing pool upon the clergy house floor. . . . However, Miss Sayers had, predictably, just the right guest for such an event, a small, brisk lady, delighted to cope. She came out on the landing and stood for a moment peering down at the unlovely mess. Not myself one to delight in hospital matters, I hovered ineffectively as much as possible in the rear. She made up her mind. "Well, I think we can manage *that* all right. Can you find me a tablespoon?"

The club room was unaccountably lacking in tablespoons. I went out and diffidently offered a large fork. "A fork? Oh, well . . ." She bent again and studied the pool of gore. "I think we can manage," she said again, cheerfully. "It's splendidly clotted."

I returned once more to the club room and closed the door; and I can only report that when it opened again, not a sign remained of any blood, anywhere. "I thought," said my husband as we took our departure before even worse might befall, "that in your oath you foreswore vampires." "She was only a *guest*," I said apologetically.

"Dear old Mr. Punshon," no vampire he, passed through a door to death in his 84th year on 23 October 1956, four years after his elder brother, Robert Halket Punshon. On 25 January 1957 the widowed Sarah Punshon presented Dorothy L. Sayers with a copy of her husband's thirty-fifth and final Bobby Owen mystery, the charmingly retrospective *Six Were Present*. "He would like to think that you had one," wrote Sarah, warmly thanking Sayers "for your appreciation of my husband's work during his writing life" and wistfully adding that she would miss her "occasional visits to the club evenings." Sayers obligingly invited Sarah to the next Detection Club dinner as her guest, but Sarah died in May, having survived her longtime spouse by merely seven months. Sayers herself would not outlast the year. As Christianna Brand rather flippantly reports, Sayers was discovered, just a week before Christmas, collapsed dead "at the foot of the stairs in her house surrounded by bereaved cats." Having ascended and descended the stairs after a busy day of shopping, Sayers had discovered her own door to death.

* * * * *

Dorothy L. Sayers's literary reputation has risen ever higher in the years since her demise, with modern authorities like the esteemed late crime writer P.D. James particularly lauding

Sayers's ambitious penultimate Peter Wimsey mystery, *Gaudy Night*--a novel E.R. Punshon himself had lavishly praised in his review column in the *Manchester Guardian*--as not only a great detective novel but a great novel, with no delimiting qualification. Although he was one of Sayers's favorite crime writers, Punshon was not so fortunate with his own reputation, with his work falling into unmerited neglect for more than a half-century after his death. With the reprinting by Dean Street Press of Punshon's complete set of Bobby Owen mystery investigations—chronicled in 35 novels, five short stories and a radio play—this long period of neglect now happily has ended, however, allowing a major writer from the Golden Age of detective fiction a golden opportunity to receive, six decades after his death, his full and lasting due.

Short Stories by E.R. Punshon

Five Bobby Owen detective short stories complement E.R. Punshon's 35 Bobby Owen detective novels, and these short stories are reprinted, one to a volume, with the new Dean Street Press editions of Punshon's *The Attending Truth*, *Strange Ending*, *Brought to Light*, *Dark Is the Clue* and *Triple Quest*. Although Punshon's Bobby Owen detective novels appeared over nearly a quarter-century, between 1933 and 1956, the publication of the Bobby Owen short stories was much more concentrated, with the first one, "A Study in the Obvious," appearing in the London *Evening Standard* on 23 August 1936 and the remaining four, "Making Sure," "Good Beginning," "Three Sovereigns" and "Find the Lady," in the *Evening Standard* in 1950, on, respectively, 15 February, 1 August, 17 October and 21 December.

"A Study in the Obvious" appeared as part of an *Evening Standard* series devoted to "famous detectives of fiction," edited by Dorothy L. Sayers. Besides Bobby Owen, fictional detectives included in "Detective Cavalcade" were Sherlock Holmes, Sexton Blake, Raffles, Eugene Valmont, Father Brown, the "Man in the Corner," Max Carrados, Dr. Thorndyke, Dr. Priestley, Dr. Hailey, Hercule Poirot, Reggie Fortune, Philip Trent, Albert Campion, Lord Peter Wimsey, Roger Sheringham, Ludovic Travers, Mrs. Bradley, Mr. Pepper, Mr. Reeder, Mr. Pinkerton, Chief Constable Sir Clinton Driffield, Inspector French, Superintendent Wilson, Inspector Head, Uncle Abner, Trevis Tarrant, Charlie Chan and Ellery Queen.

As editor of the series Dorothy L. Sayers warned Gladys Mitchell, who was contributing an original Mrs. Bradley short story, that the *Evening Standard* "will probably say they want it as short as possible and as cheap a possible! Don't let them screw you down to 4000 words, because I know they are prepared to go to 6000 words or thereabouts. . . . I have almost broken their hearts by pointing out to them that all the older people, like Conan Doyle and Austin Freeman, run out to something like 10,000 [words] and their columns will be frightfully congested."

In her *Evening Standard* introduction to "A Study in the Obvious," (2814 words) Sayers wrote:

> E.R. Punshon's detective novels are distinguished by two things: a delicate, sub-acid humour and a fine vein of romantic feeling. They fall into two groups—the stories about Inspector Carter and Detective-Sergeant Bell, and the more recent series about Superintendent Mitchell and Detective-Sergeant Bobby Owen.
>
> In this short story . . . Owen—that nobly-born and Oxford-bred young policeman—appears alone, exploiting his characteristic vein of inspired common sense.
>
> The crime here is a trivial one; those who like to see serious crimes handled with delicate emotional perception should make a point of reading some of the novels, such as "Mystery Villa" and "Death of a Beauty Queen."

"A Study in the Obvious," which appeared the same year as *The Bath Mysteries*, a Punshon detective novel that delved into Sergeant Bobby Owen's aristocratic family background, is Bobby Owen's origin story, showing how he came to be a policeman. Though light, the tale is one of considerable charm that should delight Bobby Owen fans.

The later *Evening Standard* stories are shorter affairs, though they are all murder investigations. "Good Beginning" and "Find the Lady" take us back to earlier years in Bobby Owen's police career, when he held the ranks of, respectively, constable and sergeant. "Making Sure" and "Three Sovereigns" capture something of that quality of what American mystery critic Anthony Boucher called "the obscure destinies that drive [Punshon's] obsessed and tormented characters," which so impressed Dorothy L. Sayers about Punshon's novels.

Curtis Evans

CHAPTER I
APPEAL FOR HELP

Deputy Commander Bobby Owen, C.I.D., his hands in his pockets, whistling very badly the latest popular tune from the latest American musical, was looking out of a window of the West Mercian police headquarters in the pleasant little country town of Penton, once upon a time the capital of the kingdom of Mercia, but now not even the capital of the county. That distinction had been basely stolen by some upstart of a place in East Mercia, not more than six or seven hundred years old, at a time when Penton was still recovering from having been burnt down once or twice during the wars of the barons. And what the Deputy Commander was thinking as he gazed absently into a street where Tudor, Stuart, and even earlier buildings rubbed shoulders with the latest multiple-store buildings in the latest fashionable style was that when he became a policeman he had never expected to become a schoolmaster as well.

Recently he had been giving a course of three lectures to the West Mercian police, basing them largely on the Howe edition of Gross's *Criminal Investigation*. Members of neighbouring police forces had been invited to attend, and had done so in large numbers. There had been discussions following each lecture, and finally Major Rowley, West Mercian Chief Constable, had offered small money prizes for the three best essays on these Bobby Owen lectures.

To this offer the response had been almost embarrassing in its plenitude, and as Major Rowley had not wished to adjudicate himself, for fear of being thought to show bias towards his own men, he had asked Bobby Owen to undertake the task. So here Bobby was, playing schoolmaster, as he told himself, trying to mark fairly what were in effect examination papers, and more than a little worried by the unfamiliar task, since on its competent performance so much depended for the essayists. Not so much, of course, on account of the monetary value of the small prizes offered, as because success would mean better prospects of promotion in a service in which promotion is often slow and difficult.

And very difficult Bobby was finding it to penetrate both behind the stiff and formal official language too many of the men had been trained to use, and also behind the difficulty others found in expressing themselves. Yet only thus could be formed a clear estimate of the degree of clarity of thought and grasp of essential principles lying nearly smothered beneath turgid language and muddled syntax.

Now, as he was turning back from the window to resume his task, there came a knock at the door, and Major Rowley appeared with an apology for an interruption which as a matter of fact Bobby welcomed rather than otherwise. The Chief Constable was a brisk, energetic man, of middle age, but still something of an all-round athlete, slightly below average height, but of square, strong build, with a quick, glancing eye that missed little, and a prominent nose above a firmly closed mouth. Behind him were many years of police service in India. He had the name of being a strict disciplinarian—too much so, indeed, in days when the emphasis has passed from demanding obedience to winning cooperation. Bobby had, however, found him pleasant to work with, appreciative of the lectures delivered, and, as Bobby knew, he had the reputation of having considerably improved the efficiency of the force he commanded.

"Getting on all right?" he asked, with an approving glance at a desk where the piles of essays were evidently being sorted out into groups of differing merit.

"More or less," Bobby answered, still slightly worried by his unfamiliar task. "I've weeded out about half that I don't think amount to much. I don't know if you would care to look through them yourself and see if you think any of them should have another reading?"

"Oh, I don't think so," Rowley answered. "I want to be able to say I've had nothing to do with the judging." He began to fidget in an awkward and rather embarrassed manner with the piled-up essays on the desk. "There's a local big-wig here," he said. "He wants to know if you can spare time to see him. I had to promise to ask. No confidence in country bumpkins like us. He wants the pure milk of Scotland Yard."

"Well, he can't have it, that's all," declared Bobby, well aware of all the work waiting for him in London. "There's a discipline board I've got to attend as well as the newest re-organization committee. Who is he, anyway?"

Major Rowley countered by another question.

"Ever heard of Stephen Asprey?" he asked. "You know that thing of his: 'In gold and sumptuous velvet go the stars'? Always being quoted."

"Oh, is that his?" exclaimed Bobby, surprised. "I always thought it was Shakespeare or somebody. I remember Asprey was all the go when I was up at Oxford. Hadn't heard much about him lately. Dead, isn't he? Where does he come in?"

"Mr Day-Bell," the Major went on, reverting now to Bobby's earlier question, "is the clergyman at Hillings-under-Moor, about ten or twelve miles from here. On the fringe of the Great Mercian Moor and a scattered, lonely sort of place. Janet Merton lived near there, and she is buried in Hillings churchyard."

"Oh, yes, of course," Bobby exclaimed, as old memories began to return to him. "They were lovers, weren't they? Asprey and her. Isn't there some story about Asprey having put their love-letters in her coffin to be buried with her?"

"All his last poems, too, according to one version," Rowley said. "I don't think that's known for certain, but it is certain that he wrote to her continually when they were apart, and that he published nothing during those years, though he used to say Janet had rekindled his Muse and the world would one day know what it owed her. There's always been a good deal of talk about reopening the grave and recovering the letters and manuscripts if they are really there, and recently it's been revived. There was a question about it in Parliament, and the Home Secretary said the request would receive favourable consideration if application were made."

"Well, then, that's all right, isn't it?" Bobby asked. "If the Home Office gives permission that's all that's necessary."

"Not quite all," Rowley explained. "The grave is the freehold of the Merton family, and is now in the name of Miss Christabel Merton. She's a niece of Janet Merton's, and she says she will never agree to its opening. It was what they wanted and they loved each other, and she won't have her aunt's resting-place disturbed. Mrs Asprey—Asprey's widow—backs her up, and she's a formidable old lady."

"I don't see what say she has from the legal point of view," Bobby remarked, "but Miss Christabel is clearly within her rights. Nothing doing if she holds out. What's Mr Day-Bell worrying about? He's the Vicar, didn't you say?"

"He seems to think," Major Rowley answered, "that attempts may be made to open the grave one night—without permission."

"Well, of course, that would be illegal," Bobby pointed out. "Fine or imprisonment. Or is it only a fine? I forget. And of course anything taken from the grave would have to be returned, if Miss Merton insisted. At least, I suppose so. Anyhow, it's Mr Day-Bell's responsibility if he's the Vicar."

"No, priest-in-charge, I think they call it, or curate-in-charge, or something like that," the Major corrected him. "The last Rector, not Vicar—a Mr Thorne—disappeared about two years ago. He left the rectory one night for what he told his housekeeper was to be an evening stroll before bed. He has never been seen or heard of since. The Bishop put Mr Day-Bell in charge after a time, but I gather there are legal difficulties in the way of declaring the benefice vacant. Parson's freehold, you know, and his daughter has started legal proceedings in restraint. She claims that her father may return, that his absence may not be voluntary, that there is no proof of wilful neglect and that if he returns and proves his absence was by *force majeure*, then the Bishop would have acted *ultra vires*."

"A jolly little legal fight on hand, I can see that," Bobby agreed. "Lawyers' idea of a fun fair, I should say. Who is fighting it? Costs will run pretty high, won't they?"

"It's Mr Thorne's daughter," Rowley explained. "She's married and a practising barrister, and so is her husband. The Hillings living is one of the best endowed in the country. In the sixteenth century a pasture field was left to the parish for ever, and it's where all this part of the High Street has been built. Ground rents run high, and she doesn't mean to let all that money go out of the family if she can help. And I daresay the case is quite a useful advertisement for her. Gets her well known to solicitors."

"Nothing ever found to explain Thorne's disappearance?"

"Nothing definite. Lots of gossip, of course. He was rather heavily in debt. He had lost a packet, speculating on the Stock Exchange. There were hints that he had got himself compromised with some woman who vanished about the same time. Nothing ever proved, but he had got the name of being inclined to be a little too friendly with some of his women parishioners. And suggestions that he had opened the Janet Merton grave on the quiet and gone off with what was buried with her."

"Good lord!" Bobby exclaimed. "The thing's opening out all right. But what for? What good would the buried poems be to him? He couldn't make any use of them. If he did, he would have to explain how he got hold of them."

"Well, that's another angle again," Major Rowley explained, though hesitatingly. "It's not so much Asprey's last poems, though some of these high-brow johnnies talk as if recovering them would be like recovering a lost play by Shakespeare. It's the letters—those he wrote to Janet during their intimacy. There's reason to think there's a lot in them about his friendship with the young Duchess of Blegborough. If you remember, she died from what was said to be an overdose of sleeping tablets. It was all very much hushed up. The verdict at the inquest was 'Death by Misadventure'. Probably her husband didn't want it brought in as suicide. Natural enough if that were all, but—well, ugly stories got about that the Duke knew a good deal more than he said at the inquest; and that others knew still more, but were frightened or bribed into keeping their mouths shut."

"I'm beginning to remember the case," Bobby said. "It never came up to us at the Yard."

"It was all very hush-hush," Rowley repeated. "The whispers going round were very low whispers indeed. I happened to know of them because an old Indian colleague of mine had a lot to do with handling the case and he wasn't at all happy about the whole thing. He told me the Duke wanted to take action against the whisperers, but his lawyers wouldn't let him. There was nothing he could lay hold of, and the only result would be to give the stories wider publicity and make people think there must be something in them. While if he kept quiet, they would die out of their own accord."

"You say 'ugly' stories," Bobby remarked. "What precisely were they?"

"Well, of course, you won't let it go any further," Rowley replied, still rather unwillingly, "but it was said that the Duke was jealous of Asprey, believed his wife had been unfaithful, and—well, suppose he had slipped just one or two extra tablets into the dose his wife took? Murder, in short."

"There may be evidence of some sort in the buried Asprey letters?" Bobby asked again. "You know, that's pretty serious."

"Opportunity for blackmail," Rowley said. "Presumably the Duke would pay a good price for letters like that if anyone got hold of them."

"Nice reputation this Mr Thorne seems to have," observed Bobby. "Stock Exchange gambler. Woman chaser. Desecrator of graves. Potential blackmailer."

"Very likely it's all mere malicious gossip," Rowley said uncomfortably, "except of course for Thorne's disappearance. That's a fact. It's why Day-Bell wants to talk to you. He says if you at the Yard will take the case up and find out what really happened to Thorne, then everyone will be satisfied and all the gossip will die down."

"Well, I hope he doesn't think I can do that off my own bat," Bobby protested. "I should think his best plan would be to get his lawyers to work the thing up. If they can present a reasonable case for further investigation, supported by the next of kin—there's a wife and daughter, you said—the Commissioner might take it up. I don't know. I expect he would want to consult the Home Office. I don't see there's much to be done—not after two years. Quite possibly Mr Thorne is living very happily somewhere in South America with his unidentified woman—and the Asprey documents in reserve for possible use if and when trouble crops up. It's a queer business, though. Compromising letters. Lost poems of a dead poet. A desecrated grave. A mysterious disappearance. Possible blackmail. A Ducal suspect. And all as vague and unsubstantial as a November fog."

"The worst of it," Rowley went on, "is that there's a lot of back-stairs stuff going on. The man behind that question in Parliament is a Mr Pyle. He's a chairman of the *Morning Daily* group. His brother is editor of *Morning Daily* itself. He could start one of those Press stunts any time he wanted. *Morning Daily* is an awful rag."

"Yes, I know," Bobby agreed. "We don't want them butting in if we can help it."

"Then there's Mrs Asprey—Asprey's widow," Rowley added. "She's rigged herself up rooms in an old half-ruined house near here—Two Mile End."

"What for?" Bobby asked.

"I don't know," Rowley answered. "I suppose she wants to be on the spot. Then there's the Duke of Blegborough; and a duke is still a duke, even under Socialism."

"Even more so, I'm told," Bobby remarked.

"Day-Bell himself as well," Rowley went on. "He has a big pull with the Joint Committee. Both the Days and the Bells are old local families with a lot of say in local affairs, and Mr Day-Bell has family connections on both sides. Born a Day and tacked on Bell under a family will. Rather a pushing sort, too. And a poor devil of a Chief Constable likely to come under pretty heavy cross-fire between the lot of them. I should be really grateful if you would have a chat with Day-Bell and try to choke him off, if you can. He did say something about fresh developments he would like to consult you about."

CHAPTER II
SEXTON PHILOSOPHER

MR DAY-BELL had evidently been waiting not far off to hear if Bobby would agree to their suggested talk. Not that he had had any doubts on the point—he felt himself far too important to be in any way ignored—but when Major Rowley had suggested it would be as well if he first opened the subject with Bobby, Mr Day-Bell had seen no reason to object. Only a few minutes elapsed before the Chief Constable and he appeared together and introductions began. He was an unusually tall, thin man with a long, thin face and long, thin arms and legs attached to a round, plump body, so that what with his small black eyes and small, pursed-up mouth, he bore a somewhat disconcerting resemblance, or so Bobby thought, to an enormous spider. He possessed, however, a remarkably clear, musical voice, of which he made admirable use, though whether as a result of training or by natural gift, Bobby was not sure.

'An actor's voice or a B.B.C. announcer's,' Bobby told himself, 'but hardly the physical presence for the stage.'

The moment introductions were over, Major Rowley took himself off on the plea of work to be attended to, but really, Bobby suspected, because he wished to be concerned as little as possible, in any further discussion or action. Then Mr Day-Bell suggested that as it was getting on for lunch-time, Bobby might care to join him for that meal at the Penton Constitutional Club, a little way down the High Street.

"We have a very good Chablis," Day-Bell remarked. "I'm on the Wine Committee, and I do try to keep us up to the mark. The good things of life are meant for our enjoyment."

Bobby saw no reason to disagree with this sentiment, and soon he and his host were enjoying a very satisfactory meal in the well-appointed dining-room of the club. But it was not until the coffee stage was reached that Mr Day-Bell began to talk of the reasons for which he had desired this opportunity of talking to Bobby. Even then it was in a somewhat hesitating and nervous manner—one, Bobby suspected, anything but characteristic—that he opened the subject.

"I think our good Chief Constable," he began, "has told you I am finding myself considerably worried and uneasy over certain recent developments. Major Rowley is a most efficient officer, but, if I may say so, a little wanting in drive and imagination. He tends to think all is well if only his men look smart on parade."

"It is not a bad test," remarked Bobby, who in fact had already come in private to much the same conclusion. "A force smart on parade is generally efficient in action."

"No doubt, no doubt," agreed Day-Bell. He put more sugar in his coffee and stirred it absently. "I don't care for it too sweet," he said, and then added abruptly: "I had a somewhat disturbing letter from the Duke of Blegborough this morning."

"Indeed," said Bobby, and waited for more.

"I expect," Day-Bell continued, now pushing his cup of coffee away and beginning to fidget nervously with an unlighted cigarette—"I expect you have heard of the story that the last poems of Stephen Asprey—they gave him an O.M., didn't they? just before his death—and certain letters of his were buried with a Janet Merton, a woman he had been intimate with for several years. The grave is in the Hillings churchyard. I think Major Rowley told you also of the disappearance of my predecessor at Hillings—Mr Thorne."

"I understand," Bobby said, "there was some gossip about his having got possession of the poems and letters, wasn't there?"

"I hardly think there can be any foundation for that story," Day-Bell said; "but I have heard it still goes on. I've been for a long time anxious to clear up Mr Thorne's disappearance. My own position at Hillings is difficult, though the Bishop has asked me to put up with it for a little longer. There are the legal proceedings Mr Thorne's family have begun. All very unsettling. John Hagen's suggestion is that Mr Thorne met with a fatal accident on the moor. Even a sprained ankle or something comparatively trivial like that might have fatal results. An injured man might easily lie there helpless till he died. A lonely, savage place. I do not trust it." He paused and frowned, as if he spoke of some dangerous, living entity he had reason to fear. He went on: "I should wish to secure the help of Scotland Yard in making fresh endeavours to discover the truth."

"But it was gone into thoroughly by the police force here at the time, was it not?" Bobby asked. "I am sure everything possible was done. Of course, if new facts have come to light, they would be at once followed up."

"I was a padre during the war," Mr Day-Bell told him, "and I always found the best plan was to go straight to the highest authority if action were needed—to the corps commander rather than at battalion or company level."

"I am afraid," Bobby explained, "that at the Yard we are not in the position of corps commanders. We have no authority over local police forces."

Mr Day-Bell waved this aside, evidently still convinced that, whatever Bobby's disclaimers, Scotland Yard was still the central and authoritative police force in the country.

"New developments are threatening," he said, "that go far beyond merely local matters. I mentioned that I had a letter this morning from the Duke of Blegborough, and now there's a telegram to say he is on his way here and wants to see me."

"It sounds like a sudden decision," Bobby remarked. "Nothing in the letter to explain it?"

"No. Nothing. No. He wanted to know if any further steps had been taken to get an order to open the Janet Merton grave, and if there was any possibility that it had been opened secretly and the letters taken. An unpleasant suggestion, when you remember the gossip about my predecessor. It is certainly untrue. I can't imagine any one in charge of a parish committing such a horrible outrage as violating a grave in his own churchyard."

"No," Bobby agreed. "One would want very clear, strong evidence before even considering such a possibility. Most likely rumours about these letters—Asprey's last poems, too, aren't there?—got started in some way, and then the story got tacked on to the known fact of Mr Thorne's disappearance. If one item of a piece of gossip is true, it is often taken for granted that the rest of the tale must be true as well. It looks to me as if some such story, perhaps with added detail, has reached the Duke and upset him. He must be taking it seriously, whatever it is. The natural course would be to ask his lawyers to look into it." Bobby paused, and then added thoughtfully: "I wonder if there's any reason why he's not doing that," and now he was remembering that suggestion of blackmail possibilities made previously.

"It's all very upsetting," complained Mr Day-Bell, and looked very much as if he found it so. "I shouldn't be inclined to take it seriously myself, only for what Hagen has told me. A most trustworthy man."

"Hagen?" Bobby repeated the name. "You mentioned him before. Who is he?"

"John Hagen? He is the sexton at Hillings," Mr Day-Bell explained. "An unusual character. Remarkable, indeed. Self-educated to such a degree that really you might almost call him a scholar. His library would put to shame many of us clergy. He has a knowledge of Latin fully equal to mine—he reads it easily, though his pronunciation is all his own. Quite natural, as he has had no teaching."

"He certainly sounds unusual," Bobby agreed. "Is he content to remain on as sexton? I should have thought with those qualifications he might have secured something more suitable, more to his taste. Is he a young man?"

"No, middle-aged. About fifty, I suppose. He appears contented enough. I did suggest at one time he ought to try to find more congenial employment and I offered to try to help. I find it, I must admit, a little embarrassing at times to have one's sexton correcting one's Latin or explaining the meaning of some quotation from the early fathers."

"He didn't take up your suggestion at all?"

"No. He said, quite truly, that acquaintance with Latin, or with the writings of the early fathers, hasn't much commercial value and his lack of general education didn't fit him for any academic post. Besides, he thought he was very well off where he was. He has leisure, freedom, quiet, and enough to live on. Pursuing a private line of research, he says. I believe every penny of his wages goes on books; and his garden and his hens provide enough for his daily needs."

"A sexton philosopher," Bobby said smilingly. "It sounds an ideal life for those who can live up to it. Not many, I think, and not me, I fear. You were saying he had mentioned something you thought rather disturbing?"

"Yes, when taken together with other happenings. People often come—in the summer especially—to stare at the Janet Merton grave. Even the touring coaches come. The story of the buried letters and Stephen Asprey's last poems is in all the guidebooks, and these coach tours—they seem exceedingly popular—apparently include a visit to Hillings and crossing the Great Mercian Moor among the attractions they advertise. Why crossing the most bleak, desolate spot in the whole country should be an attraction I don't know, but it seems to be considered so." There was again that odd note of hostility, of dread almost, in Day-Bell's voice as he spoke of the moor. For a moment he was silent. He resumed in rather a grudging way, as if unwilling to make the admission: "Certainly there's a fine view from Gallows Tree, the highest spot on the moor, if you don't mind the associations—it was used as a place of execution till comparatively recently, and earlier on women convicted of witchcraft were taken there to be burned alive. Hagen makes a little extra by selling postcards both of that place and of the grave. He was given permission originally by Mr Thorne, and I've made no objection. In fact I've rather encouraged it. It's an incentive to him to be on the alert when these tourists and coach parties arrive."

"You find that necessary?" Bobby asked.

"Oh, definitely," Day-Bell assured him, not much to Bobby's surprise. "It's not so much the coach parties. They are generally well enough behaved, and some of them even take an intelligent interest in the church, which goes back to Saxon times. It's the private motorists. If we weren't careful the Janet Merton grave would soon be scribbled all over with the initials of louts from every place in the country. That is, if anything were left of it. Hagen has found people—especially Americans—trying to chip off bits of the tombstone for what they call souvenirs."

"Has he noticed anything of the sort recently?" Bobby asked; as Mr Day-Bell seemed inclined to pause here, and indeed all the time he had been speaking he had seemed to show a certain hesitation, almost a reluctance, to continue, as if to do so cost him a real effort he none the less knew was necessary.

"Well, yes," Day-Bell admitted now. "Yes. I didn't think much of it at first; but now, what with one thing and another and the letter this morning, I find it disturbing. Hagen is fortunately a light sleeper. His cottage overlooks the churchyard, and he makes a point even in winter of sleeping with the window wide open so that he can hear if there's any disturbance. Two nights ago he did hear something. He got up, pulled on some clothes, and went out, first arming himself with the kitchen poker—the first weapon he could lay his hands on now he has lost his revolver. The police refused him a licence for another. He could just make out in the darkness two figures near the Janet Merton grave. He can't say what they were doing, he is not even certain there were two. They—or he, if there was only one—must have heard Hagen coming, and at once made off. Hagen shouted to them to stop and tried to follow, but that wasn't much good in the darkness. So he went back to bed. But he was up again as soon as it was light. There were plainly visible footprints in the churchyard, and they pointed in the direction of the moor. He showed them me, and he showed me, too, where it certainly did look as if the churchyard wall had been climbed. We found a few more footprints, all still leading towards the moor, but on the moor itself we soon lost them."

"Are there any cottages on the moor?" Bobby inquired.

"No, but caravans—gypsy or occasionally private ones—are sometimes parked there. Cars, too, now and then. Motorists camping out. At present there is one caravan. It belongs to a Mr Edward Pyle."

"Pyle?" Bobby interrupted quickly, remembering at once that Major Rowley had mentioned the same name. "Never mind. Go on, please, if you will."

"He came to see me," Day-Bell continued accordingly. "He seems to be keenly interested in the Asprey story. He told me he was gathering material for a biography of Asprey, and he was evidently sounding me about the possibility of opening the grave and recovering the letters and poems. He spoke of it as a matter of public interest, and hinted that he was trying to get it taken up on what he called 'top levels'. I told him there was nothing I could do and for that matter nothing I should wish to do. But after what Hagen saw, and with those footprints all clearly pointing towards where his caravan was standing, I felt it my duty to speak to him about it. I went on to the caravan, but Mr Pyle was not there. An extremely surly, unpleasant person appeared to be in charge. He said Mr Pyle had not told him when he would return. When I tried to get some more information he became extremely rude. He even called me a 'snooper', going so far, indeed, as to use threats of violence. Later on, I heard that Mr Pyle was staying at a Penton hotel, so I wrote to ask him to call to see me here. At three this afternoon. Would it be too much to ask you to be present? I am seriously uneasy, and I think I ought to know what this Mr Pyle was doing in the churchyard in the middle of the night—he and that ruffianly-looking fellow I saw, for I feel sure it was they Hagen disturbed. Not at all the sort of person one would like to meet in a lonely spot at night. One of the worst squints I ever saw and a broken nose. Bandy legs as well. I suppose the squint is no fault of his, but I shouldn't wonder if the broken nose wasn't a result of some scoundrelly brawl or another."

Bobby showed no sign of any special interest on hearing this unflattering description of Mr Pyle's caravan attendant. It is of course a matter of police discipline—almost a point of honour, one might say—to allow no hint of any knowledge a police officer may have of a man's past to escape him when he hears of a former criminal apparently endeavouring to earn an honest living. Enlightened self-interest, perhaps. 'One headache off our hands,' an Inspector of reputedly Irish descent was accustomed to say when he heard of such cases.

A thoroughly sensible comment, Bobby thought it. Nevertheless this time he could not help feeling a little uneasy. He had at once recognized Mr Day-Bell's description as that of a man named Item Sims, his father having had so many children he had grown tired of finding fresh names for them all and had decided to consider this newest arrival as just another family item. Item had not turned out well, possibly handicapped by a name that seemed to deny him a personal importance he had known no other way of emphasizing than by taking to crime. At any rate, that would probably be the fashionable psycho-analytic explanation. In underworld circles he was known as 'Sticker' Sims, from his preference for the use of knife instead of gun. 'Knives don't miss,' he was accustomed to say. 'Knives don't jam; they can't fit in a knife the way they can a bullet to a gun. Give me a knife every time.' But this, Bobby knew, was what is now called a 'rationalization'. A fortune-teller of wide repute in the underworld had warned Item that one day not too far off he would die from a pistol shot he would fire himself. Thereon he had sworn never again to touch a gun—revolver or automatic—or ever to be near one if he could possibly help it.

Item had served one long sentence, one or two shorter sentences for rather specially brutal assaults, and altogether was an extremely unpleasant item in the current police records, though at the moment there was nothing against him—except apparently being rude to Mr Day-Bell, which was most regrettable, but not a criminal offence.

But of all this Bobby gave no sign. It didn't seem likely there could be two men answering to the description given. But it was a possibility; and Bobby decided he would pay an early visit to the caravan, partly to make sure it really was Item, and partly, if it were him, to let him know that the police were aware of his presence. That might be a useful deterrent—or 'disincentive', Bobby supposed he ought to say, if he wanted, as he always did, to be up to date—should any 'unlawful occasion' be under consideration. If it was the real Item Sims Mr Pyle had with him, then it certainly seemed he had made a very odd choice of a travelling companion—very odd indeed. And oddities are always interesting, or so Bobby thought.

One of the club servants appeared—a trim little maid in a natty uniform designed by the wife of the chairman of the club, a lady who was also the owner of a 'select fashion salon' in the Penton High Street. The maid said:

"Gentleman to see you, sir—Mr Pyle."

CHAPTER III
ODDITIES ARE INTERESTING

MR PYLE was a stout, heavily built man, wearing his clothes with that kind of shabby carelessness only the really rich and important can afford. His whole manner, his rather loud, dictatorial voice, proclaimed the assurance that comes from the same sense of a safe and secure position in the world. His most noticeable features were his jaw—square, projecting, thrusting—and his large, light blue eyes, set unusually far apart; though, as he wore heavy horn-rimmed spectacles, they could not be seen very plainly. A curious trick he had was that of blowing his nose at frequent intervals, and when he did so it was like the blast of a trumpet. At first he seemed inclined to ignore Bobby, on whom he bestowed a brief glance and nod, as if wondering for a passing moment who he was and what he was doing there, and then deciding that anyhow it didn't matter much. It was Mr Day-Bell he addressed—the appropriate word—before that gentleman had been able to do more than make a few vaguely polite introductory remarks. In a loud, harsh, authoritative voice, a voice that seemed to proclaim it knew it had to be listened to with respect, he began by saying he had been pleased to receive Mr Day-Bell's note, as he hoped he could take it this meant that Day-Bell was willing to consider afresh his former position.

"It is absolutely essential," declared Mr Pyle, as if daring disagreement, "that these papers, poems, the last work of a very great poet, letters that will shed such an illuminating light upon his character and his career, should be recovered, restored to the light of day." He paused and blew his nose with that startling effect it always had upon those who heard it for the first time. "The last great poet," he resumed before his two listeners had fully recovered from the shock of that reverberating report, "England has produced for nearly two hundred years and already half forgotten by a people always only too ready to forget their past glories. That must be put right." He paused again—again as if daring them to challenge his pronouncements—and then went on: "Tennyson, Browning—merely singers of an idle day, both of them, as one at least knew very well. Even Hopkins cannot be mentioned in the same breath as Stephen Asprey. The poems must be given to the world to whom they belong. The letters, too—the letters of a great lover, an inspiration to all who believe, as I do, that the love of man and woman is the highest inspiration of the human spirit. Nor can a poet's work be appreciated as it should be till instructed criticism has made itself thoroughly familiar with his inner life—the whole truth."

A little breathless, Mr Pyle paused again, and looked severely at his two auditors, apparently to assure himself that they had been suitably impressed. Mr Day-Bell, though he had uttered no word, was a little breathless, too, overwhelmed by such a torrent of eloquence. Bobby, gravely attentive, was asking himself how much of this was genuine and how much mere professional chatter. He decided it was indeed genuine. He told himself that Mr Pyle had made for himself an idol, not with his hands but with his mind, and that he had come to consider the shrine at which he worshipped his own private property, even though subsidiary acolytes would be permitted. A dangerous worship, Bobby felt. Apparently satisfied with the tribute of their silence, Mr Pyle was about to continue his tirade when Bobby murmured, not very loudly but very distinctly:

"Difficult, don't you think, to know the whole truth about anything?"

Mr Pyle gave him a surprised look, astonished at a comment he clearly considered out of place.

"Difficult, no doubt," he admitted, "but less so to the trained intelligence," and now Mr Pyle's glance had changed from the surprised to the withering—that famous glance of his before which subordinates vanished away like that proverbial snowball so improbably finding itself in hell.

But Bobby was not easily impressed by withering glances, and to Mr Pyle's he returned his most amiable smile, while Mr Day-Bell took advantage of the momentary pause to say:

"It was a somewhat different matter which I felt it would be desirable to mention to you, and I must explain, too, that I have in no way altered the view I take."

"Indeed," Mr Pyle said, coldly surprised and without showing the least curiosity or desire to know what this different matter might be. "I must confess I am equally astonished and disappointed. I entirely fail to understand what I can only call the concerted opposition I am meeting with. It is of national—international—importance that these papers should be brought to the light of day. You must be well aware that the first recognition of Stephen Asprey's genius came when his poems during the First World War in praise of heroic France were widely quoted there. I believe originally by a Deputy in the National Assembly. Recently I have had letters from many leaders of thought, scholars, critics, from America, from France, from elsewhere, expressing the warmest appreciation of my efforts and pledging full support. I shall leave no stone unturned, no avenue unexplored, to achieve my object, and I shall I know have the support of all right thinking men and women. Yet here, where

Stephen Asprey's memory should be even more honoured than elsewhere, since here it was that his genius reached its peak in his last poems, when human love reached its highest expression in the letters to Janet Merton, that I find the most obstinate opposition," and once again he stopped to blow his nose and once again that trumpet-like challenge sounded clear and loud.

But this time his two hearers were better prepared, and Bobby took the opportunity to remark:

"I was just wondering why you rate these poems and letters so highly. No one has ever had a chance to see them, I think."

"I judge their value," Mr Pyle retorted, "by what I know of Asprey's work and career—and few know more. By what Asprey himself said when, with that last fine gesture of his, he placed letters and poems in the coffin of the woman he had so greatly loved," and Bobby's further interjected question: "Why greatly?" was ignored, not even heard, probably, for Mr Pyle continued unchecked: "It was, no doubt, the same at Stratford-on-Avon when Shakespeare retired there to write his greatest play: *The Tempest*. Not a word has come down to us to indicate that one single person in the town knew what was happening. My hope is to employ the royalties and other receipts accruing from Asprey's biography, for which I am gathering material, to found an Asprey memorial trust at Penton. Yet I find little welcome for a project which would bring to Penton some of the glory that is rightfully Asprey's alone, but in which Penton also would share, as Stratford shares in Shakespeare's."

"Instead of the concerted opposition you spoke of," Bobby said cheerfully, and, ignoring the stony stare Mr Pyle now bestowed upon him, he continued: "I don't quite see, though, how you are going to get over it. I'm told the grave is the freehold of the Merton family."

"I have," Mr Pyle retorted, "what practically amounts to an undertaking from the Home Office. I happen to be a close personal friend of the Home Secretary, and I had the privilege of giving him the whole-hearted support of the not uninfluential paper I am connected with when there seemed to be some ill-considered opposition to his appointment to his present office." He paused, and was gratified to observe that Mr Day-Bell did look suitably impressed and that Bobby appeared thought-ful. He resumed: "Nor have I failed to find among many in high positions—political, social, financial, indeed in all ranks of life—a civilized awareness of the absolute necessity of the recov-ery of documents of such importance to the cultural life of the country—of the world, indeed."

By this time his voice was trembling with excitement. He took off his spectacles and waved them challengingly in the air, and now Bobby was able to see more plainly how the pallor of those large, light blue eyes had become charged with, shone with, a kind of fanatical enthusiasm.

"I am not sure," Bobby remarked, "that the Home Office has the power to give any such permission. Not if the freeholder ob-jects. Not on its own, anyhow. I imagine it would take something like a private Act of Parliament. An Order in Council might be enough. I don't know."

"There would be no difficulty about that," Mr Pyle asserted confidently, as one who habitually went about with Orders in Council in his pocket. "But I did promise I would first of all, be-fore taking other steps, do all I could to secure the consent of all concerned. But I only meet with a foolish, ignorant, pig-headed opposition, a merely emotional, unreasoning resistance," and with every epithet he used, the light in those large pale eyes of his glowed ever more strongly. As if sub-consciously aware of this, he replaced his heavy, horn-rimmed spectacles as he re-sumed: "Only this morning I called to see Mrs Asprey in that tumble-down, dilapidated house she seems to be occupying."

"It was the only vacant residence in the district," Day-Bell interposed.

"Well, she has a flat in Bristol," Mr Pyle snapped. "She re-fused to see me there. I had no idea she had a place here as well, but when I heard, it did seem an opportunity to explain things to her. I felt she must have misunderstood my letters. But when she realized who I was—well, she became quite hysterical. She simply would not listen to a word. She ordered me out of the house. When I tried to pacify her she got a revolver and threat-ened to shoot if I wasn't out of the house before she counted ten.

She actually began to count, beating her hand up and down like a referee in a boxing match."

"What did you do?" Bobby asked.

"I went," Mr Pyle answered simply.

"Very wise," approved Bobby.

"Not that I supposed for one moment that she would ever attempt to put her threat into action," Mr Pyle explained, though now the pallor that formerly had shown in his again half-hidden eyes seemed to have transferred itself to his cheeks, so that Bobby felt that the poor man had been given a fright from which even yet he had not fully recovered.

"A formidable old lady," he remarked, slightly uneasy at this talk of revolvers—tricky things even in the hands of those accustomed to their use, as old ladies seldom are. He decided it would be as well to mention it to Major Rowley. Aloud he said: "It sounds as if housing were as bad here as anywhere. Mrs Asprey would have done well to follow your example, Mr Pyle, and use a caravan. Much more comfortable. Mr Day-Bell was saying he paid it a visit this morning."

Mr Day-Bell, so often reduced to silence by Mr Pyle's unceasing, droning voice, took advantage—as Bobby had intended he should—of the opening thus offered.

"In connection," he said, "with a certain recent incident. It is why I suggested our meeting. An incident I found disturbing, not so much in itself as because of other circumstances. My sexton, John Hagen, tells me that last night he was wakened by sounds coming from the churchyard. He got up and went out. It was about midnight. He saw two men—he thinks two, but it was dark and possibly there was only one. They were standing near the Janet Merton grave. As soon as he approached they made off. He called to them to stop, but they took no notice and disappeared in the darkness. When it was light he found footprints. He informed me and we traced them to the moor and towards your caravan. It seemed possible you might have seen or heard something; but unfortunately you were not there when I called, and I must say that the man who claimed you had left him in charge was most uncivil."

"That would be Sims," Mr Pyle said. "I expect he thought you were questioning the right of my caravan to be there. A rough sort of fellow, but useful, though you have to let him see you don't intend to stand any nonsense. I hope you made that plain," and Mr Day-Bell did not quite know how to answer this turning of the tables, this subtle suggestion that if there had been any insolence, then he was to blame for putting up with it. Mr Pyle resumed: "Your sexton—I didn't catch his name—saw these intruders about twelve. At twelve I was sound asleep in my tent. I am a great believer in fresh air, I often sleep out of doors, and I find my little tent very snug and warm once it is made secure against draughts. Sims sleeps in the caravan, and by that time would be asleep, too. If he had heard anything he would certainly have told me. So I am afraid neither of us can help. Does this sexton of yours go to bed early?"

"Well, really, I hardly know," Day-Bell answered, rather taken aback by so unexpected a question. "We are generally early folk in Hillings. Why do you ask?"

"Because," explained Mr Pyle, "I was in the churchyard about eleven, and it is possible he heard me. I was taking a stroll before bed, as I often do. It is an opportunity for thinking over the problems always arising for one in my position to deal with. On this occasion my thoughts were busy with the great work I have in hand—the biography of Stephen Asprey—and the thought came to me to seek inspiration by the grave of the woman he had loved with a passionate devotion that had raised his genius to such heights as even it had never known before. Perhaps both you and others will understand that better when my publishers give to the world the result of my labours. How long I stood there, wrapped in meditation, I am not sure, but I am sure that I was back in my tent Sims had prepared for me long before twelve. I am inclined to suspect that your sexton saw me, but has mistaken the time, as he might very easily do on wakening from sleep. Perhaps he has embroidered a little as well—discretion is often more in evidence than valour, especially at night. Certainly there was no call to me to stop, no attempt at following me. I could not have failed to hear anything of the sort. The night was quiet and I walked slowly, still musing. Of course, there may have been someone else after I left, but it hardly seems likely."

"Very unlikely indeed," agreed Day-Bell, secretly relieved at so simple a solution of at least one disturbing incident. "I must tell Hagen. Most satisfactory."

"I hope you will commend his vigilance," Pyle said. "A small gratuity would not be out of place. I must remember. Every precaution must be taken against any possible violation of the grave without due authority."

"May I ask," Bobby interposed, "if Sims was recommended to you by Sandy McKie?"

Mr Pyle swung round on Bobby and stared at him blankly, evidently considerably startled by the question.

"Do you know McKie?" he demanded.

"I know him," Bobby explained, "as, in my opinion, the best crime reporter in Fleet Street. *Morning Daily* is lucky to have him. He is your music critic as well, isn't he? Equally good, I hope, but I'm no judge there."

"You seem well informed," Pyle said suspiciously. "Are you a journalist?"

"Oh dear, no," Bobby assured him. "Are journalists well informed? They always strike me as knowing everything—wrong. No, I'm merely a policeman, merely anxious to stop trouble developing. It does almost seem as if something were brewing, goodness knows what."

"I will make it my business," said Mr Pyle, with just a hint of warning in his voice, "to inform your Chief Constable, to whom I was introduced to-day, that I have met you and of your apprehensions as well as of your interest in my caravan. Are you sergeant, inspector, or what?"

"Oh, I'm not a local man," answered Bobby. "I'm from London. And it wasn't your caravan interested me. It was Mr Sims. I rather thought it might be McKie had found him for you."

"I don't think I understand all this," put in Day-Bell, and was certainly looking from one to the other in a very puzzled way.

"It probably doesn't matter in the least," Bobby told him.

CHAPTER IV
THE IMPONDERABLES

PLAINLY MR PYLE also did not understand. He was regarding Bobby with a somewhat bewildered annoyance. He felt baffled, and he was not used to being baffled. One of the secrets of his success in life was that everything to him always seemed crystal clear. So he always knew what was the best thing to do and did it without hesitation and knew that it was right, and if anyone else didn't agree with him, then that person had to be got out of the way, no matter how. Then, again, to him a policeman had hitherto always meant a man in a helmet who directed traffic and who took every opportunity he dared to persecute motorists instead of arresting the cosh boys to be found, in Mr Pyle's opinion, at every street corner.

But somehow or another Bobby did not seem quite to fit into this category. For one thing, he appeared to speak with a certain air of authority and to be but little over-awed by Mr Pyle, as Mr Pyle expected, and generally found, all to be. Worse still, though no word of disbelief had been spoken, no sign of incredulity given, yet somehow Mr Pyle was not sure that his account of the churchyard incident had been accorded by Bobby the full and instant acceptance it had received from Mr Day-Bell. And had there been at times a graver note—a note, indeed, of warning—not so much in what Bobby had said, as discernible, as shadow following substance, behind the spoken word? Or was it substance following shadow? A disturbing thought to one who, like Mr Pyle, possessed his fair share of imagination, overlaid as it might be by pomposity and self-importance. So he sought relief by blowing his nose once more, and even more loudly than before. Not until these thunderous reverberations had died out and a startled maid had appeared in the doorway, only to be impatiently waved aside, did Bobby speak, and then it was more to Mr Day-Bell than to Mr Pyle.

"I suppose," he began, "we may take it from what Mr Pyle says that Mrs Asprey is a part of the concerted opposition Mr Pyle finds his ideas are being met with. She can have no legal standing as far as I can see, but no doubt weight would be given to any opinion she might wish to express. She can't claim ownership of the actual letters, but she can probably claim copyright both in them and in the poems, unless there is some other provision in the will, if there was one. Copyright runs out in time, but in this case it's a good long time, I think."

"Everyone knows all that, and it's all provided for, once the letters and poems have been recovered," Pyle interposed impatiently. "Questions of that sort are always subject to arrangement," and now his tone indicated that such legal quibbles would be of small importance once the documents were in his possession—and possession is, after all, nine-tenths of the law.

"Arrangements are not always so easy when emotions are concerned," Bobby suggested. "The imponderables still count," and Mr Pyle's expression indicated that he had a poor opinion of imponderables as against the ponderables of a bank account of the size of his own. Bobby resumed: "What I am trying to get at is Mrs Asprey's reason for leaving a presumably comfortable flat in Bristol to establish herself in a half-ruined house in a strange neighbourhood. It may be that she wants these papers recovered. She may think they will add to her husband's fame, and of course there's the money, too. The poems would certainly command a big sale if they were published with such a story behind them. Or it may be she wants to make sure they stay where they are. Or perhaps she wants both at once, but never knows which she wants most. On one side her husband's fame and the money. On the other side the record of his friendship, even his devotion to, another woman. Only one thing seems plain, and that is that she feels pretty strongly about it, one way or another, or both ways, if she takes to threats of shooting people. She clearly doesn't mean to have anyone interfering if she can help it."

"No one can help it," Pyle announced, as with authority. "I am not easily turned aside, least of all when every consideration of ordinary common sense supports me. No one can deny that what I suggest is right and reasonable. But I can detect undercurrents. I have reason to suspect that the attempts being made to thwart me are simply so that my project can afterwards be carried out by others in their search for notoriety and private gain. I need not, I hope, repeat that however much money the biography I am writing may bring, not one farthing will go into my pocket. Every penny will be devoted to perpetuating a great man's memory. It may be it's that petty scribbler, Chrines, who is at the bottom of it all. A mere hack. I don't know how he has the impudence to think himself capable of dealing with such a theme as the life of Stephen Asprey. You have met him very likely? He has chosen to settle himself somewhere about here, hasn't he?"

These last two questions were addressed directly to Mr Day-Bell, and that gentleman answered that he knew little of Mr Chrines and had not seen him for some time.

"Not," Mr Day-Bell added, "since I called to congratulate him on the success of his poems he brought out last year. I believe they had a considerable success and sold well."

"Is this another poet?" Bobby asked in dismay, for he knew well that poets are kittle cattle to deal with.

"Poet indeed!" snorted Mr Pyle. "Why, the *Saturday Supplement*"—and even Bobby knew the name of that leading British literary paper—"called them a feeble caricature of Stephen Asprey's worst work. And then he dares consider himself competent to write the Master's life. I lose patience when I think of it. He knows nothing of Asprey's inner life. He has not even tried to understand it, though, as I shall show, there lies the secret of all Asprey's best work. The fellow will probably succeed only in making Asprey a laughing-stock—if his stuff ever gets published. Which I doubt."

"He told me," Day-Bell said, "that he is a son of Asprey and Janet Merton. He told me in confidence, but he seems to have told everyone else, also in confidence, so I suppose it's no secret."

"Poppycock," Mr Pyle almost shouted. "A wholly preposterous story he has managed to get repeated by fools who know no better. I saw him once. I asked him to call at my office. I thought he might have something to say, some scrap of information or gossip. I was prepared to pay well. There was nothing at all, and I was soon sure—as I always had been, for that matter—that he made the claim purely for publicity purposes. Everyone connected with the Press knows what things people will do to get their names into print. Especially authors. Miss Christabel Merton gave me a most emphatic denial."

"You have called on her?" Bobby asked. "If you get her consent there wouldn't be any more difficulty."

"She seemed reluctant to agree," Mr Pyle admitted. "At first, anyhow. She listened to what I was saying, but unfortunately she was called away before I had time to press my arguments home, and then a red-headed oaf pushed his way into the room where I was waiting for her return. Naturally I refused to leave without seeing the young lady again. I wasn't going to accept messages of that sort from a clodhopper like him. The fellow actually used threats of violence. I would see the young ruffian was adequately dealt with if he were worth the trouble. At the time, rather than distress a young lady by an unseemly scuffle in her home, I judged it best to withdraw."

"Much best," approved Bobby, though inwardly wishing he had had a chance to witness such an unseemly scuffle between the portly and dignified Mr Pyle and the 'red-headed oaf' referred to. Suddenly he noticed that Mr Day-Bell was swelling, almost visibly, just like Mr Stiggins on a famous occasion, and that his face was growing redder and redder and ever redder still. In slow, precise, carefully restrained tones, Mr Day-Bell said:

"Was the red-headed clodhopper of whom you speak, a very tall young man with a slight limp in his left leg?"

"You know him?" exclaimed Mr Pyle, pleased. "Some notorious local bully, no doubt?"

"It seems probable," said Mr Day-Bell, getting rather awe-fully to his feet—one could see him as a cardinal delivering sentence of excommunication—"that you are speaking of my son, Duncan. His farm adjoins that of Miss Christabel." He paused. Bobby had the idea that this time it was Mr Pyle who was expected to wither into nothingness. Unfortunately, like the celebrated jackdaw of Rheims, Mr Pyle seemed none the worse. All he did was to spread out his hands in the sort of deprecatory gesture he was accustomed to use when sacking one of his editors who had failed to show a satisfactory increase in the circulation of the journal entrusted to his care. Still stately in his wrath Mr Day-Bell moved towards the door. Totally ignoring Mr

Pyle, he stayed for a moment on his way to say to Bobby: "As we have now a satisfactory explanation of what Hagen saw we must remember that the Duke of Blegborough"—this with a sidelong glance at Mr Pyle—"may arrive at any moment. Would it be convenient for you to accompany me to Hillings? I must confess to being still somewhat uneasy as the Duke himself seems to be. Your presence would help to show that every possible precaution is being taken."

Bobby hesitated. He, too, was uneasy. He was still aware of the promptings of that kind of sixth sense he possessed—in fact the creation and the child of long and varied experience—which now was whispering incessantly to him that more was going on than appeared on the surface. But then there were those unjudged essays still waiting for him at West Mercian police headquarters. And in West Mercia he was only a guest, without authority or responsibility. Before he could decide how to reply, Mr Pyle, who had no intention of being ignored, and on whom the reference to the expected arrival of His Grace of Blegborough had not been lost, was saying, in his blandest voice:

"Of course, I should not have spoken as I did if I had known who the young man was. Unfortunate, but I am sure you will admit I had considerable provocation. Perhaps I spoke too hast ily in a not unnatural, though passing irritation. Now I think the best thing is for both of us to simply forget all about it." He beamed and waited, expecting with confidence, for had he not gone as near to an apology as anyone could reasonably expect from a Mr Pyle of *Morning Daily*, a response that he did not receive. Mr Day-Bell's marked resemblance to an angry turkey cock did not diminish. Though a little disappointed by this, but making due allowance for a country clergyman who probably did not understand that even cabinet ministers looked anxiously to see what *Morning Daily* had to say, or, if they didn't, so much the worse for them, Mr. Pyle continued, as blandly as before: "I had the pleasure of meeting the Duke recently, and I was intending to take an early opportunity of consulting him and enlisting his support. This might be a suitable occasion, perhaps?"

"No doubt you will ask for an appointment," answered the still unappeased Mr Day-Bell.

Hastily, for he was really beginning to fear that something in the nature of an 'unseemly brawl' might develop, Bobby interposed:

"I should have to speak to Major Rowley first and see what he thinks," he remarked. "It's really his pigeon. If it is anything really serious that's brought the Duke here, couldn't you ring me up? Hillings isn't far, is it? I could easily ask Major Rowley to let me have a car, if necessary."

"My car's outside," Day-Bell said, still totally ignoring Mr Pyle. "It wouldn't take a minute to run you round to Major Rowley, and then we could both go on to Hillings. With the Major, if he would like to be present."

Therewith he swept out of the room, as he went giving, not too willingly, a curt nod and word of farewell to Mr Pyle, who, for his part, still amiable, waved a pudgy hand in response and even smiled. It was a smile of which Bobby took due note as he followed the retreating Mr Day-Bell. As they were getting his car from where it was parked by the club's side entrance, Mr Day-Bell said:

"Unfortunately, there's no telephone service at Hillings, so I can't ring you up, and I should really value your presence. I can't help thinking there must be something wrong to bring a man like the Duke here in such a hurry. His telegram sounded— no, I can't say panic-stricken. But still—well, we shall see. Most inconvenient, more than inconvenient, our having no telephone service at Hillings. No gas or electricity either. No piped water. We might be living in the Middle Ages. And every ounce of coal charged extra for a ten-mile haul. What does this Government care? Nothing. No public transport even, except for one 'bus in the early morning, one in the evening, and one about noon. At other times those who have no car, cycle; those who have no cycle, walk; those who can't walk, stay at home, no matter what their need. It is a crying scandal."

Bobby agreed politely, and as they had now arrived opposite police headquarters he alighted. Fortunately Major Rowley was in his office, and raised no objection. As a matter of fact he was more relieved than otherwise to be able to avoid responsibility a little longer. When dukes appear on the scene, comparatively lesser fry like Chief Constables may find it as well to keep out of the way. Not always easy to satisfy both intruding dukes and Joint Committees. Already, for instance, there had been suggestions that a resident constable should be stationed at Hillings, and the Major did not see how, with a force so much below strength, that could possibly be managed. In an emergency there would be no way of getting in touch with him, since Hillings had no telephone service. And on his side Bobby promised he would be back as soon as possible to get on with those so sadly neglected essays.

So it was not long before Mr Day-Bell and Bobby were on their way to Hillings; and when presently they were halted by traffic lights—not very necessary, perhaps, but Penton prided itself on keeping up-to-date—Mr Day-Bell said:

"Do you know, I almost thought at one time that that unpleasant Pyle person meant to thrust his company upon us?"

"Well, I shouldn't be awfully surprised if that isn't just exactly what he means to do," Bobby remarked. "I saw him smiling to himself as if he had something up his sleeve."

Mr Day-Bell was so startled by this that he very nearly steered the car into the roadside hedge. In recovering he again very nearly swerved into a motor coach travelling in the opposite direction—towards Penton, that is. Bobby thought or imagined he heard certain comments floating back to them from the motor-coach driver, but of these his companion was evidently unconscious.

"That fellow," he remarked severely, "was far too much to this side. Trying to occupy the crown of the road. A common trick with these coaches. I can't think Pyle would do a thing like that. He has no idea when the Duke is likely to arrive."

"Is there any other road to Hillings you can reach without going through Penton?" Bobby asked.

"Well, I suppose so; I really hardly know," Day-Bell answered. "I expect there are side roads you could use if you knew the country. Why?"

"Mr Pyle," explained Bobby, "could easily wait in Penton High Street or by those traffic lights, and sit in his own car till an important-looking car passed headed towards Hillings. It would be a fairly safe guess it was the Duke's, and Pyle could tag along and make sure of arriving at the same time or even a few minutes before. A man of considerable resource. Remember how quick was his explanation of your sexton's story."

"It was a relief to have that cleared up," Day-Bell said. "It was worrying me, taken with everything else."

"It's still worrying me," Bobby told him. "It all came out just a little too pat. We have a useful cliché in the police. I adore clichés—they are always so apt, or they wouldn't be clichés. This one is that we are not satisfied. That's how I feel. I am not satisfied."

"You don't mean he was lying?" Day-Bell asked in surprise.

"There's the lie circumstantial and the lie direct," explained Bobby. "There is also the lie imaginative, which is when it is felt that so the thing ought to have been, and therefore so it was. A form the communists have developed to the highest degree."

Mr Day-Bell, pondering this, drove on in gloomy silence. Then he said:

"I can well believe Pyle is capable of anything at all."

"Oh, well, he is a newspaper man," Bobby said tolerantly.

CHAPTER V
BOBBY LEAVES A MESSAGE

AROUND THE town of Penton the land was rich and well cultivated. But soon that changed as the road began to climb slowly towards the Great Mercian Moor, on the fringes whereof hung the church and the scattered village of Hillings-under-Moor. Scanty pastures succeeded the former fertile fields, and then in their turn these were succeeded by dense stretches of bramble and even denser stretches of bracken. A sullen, hostile land, it seemed, as though resolved to bear nothing to aid or comfort the universal exploiter, Man. One might have had the idea that it waited for the moor to creep down from the plateau where it lurked, and so resume the sway that once it had exercised up to the walls of Penton itself. No longer were visible any of the comfortable, prosperous-looking farm-houses to be seen nearer the town. Now they were replaced at long intervals by scattered, untidy cottages, some in obvious need of repair.

At one spot, when this change had become well marked, there stood upon the left of the road, going to Hillings, a building that seemed utterly derelict, with gaping, sagging roof that showed bare, charred rafters, with broken windows and smoke-stained, ruinous walls, with an entrance led up to by steps even more ruinous. From this entrance all semblance of a door had long since vanished. In front was what once no doubt had been a well-tended garden but was now no more than a tangled wilderness. To judge from its size, the place must once have been the home of some prosperous, well-to-do citizen of Penton. But now it seemed both uninhabited and uninhabitable and, coming to it, Bobby was giving it no more than a casual glance till Mr Day-Bell said:

"That's where Mrs Asprey has established herself. Two Mile End."

"You don't mean she's living there?" Bobby asked incredulously. "It doesn't look as if anyone could."

"She says she couldn't find anywhere else," Day-Bell answered. "She says she can't afford hotel charges, and besides, she likes to be on her own. She got a builder to make two or three rooms at the back fit to live in, and she pays a small rent. There was a had fire some years ago, and the place had been left entirely deserted till she came."

"Do you mind if I get down and have a look?" Bobby asked. "I won't be more than a minute or two."

Though a little surprised by the request, Mr Day-Bell complied. Bobby alighted accordingly, and, his brief tour of inspection completed, came back and said:

"Mrs Asprey doesn't seem to be there. Anyhow, I saw nothing of her. Looks to me as if the whole place might collapse any moment."

"That's what people are saying," agreed Day-Bell. "A strong wind might easily bring the whole thing down. Just as well she's not there, though," he added, "or you might have had a warm reception. There's been talk of sending some inspector or another to see if it were safe for her to remain. When she heard of it she said she would take a broom to anyone she found trespassing. I don't doubt it myself."

"A bit of a tartar," Bobby remarked. "I wonder she's not nervous, living alone in a place like that with not a neighbour in sight."

"I don't fancy Mrs Asprey is much given to nervousness," Day-Bell told him. "A rather formidable old lady indeed. Two Mile End is not in Hillings parish, but when she first came I called to see if I could be of any help. She was civil enough, but I didn't feel myself encouraged to repeat my visit."

"She doesn't stay there all the time, does she?" Bobby asked. "Mr Pyle said something about a flat in Bristol."

"She comes and goes in the most unexpected fashion," Day-Bell replied. "For all you can tell, she may be back in Bristol now. I've never been able to understand why she comes at all."

"Does she ever visit Janet Merton's grave?" Bobby asked.

"Hagen tells me he sees her there occasionally. Sitting on the churchyard wall, eating sandwiches. It rather worries him. She takes no notice of anyone and never speaks except just to answer Hagen's good day."

"Do you think she's quite sane?" Bobby asked.

"Well, there's certainly nothing you can take hold of," Day-Bell replied in a rather deprecating tone. "There was some gossip at first, I believe, but that's died down, and no one takes much notice of her. Miss Christabel Merton told me once that she thought Mrs Asprey came to triumph in death as her dead rival triumphed in life. I don't know."

"It might be something like that," Bobby agreed thoughtfully. "The living wife, the dead mistress, and life more than death. No one now to share her memories, no longer any cause for jealousy. Did Asprey return to her after Janet's death, do you know?"

"He never left her," Day-Bell said. "There was no open breach. He did not live long after Janet died."

"A strange history," Bobby said. He climbed back into the car and they drove on, his mind full of that picture of the silent wife eating her sandwiches by the side of the grave of her dead rival. He said: "It may be she wants to be sure the grave is undisturbed, the poems and the letters still there." Then he said: "I don't think it's that, exactly."

"The whole thing seems to me unpleasantly morbid," declared Day-Bell, frowning. "I think it would be better if she stayed away."

"Yes, it would be better if she stayed away," Bobby agreed.

The road was still climbing ever more steeply towards the dark, overhanging mass of the Mercian moor, the country was becoming ever more desolate, more deserted looking. Mr Day-Bell's car, of ancient date, was making heavy weather of it. They came to a notice-board where a side-track turned off. It announced 'To Canbar Farm', and underneath: 'To Skeleton Farm'. Mr Day-Bell slowed down if that which is already a crawl can be said to slow down, for here they were on a particularly steep and bad stretch of the road.

"Canbar Farm," he explained, "is Christabel Merton's place. Too much for a young girl like her. Skeleton Farm is my son's. The two used to be one farm, but forty or fifty years ago old Mr Merton, Janet's father, was obliged to give up part—the part that is now Skeleton Farm. When it came vacant recently Duncan took it. Marginal land, as they call it now and a tenant not too easy to find. But Duncan seems to be getting on very well, though even during the war there was no attempt to bring it back into full cultivation."

"Not a very attractive name," Bobby suggested.

"Duncan thinks it's most appropriate because it provides only a skeleton living and, besides, it helps with inspectors and agricultural committees and all the rest of what he calls the lunatic fringe. He claims that the name is worth a lot to him, since no one can expect much from a skeleton." Here Mr Day-Bell paused to chuckle, evidently thinking this was an excellent joke. He resumed: "The name is said to come from skeletons found in one of the fields. Possibly relics of a last stand of the Mercians against what to-day would be called aggression when Mercia was overwhelmed by the Wessex invaders. At first the name was applied only to the one field, but when the farm was divided it was given to the whole of that half—third rather."

"Old memories still live about here, then?" Bobby asked.

"I sometimes think old memories never die," Day-Bell answered. "Except in towns. But this new machine age may kill them everywhere. I really think if you raised an alarm in Penton High Street that the Welsh were coming, every man would hurry home for spear and shield and helm."

By now Hillings church tower was in sight—an old, old grey tower, said to date from Saxon days, but more likely of Norman erection, though possibly pre-Conquest. There was no sign of any village, though, for only two dwellings were visible. One was an austere, square house, in grey stone with a slate roof, facing due north and much overhung by the dark mass of the moor behind. Bobby decided it had probably been erected, on strictly utilitarian lines, about the beginning of the last century. It stood some distance from the church on the edge of the shallow depression or hollow in which the church stood, and it had rather the air of wishing to deny that any connection existed between them. Or even of trying to escape from the hollow back to the moor above.

The other dwelling was a small cottage, looking, Bobby thought, much more comfortable and habitable. It, too, was of grey stone, but it had recently been given a coat of whitewash, from the thatched roof to the ground, so that it positively shone in the late afternoon sunshine. Then, too, dormer windows broke the monotony of the flat, square façade. It faced due south, as the larger building faced due north, and also, farther removed from the moor, it seemed by it less overhung—overwhelmed might be a better word. It was adjacent to, and overlooked, the churchyard, and Bobby took it to be the dwelling of the sexton, John Hagen, Mr Day-Bell had mentioned more than once. The larger house was no doubt the rectory.

Before it, Mr Day-Bell brought his car to a standstill, and he and Bobby alighted. Mr Day-Bell went off to open the door of a shed that evidently served as garage, and Bobby stood looking up at the moor above and wondering what had become of the village this church was presumably intended to serve. Day-Bell came back and, guessing Bobby's thoughts, observed:

"There was a much larger population here in earlier days. Always very widely dispersed; but the church served as a rallying point, the centre of all interests, as it should be still. To-day there are only between a hundred and a hundred and fifty inhabited houses in the whole parish. Once the moor provided a living for the cottagers. Gathering reeds for rush-lights or thatching. Material for brooms, too, or cutting peat or keeping flocks of geese. Innumerable activities of that sort. And of course seasonal work on the Penton farms. All dead now, but while it lasted an independent life for which there was much to be said."

Bobby made some conventional remark about it being a pity. Then he said:

"You were speaking of Mr Pyle's caravan being parked on the moor. Is it far?"

"About a quarter of an hour's walk or thereabouts. You see it as soon as you get to the crest of the moor."

"I think I should like to have a look at it," Bobby said. "That is, if I may leave you for a few minutes."

"You don't think Mr Pyle can be there already?" Day-Bell asked, slightly alarmed. "He couldn't have started before us, could he?"

"Oh, it's not that," Bobby said reassuringly. "But I do feel a little curious about the man you saw, the chap who told you he was in charge. I'm wondering if he is as rude to everyone as he was to you, and there is the bare possibility that he wasn't in charge at all, but only a sneak thief taking advantage of an unattended caravan to see what he could pick up. By your description he hardly seems the sort of person a man in Mr Pyle's position would be likely to employ."

"I never thought of that," Day-Bell said. "He seemed so very much at home."

"Well, I think I had better make sure," Bobby said. "And I am rather wondering what made Mr Pyle take to caravanning. I should have expected a Rolls-Royce and a smart hotel would be more in his line."

He went off then with his long, swift strides. The quarter of an hour by which Mr Day-Bell had measured the distance seemed, reduced to terms of length, to be about a quarter of a mile, and Bobby, who thought he was almost standing still if he went at a rate of less than four miles to the hour, covered the distance in five minutes or less. No one was visible at first, but as he drew nearer the door opened and there appeared that unprepossessing individual of the bandy legs and the broken nose Day-Bell had described with such feeling. With a fair degree of accuracy, too, though the fearsome squint was in fact not much more than a cast in the left eye. Indignation at the reception given him had no doubt led Day-Bell unconsciously to elaborate just a little. Not that there was much need, for a more scoundrelly looking ruffian no one could wish to see or be more reluctant to meet on a dark night in a lonely spot.

He stood there at the head of the short flight of steps leading up to the caravan door, hostile and sullen, clearly preparing no warm welcome, when all at once his expression changed, at least as far as the truculence went, for that dropped from him like a superfluous coat thrown off in a hurry. The sullenness remained; and a glance first over his shoulder and then another sideways suggested that he was meditating taking refuge in the interior of the caravan, or else perhaps in flight. But it was too late now for either alternative; and he stood there, with his shoulders hunched and his head down, like a baited bull waiting for a fresh assault.

'Item Sims, and he knows me all right,' Bobby said to himself and then called out cheerfully:

"Oh, good afternoon. Mr Pyle's caravan, isn't it? Is he there?"

"No, he ain't," Sims replied, eyeing Bobby distrustfully. "Not come back yet and not expected. Left me in charge, he did."

"Oh, well, it doesn't matter," Bobby said. "Tell him Mr Owen called, will you? and say I'll write. Don't forget. Tell him it was Mr. Owen. I met him in Penton this afternoon, and there was something I forgot to say. Good afternoon. Sorry to have troubled you."

With that he turned and went, and as long as he was still in sight that sullen, watchful, waiting figure remained motionless in the caravan doorway.

CHAPTER VI
MR PYLE'S ENTERPRISE

Mr Day-Bell was just completing the garaging of his car as Bobby came swinging down from the moor, and he looked very surprised to see Bobby back so soon.

"Isn't the caravan there now?" he asked. "Couldn't you find it?"

"Oh, yes," Bobby answered. "It's there all right, and the same fellow you saw is still in charge, so that's all right, too. If he were a sneak thief of any sort, he would have cleared off long ago. An ugly-looking customer. Looks are nothing to go by, though, and I didn't give him any chance to be rude. I asked if Mr Pyle were there, and when he said he wasn't I came away."

Mr Day-Bell was secretly disappointed at so tame a conclusion. Deep down in his unconscious there had existed a kind of wistful hope that the unpardonable insolence shown to him might be shown to Bobby, too; and, if so, that then Bobby might return, bringing with him a handcuffed prisoner under arrest for obstructing the police in the execution of their duty or something of the sort. Not much good being a high police officer if you couldn't arrest people like this rascally caravan attendant. Probably the next thing would be the discovery of Mr Pyle with his throat cut. Or perhaps never heard of again. Like Mr Thorne, the former incumbent. A dead body lying in those remote and lonely recesses of the moor might well not be found for years, or never found at all. Mr Day-Bell said something to this effect, and Bobby did not contradict him, for he himself was aware of misgivings not very different.

Nothing to be done, though. Mr Pyle would certainly have been informed by Sandy McKie of Sims's background and record, since it was through him that Sims had been engaged. No use repeating a warning already given; even if Bobby had felt, as he did not, that he would have had himself any right to speak of Sims's past while there still remained the possibility that Sims was being offered, and was availing himself of, an opportunity to make a fresh start. Now also Sims knew that whether Bobby had actually recognized him or no—and of that he could not be sure, since Bobby had been so careful to give no sign of being aware of his identity—he had at least been seen and spoken to by an officer of police. If good cause arose he would be quickly identified. 'Of distinctive appearance', as had been said once in a Court of Justice. Or, as it had been more crudely put from the witness-box:

"Know 'im again? Of course I do. With a mug like that as is more like the Zoo than anything 'uman."

Warning had therefore been given in both quarters, and no other action could be taken. As always, the initiative was with the criminal. Nor in this case was there any real evidence that anything of an even remotely criminal nature was being planned, only the vague misgivings hovering as it were in Bobby's mind. The Duke of Blegborough's telegram. The unexplained disappearance of Mr Thorne and the rumours concerning it still current, it seemed. Mr Pyle's arrival on the scene with so unlikely a companion as Item Sims. Old Mrs Asprey's reported threat to shoot. Did all that add up to anything really serious? And if it did, what?

Troubling, Bobby thought, even though most probably there was nothing in it, and now Mr Day-Bell was saying something about having a cup of tea while they were awaiting the arrival of the Duke of Blegborough.

"If he comes, that is," Day-Bell added, a little doubtfully. "He may have changed his mind, though the telegram didn't read as if that were likely. Anyhow, I'll light the oil-stove and put the kettle on. With the price we have to pay here and the difficulty of getting coal, I find oil more convenient and cheaper. I prefer it to the calor gas Duncan uses. You would like a cup of tea?"

"Oh, I'm the complete old woman when it comes to cups of tea," Bobby told him. "I was wondering which part of the churchyard Janet Merton's grave is in? I should like to see it."

"It's near Hagen's cottage," answered Day-Bell. "Visitors have worn a path to it you need only follow. If Hagen's there, he'll probably appear, if only to sell you postcards."

Bobby went off accordingly, and as he went he tried to impress upon his memory every detail of the scene. Not at all probable, of course, that he would ever have to return, but if that should become necessary, in fog or mist or rain, perhaps, it would be well for him to have as clear a picture in his mind as possible. Unnecessary precaution, probably, but it was to this habit of trying to prepare for every possible contingency that he owed much of his success.

As he came nearer, he saw a motor-cycle leaning against the churchyard wall, near the small entrance gate. Coming towards him, from the direction of the cottage and the grave, was a tall, shambling young man with a long, narrow face—so long and narrow, indeed, it almost seemed as if Nature had experienced difficulty in fitting nose, mouth, and eyes into so restricted a framework. At any rate, these features were all disproportionately small, the mouth miniature, the nose little more than a blob, the eyes tiny, though sharp and intent-looking. There was a high, narrow forehead, its height accentuated by a tendency to baldness, and the face terminated in a chin equally long, narrow and pointed. He was wearing a loose jacket, a flowing tie, corduroy trousers. Taking no notice of Bobby, he hurried by, and soon Bobby heard the sound of the departing motor-cycle.

Walking on, Bobby came to the grave. A simple tombstone bore a conventional inscription, giving the dead woman's name, and the dates of birth and death. The customary Scriptural text was missing. A stone kerb surrounded a grass centre, well tended, and a wreath, placed there presumably by admirer or sympathizer, was beginning to wither.

No quieter or more peaceful spot could have been found for the conclusion of so passionate a tale of love, one that even yet had not entirely lost its power to move. Bobby was still standing by the grave, thinking how much of uncontrolled emotion had ended here, when the door of the cottage opened and a man came out and began to walk towards him.

John Hagen, the sexton, no doubt. He was short, strongly built, but with something of the scholar's stoop, as of one who spent many hours bending over books. His head was noticeably large, his features good with clear blue eyes set, like Mr Pyle's, unusually far apart, a high Roman nose, and a largish mouth cut in firm, straight lines above a strong, square chin. The whole impression was of strength and an almost ruthless determination that would allow nothing to stand between it and its goal. Bobby told himself that here was a man who could have made his mark in the outer world had he not chosen to follow his own private way—knowledge rather than success. As he came nearer, Bobby noticed that though he walked briskly, there was a slight tendency to drag one foot and that he held in his hand what looked like postcards.

"Mr Hagen, isn't it?" Bobby asked as the other came up. "Mr Day-Bell has been telling me about you. My name is Owen."

"The police gentleman?" Hagen asked. "You'll excuse me, sir, but when I saw you I thought it was the Duke of Blegborough. Mr Day-Bell told me he was expecting him."

"He still is, I believe," Bobby remarked. "Sorry if you're disappointed, Mr Hagen. I'm afraid a policeman is a poor substitute for a duke. Mr Day-Bell seems to think he's coming about Janet Merton's grave. Something to do with the manuscript poems and the letters said to have been placed in her coffin. Illegible by this time, I should think."

"Well, no, sir," Hagen said. "Not if it's true that they were enclosed in a leaden casket."

"Oh, I didn't know that," Bobby said. "Looks as if Asprey had his reservations at the back of his mind. I wonder. May I see your postcards? I must have one or two. Do you sell many?"

"It all helps," Hagen admitted. "Stephen Asprey's poems, too, but not many buy them. Most seem to think ten and six is a lot to pay just for a book. Mr Chrines wanted me to sell his poems, too—those he published last year. Very successful, too, he tells me."

"Mr Chrines?" Bobby repeated, puzzled for the moment. "Oh, yes. The young man who claims to be a son of Stephen Asprey and Janet?"

"That's him, sir," Hagen said. "Mr Samuel Chrines. He was here just now; perhaps you saw him leaving? A tallish young man, going bald, in corduroy trousers and a loose jacket?"

"Oh, yes," Bobby said. "He went off on a motor-cycle. You sell his books, too? Do visitors buy them at all?"

"Well, sir," Hagen answered, "I thought it best not to try. I don't think Mr Day-Bell liked the idea any more than I did. It might have looked as if we endorsed his story about being the son of Stephen Asprey and Janet Merton.”

“Is that at all generally believed, do you know?” Bobby asked.

“I don’t think so. Mr Chrines is a very pleasant young gentleman, and there’s nothing against him that I know of, but most seem to think he’s only trying to attract attention to his own poetry. I’m no judge of poetry—never read it”—this with a slight accent of contempt—“but a good many papers said he was only imitating Asprey’s work. Miss Christabel was very angry about the story. She got her lawyers to write to him. They called it a libel. I didn’t know you could libel dead people.”

“In some circumstances you can, I believe,” Bobby said. “It depends. Did it have any effect on him?”

“Well, sir,” Hagen answered, smiling a little. “At any rate, now he always says he is telling you in confidence and you mustn’t repeat it. He told me he had proof and he would show it when he was ready—documentary proof he called it. I must say it rather impressed me, what he said. He seemed so confident that some day he would have complete evidence and that was all he was waiting for. He said, too, there were references in one of Asprey’s poems, ‘The past still lives’, that meant him.”

“I see,” Bobby said, looking thoughtfully at this grave where perhaps more secrets than one were hidden. “Mr Chrines lives near here, doesn’t he?”

“Well, it’s not very far. He has a cottage where there’s what’s left of the village,” Hagen explained. “Rather more than a mile and a half from here. There are a few other cottages, and the post office and the ‘Green Man’. If things go on the way they are, Hillings will soon be a parish without inhabitants—except the dead,” and his glance, too, wandered to the grave by which they stood.

“How do the people live?” Bobby asked. “Small-holdings or what?”

“Well, sir,” Hagen answered slowly. “Maybe it’s just as well not to ask. We’ve a bad reputation here. Always have had. It’s said Hillings-under-Moor means the men of hell near the moor, and that in some old maps the place is simply marked ‘Hell’. I don’t know about that. I’ve never tried to go into it. Too busy.

But if there's sheep disappear from a farm, or a poultry run is raided—well, it's always blamed on Hillings. There's been talk of having a policeman stationed here, but it's never come to anything. He would have a bad time, I'm afraid, if it ever did."

"What about Mr Chrines?" Bobby asked. "How does he get on?"

"Oh, no one minds him," Hagen said. "He doesn't interfere and he's left alone. He stands treat at the 'Green Man' sometimes, and plays a game of darts now and then. Otherwise he keeps himself to himself—busy with his writing, he is. What he calls an 'An Epic of Despair and the Modern Age'. It's to be his masterpiece, he says. He used to come here and read bits of it to me, but he's stopped now. I haven't the time to listen, and anyhow I couldn't make head or tail of it, so I started to read him parts of my own work, and that choked him off. He said he couldn't make head or tail of it, and I daresay he couldn't. Not very well read or highly educated, I think, and wholly ignorant of the subjects that happen to interest me."

"Mr Day-Bell told me you had a remarkable library," Bobby said.

"Well, sir," Hagen answered with something of an air of defending himself against possible criticism, "in a place like this you have to have something to keep you occupied, and with me it's always been books and trying to puzzle things out for myself. I can't claim to be a scholar in any sense. That's not possible when you've had no proper education, but I like to read and think. And I rather fancy, sir, this must be the Duke of Blegborough Mr Day-Bell said he was expecting."

Bobby turned sharply. An imposing-looking car was drawing up before the rectory. Two men alighted, and in one of them Bobby recognized Mr Pyle. From the rectory Mr Day-Bell was emerging, all bland welcome. But now he stood motionless upon the doorstep, bland welcome changed to an indignant, bewildered dismay as he recognized Mr Pyle, already, as it appeared, snugly established as the Duke's companion. Bobby devoted one moment to entranced admiration of Mr Pyle's enterprise—no wonder he was a great figure in Fleet Street—and then decided that he had better join them. With a word of farewell to Hagen, he went quickly back to the rectory.

CHAPTER VII
DUCAL VISITOR

WHEN BOBBY, hurrying, reached the rectory, Mr Day-Bell was still standing frozen in that attitude to which his first dignified yet deferential, welcoming approach to his ducal visitor had changed as he recognized that visitor's companion. The two of them, the Duke and Mr Pyle, had paused by the side of the car, and Mr Day-Bell could see with anguish that the Duke was listening attentively to whatever Mr Pyle was saying. To Bobby, as he came up, Day-Bell said with fierce intensity:

"It's Mr Pyle—Pyle. How dare he . . . intolerable . . . Pyle," he repeated as one who could have said so much more had not his cloth forbad.

The Duke and Mr Pyle had finished their little preliminary talk now and were quite close; Mr Pyle wearing the smug, complacent air of the man who has just trumped his opponent's ace. The Duke was a portly, middle-aged man with a long, melancholy face and a manner at once aloof and ingratiating; as of one who knew well that in these days dukes and such like exist only on sufferance, but knew also that while they did exist, they existed by a natural right nothing could change or take away. Indeed, he so much, in so many ways, corresponded to the American idea of the British butler, at once subservient and dictatorial, perfectly sure of himself in his environment, but aware he may be given his final discharge at any moment, that had he appeared in Hollywood he would certainly have been offered such an engagement on the spot.

"The Duke of Blegborough, no doubt," Mr Day-Bell said, advancing in as stately a manner as his inner dismay permitted, and trying at the same time to offer a respectful greeting to the Duke and to ignore as completely as possible his companion. "I received your telegram earlier to-day."

"I hope I'm not inconveniencing you by turning up like this," the Duke said, with his odd mixture of apology and authority. "You have met Mr Pyle already to-day, I think? I was lucky enough to be able to offer him a lift when his car broke down on his way here."

Mr Day-Bell ignored this, and proceeded to introduce Bobby as a high official of Scotland Yard.

"I considered his presence and assistance might be of value, and so I asked him to join us," he explained; and he would have dearly loved to add: 'As I did not Mr Pyle', but then thought he had better not.

"In my view," interposed Mr Pyle, who seldom thought he had better not, "it is somewhat premature, even undesirable, to invoke police aid at this stage. I personally see no good reason for it."

"I am afraid," Bobby interposed in his turn, "the presence of the police is often felt to be undesirable. Quite a natural attitude, but one that on our side we are apt to notice."

"I can assure Mr Owen," declared the Duke, speaking now with the firm yet deferential authority of the butler laying down the correct order of serving the wines, "that his presence is more than desirable. But I trust it does not mean there have been fresh developments?"

"No doubt your Grace is right," Mr Pyle cut in. "Possibly I was a little over-anxious in fearing the police being here might mean unwelcome publicity. My journalistic training, no doubt. One has to be so careful—so strait-laced, I might say—in our profession."

"I was in the act of preparing a cup of tea for Mr Owen and myself while we were waiting," Mr Day-Bell said, in his confusion forgetting to answer the Duke's question. "If, sir, you would care to join us we could talk more comfortably," and it was by no means forgetfulness that made him fail to include Mr Pyle in this invitation—though after all 'you' is a plural and may be so regarded.

Nor had Mr Pyle any intention of not so regarding it.

"A cup of tea is the one thing we were both longing for, wasn't it?" he declared, appealing to the Duke for confirmation.

"Yes, indeed; it is most kind," agreed the Duke, though in fact he had not known till then that thoughts of tea had entered into his somewhat troubled mind.

Mr Day-Bell, baffled, defeated, and well aware of it, led the way back into the house; followed by the Duke, faintly puzzled by exchanges he did not quite understand; by Mr Pyle, grimly persistent; and by Bobby, in full enjoyment of this little scene of high comedy whereof no detail had escaped him, the flavour of it for him so much enhanced by his dark foreboding that behind it might well lie grim issues of life and death. But, then, often had he had occasion to observe how strangely in life tragedy and comedy become inextricably intermingled.

His Grace of Blegborough had already forgotten his desire for a cup of tea whereof Mr Pyle had so recently reminded him. Mr Pyle seemed equally forgetful, for his cup, too, stood untasted before him. Bobby alone showed signs of appreciation as he stirred and sipped and sipped again. True, it was a somewhat weak brew, for Mr Day-Bell had either forgotten or ignored the fact that a pot of tea prepared on economical lines for two is hardly adequate for four.

At first no one seemed inclined to speak. Bobby waited to see who would begin. Mr Day-Bell, exhausted perhaps by his efforts to press a plate of extremely stale-looking currant buns on his guests, had subsided into silence. The Duke was looking more melancholy than ever and was evidently ill at ease. To Mr Pyle, the Duke was equally evidently the only one of those present who had for him a real worth-while existence. It was Mr Pyle who broke a silence beginning to grow a little awkward.

"Difficult as it all is," he said suddenly, "I see no reason why it should not be dealt with satisfactorily. My utmost efforts—" He paused and bowed to the Duke, who looked rather startled and did not seem sure whether or not to bow in return. Mr Pyle continued: "The thing is to avoid undue publicity. I shudder to think of some of the less responsible organs of the Press—such as *Daily Intelligence*—getting to hear of and exploiting all this. I am inclined to suggest we should each undertake formally to observe the utmost privacy. I hope we all agree. For my part most willingly. And you, Mr Owen?"

"Certainly not," Bobby answered, handing up his cup for more tea and helping himself to another of those stale and uninviting buns; for he was beginning to feel that prospects of dinner were slowly but surely fading away, leaving not even a grin behind. "I never," he told Pyle, "make promises I might not be able to keep."

"In that case," Mr Pyle said, slowly and weightily, "may I suggest that it might be as well if Mr Owen left us to discuss this matter between ourselves, less bound as we are by what perhaps I may venture to call official red tape?"

"I am here," Bobby said, "on the invitation of Mr Day-Bell to see if I can be of any assistance—a kind of watching brief, so to say. Of course, I am perfectly willing to retire, if that is Mr Day-Bell's wish. But in that case I shall advise Major Rowley that I am not satisfied, and that in my opinion he should take further action. Of course, it would be for him to decide."

"Oh, we don't want that, not at all," exclaimed the Duke, fluttering protesting hands. "It's not in any way secret. It's merely that I've had two anonymous letters, a 'phone call as well, and there was a pretty plain hint that an old absurd and most offensive story might be raked up again soon and would I like it stopped?"

"Was any specific sum demanded?" Bobby asked.

"No. No. I don't think so," the Duke answered. "It was all put rather vaguely, but the meaning was clear enough."

"Have you the letters with you?"

"I tore them up at once and threw the bits into the waste-paper basket," the Duke answered, and it was exactly the reply Bobby had expected.

"If you get any more," he said, "please be very careful to keep them, especially the envelopes. There might even be finger-prints—'dabs' we call them—we could trace. If there's another 'phone message at any time, keep the line open as long as you can and arrange to let us know, so that we can try to get who ever it may be. A thin chance, I know. People who make those sort of calls don't hang about. But worth trying, all the same."

"My own suggestion," put in Mr Pyle, "would be that one of my staff should remain permanently by his Grace's 'phone—Mr

McKie, I think. A most able experienced man with a wonderful knowledge of the underworld. The moment McKie—"

"Most undesirable," Bobby interrupted curtly, "and might indeed come very near to interference with the course of justice."

"Nothing like that could possibly happen; in any case I would take full responsibility," Mr Pyle declared, looking hopefully, almost pleadingly from Bobby to the Duke and back again, his mind full of exciting dreams.

If once he could get his foot in—or rather Sandy McKie's—the rest would follow automatically. A vision of vast headlines floated before his eyes—'My stay at Blegborough Castle', 'Waiting for the fatal 'phone call', 'My race to the call-box and what I found'—each one more alluring, more 'reader creating' than all the others. The Duke was looking somewhat bewildered. His less alluring vision was of a reporter camped permanently in his study; and he did not like it very much, but was half afraid it was going to happen, unless someone came to his aid. You never knew where you were with these Press johnnies. Bobby took no notice of Pyle's last remark. If the Duke were fool enough to admit one of Pyle's staff to his house, that was his affair. At any rate he had been warned against it. Bobby said:

"May I take it that the scandal in question is concerned with Stephen Asprey and the letters said to be buried in Janet Merton's grave?"

The Duke nodded gloomily.

"I think I had better tell you the whole thing," he said, speaking directly to Bobby, for he was really beginning to be a little afraid of Mr Pyle and of what action that gentleman might next propose. "My wife, the late Duchess, was greatly impressed by Stephen Asprey. I don't know why. The man struck me as an ill-conditioned bounder. These literary geniuses often are. Asprey may have been one—a genius, I mean. My wife seemed to think so, and there is one thing of his very well known—something about 'to hold the gorgeous East in fee', I think it runs."

"Wordsworth," murmured Bobby, unable to let this pass.

"Yes, yes, of course," agreed the Duke. "I meant the one beginning 'In gold and sumptuous velvet go the stars'. Always coming across it. Very fine, no doubt. But all the same I would have soon kicked the fellow out if I had had my way. But you know what women are, and he wasn't worth quarrelling over. Any idea that I ever thought of being jealous is merely silly. One isn't jealous of people of that sort. I understand Asprey's father was a plumber—no doubt a most worthy man," the Duke hastened to add in deference to the democratic standards of the age. "Asprey was staying with us when I had the misfortune to lose my wife. It was most sudden, wholly unexpected. I strongly suspect that it was Asprey who started the abominable lie that I was responsible. I've been told he was very resentful of the speed with which I got rid of him. As if at a time like that I wanted perfect strangers hanging about. He may even have believed the lies he spread. The man's vanity was so colossal he was capable of believing—or imagining—anything to flatter his self-importance. I wanted to take proceedings. My lawyers advised against it."

"It was good advice," Bobby told him. "Much better to let groundless scandal die of its own falsehood rather than spread it further."

"I happen," the Duke said, "to have been fond of my wife. I have never married again and I still miss her—I think at times I even miss her very often highly objectionable protégés she used to have to stay with us," and quite suddenly he blew his nose— loudly, and Mr Pyle blew his more loudly still, probably as a sign of sympathy. "You can imagine," the Duke went on, "my feelings when I found it was being widely hinted that I"—he hesitated and resumed—"that I had murdered her, for that is what it came to."

"Was that said?" Bobby asked, startled.

"Disgraceful," said Mr Pyle. "The whole Press would cry out against such an outrage."

"Evil speaking, lying, slandering, the greatest evil of the day," declared Mr Day-Bell.

"I take it," Bobby said, "the writer of the anonymous letter means it to be understood that he has these Asprey letters in his possession and that they make some definite accusation?"

"That was certainly what was implied," the Duke admitted. "Is it in any way possible that the grave has been opened at some time and the letters removed?"

CHAPTER VIII
LEGAL DIFFICULTIES

BOBBY LOOKED at Mr Day-Bell, who hesitated, waited, spoke at last with evident reluctance.

"It does seem," he said finally, "that there are rumours of that sort in existence. Mere gossip. Entirely baseless. In connection with the extraordinary disappearance of my predecessor here, the late incumbent. I was not, I fear, on very good terms with Mr Thorne. He chose to believe that I was animated by unworthy motives in supporting a scheme for the amalgamation of this parish with St. Mary's at Penton. He got it into his head, quite erroneously, that I was the prime mover in the matter, and I resented that, and said so openly. But I am absolutely sure that whatever caused his disappearance, it had nothing to do with these Asprey letters, or the manuscript poems either. It is out of the question that any priest would permit the violation of a grave in his own churchyard."

"I think we may all accept that," Bobby said. "Besides, what motive could there be? And then it's two years since Mr Thorne vanished, and only now that all this has started up again."

"We newspaper men," declared Mr Pyle, "do come to know of so many utterly incredible happenings that we dismiss nothing as impossible. What is needed is proof; clear, positive proof. It would be most unfair—unEnglish, I might say—to expect any man, duke or dustman, to rest content while such stories are in circulation. The letters must be recovered. They must then be placed immediately in the hands of a competent and responsible, wholly impartial third person, already well acquainted with all the circumstances." He paused here and looked round at the others. When none of them said 'Such as yourself', as he had hoped and expected, he went on: "Presuming, as one is sure would be the case, that the letters are innocuous, they could then be given to the world. If they did contain any irresponsible, malicious gossip, they could be at once destroyed. But I feel it is necessary in the interests of all concerned that they should be recovered and examined."

"I think you may have forgotten," Bobby put in drily, "that there are certain legal difficulties in the way. I think I pointed some of them out."

"In so good a cause as this, for such good and sufficient reason," asserted Mr Pyle, speaking with the superb self-confidence of the Press magnate who knows his power and has exercised it but has not yet recognized its limits, "I should not hesitate to go a little further than the strict letter of the law would permit—to anticipate, in fact, its very often slow, doubtful processes. I should suggest to our friend from Scotland Yard that he should devote himself to tracking down and prosecuting whoever is guilty of this attempt at blackmail."

"Unfortunately that is for the moment impossible," Bobby told him. "Our information is insufficient as yet, and so far there seems to have been nothing in the way of a criminal offence."

"And since when," demanded Mr Pyle with heavy irony, "has blackmail ceased to be a criminal offence?"

"There is certainly a disturbing suggestion of blackmail," Bobby agreed, "which very naturally you, sir"—he was speaking directly to the Duke now—"find very upsetting. But a suggestion is not enough. There must be a definite attempt to obtain, under menace, a specific sum of money. As things are, if we made an arrest, it could be pleaded, and probably would, that there was no idea of getting money, all done out of pure goodwill and kindness of heart."

"You will, I hope, permit me," said Mr Pyle, his irony heavier still—several tons heavier, in fact—"to regard that as a piece of characteristic official red tape?"

"You don't need my permission," retorted Bobby sharply, for he was growing a little tired of Mr Pyle, "to regard anything on earth or in heaven in any way you like. I am merely telling you what is the law, and I may remind you that people disregarding the law do so at their own risk. But that's your business, not mine."

"I am sure," put in the Duke, rather plaintively, "none of us would ever dream of breaking the law. At the same time—well, it's all very difficult, and what can I do if I don't know what Asprey chose to say in those letters? If he said anything at all, that is. Most difficult. One feels at times like taking the law into one's own hands—though of course one wouldn't," he added hastily.

"There is one other thing," Mr Day-Bell interposed. "It has struck me as possible that these letters and so on were never really there at all. Never placed in the coffin, I mean. It seems to me the sort of dramatic gesture Asprey—to judge by what I've read of him—might have indulged in to impress the public. Or posterity, for that matter. I rather thought the introduction to his collected poems hints at something of the sort. It does admit that all his later work showed a great falling off—like Wordsworth, if you remember."

"We have the account of eye-witnesses," interrupted Pyle. "They actually saw the casket deposited in the coffin and the coffin sealed up. As for that introduction—a mere exercise in the debunking which was so popular at one time. No importance can be attached to it. I shall deal with it very adequately in my forthcoming biography."

"I don't think any of the witnesses you mention claim to have seen what the casket contained," Mr Day-Bell persisted. "The casket was certainly put there, but what was actually in it we can't be sure; there's nothing to show. It's only a suggestion, I know. But if Asprey realized that there was a great falling off, and his later work very much inferior to his earlier, or if possibly his inspiration failed entirely and he had stopped writing altogether, he might not have wished it generally known, and so have invented this legend of buried masterpieces lost for ever to the world."

"I don't accept that as even remotely possible," almost shouted Mr Pyle, for the reputation of Stephen Asprey had to remain at its highest if the Pyle biography was to attract the attention it deserved.

"That wouldn't apply to my letters," the Duke said. "Could it?"

"I was thinking chiefly of the poems," Mr Day-Bell admitted. "But Miss Christabel told me once there was a family belief that her aunt destroyed Asprey's letters when she felt her end was near."

"Good God!" cried Mr Pyle, almost in tears now. "No woman could. Not letters of such passionate intensity as only one of

England's greatest poets could write. Her claim to immortality and his as well. I don't, I won't believe it."

"A most interesting idea," Bobby put in, "but there is one objection. No author ever believes his work shows any falling off. Very often the worse it is, the more he likes it. The mother's favourite, the most backward child. Another thing, if Janet Merton destroyed her letters, how are you to account for these blackmail approaches? Not the most sanguine blackmailer could try it on letters that didn't exist. It seems puzzling. I think we must take it that both letters and poems were really placed there."

Mr Pyle cheered up wonderfully at this pronouncement. He even bestowed on Bobby, and for the first time, an almost friendly smile. The Duke, however, looked even more worried than before. A passing gleam of hope he had experienced that these probably highly unpleasant letters were no longer in existence had been extinguished as swiftly as it had been kindled. He said rather helplessly:

"Well, what's to be done?"

"We can only await developments," Bobby said. "We can try to trace your anonymous correspondent if you get any more letters and let us see them. And warn us in time if any more 'phone calls are made. If we can effect identification that would be a big step forward. We can't arrest at present, but we can question. It might even be someone we know. No telling. And I will have a talk with Major Rowley and see if he agrees that the situation needs watching. I do feel that there's a good deal going on behind the scenes, and I don't like it. Too many cross-currents. Poets generally make plenty of trouble while they are alive, and it may be this one is going to make still more now he's dead." He glanced at his wrist-watch. "I think I must be off," he said. "I've got a lot of desk-work waiting for me," and he looked almost as depressed as he felt when he remembered those piles of essays all waiting careful conscientious adjudication.

"Have you a car?" the Duke asked, "or can I offer you a lift?" and he said this quite eagerly, for Bobby's presence gave him a sense of security and support he found really comforting.

But Mr Pyle frowned, regretting deeply that friendly smile into which he had been untimely betrayed. What he chiefly wanted was to have the Duke to himself and persuade him to agree to a plan already forming in his mind, one of which he did not think it desirable that Bobby should have even the faintest inkling. And then, if this plan did go wrong—not that that was in any way likely, but still one never knew—then it would be very convenient to be able to say that there had been ducal approval and support. However, his frown vanished like mouse before cat when Bobby expressed his thanks for so kind and thoughtful an offer but explained that he wished to walk.

A sensation. Had he said he intended to fly, neither the Duke nor Mr Pyle would have experienced any surprise. They would merely have wondered where he had parked his aeroplane and what make it was. But—walking! Their eyes opened, their mouths gaped, they disbelieved their ears.

"Walking," murmured the Duke, as in awe-struck reference to some quaint, long-forgotten, prehistoric practice.

"Ten miles or more," said Mr Pyle, almost equally awe-struck. "Take three or four hours at least."

"Oh, I shan't allow myself more than two," Bobby told them cheerfully. "A policeman has to keep fit. You can't afford to let yourself get out of condition, and I feel I need a little exercise and fresh air. None so far all to-day."

"It'll be dark soon," Mr Day-Bell said warningly.

"Just as well to be as used to the dark as possible," Bobby explained. "Scraps happen in the dark as often as not."

Mr Pyle was on his feet now, deeply anxious lest Bobby should change his mind. He bustled the Duke away with all possible speed, fearful of losing this happy opportunity for a confidential chat thus offered him. Even Mr Day-Bell, not usually excessively perceptive, remarked, when the Duke's car with its two occupants had finally vanished from sight, that Mr Pyle had fairly jumped at the chance of having the Duke to himself.

"Yes, I know," Bobby agreed. "He wanted it very badly indeed. That was plain enough, and I thought it would be a pity to disappoint him. I'm sure he has something up his sleeve, though I've no idea what, and I rather think he means to haul in the Duke if he can. If he does try that, I don't think it will be difficult to get what it is out of the Duke later on, very likely without his even knowing it. A simple-minded, slightly bewildered gentle-man, our Duke, I think, and finding it rather difficult to adjust himself to present-day conditions. And it may be as well to get a pointer from him to what Pyle is up to. I'm not too easy in my mind about Pyle and his proceedings."

Mr Day-Bell pondered this. Then he said with a faint accent of rebuke:

"The wisdom of the serpent."

"Not at all," Bobby said—with a faint accent of protest. "Merely letting those who wish to do so to trip themselves up over their own feet. And now I'll be off. I don't really want to be caught in the dark, but I'll have one more look at the Janet Merton grave first," and therewith he departed, while Mr Day-Bell turned back into the house and the task of washing up the tea-things waiting for him there.

<h1 style="text-align:center">CHAPTER IX
THE VICTORY SIGN</h1>

By the grave, when he reached it, Bobby stood for some min-utes, regarding it with such a fixed intensity of gaze as if he thought that thus he could force it to reveal the secrets it seemed to hold—the secret of Janet Merton's relations with Stephen As-prey; of what, if anything, had been deposited in the dead wom-an's coffin, even perhaps of what had happened to the missing Mr Thorne. And, more immediately important, what plans were hatching in Mr Pyle's busy, scheming, confident, ambitious mind. But though more than once this concentration of his into the same kind of patient, silent waiting had brought unwilling words from those he was interrogating, now the silent patience of the grave more than equalled, more than baffled, his own.

He became conscious that he himself was being watched from behind the curtains in the window of Hagen's cottage, just on the other side of the churchyard wall. No doubt Hagen was wonder-ing about the aim and result of the visit of the Duke. No harm, Bobby decided, in satisfying so natural a curiosity, especially as it was certain Mr Day-Bell would be sure to tell Hagen all about it. Bobby knew well, too, that to appear to be fully and frankly informative yourself is always the best way to get in return the information you need. And to secure Hagen's full co-operation might be very useful should there occur in fact those developments of which Bobby was vaguely and uneasily expectant.

The stage was set, he thought, the actors in position; but how the drama would develop, that he could not even guess.

He turned away and followed the well-trodden path that led through a small swing gate in the churchyard wall towards the sexton's cottage. As he drew near, the door opened and Hagen appeared.

"I saw you were there, sir," he said. "I hope there's nothing wrong to bring the two gentlemen here like this. Will you come in, sir? One of them was the Duke of Blegborough, I take it?"

"Yes, the taller one," Bobby answered, accepting the invitation. "The other man was the owner of the caravan parked up there on the moor. A Mr Pyle. The Duke seems a good deal worried. He's been getting anonymous letters. Nothing very definite so far, but clearly meant to soften him up and make him readier to pay blackmail."

"Blackmail?" Hagen repeated. He pushed forward a chair. "Blackmail?" he repeated once more. "Over the Asprey letters?" he asked.

Bobby nodded and seated himself. He looked slowly round the room, following his usual practice of trying to deduce from its contents something of the character of its occupant. It was small, plainly and sparsely furnished, with two or three kitchen chairs, a deal table before the window. Everything was scrupulously clean and tidy. The floor of plain, uncovered boarding gave the impression of being well scrubbed every morning. The walls were nearly hidden by apparently home-made shelving filled with books, many of them with slips of paper sticking out, presumably for purposes of reference. They gave the impression of being a workman's tools kept in readiness for instant use. Near the fireplace in a corner stood a big filing cabinet, and there were two large wooden packing-cases close by. The table in the window was covered with piles of neatly written manuscript. In one corner stood a great heap of exercise books and there was a blotting-pad on which one of these exercise books lay open, one page half covered with writing not yet dry.

An interesting room, Bobby thought, and one that seemed to proclaim aloud the old maxim, 'Plain living and high thinking', in complete devotion to learning and research. What strength of resolution, what avidity to know, what determination, must not have been shown to overcome the obstacles that a man in Hagen's position would certainly have had to face. Bobby found himself looking at Hagen with a respect that was almost awe, as he thought of the path Hagen had set himself and followed with such persistence.

Hagen had seated himself by the table in front of the window, but he did not seem inclined to speak. Bobby said:

"The Duke seems to be afraid that the letters said to have been buried in Janet Merton's coffin may have been removed."

"There were stories like that going about after Mr Thorne's disappearance," Hagen said slowly. "Now they seem to have started up again. I don't know why."

"It wouldn't take long, would it?" Bobby asked. "I think I remember it was said at the time that the resurrection men at the beginning of the last century could open a grave and remove the body in less than an hour—and in complete darkness."

"Not without my hearing," Hagen said confidently. "My bedroom is the one above this, overlooking the churchyard just the same. I'm a light sleeper. I always keep my window open. I should hear at once if there was the slightest sound." He spoke more slowly, almost as if to himself, saying softly, "I should hear, I think, even if the dead arose. But they don't; they never do. The dead lie quiet and still in a silence like the thunder of the voice of God."

Bobby looked at him quickly. He did not understand this last sentence, he did not understand the intensity with which it had been spoken; he wondered what it was that made Hagen stare with such fresh intensity—was it challenging intensity?—out there where Janet lay in her quiet grave. Hagen turned to him suddenly.

"Sorry, sir," he said in quite a different tone. "I suppose one gets ideas, living so much alone and having so much to do with graves. Sometimes I think the dead waiting out there for me to join them are nearer to me than the living." He got up abruptly and shook himself, as if to get rid of such thoughts, as a dog will shake itself to get rid of the water in its coat. "Quite out of the question," he declared briskly, "for anything like that to happen to any grave in my charge without my knowing. I can swear to that."

"Couldn't something of the sort happen when you were away?" Bobby suggested. "You can't be always here. Holidays, for instance?"

"Well, sir," Hagen answered, smilingly, "I'm not much of a one for holidays. I go to London sometimes. Very rarely, though. And now and then I go into Penton to the library, if they've some book there I want to look at, or if they've been getting one for me from some other library. They're always very good about that. Once they got me one I needed from the John Rylands Library in Manchester. But any grave-robbers would have to wait a long time for the chance. I don't think it's feasible. Besides, one thing's certain. Nothing like that could possibly happen without my knowing. There would be plenty to show—trampled grass, disturbed earth, the headstone not quite in the same position. It's not an ordinary grave. It's part of my livelihood—selling postcards and so on. If a blade of grass were disturbed near it I should notice it. For that matter, so I should, I think, anywhere in the churchyard; I know it so well. No, sir. You can dismiss that as even remotely possible. Not without my knowing, at least."

He spoke with an air of absolute certainty that carried conviction with it, and Bobby nodded in agreement, feeling he could accept this.

"If I get in touch with the Duke again," he remarked, "I'll tell him what you say. But I don't wonder the poor man's worried. It seems there were hints that an application might be made for permission to exhume his wife's body. You can imagine what the cheap Press would make of it if they got hold of a story like that."

"But surely," began Hagen, "surely that isn't likely. After all these years."

"Oh, I've no doubt it's mere bluff," Bobby agreed, "but disturbing, all the same. Well, I must be off. Got to get back to Penton. You have a fine library, Mr Hagen. May I have a look?"

The titles of some of the books were familiar—to Bobby, sad to say, more familiar than their contents. Others he had never heard of, nor could he even guess at the subjects they treated of. A number were in Latin, and Bobby, who had long ago forgotten his 'mensa—a table', and his 'Hic, haec, hoc', regarded these with a doubtful eye. He had a feeling he might suddenly be called upon to do an unseen translation and probably get kept in as a result. There were a few of those early books known as 'incunabula', and others were in black letter. Generally the subjects dealt with seemed to be philosophy, theology, comparative religion, mysticism; this last appearing to be the largest separate class. There were many medical books, too, mostly treating of abnormal mental states.

"You read a great deal, Mr Hagen," Bobby remarked. "Do you write as well?"

Hagen made a gesture, a somewhat deprecating gesture, towards the manuscripts on the table before the window.

"A beginning," he said. Then he pointed to one of the great wooden cases near the filing cabinet. "Material. Memoranda. Notes," he said. "Preparatory. *Thought* has published one article of mine, and there have been two in the *Herbert Trust Quarterly*. And only this week I had one back from *The Eastern Road* they had sent me a proof of, though they did warn me that did not necessarily mean they meant to publish it. To send round to members of their editorial board, they said."

"Too bad," Bobby remarked.

"I may try to recast it," Hagen observed meditatively. "It's an attempt to compare Bergson's approach to intuitive knowledge as a universal sympathy, giving complete insight, with Spinoza's theory of intuitive recognition of a thing's essence through immediate union with the perceived object. I feel now I did not go deep enough."

Bobby, gasping a little under the influence of this pronouncement, which he was sure meant something, though he was not sure what, picked up his hat and said it was very interesting, but he must be off if he were to get back to Penton before dark. Hagen, still apparently wrestling with Bergson and Spinoza and getting, it seemed, rather the worst of it, went to open the door, where a splash of rain driven in by a gust of wind served to recall him from his philosophic heights to the more common needs of humanity.

"It's raining," he said.

"Rather a nuisance," Bobby remarked. "I never did like getting wet through. May I wait a few minutes, to see if it clears off?"

Hagen had stepped outside and was looking up at the clouds now veiling the declining sun.

"I don't think it will last," he said. "If it does come on heavily I'm sure Mr Day-Bell would let me have his car to drive you into Penton and then bring it back. It would be a long walk in the rain." He stepped back into shelter and closed the door upon the driving rain. "The other gentleman—Mr Pyle—did he go with the Duke or back to his caravan?" he asked. "I intended to mention it before, but I forgot. I think perhaps he might be told that that man of his isn't making himself at all popular."

"Oh. What's he been up to?"

"Well, sir, the people round here don't like gypsies. Gypsies have a name for picking up unconsidered trifles, and our villagers feel they can do all that's necessary in that line—and rather more, too, for that matter. So when they heard there was a caravan parked on the moor near the church, Mrs Davis—she lives near the 'Green Man'—thought she would see if it was gypsies, and give them a hint to move on before there was trouble and the Penton police coming to see what it was all about. She came back rather fussed and complained about being sworn at and told to get out unless she wanted a clip on the ear. I don't want any trouble either, so I went myself—the caravan's only a few minutes' walk away—and told a man who was there about the time when caravaners quarrelled with our villagers and woke up in the middle of the night to find a bonfire blazing under the caravan. It didn't do any great harm, but it might have been nasty."

"Yes, indeed," Bobby agreed. "Looks to me as if it would be rather a good idea to station a constable here. I hope the chap you saw was grateful for your warning?"

"Not him, sir," Hagen answered. "I fancy he had had a drop too much. Been visiting the 'Green Man', probably. He used a good deal of bad language and showed me a revolver he was busy cleaning, I suppose. He said anyone trying tricks like that on him would get a pill to stop him ever needing another."

"Did he, though?" Bobby exclaimed, so startled and surprised that Hagen in his turn seemed almost equally surprised. "I think I had better tell Major Rowley. He may think it worth while to find out if the chap has a certificate—or Mr Pyle either. I don't like people who take a drop too much and flourish guns. It looks as though the rain was stopping now, thank goodness. By the way, Stephen Asprey's widow has a place somewhere about here, hasn't she? Does she ever visit Janet Merton's grave?"

"Oh, yes," Hagen said at once. "I've often seen her. She doesn't speak much, except to answer, and not always that, if you say something. I remember once—"

He paused and seemed doubtful whether to continue.

"Yes," Bobby said as Hagen still hesitated. "Yes?"

"It was one time," Hagen said. "It was strange. It's stuck in my memory somehow. I don't think she knew I was there. She had been sitting perfectly still, there on the churchyard wall, not moving a finger, just sitting. All of a sudden she got up and went to the grave and stood for a minute, rather like a statue, so still and motionless she was, and then she straightened herself up, so she seemed to grow taller, and she made the victory sign they used in the war—you remember? Two fingers held up like a 'V'. She stayed like that for a minute and then she went away."

CHAPTER X
TRAGIC MEMORIES

WITH THIS strange, tragic picture in his uneasy mind of the widow, watchful and waiting, by the grave of her rival till at last she came to make above it her sign of triumph and of victory, did Bobby begin his long walk back on the lonely Penton road.

The triumph and the victory of the living over the dead? You, you have gone, it seemed to say; but I remain. But was it not rather, Bobby asked himself as he strode along, more truly that the triumph and the victory lay with the quiet, untroubled dead?

He put that question aside. One of the many which must indeed be asked, but to which no answer can be given, unless indeed it is that triumph and disaster are equally the impostors they have both been called. More useful, more necessary, he felt, if ill things that threatened were to be stayed, for him to consider what might lie behind that strange gesture and for what reason Stephen Asprey's widow had left her Bristol home to establish herself for long periods in two or three barely habitable rooms of a house that was nearly a ruin. Was it merely some kind of morbid attraction that drew her to the grave of a woman she had never seen in life? Or was it because of those buried letters and their rumoured or possible recovery? Or was it rather a belief that in fact they had never been there to recover? Was it conceivable that she was the Duke's anonymous correspondent?

Fortunately the gust of rain and wind that had delayed Bobby's departure had died away as quickly as it had arisen. For though he had, perhaps a little boastfully, declared his indifference to the risk of being overtaken by darkness during his long walk, it was not, all the same, an experience he was in any way anxious for. Especially if the rain came on again. The road was not in the best possible condition, and bad weather and consequent mud would soon reduce his present five-mile-an-hour pace or over to a much more moderate speed.

But now first he heard and then he saw a motor cyclist speeding towards him. As they neared each other the motor cyclist dismounted and stood waiting. Bobby, close now, could see that he was a fair, red-haired youth and that he had a slight limp in his left leg. That answered to the description Mr Day-Bell had given of his son, and Bobby, as he came up, was the first to speak.

"Mr Duncan Day-Bell, isn't it?" he said.

"Why, yes; how did you know?" the other countered. "Are you the man from Scotland Yard my father has been talking about?"

"I am," Bobby agreed. "I might ask how you knew, but I won't. A fair guess on both sides, perhaps. As another guess, you are on your way to ask what the Duke of Blegborough wanted?"

"Well, it's all been worrying Dad quite a lot," Duncan admitted. "Dukes aren't everyday birds in Hillings, and it did rather look as if something fresh had turned up about those Asprey letters."

"So it has," Bobby told him. "In confidence, it's not a story that ought to be allowed to get around too much, but your father is sure to want you to know; there's been what looks like the beginning of a blackmail threat."

"Has there, though?" Duncan exclaimed. "Do you know, I half expected there was something like that in the wind. There's been a lot of talk about those letters, and more than ever lately. Sort of started up again. The idea seems to be that it's all mixed up with Mr Thorne's going off the way he did and that he or someone else had got hold of them. Cracked sort of notion, if you ask me."

"Could the grave have been opened secretly, do you think?" Bobby asked, "and the letters recovered?"

"No, I don't," Duncan answered. "Quite impossible. You can trust old Hagen. He keeps a pretty close eye on that grave. He says if he didn't, soon there wouldn't be any grave at all, what with souvenir hunters chipping bits off and pocketing handfuls of earth and all that sort of thing."

"I've been having a long talk with Hagen," Bobby said. "He seems a remarkable character."

"He jolly well is," Duncan agreed. "Never been to school to speak of, and now reads Latin right off, the way you or I read the morning paper—I mean me, of course."

"Oh, you can count me in," Bobby said smilingly. "He has a fine library—must have cost something to collect."

"You can buy a lot of books if you buy nothing else," Duncan pointed out, with great truth. "His idea of a really cosy evening is sitting by the fire reading blokes like Kant and Hegel. Just now he's exchanging letters with some howling swell of a Jesuit father about Thomas Aquinas. I can't for the life of me imagine why he hangs on here."

"I wondered about that myself," Bobby said. "Your father told me he refused offers he's had because his knowledge of Latin has no commercial value and his lack of general education would make him unfit for any academic appointment."

"Rubbish," declared Duncan. "Dad got him an offer from old Sir Thomas Alexander, who is about the leading classical scholar of the day, even if he hasn't a bean to his name. He was looking for someone who was a Latin scholar, didn't mind living in the country miles from anywhere, wouldn't be too proud to help in the washing up, and all for thirty bob a week, board, lodging and washing included—and never want to stop working. Not too easy to fill that bill, especially with a snag like that thirty bob a week. Hardly enough to keep most people in cigarettes today. The very thing for Hagen, you would have thought, but he turned it down—God knows why."

"Probably," Bobby agreed. "Probably He does. I suppose Hagen had his reasons. I always tell our chaps there's a reason for everything if they do but diligently seek it out. Your father told me he found it a little embarrassing to have so learned a sexton."

"I know," Duncan said, grinning. "A bit awkward, if you see what I mean, being the boss of a bloke like Hagen. I believe Mr Thorne felt that way, too. No one could help. Hagen seems quite content, though, and you can't sack him."

"Did Mr Thorne ever try to get him other employment?"

"I don't know—couldn't say, I'm sure," answered Duncan. "I believe he used to complain sometimes that Hagen was getting too big for his boots. Jealous, perhaps, and rather more than didn't like it when Hagen put him right over a quotation from some old johnnie or another—St Jerome, I think it was. It got into the papers somehow. Hagen wasn't too tactful, and Mr Thorne was peeved, and Dad says he's always jolly careful to keep off the classics when Hagen's near."

"Mr Thorne's disappearance has never been explained, has it?" Bobby asked.

"Well, the general idea," Duncan answered, "is that he did a bunk. Got into a mess about money and went off with a woman who left Penton about the same time. Dad says it was the moor, and I expect that's about the size of it. Dad nearly had his there once. He got caught in one of the moor mists that can come up before you know, and if it does you can easily lose your way and wander round in circles till you die from cold and exposure. Luckily for Dad, the mist cleared, but he's never trusted the moor since."

"It sounds a likely explanation," Bobby said. "I expect you know a young man named Chrines?"

"Oh, yes. Why? You mean the chap who tells everyone he is the son of Stephen Asprey and Janet Merton, only you mustn't say so to anyone else. Has he been pitching you that yarn? Miss Christabel Merton is very angry about it, and I told him to lay off or I'd break every bone in his body."

"What did he say to that?"

"Bought himself a gun and sent a note to tell me he wouldn't hesitate to use it if he were attacked," answered Duncan, grinning widely. "So next time we met I stood him on his head to see if he really had a gun with him. He hadn't, but what he says is that I took him by surprise, and now he always carries it. Miss Merton got to hear and made me swear blue black and white to lay off myself, so that's that."

"Then Miss Merton doesn't accept his story about being Asprey's son?" Bobby asked.

"No. I told you. She's really angry, and when she gets that way—well, you have to look out for squalls. She went off to her lawyers, and they wrote to Chrines and charged her six and eight, I expect. I would have shut Chrines up free gratis and for nothing if she had let me. You never know with women."

"Do you know if Miss Christabel has any definite reason for disbelieving Chrines's story?" Bobby asked.

"She told me her aunt—Janet Merton, you know—said when she was dying that there had been nothing physical between her and Asprey. They had only met very occasionally and their friendship was entirely intellectual and spiritual. I can't say I put much stock in the spiritual and the intellectual when it's a pretty girl on one side and a chap like Stephen Asprey on the other. Only I suppose on your death-bed you do rather tend to speak the truth. No reason not to, and then you feel you're going where it's all known already."

"Death-bed statements have always been taken seriously," Bobby agreed. "More so in earlier times than to-day, perhaps. I must be getting on, though. I don't much like the look of those clouds."

"Walking?" Duncan asked.

"Eccentric, isn't it?" Bobby said. "Practically antediluvian. I feel as if I ought to charge for admission. Might I ask you again to say nothing about the Duke of Blegborough's complaint of what looks like a hint of blackmail in the wind? I can't help thinking there's more behind all this than we know of and the less said for the present, the better."

He nodded and went on, leaving Duncan standing thoughtful by his motor-cycle, and it was some time before the distant rhythmic beat of the engine told him that the young man was once more on his way.

It was growing dark now, not only because the hour was late, but because of those heavy clouds Bobby had remarked piling up overhead. The rain still kept off though, and there was even a gleam of the westering sun breaking through by the time he came to Two Mile End, that three parts ruin where Mrs Asprey had made a lodging for herself.

A light was showing at the back of the building, so presumably Mrs Asprey had returned. With a somewhat hesitating glance at those still threatening clouds, and another in the direction of Penton and shelter, Bobby left the road and started to pick his way across the tangled growth that once had been a garden and on to where the light showed. It might be, he reflected—in fact, it almost certainly would be—his last opportunity to see or talk to Mrs Asprey, and he was curious to meet the woman of whom Hagen had told that strange story of the victory sign made above a rival's grave. To-morrow would be too late, for he must be back at the Yard as soon as possible, and there were still those unread essays heavy on his conscience, only barely placated by his promise to it to sit up till all had been read, no matter how late the hour.

His approach had evidently been heard, for now a door opened, a ray of light shot out, and a harsh voice called:

"Who's that? What do you want?"

"Mrs Asprey, isn't it?" Bobby asked.

"Well, if it is, who may you be?" came the challenging response.

"My name is Owen," Bobby said. "I'm a policeman. From London. Down here on special business. There seems to have been a good deal of talk just recently about Mr Stephen Asprey and his letters and poems said to have been buried with Janet Merton in Hillings churchyard. I was wondering if you knew of anything likely to have started people talking again?"

"Start," she retorted. "They never stop, do they? So how can they start? I suppose it's the Duke of Blegborough's being here has brought you along? You had better come in. The rain's starting, anyhow."

She moved back into the house, and Bobby followed. It was a bare, comfortless room he entered, with little furniture beyond a chair or two, a deal table, a very rickety-looking sofa, shelves on which were a few household utensils, and a cupboard with a door swinging half open and affording a glimpse of crockery within. The room served apparently both as kitchen and living-room, for in one corner a kettle was boiling on an oil stove, and there was also an oil heating-stove. It was well lighted by a lamp standing on the table, and the only sign of feminine occupation was knitting thrown down on one of the chairs. Nor did it show any such signs of a meticulous care that Hagen's cottage had displayed in well-scrubbed boards, a shining table, polished chairs, everything in its place.

Mrs Asprey was a tall, gaunt woman with a thin, angry face, the features prominent, the narrow mouth so tightly closed one felt it was kept like that to hold back words better left unuttered. She seemed to take but little thought for her personal appearance, for the woollen jacket and the skirt she wore were old and shabby and not too clean, and she displayed no ornament of any kind. It was said that once she had been an exceptionally pretty woman, but small trace of such beauty now remained. Only her eyes attracted and held attention, still vivid, still quick and questioning, and piercing when they came to rest on anything, as now on Bobby. There was somehow, it was hard to say why, an air of dignity about her as she stood upright and waiting, in the centre of that bare and austere room. Perhaps it came, Bobby thought, from much suffering silently endured, and yet this air of sombre dignity went not well with Hagen's tale of her futile gesture above Janet Merton's grave—futile, for what care the silent and unknowing dead for the gestures of the living? But that strange dignity was plain about her as now she lifted one hand and uttered the single word:

"Well?"

CHAPTER XI
FORGOTTEN POET

BOBBY DID not answer at once. He scarcely knew how to begin, and he had an instinctive feeling that on how he began would depend entirely whether this darkly attentive woman would respond or not. She was still waiting with something of that slow, implacable patience he himself could show upon occasion. Then when it came to him that this silence must last no longer, he said:

"You knew of the Duke of Blegborough's visit here this afternoon?"

"Why should I not know," she retorted, "what everyone in Penton knows?"

"You can probably guess what brought him," Bobby suggested.

"The letters and manuscripts my husband put in Janet Merton's coffin, I expect," she answered. "There was some meddling twopenny-ha'penny journalist wants to get hold of them—to make a Sunday newspaper holiday. Does the Duke want to help him or to stop him?"

"I don't know," Bobby said. "I don't think he knows. Which do you want?" But to that she made no answer, her lips more tightly pressed together than before. When he saw no reply was coming, Bobby made no attempt to press her. He knew it would be useless. Instead he said: "Of course, I needn't assure you there is no question of any official action. But there are some disturbing rumours in circulation—the Duke is certainly very disturbed indeed."

"What sort of rumours?" she asked, eyeing him closely, but yet apparently with less hostility.

"Rumours that these papers were either never buried at all or else that somehow they have been recovered," Bobby answered. "There seems to be some sort of idea that it's all linked up with the disappearance of Mr Thorne two years ago—he was the clergyman here."

"That's all nonsense," she declared contemptuously. "They couldn't matter to him. They could to the Duke if Stephen's letters are anything like what he told me." She pushed forward a chair. "Sit down," she said and seated herself, upright in her chair as she had been upright while standing. "That's why he came to-day. Did you know?"

"I understand the letters may contain gossip about the former Duchess," Bobby answered. "What is disturbing the Duke so much—very naturally—is some sort of vague suggestion that application may be made for an order of exhumation to be issued."

"That will be the work of the journalist who came here—I forget his name, he told me; Pike or Pyle or something."

"Mr Pyle," Bobby interposed. "Of *Morning Daily*. If statements are made in these letters, it may be very awkward. It depends, of course."

"Anyone who takes Stephen's letters seriously doesn't know much about him," Mrs Asprey said. "It's quite possible he said all sorts of things in them. It's possible he really believed that the Duchess had been murdered because her husband was jealous of him. He could believe anything that flattered his vanity."

"Did he tell you anything like that?"

"I expect so; I didn't pay much attention if he did. I'm sure he would have tried to make love to her if he had been given a chance. It's quite likely he did try, and that the Duke didn't approve—or the Duchess either. I don't know."

"Accusations of murder, hints of murder, are serious things," Bobby said. "I gather you didn't take them seriously in this case?"

"I never took seriously anything he said," she retorted, and Bobby noted that this was more or less in the nature of an evasion of his question. "I never believed a word he said. Except, of course, when he told me that he loved me. That's a tale every woman is always ready to believe—till they know better, poor fools!" Her voice softened, and for a moment she seemed lost in old memories. She resumed: "I daresay I still believe it was true—at intervals. I went to see my lawyers the other day. They say the paper the letters are written on belongs to Janet Merton's niece under her will, but the copyright in what's written on the paper is mine, so I can stop publication of the letters themselves. But it would be difficult to prevent publicity being given to anything said in them. Allegations that the Duke poisoned his wife could come from anywhere. If challenged, then the letters could be cited as supporting evidence and an order made for their production. I told them what I thought of that sort of legal quibbling. I asked the Merton girl if she would promise to burn them if she ever got them. She said she must ask her lawyers, and they told her she mustn't on any account promise anything till she knew what they really contained. What do you think of silly hair-splitting like that?"

"I suppose it's how the law stands," Bobby said, "and nothing you can do about it. It does seem all rather confused. The law often is."

"Or else lawyers would starve, and a good thing to," she commented. "Is there any chance this Mr Pyle will manage to get the grave opened? He seemed to think he could. He wanted my support. He tried to argue; talked about money, promised me some. I chased him out. Well, could he?"

"I don't know, I'm sure," Bobby said slowly. "I suppose it's possible. The Press can do a lot when it gets going. His idea seems to be to get a Home Office order, and I've an idea he's begun to work on the Duke already. There are two lines he could follow. He could say that the poems are of such great literary value the world cannot afford to lose them. Who would hesitate to open a grave to recover, say, a new play by Shakespeare? Or a new sonnet sequence telling us who the dark lady was? And then he could suggest that the letters contained an accusation of murder that ought to be investigated, if only to clear the ancient house of Blegborough from so intolerable a stain. I think it's at any rate possible that he might bring it off one way or the other.

My impression of the Duke from what I saw of him this afternoon is that he could be easily influenced."

"What's this Mr Pyle really want?" she asked. "I thought Stephen was as good as forgotten. His books don't sell any more. You see them on the top shelf in second-hand bookseller's shops. The last time I heard from the publishers they had sold under a dozen copies of his collected works."

"Mr Pyle intends to write your husband's life," Bobby explained. "He seems to think he can make him famous again. He was once, and Mr Pyle argues he might be again."

"Fallen idols generally stay fallen," she commented. "A good thing, too, or there would be no vacant pedestals for new ones. Another biography? I remember an offensive young fool came to see me. A long time ago. I had almost forgotten. He claimed he was Stephen's son. He seemed to think that gave him a claim on me. He said he meant to write a life of Stephen. He wanted my help. I think he wanted me to write the whole book, for that matter. I chased him out, too. The dead are best left dead."

"That would be Mr Chrines, I take it?" Bobby said. "I've heard about him. Do you think it's true? That he is a son of Mr Asprey's, I mean."

"He wouldn't be the only one if he were," she answered moodily. "How should I know? He said Janet Merton was his mother, and he told me he has written poems all the critics recognized as having the Asprey touch. Monkeys can always imitate, and so I told him."

"I saw him in Hillings churchyard. I understand he brings flowers to put on Janet's grave," Bobby remarked. "You go there, too, sometimes, don't you?"

"I expect Hagen told you that?" she countered. "He watches all the time. He might be afraid the grave would open suddenly and the dead arise. Well, what are you staring at?"

"You startled me, that's all," Bobby said. "I had the same idea myself, and Hagen said something of the same sort—something about the dead lying quiet. Well, why shouldn't they?" he went on, without waiting for an answer. "There's one thing more I would like to ask if I may. Do you think it's absolutely certain these papers were really placed in Janet Merton's coffin to be buried with her?"

She took a little time to answer, and it was apparent she was hesitating how to reply. She said presently:

"It's strange you should ask that. At first I didn't believe it. I knew how Stephen loved playing to the gallery, striking attitudes in public. It would have been like him to make a gesture and then go back on it." Again she was silent. Then she said: "Yes, it would be like him, but still more like him to make the gesture and be quite sure posterity—he always talked of Posterity with a capital 'P'—would never consent to lose what he told everyone was the best work he had ever done. The *King Lear* of his compos, he said. He certainly believed it was. I never knew him so confident. He always was in public, but I knew. The last thing he wrote was always his best, and he tried to make the public think so, too. But alone with me at night, then sometimes he would break down and cry."

"Cry?" Bobby repeated.

"For fear his gift had left him," she said.

"Had you read them?" Bobby asked. "These last poems, I mean?"

She shook her head.

"One or two, perhaps," she said, "but he never liked to let his work be seen till it was ready for publication. 'Only my best is good enough for the public,' he used to say, but really it was a sign of how unsure he was inside him. No," she said, "I think it is certain the buried casket did really contain both the last poems he wrote as well as the letters." She sank again into silence. He did not attempt to interrupt her thoughts. He had an idea that they went a long way back, and perhaps as well a long way into the future, too. At last she said, a little as if musing aloud: "If the poems could be recovered they might make Stephen famous again. How he would have loved that! By themselves? But that could not be. Could it?" she asked, now addressing Bobby as if suddenly remembering his presence.

"You mean the poems recovered, but the letters left?" he asked. "Is that what you would wish?"

"Do you think," she flashed with a sudden fierce intensity of passion one would hardly have thought that old and tired frame could contain: "do you think I want every gaping fool to read what he should have said to me, but said to her instead? She stole his body from me. Let it go. Others had done as much before. What did I care? I didn't marry him for his body. I married him for his poetry. He married me for my money. He had it and he spent it. I knew he would. But I didn't know when I went to the altar that I was committing bigamy. Two Stephen Aspreys. A poet who died young, for the gods loved him. And a man. A common man. A mean man. He lived longer."

After that she would say no more, and finally Bobby left her sitting there alone with her memories and her griefs.

CHAPTER XII
MURDER

NOT LONG after Bobby had left Mrs Asprey's strange dwelling-place the rain, threatening so long, began to fall. At first only heavy scattered drops. Bobby increased his speed. At times he ran. It became a race between him and the rain. The rain won, hands down. Or rather, sheets down.

It was indeed a very bedraggled Bobby Owen, who, drenched and sorry, at last reached his hotel. However, a hot bath and a good dinner, which he ate in his room, attired in dressing-gown and pyjamas while the hotel did its best for his soaked garments, served to restore his energies. A message to police headquarters brought him those so long neglected essays; and, by dint of sitting up till three next morning, he managed to sort them out in fair order of merit and to select those he thought worthy of awards. He was up again by seven, spent another hour or two in confirming by re-reading his previous night's judgments, communicated his decisions to Major Rowley, and just managed to catch the 1.15 p.m. London express. Most of the way he dozed, awakening though every now and then with a troubled and uneasy conviction that he had left behind him in Penton problems to which the solution would have one day to be sought most urgently.

Fortunately he found, when he reached the Yard, nothing very pressing on his desk, and he was able to get home fairly early, persuade a somewhat doubtful wife that the condition of his coat and trousers did not indicate that he himself was equally the worse for wear, and agree that the sooner the said coat and trousers went off to the cleaners, the better—and whether the cost would go through on the expense sheet could only be discovered by the method of hopeful experiment.

Next day one of the first things he did was to put through to *Morning Daily* a call asking if Mr McKie was disengaged, and, if so, could he lunch with Bobby at the 'Golden Grasshopper', the well-known and not too expensive restaurant in Whitehall. The call was answered in person by a pleased but slightly apprehensive Mr McKie. Pleased because it would add to his prestige, both with *Morning Daily* and with the rest of the world, to lunch with a high Scotland Yard official; apprehensive, because he knew the Yard did not consider he was always so co-operative as could have been desired and had found occasion more than once to hint that there was such a thing as being an accessory after the fact. He would, he assured Bobby, accept the invitation with the greatest pleasure. That settled, he sat down to examine his conscience—or what with a newspaper man stands for that inconvenient and nearly obsolete appendage—and decide whether he had been in any way less co-operative than usual. There was, of course, the little affair of the Spanish Emeralds, but the Yard, not even Bobby Owen himself, could hardly have got hold of that yet, and anyhow, if by some miracle they had, there was nothing they could really make a fuss about. So it was in a fairly confident mood that he arrived in good time at the 'Golden Grasshopper', ordered a cocktail for himself with the hope that Bobby would treat him to another on arrival, and settled down to wait.

Mr McKie, known in Fleet Street as 'Sandy Mac', to the readers of *Morning Daily* more simply as 'S. M.' when he was writing about crime, and more grandly as 'Alexander' when the subject was music, was a round little man with large spectacles he did not need in the least, a mouth that gaped open on the least provocation, and a general air of such sweet innocence

that confidence tricksters—except those who had met him before—made for him at first sight, confident that at last they had
found their *beau ideal*. He wore his hair long, as befitted one
who mixed much with musicians, and he was probably the best
performer on the mouth-organ to be found in the whole country. A useful accomplishment, for who could imagine that the
little man sitting quietly in an East End pub or a Soho café and
showing himself such a virtuoso on the mouth-organ, was really
hot on the trail of a crime exclusive for *Morning Daily*?

Bobby, a little late in arriving, duly apologized for the delay,
provided the expected cocktails, and not till they were seated at
table did he ask abruptly:

"What's your Mr Pyle up to?"

"Why?" McKie countered. "All sorts of things probably, from
changing the course of world history by just one article in *Morning Daily*, to sacking your humble servant. You never know.
Restless sort of cove. But you don't imagine he confides in his
reporters, do you? Theirs not to reason why, theirs but to do and
die. Tennyson. Wasn't it?" he added doubtfully.

"I imagine," Bobby retorted, "that his reporters know quite a
lot without being confided in. Especially when they recommend
him a man like Item Sims."

"Oh, that's it, is it?" McKie asked. "I wondered myself what
he wanted a bloke like Item for. How did you know? Eddy Pyle
hasn't been confiding in you, has he?"

"Far from it," answered Bobby. "And not likely to. I don't
think I made myself awfully popular with him. I saw instant dis-
missal in his eyes more than once. Fortunately it had to stay
there, and he had to content himself with hints about how he
carried the Home Secretary around in his coat pocket. Well,
what about Item? Do you really think he is a suitable companion
to send off with a respectable citizen on a caravan tour?"

"Caravan tour?" McKie repeated. "I didn't know about that.
It doesn't sound like our Eddy. Rolls-Royce tour is more in his
line. What's it all about?"

"Did you warn Mr Pyle of Item's character?" Bobby asked,
without answering the other's question.

"I did," McKie answered. "I told him Item would be fully equal to knocking him on the head and clearing off with all the loose change available. That's not what's happened, is it?" he asked hopefully; and, when Bobby shook his head, McKie said: "A pity. What a story it would have made! Eddy can generally look after himself, though; I will say that for the little blighter. He said there was no risk of Item playing tricks if it was made worth his while not to. Sound philosophy. What have they been doing? Take a tip from a pal and, whatever it is, watch out when you are handling Eddy. He can't sack you and he hasn't the Home Secretary in his pocket, even if he thinks he has. But he can do a devil of a lot. More things are wrought by Eddy Pyles than this world dreams of. Tennyson again."

"The power of the Press?" Bobby asked. "You know, I think newspaper men are a bit apt to exaggerate that. More and more every day are caring less and less about what the papers say. Not Tennyson. Just me—plagiarized and adapted."

"Don't say that," McKie urged earnestly. "Or you will see what none has ever yet beheld—a Fleet Street man in tears. Anyway, what's making you so interested in Eddy? He's not such a bad bloke at bottom—a slight tendency to confuse himself with Almighty God, that's all."

"Not quite all," Bobby said. "Why Item? What possible reason can a man like Mr Pyle have for wanting to take a man like Item caravaning with him?"

"Not knowing, can't say," McKie retorted. "Couldn't care less, for that matter. I warned Item, too, by the way. I told him to mind his step. I think he would. You haven't told me yet what it's all about. Or is that one of your Yard top secrets?"

"Not exactly," Bobby answered. "Did you know Mr Pyle was writing a biography of Stephen Asprey?"

"Couldn't help knowing," McKie declared. "He tells you every time he sees you. *Morning Daily* has a par. every week or so about the progress of the great work and the passionate interest the literary world is taking in it, and how Hollywood is already negotiating for the film rights, and all the rest of the guff publicity agents put out for the public to lap up—as they do and ask for more, bless 'em. But Eddy's trying his hand at biography and digging up a poor defenceless dead poet isn't criminal, is it? Though very likely it ought to be. Why so interested?"

"Why did you say digging up?" Bobby asked, a little startled by an expression he had thought for the moment might have been used intentionally.

"Well, isn't that what it amounts to?" McKie demanded. "I thought Asprey was dead beyond all hope of resurrection. But I don't know. Wait and see what our Eddy can do—power of the Press, my boy."

"What's worrying me," Bobby said, "is what he wants a man like Item Sims for, if it's only a purely literary project he has in mind."

"I don't know," McKie repeated; and for the first time he began to look uneasy, for the first time to let his attention wander from the excellent lunch provided. He went on, but still uneasily. "The thing is Eddy's not satisfied with being chairman of the *Morning Daily* group, and cabinet ministers shaking in their shoes at his approach—at least, that's what he thinks. What *Morning Daily* says in the morning, all England thinks by afternoon. That's Eddy's credo. What he really wants is to be as big a pot in highbrow literary circles as he is in journalism. The Stephen Asprey biography is to bring him in at the top of the tree. His claim to immortality. Journalism for to-day, the book for future ages. He's quite serious about it, and if he heard there was anyone else trying to get in ahead on the Stephen Asprey story, my guess would be that he wanted Item to beat the other bloke up."

"As a matter of fact, there is someone," Bobby told him. "A young man, a Mr Chrines—Samuel Chrines. He lets people know in confidence that he's a son of Stephen Asprey and Janet Merton."

"Oh, him!" McKie exclaimed. "I know. He called at the office once and tried to wangle an extra long notice for some piffle he had written by telling that yarn. We went into it rather thoroughly. The Asprey and Janet Merton affair isn't quite forgotten even yet, and there was some idea that it might be worked up into a good story—the world's greatest love-tale. Grand headline. We dropped it. We aren't stuffy about it, but we do like some sort of foundation for a story. Chrines hadn't a thing to show except one or two letters Asprey might have written to any woman he was chasing—plenty of them, apparently."

"Can you tell me anything about the poems Chrines published?" Bobby asked. "They had some success, hadn't they?"

"Well, yes," McKie agreed. "You could say so. I daresay they've even brought him in a few pounds, and not many poets can say that much. The last thing he did got an awful slating from the critics—'weak imitation of Stephen Asprey at his worst', was what they said. The public bought a few odd copies, all the same. The funny thing is that it was a complete change of style and method. The first stuff Chrines published was in the best modern style—all the lines different lengths, no rhyming, no scansion, no capitals, no sense. You can't understand a word of the stuff, and if you say you can't, you're out with the other thick-skinned philistines; and if you say you can, then you're a brother intellectual well inside the pale. It brought him some kudos in the really swell circles. He tried again, and it was such a complete flop—even the highbrows know the limit when they see it—that he couldn't get his next stuff looked at. So then he came out with his last. Imitation Asprey. Critics snarled, but the public bought—more or less, chiefly less."

"Thank you," Bobby said. "It's what I wanted to know, and it's interesting."

"Why?" McKie asked, looking at him distrustfully. "Look; if Chrines is really trespassing on what Eddy thinks is his private domain, Chrines is heading for trouble. If he's got hold of some fresh material for his biography that Eddy knows about and wants and Chrines won't part—well, could that be what Item's for?" He paused, and again he looked uneasy. "No," he said finally, "I can't believe Eddy would ever go in for strong-arm methods. Plenty of other ways he could get what he wanted."

"You know about Asprey's last poems and his letters to her being buried with Janet Merton?" Bobby asked.

"Is that another slant to it?" McKie asked in his turn, more uneasily still. He was silent for a time. Bobby had made no reply, and McKie did not seem to expect one. He resumed: "You mean if Eddy can't get permission to open the grave and recover the poems and letters, he might hire Item to do it without bothering about what he calls mere red tape. Is that it?"

"It's where you come in," Bobby said. "Could you drop a hint to Mr Pyle that it would be a criminal offence and a first-class scandal?"

"It would be a first-class story—rate the biggest headline ever. But no good to us. No," he decided. "I'm not playing. Tackling our Eddy like that wouldn't be too healthy. Nothing doing."

"Asprey's widow is living near Penton at present," Bobby remarked. "Mr Pyle went to see her. He says she got a pistol out and wanted to shoot him."

"Well, why didn't she?" interjected McKie. "Good idea, if you ask me. Top line story."

"It may turn out that way," Bobby told him. "I've just got back from Penton, and I can't help feeling there's trouble brewing and that your Mr Pyle is likely to burn his fingers, or worse. The whole thing seems to be mixed up with the mysterious disappearance of the former rector. It seems he walked out of the rectory one night for an evening stroll and has never been heard of since."

"He wasn't writing Asprey's life, too, was he?" McKie inquired, rather flippantly.

"Not that I know of," Bobby answered. "This is in confidence as coming from me, though I expect plenty of people know. There seems to have been some sort of hint of a coming attempt to blackmail the Duke of Blegborough. He is at any rate thoroughly alarmed. He was at Penton yesterday, and your Mr Pyle got hold of him. They had a long talk together."

McKie was all alert now. He sat up with bright shining eyes; his very hair seemed to bristle.

"Good Lord!" he said slowly. "That means—that means—"

A waiter came up and whispered. McKie got up.

"Call from the office," he said. "I'll be back in a minute. Wait for me, will you? You know, this may turn into the biggest ever."

He hurried away, and was back almost at once, and Bobby could see that he was shaking with excitement. He could hardly speak. He stammered out:

"Pyle's been found dead on the Great Mercian Moor. Shot. They want me to go down there at once. A car's coming to pick me up."

CHAPTER XIII
INQUIRY BEGINS

BOBBY, A LITTLE shaken by so swift, so tragic, a justification of his forebodings, a little envious of Sandy McKie, now doubtless speeding on his way to Penton, returned reluctantly to a desk that seemed more dull than ever when there was so strange a problem waiting solution.

Nor could he help wondering if there was not a chance that he might be called in to help. Major Rowley was a highly efficient officer of police, but without experience in handling serious crime, Penton was a quiet little town, not much troubled by anything worse than occasional rowdiness or petty thieving. Highly probable that he was feeling a trifle bewildered, even a little nervous, at the prospect of becoming, as he certainly would, a centre of public attention and a target of universal criticism. What more natural, Bobby thought—hoped—than that he should turn for help to one who had so much experience in such cases, and in addition knew already something of the background involved?

This vague hope—an unfair word—knowledge rather of the possibility that duty might presently support desire, soon translated itself into fact. Major Rowley was already on the 'phone, wondering, rather timidly, if Mr Owen could be spared, and by evening, Bobby, a somewhat grudging consent given, was back in Penton, talking to a worried and apologetic Major Rowley, who was explaining that he had not been able to secure Bobby a room in any of the Penton hotels.

"Every journalist in the country is here," the Major said sadly. "I found a chap who said his name was Sandy McKie sitting in my office. He said he knew you, and you had mentioned me to him. It doesn't pay to be rude to journalists, or I would have thrown him out pronto. I had to leave him there while I talked to my men in the canteen."

"Too bad," Bobby sympathized. "No, never be tough with journalists—kind, but firm. That's the idea. Did McKie say that I also knew him? Only too well. If I mentioned you at all, it was only as Chief Constable here. I'm not sorry not to go to an hotel, though. It would be full of crime correspondents, and if I said 'good evening' to one of them his paper's next issue would feature an 'Exclusive interview with officer in charge'. 'Exclusive' is a word the papers love the further side of idolatry. Isn't there one of your men could put me up?"

"Sergeant Wiggins might have a spare room," Major Rowley answered. "I could ask him, and I'm sure Mrs Wiggins would look after you all right."

"If you would fix that up for me, I should be grateful," Bobby said. "All I really want is to be able to hold the Press sleuths at bay. Now could you tell me what you know so far?"

"Just about nothing," Major Rowley answered, more sadly still, "except the bare fact that Mr Pyle has been murdered, and as he was someone very important in the newspaper world, every paper in the country is fizzing with excitement. First thing this morning Duncan Day-Bell came tearing up on his motor-cycle to say young Chrines was telling people there was a dead man on the moor in a burnt-out caravan and he thought it was Mr Pyle. I didn't believe it at first. I thought Chrines must have been drunk or dreaming or someone had been playing a practical joke on him, but of course it had to be seen to. I got hold of Chrines first, drove straight there. His story is that he saw the light of a fire on the moor. He said he had been on the moor last night for a walk before starting writing—it seems he likes to get on with his poetry at night. Thinks the quiet and dark help him. He was near the caravan. There was a light in it, and he saw someone moving close by. He didn't go any nearer or attempt to speak, and he saw no one else except Mr Day-Bell—Duncan's father— who was going towards the caravan. Chrines returned home and started on his poetry. About midnight he saw the glow of what seemed a big fire on the moor. He watched for a time because, of course, moor fires are sometimes serious if there's been much dry weather. As it happens, there's been plenty of rain lately."

"So there has," murmured Bobby, sadly reminiscent of that race with the rain in which he had been so signally defeated.

"Anyhow, the glow soon died out," Rowley continued, "and Chrines went to bed. But he woke early, and decided out of curiosity to see what had been burning and if any damage had been done. He soon found a burnt-out caravan. When he looked inside he saw a dead body. Apparently he was then very sick, and he scuttled away home as fast as he could. He says his first idea was that the dead man was Mr Day-Bell, but then he saw it wasn't. When he got home he went to bed—after first being sick again. But he did tell the woman who keeps the Hillings Post Office what he had seen. She sent a message to her husband, who is cowman to Duncan Day-Bell, and who told Duncan, and Duncan came full speed to us. There's no 'phone in Hillings—Post Office won't put any in. Those are the bare facts, and I needn't go into the background because you know it already. That's why I thought your help would be so useful."

"I take it," Bobby said, "that Mr Pyle's body has been identified?"

"Oh, yes, there's no doubt about that. It was terribly burnt. Pyle had been shot three times, once in the head and twice in the body. The murderer meant to make sure. Death must have been instantaneous. Mr Pyle had a chauffeur or attendant to look after the caravan. A man named Sims. He has disappeared."

"Well, then," Bobby said.

"Quite so," said Major Rowley. "First thing everyone noticed. Only if Chrines saw the fire about midnight, it is reasonable to suppose that that would be about the time of the murder. But Hagen, the Hillings sexton, states that Sims, about eight on Thursday evening, or a little later, borrowed his bicycle to go into Penton. Sims said he had been sacked, called Pyle a few names, said he wasn't going to do Pyle's dirty work for him and be left holding the bag, and that some things Mr Pyle wouldn't like told, but told they might be. Hagen asked what he meant, but Sims didn't explain. Hagen says his impression was that Sims had been drinking, and he didn't pay much attention. Sims paid a three pounds deposit, and Hagen, who didn't trust him overmuch, gave him a note to collect the amount of the deposit, less five shillings payment for the hire of the machine, from the landlord of the 'Bull and Bell'. Hagen is a cousin of the landlord's. Sims called accordingly, left the bicycle, was paid the deposit less the amount of the hire, had a drink and went off. We've traced him to the railway station. He got there just before the last train for Bristol—the nine fifty-five. He bought two third-class tickets for Bristol, singles, and was seen on the platform just before the Bristol train drew in. No one seems to have noticed if he had a companion and no one can swear that he boarded the train, but he was not seen after it left. He is not remembered at Bristol, and there's nothing to suggest that he left the train on the way. It would have been possible, no doubt, for him to have done so without being noticed or, for that matter, never to have boarded the train at all, but to have slipped away from the Penton station without being noticed. If so, it would be possible, if he got hold of another bicycle, or even if he ran most of the way, to get back to the moor in time to murder Pyle, set fire to the caravan and make off. But nothing to show he did anything of the kind, and as it stands it all seems to give him a very fairly complete alibi."

"Looks like it," Bobby agreed. "Curious about his taking two tickets."

"Probably had a pal waiting for him he didn't want to be seen with," the Major suggested. "So he gave him one ticket, and they boarded the train separately."

"It could be that way," Bobby agreed thoughtfully. "You'll see if you can pick him up?"

"Oh, yes," the Major answered. "He'll have to be questioned, of course."

"I don't expect it'll be too easy to find him," remarked Bobby. "Not the first time he's gone underground, as they say now, and he knows all the tricks. I've heard that the Hillings villagers don't like caravans parking on the moor. Suspicious of interference with their private proceedings—lawful or not—and that sometimes they emphasize their objection by lighting a fire underneath the caravan as a hint that welcome has been outstayed. Do you think that is possible in this case? It would make the time of the murder more doubtful. It's just possible the murder had been already committed and that the fire-raising was subsequent but not consequent. No connection, in fact."

"Well, there's that," Major Rowley admitted, annoyed he had not thought before of such a possibility. "Rather upsets Sims's alibi."

"The last time I saw Pyle was when he left Hillings on Wednesday afternoon," Bobby went on. "He drove away with the Duke of Blegborough in the Duke's car, the Duke driving. Do you know anything of his movements that evening?"

"On the Wednesday evening," Rowley answered, consulting some papers on his desk, "he and the Duke dined together at the Grand Hotel. They seemed to be talking rather excitedly and not to want to be overheard. They always stopped when a waiter was near. One of the waiters thinks the Duke was objecting to something Mr Pyle was suggesting. That may be an afterthought. They left separately. The Duke drove away in his own car—a Rolls-Royce. Mr Pyle left in a car he had hired. It is still there, untouched, near the caravan. His own car had broken down on the Hillings road earlier, and he had left it there. The garage people were to collect it and carry out repairs. An odd thing is that according to them, though the damage was only slight and easily repaired, they can't think what caused it. They say it looked as if some one had taken a hammer to it."

"Mr Pyle," Bobby explained, "probably wanted to make sure of getting a lift from the Duke. He knew the Duke's car would be coming that way, and he meant to have a good reason for asking for a lift. By way of a spanner, I expect, applied where it would do most good. We shall have to ask what that last conversation was about."

"Yes, but it wasn't the last," Rowley said. "Hagen also says that late on Wednesday night he saw Mr Pyle in company with a man Hagen believes was the Duke. They were standing near the Janet Merton grave and talking in what Hagen calls a confidential sort of way. The Duke, if it was him, kept shaking his head, as if doubtful of what the other was saying. There is also independent evidence that a large car was seen on the Hillings road, travelling toward Penton. It was not noticed in the town itself. Of course the main road can be reached by by-passing the town."

"So far as is known, then," Bobby asked, "the Duke was the last person to see Pyle alive?"

"Well," Major Rowley answered, looking very uncomfortable—"well, Chrines says he saw Mr Day-Bell on the moor late Wednesday evening and some one else he can't identify near the caravan."

"That may have been Pyle," Bobby said slowly. "Or it may have been his murderer, or even a villager—possibly the one who started the fire under the caravan, if there's anything in that idea."

"Sims," the Major said. "If his story's true."

"Yes," Bobby agreed. "There's Sims. Seems to lie between him and the Duke." There was a box of cigarettes on the table. Bobby drew it towards him, selected a cigarette with great care, and then with equal care put it back. "Early days," he said abruptly. "No weapon found, I take it?"

"None," the Major answered. "The murderer may have thrown it away somewhere on the moor. I'm offering a pound reward for its recovery. I can't spare men to make a thorough search of the moor—it would take whole battalions. But a reward may set people searching. Especially over the week end—especially small boys."

"Good idea," applauded Bobby. "After all, one has to admit that even small boys have their uses—and sharp eyes. Oh, by the way, do you think you could let me see the dossier of the Thorne disappearance case? It was gone into very thoroughly at the time, I know, but somehow I can't help feeling a re-reading in the light of what's been happening just now might help. I can't think how. Just an idea."

"Well, yes, of course," Major Rowley agreed. "I'll have it got out for you. But surely—I mean I can't see how there can possibly be any connection."

"No more can I," Bobby said. "Just an idea," he repeated.

CHAPTER XIV
BURNT-OUT CARAVAN

Never certainly through all the years had the Penton–Hillings road carried such a press of traffic. An almost endless succession of cars fled up it and down it and back again. And never probably had so many disgruntled journalists said so many and such varied things about the Post Office authorities when they discovered they had to return to Penton to find a telephone. For indeed a journalist without a telephone to hand resembles nothing so much as a modern Bo-Peep without her sheep.

To this swift panorama of flying cars two more were now added: a small one carrying Bobby and Major Rowley, a larger one for more of the West Mercian police, destined to reinforce those already on the spot.

"My chief superintendent is in charge," Rowley was explaining. "Evans. Good man. Very thorough. Not long since he was pounding a beat, but the war gave him his chance, and he took it. Hustles the men a bit too much at times, but that's all."

Bobby made some conventional reply, but his thoughts were far away. Already ideas and theories were flitting through his mind like butterflies on a summer afternoon, vanishing, reappearing, vanishing again. One or two of the cars pelting back to Penton in search of a 'phone abandoned that errand when the police cars passed and turned to follow, the hope of being in on some fresh development preferred to the earlier sending off of such scanty material as would tax even the most expert re-write man to work up into a really good, public-rousing story.

Already there was something like a beaten trail to guide newcomers to their destination. There half the population of Hillings stood and stared at the burnt-out caravan, and nearly as many journalists, with itching pencils and open notebooks, stood grouped together, almost but not quite, projecting themselves by sheer force of will-power and desire into the roped enclosure within which the police were going stolidly about their grisly business. As Bobby and the Major drove up, there came forward to greet them Superintendent Evans, a burly, bustling, red-faced man, energetic and eager-looking still, even if he had grown a little fat since leaving his beat.

"We are going over the ground inch by inch," he said. "'Look under every blade of grass,' I'm telling the lads. Not that the fire has left much, but I've something to show you." As he was speaking he led them to a spot that had been carefully marked off within the larger, roped-off enclosure surrounding what was left of the caravan. "Unluckily," he went on, "a lot of 'em got here before us. It doesn't take long for news of this sort of thing to get round, and as per usual they've been tramping all over everywhere. They've even been poking about in what's left of the caravan, and I shouldn't be surprised if some of them haven't gone off with what they call souvenirs. I'd like to souvenir them! Destroyed vital clues, as likely as not. But they don't seem to have noticed this. Bit of luck, and a bit of luck it's been raining so hard the last day or two."

"Yes, indeed," agreed Bobby, even if poignant memories now brought forth from him a violent sneeze and then another.

"Caught a cold?" asked the Major with sympathy.

"I never catch cold," declared Bobby with dignity; and, what's more, when he made this statement he firmly believed it to be absolutely true.

Then he sneezed again, and after that was able to give his full attention to what the Superintendent was showing them. This was a spot which owing to the configuration of the ground, had remained damp and muddy from the recent rain much longer than had been the case elsewhere. Crossing it diagonally were the tracks of a large car, plainly visible.

"I've had inquiries made in Penton," Evans was saying. "The only car I could hear of, of this size and with Hardwear tyres—you can always tell 'em—was at the Grand Hotel. Their garage attendant spent most of the time it was there admiring it—and hoping for a tip most likely." He paused and went on with studied indifference. "It belonged to the Duke of Blegborough. Seems he and Pyle had dinner together. Of course, it can't be him—dukes don't commit murders—but it might be as well to ask him if he could help us."

"Necessary," Major Rowley said firmly. "Quite necessary." He looked depressed. "What a case!" he sighed, "with dukes and poets and newspaper proprietors and Lord knows what, all mixed up together."

"There's something else," Evans said, rather with the air of a conjuror who, having produced one rabbit out of a hat, now proceeds to extract a second. Stepping carefully, he showed them where on the edge of the damp patch of ground a piece of board supported at each end by stones, protected what was underneath.

"Woman's footprint," he said, lifting the board for them to see for themselves. "Not one of the villagers. They don't wear shoes like that in the ordinary way. Only when they are going to a dance or somewhere. Size, a number four, I should say. She didn't come in the car. Footprint too far away and none in between. Who was she and what was she doing? I'm having a plaster cast taken."

"Good," Bobby said, approving this obvious, but occasionally forgotten bit of routine. "Have the doctors said anything fresh?"

"Only the usual 'further examination necessary before pronouncing a definite opinion'—as if doctors ever gave a definite opinion. Breach of professional etiquette, most likely, if they did."

Bobby nodded absently and walked over to what was left of the caravan—little more than a charred and jumbled heap of debris. It told him nothing. The fire had done its work well. A more careful and detailed examination would presently be given, but not much hope of any useful result. Bobby asked if anything in the nature of a cash-box or anything else of value had been found, and was told only a gold wrist watch, much damaged by fire, and a signet ring. He suggested then that special care should be taken to see if among the ashes any trace of money could be found. A tight, thick wad of pound notes, he remarked, such as Mr Pyle might have had with him for current expenses, takes a good deal of getting rid of 'without trace', and Evans nodded in full agreement.

"That's not been overlooked," he said, pleased to show this Scotland Yard man that West Mercia knew things, too. "It may be the motive for the murder if this man, Sims, had been helping himself and Mr Pyle found out, or even if Sims had to put him out of the way to get hold of it. May have been quite a sum."

"Sims has a fairly sound alibi," Bobby observed, and when Evans's expression showed clearly what he thought of alibis, Bobby added: "From what I know of him, he hasn't brains enough to think out anything that would need careful planning. Of course, he may have had an accomplice, but no sign of one, and he generally works alone."

"Yes, sir," agreed Evans with the touch of deference naturally due to a high-ranking official from Scotland Yard, and then added to show he could keep his end up: "Sims is my man at present, though, and once we can bring him in, we ought to know a lot more."

Bobby nodded in full agreement and then became 'tranced', as they say at the bridge table. Evans went off to talk to Major Rowley and to express a guarded opinion that this Scotland Yard swell spent rather too much time with his hands in his pockets, staring at nothing.

"Action," he told the Major. "That's what I say. Get going, and then you know where you are."

Major Rowley expressed qualified agreement with this sentiment; without adding that knowing where you are, and knowing your right destination, are possibly different kinds of knowledge. He proceeded to explain his plan for enlisting the aid of small boys in a search for the missing murder weapon. Evans expressed approval, also qualified, for, having four of them himself, he was inclined to regard all small boys with but a wary and a doubtful eye. Then Bobby woke up from his trance, removed his hands from his pockets, and, aware as he was that the others were now talking about the missing revolver, since however deep his 'trance' he always remained fully conscious of what was going on around him, he said abruptly:

"Hagen told me he saw Sims with a revolver. Sims was in the caravan. He had taken the revolver to pieces and was cleaning it."

"To my mind," declared Evans, "that about clinches it."

"Hagen might be able to tell you more," Bobby said. "I didn't press him for details. It didn't seem important at the time. Now it does. It is what was in my mind just now—very much in my mind. I was trying to think out what it might mean." He paused, and Evans only just stopped himself from saying: 'Plain enough what it means. Not much thinking needed to see that.' Unaware of this piece of criticism of unnecessary thinking, Bobby continued: "Not the only gun I heard of when I was here before: Mr Pyle complained that Mrs Stephen Asprey had threatened him with one."

"What on earth for?" demanded Major Rowley in a very surprised tone. "What was she doing with a gun, anyhow?"

"There's that woman's footprint we found, not a villager's," said Evans, and looked thoughtful.

"So there is," agreed Major Rowley, and also looked thoughtful.

"She lives alone; no neighbour for miles, is there?" Bobby remarked. "She may have thought she needed it for self-protection."

"She never applied for a certificate," the Major said with severity. "What was she threatening Pyle about?"

"Over his plan for opening Janet Merton's grave," Bobby explained. "Pyle wanted her support, and she seems to have objected—strongly. When he tried to argue she chased him away at pistol point. I only know what he told me. Then there is Mr Chrines, the young fellow who claims to be a son of Asprey and Janet's, and tells everyone—in confidence."

"He hasn't a gun and been threatening people, too, has he?" demanded Major Rowley.

"It was Chrines discovered the murder," observed Evans, and once more he was looking thoughtful.

"So it was," agreed Major Rowley. "Who was he threatening?" he asked Bobby.

"Duncan Day-Bell," Bobby answered. "Miss Christabel Merton wanted Chrines stopped talking about being her aunt's son. Young Day-Bell constituted himself Miss Christabel's champion."

"Sweet on her," interposed Evans. "Everyone knows that. Young man in love always liable to make even a bigger fool of himself than as per usual."

"He's evidently a believer in direct action," Bobby said. "He told Chrines he would give him a good thrashing if he didn't dry up. Chrines retorted that he had a gun, and if Duncan tried that on he would get a bullet in him. Once again I'm only repeating what I've been told."

"It was young Mr Day-Bell brought us the first news of the murder," observed Evans moodily. "Have to take a statement. Guns and that footprint and Sims on the run," and he frowned angrily at a problem he was evidently beginning to feel was less simple than he had at first thought it.

"If he believes Janet Merton was his mother," Major Rowley put in, "he may have objected to this grave-opening idea."

"I believe he did, from what Pyle said," Bobby answered. "Another thing. Pyle was writing a Life of Asprey. So was Chrines. There seems to have been quarrelling over that. I suppose each thought the other was queering his pitch. Apparently, too, Chrines had got hold of some fresh material Pyle badly wanted for his own book. Chrines wouldn't part. Wanted it himself. Probably thought that it would put his book definitely ahead."

"Looks," said Evans, frowning harder than ever, "as if it might be this grave-opening and the papers said to be in it, as might have something to do with it. Only, if it's like that, why has Sims done a bunk?"

"Panicked, perhaps," suggested Bobby. "Likely enough, with the record he has. I take it most of the farmers and so on round here have shot-guns. Have any of them certificates for pistols?"

Major Rowley and his Superintendent looked at each other.

"I hadn't thought of it before," Major Rowley said slowly. "Duncan Day-Bell has one. Service type."

"Same," put in Evans, "as was used, judging by the bullets the doctors dug up."

"Have to ask him to produce it for testing," Bobby said.

"He was the first as came along to tell us," remarked Evans.

"There's nothing in that," Major Rowley said testily. "For God's sake don't bring in any more than you have to."

"The Duke of Blegborough," Bobby said. "He may have had the strongest motive of all, if the letters Pyle wanted dug up did contain allegations that he poisoned his wife. And," Bobby added, "this looks to me very like his car. Hasn't taken him long to get here."

CHAPTER XV
SUSPICIONS

MAJOR ROWLEY and his superintendent had been too busy talking and discussing to pay attention to anything else. But Bobby, who could combine intense mental concentration with a curiously alert awareness of his surroundings, had remarked a stir among the bystanders—especially the journalistic bystanders—and then had seen the Duke's imposing Rolls-Royce bumping its aristocratic way towards them over the rough plebeian surface of the moor.

It came to a stop. The villagers stared. The journalists swooped. The Duke looked alarmed. Bobby said:

"Better rescue the poor man, or he'll be torn to pieces to make a journalistic scoop. No telling what they won't get him to say."

Major Rowley nodded agreement. The superintendent beckoned to two of the constables to follow him; and so advanced with all the dignity and authority of the law. The Duke was repeating somewhat helplessly:

"Really, gentlemen, really . . . please . . . one moment."

The superintendent appeared, brushed aside the journalists; taking most of them unawares as he did by advancing on them from the rear. He nearly said: 'Move along there, please,' but remembered in time that this was an expression used, not by superintendents, but by constables on the beat that he for his part had left so far behind. Instead he said:

"Now, gentlemen, now, if you please. His Grace isn't here to give interviews. Not at present. Afterwards, perhaps," he added tactfully. To the Duke he said: "Would your Grace please come this way? The Chief Constable would be most happy to have your assistance."

"I don't know if I can give any," the Duke said, but relieved all the same to find himself thus taken as it were under the wing of authority. "A dreadful business. We dined together only last night," and at this all around pencils grew busy and note-books fluttered. "I could hardly believe it when I heard."

The two constables formed an escort. Too eager journalists were politely but firmly repulsed. But nothing could stop the cameras already hard at it. Major Rowley shouted an order, but for that not a camera ceased its busy clicking. Major Rowley came running. He clearly meant business. The cameras bolted for their cars, fearful of impending seizure. The descriptive writers, with professional solidarity, formed themselves instinctively into a protective and delaying squad. Successfully. Some excellent photographs appeared in next morning's papers. Nobody's fault if the best of them all was a shot of the Duke walking between two policemen and giving an unfortunate first impression. The *Red Toiler* used it on its front page, and later it appeared in every Russian newspaper as proof decisive of the crimes and villainy of the governing class holding Britain in its relentless cannibal's grasp. But that was in a future at present unforeseen, and now the Duke said simply:

"My God."

Evans pulled down some of the roping round the burnt-out caravan and got him safely within. To the two constables he said:

"If any of that lot try to follow, take him in for obstruction."

"Yes, sir," said one constable, and the other said to the Duke:

"Your hat, sir."

"Oh, thank you so much," said the Duke, gratefully accepting it—it had been old before, and now it looked much older, but he didn't notice. Reflectively he added: "Really, they must be all quite mad."

"Well, journalists," Bobby explained. "A purely formal distinction, no doubt. Very good of you, sir, to come along so promptly. I'm beginning to think we shall need all the help we can get."

"I'm afraid I can hardly hope to be of much assistance," the Duke repeated, and Bobby, now that he was nearer, noticed that he looked pale and anxious. "Indeed, I am not quite clear what has really happened. Do I understand that this dreadful business is connected with an attempt to open Janet Merton's grave? Has it been opened?" and as he said this the anxiety he showed became even more apparent.

"No, no," Bobby assured him, answering his last question. "There may be some connection somewhere. Or it may be a case of robbery and murder. Major Rowley has hardly begun his investigation yet. So far we know very little beyond the bare fact that Mr Pyle's caravan has been burnt, he himself shot, and that the man he had with him—a sort of handy-man, apparently—has disappeared, but with what on the face of it seems a sound alibi for the time of the murder. Might I ask how you came to hear of it? It was only discovered early this morning."

"A Mr McKie informed me," the Duke explained. "He rang me up from London. A colleague of yours, I understood. He mentioned your name; he said you had often worked together on such cases."

"Oh, he did, did he?" growled Bobby. "Did he say anything else?"

"He wanted me to meet him at the Grand Hotel in Penton," replied the Duke. "I said I would. He promised to give me what he called the inside story I ought to know. I don't know exactly what he meant, but he said he would explain when we met, and he rang off then. I was on my way, but I stopped at a garage to fill up, and the attendant there told me it would be shorter if I went through Hillings first and that was what most cars passing that way were doing. He seemed to take it for granted it was all about this dreadful affair. A most intelligent man."

"Yes, much quicker coming that way," agreed Bobby, though speaking more by faith than by knowledge. He paused for just one moment to contemplate rather happily a mental picture of the enterprising Mr McKie waiting and waiting, alone at Penton, while everything was happening at Hillings. Evidently he had planned to get the Duke there all to himself, establish a special and confidential relationship, and secure an 'exclusive' for his paper. A very good plan, too, and would have been highly successful but for the unforeseen intervention of the garage attendant. But, then, that is always the worst of the unforeseen—it is so very unforeseeable. A profound reflection, and, having made it, Bobby went on: "It is important to establish Mr Pyle's last movements. Could you tell us when you last saw him?"

"Last night," the Duke replied immediately, and with no trace of self-consciousness. "I drove over from Blegborough after dinner."

"Was there any special reason for that?"

"Well, he had been pressing me to support certain plans he had in view. He urged me very strongly to do so when we had dinner together in Penton. He laid great stress on the influence he said he possessed through his papers. I told him I would think it over. I made up my mind after I got home to tell him at once I would not only not support him, but would do all I could to oppose his plans. He was inclined to be what I considered unreasonably angry."

"May I take it the plan you mentioned had to do with a project for opening the Janet Merton grave?"

"The idea seems to me undesirable from every point of view," the Duke declared with unusual energy. "Objectionable. Unnecessary."

"Were suggestions made that the Stephen Asprey letters might contain certain allegations reflecting on yourself?"

"Oh, you knew that—I expect everyone does," the Duke said. He was beginning to show signs of impatience and anger. Generally placid, acquiescent, almost apologetic in his manner, as if he felt that to-day dukes and earls both had to recognize how small was their right even to exist, he now burst out: "The fellow told me I didn't want the letters got back because I knew they accused me of poisoning my wife out of jealousy of Asprey. We were talking in my car. Because he was afraid his chauffeur might get listening, he asked me to drive a little way away. I am afraid"—now his tone became really apologetic, even more so than usual—"when Pyle said that about my being jealous of Asprey I told him to get out. He said I must drive him back to the caravan first, so I threw him out. He went sprawling. That is the last I saw of him. Sprawling." The Duke smiled with a certain complacence. "Sprawling," he repeated, as if he could never savour the word too much. Then he stopped as if suddenly remembering he was speaking of a dead man. "I lost my temper, I suppose," he admitted. "Unfortunate. Unforgivable, especially in view of what has happened. I don't think I do very often," and now he was returning to his more familiar apologetic tone.

"Could you say precisely what time this would be?" Bobby asked.

"Between nine and ten," the Duke told him after reflection. "About the half-hour, I should say. I didn't notice particularly. When I'm alone I generally have dinner about half-past seven. It's not much more than an hour's drive here from the castle."

"It's very important to have all the times as exact as possible," Bobby explained. "We must get everything as accurate as we can, so as to have a complete time-table of Mr Pyle's movements last night. Would there be anyone at Blegborough Castle likely to have noticed the precise time you returned?"

"Well, you see," the Duke answered, "most of the castle has been taken over by the Wessex Agricultural Training College, so there's never anyone there after hours. I've been able to keep a few rooms for my own use, and my old butler, Hopkins, and Mrs Hopkins, look after it and me when I'm there. The W.A.T.C. employ a night watchman. But Hopkins and his wife would be in bed when I got back, and then they are both rather deaf. I don't expect they heard anything. The night watchman wouldn't be likely to, either. He patrols the other side of the castle generally."

"Yes, I see," Bobby said. "Thank you so much for being so helpful. We shall just have to do our best with what we know already. I'm sure if we need more details we can rely on you. You didn't see anyone else on the moor near the caravan?"

"No one at all," the Duke assured him. "I'm only sorry I've not been of more help."

Both Bobby and the two West Mercian police officers expressed polite appreciation of his assistance. He was also very earnestly advised to avoid saying anything to any journalist—especially on the telephone.

"As things are at present," Bobby remarked, "anything said—anything at all—can be so easily misunderstood, and in the interests of all concerned the less your name is mentioned the better. If I may say so, sir, your name and title would throw everything out of proportion. It would set every tongue wagging in a most undesirable way."

"Yes, indeed," the Duke said sadly. "I've enough experience of that. But there's your friend, Mr McKie. I promised to meet him in Penton. He may be waiting there still."

"Very likely," agreed Bobby, cheerfully and fully appreciative of that fact. "I'll tell him how it is. Good chap, McKie, when he's not too busy being a journalistic live-wire."

"If you'll explain, I shall indeed be grateful," the Duke said, though not quite certain what this last sentence meant. "I should be most sorry if he thought I had been guilty of any discourtesy," and after one or two more questions—unimportant ones—had been asked and answered, he departed.

For some moments the other three stood and watched in silence as the Rolls-Royce passed out of sight over the edge of the moor. Then Evans said:

"It can't really be him, can it? But when it's jealousy, I daresay a duke is much the same as the rest of us—and then poets. Poets and women seem to take to each other natural like. If he did do in his wife and he knew Asprey knew and had said so in these letters—well, there's your motive, and when you've got your motive I always say you've got your man."

"Only," Bobby pointed out, "a perfectly innocent man, especially one in the Duke's position, might equally well object to such a story getting about."

"Same motive from another angle," Major Rowley said gloomily. "It would set tongues wagging like hell."

"So it would," Bobby agreed. "Just like hell. We must try not to let that happen if we can help it—unless it becomes necessary," he added, with almost equal gloom.

"Looks to me as if it's going to be," Rowley said, half to himself, and then, more loudly: "I don't like the way things are shaping, and that's a fact, and then those 'phone messages hinting at blackmail the Duke talked about. If that tale's true, of course. No corroboration. But it does rather look to me as if there was someone in the background knew more than he ought to." He looked at his watch and thought of his dinner, for he was a man with a healthy appetite. "Getting late," he said.

Recovering abruptly from the fresh trance into which he had shown signs of relapsing, Bobby said:

"I expect you've noticed there's a small discrepancy in what the Duke told us. It may mean nothing, but it's there, and it'll have to be remembered and cleared up if possible. I never like discrepancies, even if they are only small, and then it's the second I've noticed in all this. Two of them is at least one too many."

The Major looked puzzled, but Evans nodded in full agreement.

"Yes," he said at once. "Yes. I noticed that. Puts it across he wouldn't ever dare say boo to a goose and then lets out he doesn't think twice over throwing you out of his car to find your own way back as best you can. Easy to get lost on the moor and just die of exhaustion, same as happened to Mr Thorne, most likely. That's what John Hagen thinks and so do I."

CHAPTER XVI
DEFENCES DOWN

BUT THIS theory of the Duke's deliberately deceptive character was not what Bobby had had in mind. However, before he could explain himself, there came up to them the sergeant who was supervising the careful examination, bit by bit, of what was left of the caravan and its contents. He was holding two pieces of twisted metal he offered for their inspection.

"Looks to me," he said, "like it's been the blade of a spade and the head of a pick-axe. Not what you would expect to find in a gentleman's touring caravan."

"Suggests," Bobby remarked, "that Pyle didn't mean to be held up for lack of tools if permission to open the grave came through—or even if it didn't."

Too little daylight remained for much more to be done. A few fresh arrangements were made—including the stationing of a man to remain on watch all night. ('Or there won't be a thing left by morning,' Evans had remarked in an aside, adding bitterly the one word 'Souvenirs'.) Then Major Rowley observed, rather too carelessly, that they had better be getting back to Penton and, if possible, snatch a bite to eat before sitting down to deal with all the paper work awaiting them.

"Shan't get to bed till Lord knows when," he said, with a sidelong glance at Evans, intended to warn him he would have to take his full share, and another at Bobby to see if he looked ready to come in as well.

But Bobby surprised them both by saying suddenly:

"I've never seen Miss Christabel Merton. Janet was supposed to be a beauty, wasn't she? Does Miss Christabel take after her aunt in that way?"

"Well, you could hardly call her a beauty," Major Rowley said doubtfully, and Evans told himself primly that this was a wholly frivolous question. Police were not concerned with the looks of young women. "A fine handsome girl, well set up," Rowley decided. "Takes her share in the farm work, I believe. Drive a tractor or pitch all day in the hay-field. That sort of thing."

"You wouldn't expect her to wear a number four shoe the size of the one making that print Mr Evans found?" Bobby asked.

"No," Rowley said at once. "No, I should say that could hardly be hers."

"Hard to trace identity from a single footprint," Evans put in. "How do you start? Mr Pyle doesn't seem to have been in touch with anyone in Penton. Of course, we can inquire."

Bobby nodded, approving this suggestion, and then said: "If you could put me down at Two Mile End, I might have a try at getting Mrs Asprey to talk. My idea is it might be easier for one alone than if we all three went together. How do you feel?" he asked Rowley.

The Major fully agreed. Privately he thought that Mrs Asprey would be a tough nut to crack, whether tackled by one or by three. But, he suggested, oughtn't Bobby to have a bite first? Of course, it was part of police training to go without food or drink as and when required—at this, all three of them looked sad—but was it necessary this time? Why not come back to Penton with them, get a bite there—and then borrow a car and drive back to Two Mile End? But Bobby said he thought it would be better for him to call before it got dark.

"The lady seems a trifle ready with her gun," he remarked. "Just as well not to give her any excuse for target practice. If she's heard of what's happened she may be a bit jumpy."

So it was settled; and when Bobby alighted near that desolate ruin where Mrs Asprey had chosen to take up her abode for the time being, there was still an hour or two of daylight left. He had taken care she should have full warning of his approach by one or two hoots from the Major's car before he got down, a shouted farewell when it started off again, and by a certain amount of unnecessary stumbling as he made his way across the wilderness that once had been a garden and the pride of Two Mile End. These precautions were so far successful that, as Bobby got nearer the side door Mrs Asprey used, it opened and she herself appeared on the threshold. He noticed that she was dressed more carefully than when he had seen her before, and he noticed also that she was holding one hand behind her back. He decided that if he had to go he would rival the unfortunate Mr Pyle in the speed of his departure. She was looking, he thought, as gaunt, as formidable as ever. Motionless and silent, she stood there watching his approach, still giving that impression of a tense and angry expectation he had noted in her before. But she seemed to relax a little as he came more into view.

"You, is it?" she said. "I thought you wouldn't be long. Well?"

"You will have heard what's happened?" Bobby asked.

"Of course I have. Who hasn't? Well, what have you found out? Do you know who did it?"

"If I did I should not be here to ask you if you can help," Bobby said, and she responded with an angry and contemptuous grunt.

"Doesn't interest me," she told him. "You had better come in, I suppose."

She turned as she spoke and went back into the room behind, thus allowing Bobby to see, rather to his relief, that what she had been holding behind her back had been not a gun, but a poker. Bobby followed her. He said:

"Are you not still interested in any possible opening of the Janet Merton grave?"

"Well, that won't happen now, will it?" she asked sharply, apparently a good deal taken aback by this remark. "Why should it? Nobody wanted it except this wretched man. Now there's no one."

"All that may depend on how the investigation goes," Bobby said, watching her closely.

She sat down then and he followed her example. She seemed to be both troubled and surprised by his last remark. She did not speak for a few moments, and then she said, speaking apparently as much to herself as to him:

"I thought it was all over."

"We are inclined to think there may be much that hasn't yet come to light," Bobby told her. "It seems possible the motive for the murder may go a long way back. The past still lives."

"Why do you say that?" she demanded, startled. "That's the title of one of Stephen's poems—one of his best."

"Yes, I know," Bobby said. "I expect I was remembering. I heard it mentioned once, and the title must have stuck in my mind."

"I suppose all this means there's someone you do suspect? Who is it? The Duke of Blegborough? He's a poor fish. He's not got the guts to shoot. It can't be the Chrines boy. Not possible. Or Mr Day-Bell? There were hints about him and Mr Thorne. You know that? Well, well, well?" and each successive 'Well' she snapped out with an increasingly angry impatience.

"I didn't say there was anyone we had any reason to suspect at present," Bobby reminded her. "All I said was that the course of the investigation might make opening the grave necessary."

"I don't see why, I don't see how that can be," she muttered moodily. "You mean the Duke may have known he had to stop those letters being read because of what might be in them and that was why he was there that night?"

"You, too, I think," Bobby said, "might be almost equally anxious to prevent their recovery. You would not like their contents being made generally known?"

"If anyone else tried again—" she began and then paused. "They ought to be burned," she exclaimed with fierce intensity. "They are stolen letters. They should have been mine, they were mine; they only said again what he had said before to me. She's no right to have them there with her where she lies so snug and safe, even if she's dead and I'm alive, and I have memories and she has none. That's why I'm here, so as to be sure nothing's done without my knowing." She sat back in her chair as if exhausted by the intensity of her feelings. In a slightly different voice, though one still vibrant with emotion, she went on: "Stephen's last poems. They ought to be recovered. They ought to be published. Then the world would begin to remember him again. It's his right to have them published. That's what he really wanted. When he put them in her coffin it was only a gesture, only a gesture. You had to know him all through, as I did, to be sure what was gesture and what was real. I knew as no one else did or could—no one."

Once more she was silent, and Bobby saw an unwilling hesitating tear and then another creeping slowly down her cheeks. He got up and went to the door and opened it and looked out. He stood like that for two or three minutes. Then he came back and said:

"I thought I heard rain, but it's quite clear. I didn't want to get another drenching like the one I had that other time."

"Thank you," she said and sat upright once more, to all appearance as grim, determined, formidable as ever.

But he had seen her now with her defences down, and he knew better. He said:

"There are more questions we may have to ask you. But they can wait if you prefer it. You may have to be asked to make a formal statement. Of course, you can refuse to answer. Or if you wish it, your solicitor can be present."

She was hardly listening to him, still struggling as she was to recover her earlier poise.

"Questions?" she repeated. "Ask as many as you like. It doesn't follow you'll get any answer. What questions? What for?"

"Murder has been done and questions must be asked," Bobby told her. "Even perhaps questions that may not seem to have much to do with it. Have you a pistol?"

"A pistol? No. Of course not. What should I want a pistol for? I can look after myself."

"I saw you brought a poker with you to the door," Bobby said, smiling slightly. "Mr Pyle told me the last time I saw him that when he came to visit you it ended with your producing a gun and threatening to shoot him if he didn't go. I think he did go—quickly."

"Oh, that," she said. "He tried to argue, bribe, bully. I'm not sure which. I told him to go away, and he wouldn't, so I opened a drawer and put my hand in and I told him if he wasn't gone before I counted three I would fire. He went before I got as far as two. He was really frightened."

"If he had not gone," Bobby asked, "what would you have done?"

She smiled grimly and nodded towards the poker lying by the oil-stove that stood before the old fireplace. Bobby accepted this as an answer and asked next: "Have you ever possessed a pistol?"

"Stephen had one I remember," she answered. "He wrote to the police, and they gave him a paper about it to say he might keep it. I don't know what became of it after he died. I don't think I ever gave it a thought. It got lost or stolen, perhaps. Plenty of things were."

"I see," Bobby said. "You spoke of the Duke of Blegborough visiting Pyle the night he was shot. How did you know?"

"Well, I saw his car going that way," she answered.

"About what time?"

"I don't know exactly. It was late—beginning to grow dark. I didn't take much notice."

"Did you follow him? Or were you already there when he arrived?"

"Why should you think so? I couldn't be, could I? when I saw his car pass. I can't go as fast as a huge car like his. Why should I follow him?"

He countered with another question.

"Could it be that you felt you must be there, as you said just now, if anything was happening? Well, death happened, and a woman's footprint has been found near by."

"I don't think I believe you," she said after a pause. "There's been no rain for a day or two. The moor dries quickly, and it's all rough grass nearly."

"All the same, a footprint's been found," Bobby said. "You could see it for yourself if you wished. Would you care to let me have one of your shoes to see if it fits?"

"Well, suppose it did?" she retorted with much of her former angry impatience. "What would that prove? There must be thousands of people wearing shoes like mine. All shoes come from the same lasts. Mass production."

"It would help if you let us try. Will you think it over? We should appreciate your help."

But she still shook her head.

"You'll find out without my help—if you ever do," she told him. "I happen to know, but I'm not going to say."

"Was it you?" he asked.

She made no answer. Very upright she sat and watched him, and there was silence in the room till Bobby rose to his feet. Then she spoke abruptly, without moving, her expression unchanged, almost as if the words were forced from her by some power not her own.

"Get one of Christabel Merton's shoes and try that," she said. "Ask her if it's possible anyone saw her on the moor near the caravan last night."

"This print was made by a small size shoe," Bobby said. "I'm told one much smaller than any Miss Merton could wear."

"One can always squeeze a bit," she answered carelessly.

CHAPTER XVII
ARREST IMMINENT

BOBBY COVERED the two miles back to Penton at a speed not much less than that he had displayed on a previous occasion, though this time he was spurred on not by fear of a threatening deluge, but only by a lively appetite.

At the first call-box he came to he paused to ring up Mrs Wiggins, where he was lodging, to ask if some cold meat or some bread and cheese could be left out for his supper.

"I don't know when I shall be able to get in," he explained, "and I don't want to keep you up."

But a motherly voice at the other end of the line assured him that whatever the hour of his return, sausages—pork—and mashed potatoes would be waiting.

"You can't ever go wrong with a man," the voice assured him, "if it's sausage and mashed and no trouble at all to hot up."

So Bobby expressed his thanks and felt much cheered by the prospect of so fortunate a conclusion to such a long and tiring day. Next he rang up the Penton police headquarters and asked if it could be arranged for Mr Sandy McKie, of *Morning Daily*, Mr Pyle's paper, to be there to meet him on his arrival, which would be soon.

"There are one or two small points," Bobby explained, "McKie might be able to help in; but for the good Lord's sake don't let any others of the Press Gang know. They are all as jealous of each other as a lot of girls after the same film star, and they would be dead sure we were giving him an exclusive. As cover, you might give him a hand-out to distribute to the rest of them, only take jolly good care it doesn't say anything. Lots of words and no facts."

Superintendent Evans, who had answered the 'phone, said he quite understood, hung up, remarked in the hearing of two sergeants and a constable that he didn't know what on earth the London chap thought he was up to, was conscious of a murmur of approval from the two sergeants and the constable, rebuked them severely for listening, and proceeded to draw up a suitable 'hand-out' as requested.

When therefore Bobby appeared he found McKie waiting for him and looking all at once sulky, apprehensive, and expectant—the first, because of his wasted afternoon spent waiting for the Duke and suspecting Bobby had somehow intervened; apprehensive, because he felt his little attempt to get a kind of pre-view of what the Duke was likely to say might not have been approved of; expectant, because of a faint lingering hope that Bobby might just possibly be going to tell him something important. As the second of these contingencies was the one uppermost in his mind, and as he knew that attack is always the best defence, he, as soon as Bobby entered the room where he was waiting, began indignantly:

"I suppose it was you worked it with the Duke. I do think you might have let me know. I spent all afternoon waiting for him to turn up so I could bring him along to you."

"I noticed that for once you weren't on the spot," Bobby answered amiably. "A pity. Not slipping up, I hope? But nothing to do with me. Jolly good idea, I know, nobbling the poor man and turning him inside out before anyone else, even the police, had a go. I'm not altogether sure, though, that it mightn't have looked just a little wee bit like tampering with an essential witness. Academic point now. What happened was that he took a short cut to Hillings, instead of coming through Penton. He asked me to give you his sincere apologies. But I wouldn't try anything of that sort again. We're apt to be touchy when it's a case of murder. I've asked the Super here to give you a handout on how things stand at present—on condition, of course, that you pass it on to all the other chaps. No favouritism, and now I want to ask if you can tell me what literary bloke is likely to know Asprey's work best?"

"Well, old Tom Long, I should think," McKie answered, slightly mollified by this appeal for assistance. "He's professor of poetry at one of the red-brick universities." (McKie himself was a Balliol man.) "The old boy is said to know by heart every poem published this century and most of the earlier stuff as well. He's always stood up against the debunking of Asprey by all the smart young men who want to play Macaulay to his Robert Montgomery."

"Sounds just the man I want to get hold of," declared Bobby. "He would know about Chrines's work, too, would he?"

"Oh, yes," McKie agreed. "He wrote the notice in the *Saturday Supplement* denouncing Chrines as 'Asprey and ditch water'. I went to see him when we were going into Chrines's claim to be a son of Asprey and Janet Merton. He was very interested, and he told me there was one sonnet in Chrines's book so different from the rest, it might easily have been the work of Asprey at his peak—in the early days, when he did show a touch of genius before it died out as he grew older. Bit of a tragedy, that, you know, even if he did help to kill it by complacence and swelled head."

"A tragedy," Bobby agreed. "All the more a tragedy if complacence and swelled head were the cause."

"The old boy," McKie went on, "seemed to think the sonnet was so good it could even be accepted as evidence that Chrines was in fact a son of Asprey's. Heredity at work, perhaps, or it might be it really was an early effort of Asprey's, and Chrines had got hold of it somehow—perhaps from his real mother, if she were one of Asprey's loves. If he did, he might have thought he would pass it off for his own. But if his mother wasn't Janet Merton, we weren't interested. Couldn't work it up then into the most glamorous story of all time, with the grand climax of the burial of the heart-broken poet's finest work in the coffin of his dead love. How the great B.P. would have lapped it up."

"If it didn't make them sick instead," Bobby suggested, and, ignoring McKie's interjection: 'You couldn't. Impossible,' went on: "Anyhow, very many thanks for what you've told me. You've helped enormously."

"Have I?" McKie asked, surprised, and he added wistfully, "Well, if I have, oughtn't you to tip me off how?"

"Shouldn't be necessary," Bobby retorted. "Besides, I wouldn't dare. I've far too much respect for the power of the Press. I'm not going to risk getting in the bad books of all the rest of you by giving them a chance to say I favoured one. Sorry and all that, but there it is."

"The labourer not worthy of his hire," McKie said sadly. "It's a hard world."

"Well, I'll tell you one thing," Bobby said, "and you can tell the others. I'm working on a theory founded on facts they all know perfectly well. You might even say an early arrest is possible. I don't see why you shouldn't work it out for yourselves, if you like to take the trouble. Of course, you wouldn't dare use it because of libel if it turns out to be wrong. And I can't say anything even to the chaps working with me for much the same reason. My suspect may be perfectly innocent, and it doesn't do to throw suspicion on the innocent or prejudice the investigation by giving it a slant the wrong way."

"Just say a little more," McKie pleaded.

But Bobby shook his head, and McKie had to retire disconsolate; and all his colleagues, when he told them, decided that it was only swank, and what Bobby really meant was that neither he nor any others of those working on the case had discovered the faintest clue or had even the remotest hope of bringing it to a satisfactory conclusion. All the same, they were generally content to ring up their respective offices with the message: 'Police confident of early arrest.' Only one risked instead: 'Police at dead end. Yard man baffled.'

Meanwhile Bobby had been given the file, dealing with the still unexplained disappearance of Mr Thorne, which he had asked should be ready for him. A bulky collection. Immersed in it, making frequent notes, he remained for long, oblivious of the passing hours, even forgetful—incredibly—of that 'sausage and mashed' awaiting his attention and so easily 'hotted up'. But when he had turned the last page and made his late note, his appetite re-asserted itself with sudden and even violent vigour. So he departed forthwith, though not before making sure that the file would still be there next morning, all ready for further study.

"I want to sleep on it," he explained to the station sergeant. "You'll see it's available first thing in the morning?"

The station sergeant promised he would see to that. Bobby said good night and made for the door, turning suddenly, however, before he reached it.

"Oh," he said, "there's that young fellow—Chrines, isn't his name? He was the first to discover what had happened, wasn't he?"

"That's right," the sergeant said. "A statement was took, but he didn't seem to have much to say, except what a shock it was and his nerves all gone to pieces from it."

"No wonder," Bobby said. "Enough to upset anyone. Has he been living long at Hillings? Do you know anything about him?"

The station sergeant didn't. Chrines had never come under the notice of the police in any way.

"Literary gent.," the sergeant said. "Writes poetry. Doesn't do anything for a living, but pays his way O.K. Plays a good game of darts and gets tight so easy some of the Hillings chaps as could down beer all day and never show it say even him looking too hard at a glass will knock him over. Sort of a standing joke up there."

Bobby remarked that there were some like that and would the sergeant try to find out the exact date when Chrines first became a Hillings resident. The sergeant undertook to do so,

though evidently wondering what on earth so apparently irrelevant a piece of information was wanted for, and what connection it could possibly have with recent happenings. Bobby
thanked him and hurried off to his now passionately longed for
supper. Not till he was half-way through it, and the first keen
edge of his appetite blunted, did it occur to him to ask the be-
nevolently watching Mrs Wiggins if she chanced to know exactly when Chrines made his first appearance in the district. As it
happened, she did. When he first came to Penton he lodged for
a time with a neighbour of hers while looking out for a more
permanent residence. This he had found in the Hillings cottage
he now occupied, but he had had to move into it before it was
really ready for occupation. That was because of the unexpected early arrival of a new baby in the neighbour's house. As the
child, now a lusty and healthy infant, was exactly two years old,
it followed that Mr Chrines had been a Hillings householder for
just two years.

"A very nice young gentleman," declared Mrs Wiggins. "He
writes poetry and such like for the papers and seems he has money of his own so he don't need to work. You don't think he had
anything to do with it, do you? Wiggins always says that them as
finds the corpse is often them as put it there. But I didn't ought
to ask, I know. Wiggins would give me a wigging if he knew."

Bobby rewarded this mild jest with a smile, remarked that
it was early days to say if anyone had anything to do with anything, complimented Mrs Wiggins on her skill with sausages,
and retired to bed, determined to get a good if short night's rest.

And short it was; for the story is still told in the West Mercian police force of how he was back again at headquarters
and deeply immersed once more in the Thorne file, before five
o'clock next morning.

CHAPTER XVIII
THE THORNE FILE

ONCE MORE therefore, in the stillness of the early morning,
Bobby read through from beginning to end, from end to beginning, the accumulation of reports, statements, rumours, what

not, that together went to make up the formidable mass of material known as the Thorne file. Much of it seemed wholly irrelevant, most of it contradicted the rest of it, it came to no conclusion, it pointed nowhere, and over every paragraph, every sentence almost, Bobby pored with concentrated attention. And the pile of notes at his side grew steadily higher.

There had been, of course, as was only to be expected, an overwhelming spate of rumour. All had been carefully tested, for Major Rowley's methods, if lacking in imagination, were at least thorough. If steady, sober, painstaking, plodding work could have revealed the truth, Major Rowley would certainly have brought it to light. One fault Bobby was inclined to find was that too much attention had been paid to what were clearly malicious rumours and too little to the motives inspiring them. Some, of course, were clearly mere invention, as for instance the one linking Mr Thorne's name with that of a girl, a parishioner, who had vanished at the same time, but had simply gone off without telling her family to marry a man of whom they disapproved. There seemed to be more foundation for the reports that Mr Thorne had been losing money in rash speculations—he had, for instance, bought a farm near Penton without discovering that he had also bought very heavy financial obligations—but there seemed nothing to show that with care and economy over a few years he would not have been able to recover his position entirely. Hillings was probably much the richest living in the country for so small a parish, in which hardly more than a tenth of the two or three hundred inhabitants made even a pretence of attending church—or chapel either, for that matter.

Nor could these pecuniary difficulties have been in any way pressing or immediate, since in Mr Thorne's desk in his study was found a sum of fifty pounds in Treasury notes, just repaid to him by John Hagen in part settlement of a loan.

"Mr Thorne," Hagen had explained in a statement duly recorded and signed, "had been good enough to lend me a hundred pounds for the purchase of books I badly needed for my studies. He was always very interested, and I owe a great deal to the encouragement and help he gave me. I saved up till I had enough money to pay him back, but he would only take half, and that without interest. He said I was to go on saving till I had put by a full hundred pounds again, and then I could repay him the rest of my debt. Now it must wait till he returns, as no doubt he will one day, and then the money will be waiting for him. A very generous gentleman, and he was always very kind in taking such an interest in my studies."

It appeared also that Hagen had been very active in searching the moor, and Bobby remembered that Hagen had told him that it was generally believed Mr Thorne had lost his way on it during the night or met with an accident. Even a comparatively trivial mishap might have resulted in that lost and desolate country, as lonely as any in the land, in death from hunger and exhaustion.

The only other names mentioned, with which Bobby was acquainted, were those of Duncan Day-Bell and his father, and every reference to them Bobby read with special care. It did seem there had been a certain amount of ill feeling between the two clergymen over the proposed amalgamation of the Hillings parish with the one in Penton in which lay the piece of ground, once a pasture bequeathed to Hillings in the Middle Ages for the benefit of the Hillings poor, but now built over and producing a very satisfactory revenue. An unfortunate public reference by the elder Day-Bell to a 'comfortable sinecure providing a very good living without any duties' had been bitterly resented by Mr Thorne, and produced counter allegations about underhand intrigues intended to secure possession of these revenues for the benefit of a parish to which it was well known Mr Day-Bell was to succeed very shortly, since the present incumbent was over eighty, wished to retire, and the advowson was in the gift of a member of the Day-Bell family. An added sting was an insinuation that the money was needed for the benefit of a ne'er-do-well son who had 'already seen the inside of a London gaol'. All very unseemly, and high ecclesiastical authority had had to be invoked to bring the controversy to an end. However, on Mr. Thorne's unexplained and disconcerting disappearance, the Day-Bell family influence had been enough to ensure Mr Day-Bell's appointment to the charge of Hillings parish.

Much of this was hinted at in the file rather than explicitly stated; but feelings had evidently run high, and apparently Duncan Day-Bell had exchanged blows with a young relative of Mr Thorne's, though this had been smoothed over by expressions of regret from both the young man and a final handshake.

From this intense concentration on the record of events more than two years old, Bobby turned to the recent statements taken from Duncan Day-Bell and from Samuel Chrines by the West Mercian sergeant who had interviewed them. Bobby found them of little interest; they being merely factual statements of what had happened, of the discovery of the murder by Chrines and of the resulting action taken by Duncan. So Bobby turned his attention to breakfast; and, that agreeable interlude over, had a long talk with Major Rowley, with whom he settled various details of the day's projected activities.

For his own part, Bobby explained, he would like to have a further talk with some of those whose statements he had just read.

"Oh, yes," he said in answer to a rather hesitating question from Major Rowley, "I'm working on a theory, but I would rather not say anything about it yet awhile. Doesn't do to risk putting chaps working with you on a wrong line when they may have a better one of their own to follow up, and so far I haven't got hold of a single bit of concrete evidence."

"Had you any idea of finding it in that old Thorne file I'm told you've been studying ever since some ungodly hour this morning?" and in Major Rowley's voice as he asked this there was the faintest possible touch of a discreet amusement that changed, however, to less discretion and more amusement when Bobby nodded an assent.

"I thought there might be something to show if I was really on the right track," he said. "One thing is quite clear, anyhow," he went on. "Several people disliked very much, and for very good though varying reasons, Pyle's plan to open the Janet Merton grave. The motive for the crime may have been there."

"Surely no one would go to such extremes simply for that?" Rowley protested. "Simply to prevent a few poems and letters being recovered. They may not even be there at all. No one knows for certain what was in the casket Asprey is said to have put in the coffin."

"No," Bobby answered. "No, no one knows for certain what secrets Janet Merton's grave may not hide," and Major Rowley looked uneasy, for there was a note in Bobby's voice that he did not understand and that troubled him vaguely.

"You don't mean," he asked, "you are taking seriously this nonsense about Asprey's letters saying that the Duke poisoned his wife? How could there be any real evidence in them—anything you could take seriously? Gossip and servants' tittle tattle, perhaps, but that's all it's likely to amount to. Besides, look at the Duke himself—well, not that kind. A bit of a sap, I should say. Look how he caved in at the first hint of blackmail. All in a twitter at once, instead of standing up to it."

"I don't feel myself," Bobby remarked, "that he's a man it would be altogether wise to forget. Or to under-estimate. That apologetic manner of his I should take to be merely his way of trying to adjust himself to a world that's turned upside down since he was a child. People in his position have often had what is called to-day a guilt complex about their privileges. Formerly they could work it off by giving a lot of their time and money to public service, but now—well, many of them are the lost, bewildered children of present-day conditions. And lost, bewildered children are sometimes capable of very unexpected behaviour."

Major Rowley looked both very puzzled and entirely un-convinced. He told himself that this sort of social theory had nothing at all to do with the practical task on hand—that of bringing to justice Mr Pyle's murderer. Nor did he realize that Bobby had been deliberately turning the talk away from any consideration of possible suspicion attaching to the Duke be-cause that was not a subject he wished brought up just yet. For-tunately, neither did Major Rowley wish to pursue it. He felt that now full responsibility for the direction of the inquiry rest-ed with Bobby, with whom, for his part, when that responsibil-ity had to do with people like dukes, he was perfectly willing to leave it. If the Joint Committee started asking questions, he had his reply ready—the Yard had been asked to help, and that was one form their help had taken.

"There's another point to be cleared up," Bobby went on. "I've come across references to revolvers several times, but they seem a bit difficult to check up on. Hagen told me he had seen Item Sims cleaning one and I must ask our people in London to ascertain if Mr Pyle had any gun and if so if he is known to have had it with him."

"That's important," Rowley said, looking almost excited. "Hagen ought to have let us know at once. Suggests Sims may possibly have got hold of it or got one himself in preparation. Premeditated? It does seem to indicate very strongly that Sims—" He paused, hesitated, looked worried. "Only there's that alibi. Got to break that. Anyhow, he will have to be found."

"Priority number one," Bobby agreed. "But he's an old hand at the disappearing game. We were looking for him for over a year once, and then found he had been lodging opposite a police station all the time."

He went on to say that his own plans for the day included a further chat both with young Mr Chrines and with the Day-Bells, father and son.

"You can sometimes get more out of people in a friendly sort of chat than by taking formal statements," he remarked. "Trifles that come out casually may put you on the right track, and you do get an idea of what's in their minds. Note-books are apt to inhibit, don't you think?"

Major Rowley looked doubtful. He suggested, on the other hand, that people were apt to be more careful in what they said when they knew it was being taken down in writing, and Bobby said that that was what he wanted to avoid. He liked those he was questioning to be off their guard, to let it all come out, not only what they thought and believed, but also the background of such thoughts and beliefs.

"Especially gossip," he said. "A trump card, gossip, if you know when to play it."

Major Rowley said politely that every man had his own methods and the test lay with the results secured. He did not add that he had small faith in Bobby's methods and still less in any useful results being secured by them. Bobby was well aware that that was what was in the other's mind, but that was all right by him, and when he asked for the loan of a motor-cycle on which to cover the ten miles to Hillings, Major Rowley was quite willing to supply it, grateful that he would not have to supply as well one of his over-worked and scanty force to accompany Bobby as chauffeur. Also after Bobby's departure, he would be able to turn to his own safe solid routine, which so far at least in his career had produced by no means unsatisfactory results.

And Bobby as he sped on his way was wondering whether it would be best to tackle Chrines first or the Day-Bells, and if the last, whether separately or together. He had a vague idea that the order of approach might be important.

CHAPTER XIX
CANBAR FARM

NOT INDEED till Bobby came to where a sign-post announced a turning that led to the Canbar and Skeleton farms, did he decide that there he would pay his first visits.

So for another two or three miles or so he bumped over ruts and stones and splashed through puddles—for this he had now entered on was little more than a rough farm-track—till he came to a well-kept, prosperous-looking farm-house. He noticed that the small lawn and flower-beds before it were carefully tended and at the moment showed a rich display of blooms. Unusual, he knew, for most farmers tend to regard it as slightly unethical to give up good land for the production of anything so purely frivolous as flowers, and most farmers' wives have neither time nor leisure for any such pursuit.

Bobby made a little mental note of this detail. It might be useful to remember it in the future when trying to estimate character and motive. He leaned his motor-cycle against the garden gate post and was walking up the path towards the house when he heard a man shouting to tell him that if he wanted to see the 'missis' she was over by the old barn. Towards therefore what from its appearance he took to be the 'old barn' he made his way. From it there came striding to meet him a tall, vigorous-looking young woman, wearing breeches and gaiters and such substantial shoes as could certainly never have made those footprints found on the moor.

Not perhaps a very pretty girl in the ordinary sense, with her large, irregular features and highly coloured complexion, for which one guessed the only cosmetics used had been sun, wind, and rain. But the eyes were bright and clear beyond the usual; and she was certainly a fine, handsome, upstanding lass, with about her, too, an air of authority and decision a little strange in one so young, but coming to her naturally as responsible for the working of a fair-sized farm and the employment of some seven or eight men, more at busy seasons. In a clear, strong voice tuned by use and custom to carry far in the open air she greeted him and asked:

"Are you the police, the man from London? Mr Day-Bell told me I might have a visit."

"Well, we do rather want to know if you can help in any way," Bobby answered. "I take it you are Miss Christabel Merton? Could you spare me a few minutes, do you think?"

"I suppose so," she answered resignedly. "You had better come up to the house. I don't know what I can tell you, though. Anyhow, police can't be worse than those awful inspectors nosing round and wanting to know why a cow that hasn't calved isn't giving any milk any more and will you please fill in a form in triplicate to explain."

She led the way to the house, entering by a side door, and then introducing Bobby into a fair-sized room that looked as up to date an office as any all London town could show. All the usual office appliances were there—card indexes, filing cabinets, a huge safe, typewriter, a small calculating machine, and so on. There was even a telephone, but this, Miss Christabel explained, when she saw him looking at it, was not a Post Office instrument, but for farm use.

"It's very useful," she said. "The men can call me at any time from almost any field."

She sat down at a big desk that occupied the middle of the room, motioned Bobby to a chair, produced cigarettes, offered him one, took one herself and said:

"I don't see what I can do to help. I've only seen the poor man once. It's a dreadful thing, and I wish I had been a little nicer to him. You know what he wanted?" She paused, and her fresh young face seemed to grow harder, older, harsher. It was as though a sudden cloud passed over it. Even her voice was different, fierce, intense, as she went on: "I told him plainly I would use every means in my power to stop him from violating my aunt's grave. I think I told him I would rather see him in his own grave first." She paused. "Oh, well," she resumed, "I suppose the truth is I lost my temper altogether. I never knew I could get worked up like that. Well, that's what happened, and you had better hear all about it from me. You would soon enough from the men. They are such gossips. It was all over everywhere that Mr Pyle had to run for his life. And now this awful thing has happened."

"I gathered," Bobby said, "from something Mr Pyle told me that young Mr Day-Bell was present part of the time?"

"Oh, well, not really," she answered, a slightly heightened colour now apparent. "Mr Pyle simply wouldn't go. He started writing cheques and waving them at me. He seemed to think no one could resist a cheque, if only it was big enough. I didn't want to call any of the men to make him go—there would only have been more talk—and I rang Mr Day-Bell. We carried the line to his place. It's handy if we are working in together. We do sometimes, and he's awfully good with machines when the silly things break down. He cycled over at once, and Mr Pyle went away then."

"I rather gathered that he used threats?"

"Oh, no," she protested. "All he did was to take Mr Pyle by the scruff of his neck, run him down the garden path to his car, and tell him to get going."

"I see," said Bobby. "Direct action. But I meant threats by Mr Pyle?"

"Oh, well—yes, he did. Something about how influential he was, and we might find our farms being inspected to make sure the best use was being made of them."

"Did either you or Mr Day-Bell take that very seriously?"

"Well, it's the one thing every farmer dreads. Feather bed indeed." She snorted indignantly. "Bed of dynamite, more like.

You can always find fault with other people's work if you try, and Duncan is rather fond of experimenting, and it doesn't always come off, and then you get told you haven't put that field to the best use." Abruptly she said: "It may mean ruin, and no one's safe."

"It comes to this," Bobby said, rather gravely, "Mr Pyle's death has relieved you from anxiety in two respects— the threat to your possession of your farm and the threat to open your aunt's grave."

"Well, yes, if you like to put it that way," she admitted. "It was rather a relief when I heard. I'm sorry it happened in such a dreadful way."

"Yes," Bobby said thoughtfully, uneasily even, for the talk had not gone as he had expected, and he knew enough of the power that can be wielded by a man in Mr Pyle's position to feel that threats he made had to be taken seriously. Again, Miss Christabel had made it clear that her feeling against the opening of her aunt's grave was both deep and passionate.

Bobby found himself asking himself—and not liking the question—what might not have come from the union of two such strong currents of emotion. There was fear of losing the farm, there was strong resentment at the proposed violation of a grave. He had uncovered, he felt, more than he had expected, more than he had wished. He said abruptly:

"Do you think it absolutely certain these manuscripts Mr Pyle wanted were in fact buried with your aunt?"

The question seemed to astonish her, and it was a minute or two before she answered.

"Well, yes," she said finally. "It's always been understood, and my father saw the casket put in the coffin before it was fastened down. It couldn't possibly have been taken out afterwards without people knowing. Besides, if they aren't there, where are they? I have all her things, and this is where she lived. She left me everything."

"No one seems to have actually seen what was in the casket," Bobby remarked. "We have Stephen Asprey's word, but that's all. I was only wondering. We get like that in the police. Want corroboration for everything. Only, as you say, if they aren't there, where are they? Or could the grave have been opened without anyone knowing?"

"Good gracious, no! What an idea!" she exclaimed, startled.

"There's some evidence to suggest," Bobby told her, "that some such idea was in Mr Pyle's mind. There seems to have been a spade and pick-axe in the caravan, and he had with him a man with a criminal record. He may have been chosen for that very reason—to help in opening the grave without authority. A criminal offence."

"You mean the man who has run away?" Christabel asked. "Isn't he the man who did it?"

"We think he may be able to help, and of course we are doing our utmost to find him," Bobby answered. "Running away isn't proof, though it is good cause for suspicion. But it does rather look as if he had an alibi we may have to accept. And there do seem to be some curious leads going back to before Item Sims came on the scene and hinting at a connection with Mr Thorne's disappearance."

"Oh, that can't be," she protested, and was there now just a shade of doubt and of uneasiness in her manner?

He thought so, but he was not sure. He resumed:

"It's only an idea. But when two things like this—murder and unexplained disappearance—happen within what might be called the ambit of your aunt's grave, it does look as if they might have something to do with each other. Of course, that will have to be worked out one way or another. You know Mrs Asprey has come to live at Two Mile End? Have you met her?"

"I've seen her sometimes," she answered, "but I try to keep out of her way. I think she hates me for my aunt's sake. I spoke to her once in Hillings churchyard. It seemed silly not to. I just said good afternoon. She didn't take any notice at first. She just stood. It was rather frightening. I know I was quite glad when Hagen came out of his cottage. I don't believe even a sparrow goes near my aunt's grave without his knowing. When Mrs Asprey saw him coming she went away. But she said something horrible first, so now if I see her in the churchyard when I go there, I wait till she's gone."

"How do you mean—frightening?" Bobby asked.

"Well, just that—frightening. She looked—oh, I don't know, I can't explain. As if she knew something was going to happen and she couldn't stop it and didn't want to. Mr Hagen said afterwards that he didn't think she was quite sane. But I don't think it was that. I've seen a madman. He was working here. What I felt was that he had become someone different—he wasn't any more the quiet, hard-working man I knew. He was changed. He wasn't any more his own real self. But it wasn't like that with Mrs Asprey. She seemed all at once to become much bigger, as if something had been added to her so that she was greater than before—if you know what I mean," Christabel added doubtfully.

"I see," Bobby said, though he didn't.

But it was a useful expression, and then he had had something of the same impression himself during his last interview with her. He, too, had felt there was within her an intensity of emotion held in fierce control, but that, all the same, might at any moment break out as breaks out the mountain torrent when it frees itself from banks or dam that till then had held its waters in restraint. More than a little worrying. A wholly unpredictable element seemed to have come into the investigation, one that could not be evaluated. Before he could say anything more, Christabel spoke again, quickly, in a low voice. She said:

"There was nothing like that between Aunt and Stephen Asprey. Like what she said, I mean. Father had been angry about it, but when Aunt was dying she told him again it had never been like that. They had only been friends, never anything more. You can believe what people say when they are dying." Christabel paused, and then said, but a little less certainly, a little more doubtfully: "A marriage of true minds. They were her last words. Only that, nothing more."

"It may be it was enough, it may be that that made the deepest wound," Bobby said. "It may be that, no more, that she is brooding on," and he remembered how bitterly Mrs Asprey had said that others had taken her husband's body from her, but Janet Merton had stolen his soul away as well. He went on: "Then you don't accept the claim of Mr Chrines to be their child?"

"No," she answered immediately, with emphasis and anger. "It's only that he wants to be talked about and to get people to buy his own silly stuff. I went to my solicitors, but they said there wasn't much I could do. They did write to him. It made him more careful what he said, but he still has great enlarged photographs of Mr Asprey and Aunt he had stuck up for everyone to see. There's nothing I can do, though it's awfully horrid."

"Young Mr Day-Bell tried to do something, didn't he?" Bobby asked.

"Have you heard about that, too?" she asked, looking annoyed. "I told Duncan he mustn't any more, and he hasn't."

"Mr Day-Bell does seem to be rather an advocate of direct action," Bobby remarked as he rose to go.

CHAPTER XX
MISSING REVOLVER

PROCEEDING (OFFICIAL), going (normal), or bumping (factual) on his way to Skeleton Farm—for now the road was worse than ever—Bobby could see how the house telephone wires spread to every Canbar field. He could pick out, too, the one that led to the Skeleton farm-house. Easy to guess that it was at the moment carrying a good deal of eager talk and careful warning.

Well, that was all right—nothing to object to in that—and no surprise, therefore, to see when he arrived young Duncan Day-Bell waiting to greet him.

But not quite such a prosperous-seeming farm, this, as the one he had just left. In good order, certainly—no trace of neglect—but all the same a general suggestion of an overriding necessity to think in terms of strict economy. Old fences, for instance, had evidently been not so much repaired as patched. The house was smaller, too, and badly needed fresh paint, as if its requirements came well behind those of the outbuildings; and the ground before the house, once perhaps a garden, had now been given over to potatoes. Bobby wheeled his cycle up a path not entirely devoid of weeds to the open door where Duncan stood waiting. He nodded a greeting as Bobby came up and led the way to a room that was not like the one at Canbar, totalitarian office, but rather trinitarian—part office, part living-room, part bachelor's den with two old, shabby but comfortable armchairs, fit, as armchairs should be, for sprawling in; such things scattered about as cricket bats, fishing-rods, riding-boots; a double-barrelled shotgun over the mantelpiece; and a well-filled bookcase containing both many books dealing with farming and a liberal supply of popular, paper-covered novels and stories. Duncan pushed forward a chair for Bobby, seated himself, and said rather grumblingly:

"I thought most likely you would be around again. What about this chap they say's cleared out? There's some sort of story going round that you don't think he did it? If he didn't—well, why has he run off?"

"That," Bobby answered, "is exactly what we want to ask him as soon as we can find him."

"The sooner the better," Duncan said gloomily. "Not very jolly to have police all over everywhere and tongues wagging away nineteen to the dozen."

"Murder's seldom jolly," Bobby said.

"Well, yes, of course, I didn't mean it was," Duncan muttered, looking a little disconcerted. "Well, go ahead. I'll do my best to tell you everything I know. It isn't much. I would rather you got it from me than for you to pick it up anywhere. I only saw Mr Pyle once. We didn't like each other, and my father didn't like what he said about me. Not that I minded. I expect you've heard all about it and everything else as well. Nothing much happens in Hillings, and, when it does, they make the best of it. I can't get a stroke of work out of my chaps to-day. I chase them back to their jobs, and the moment my back's turned they are in a huddle again, telling each other all about it all over again. Look, I wish you would tell me what you have heard."

"Oh, well, you know," Bobby answered, "my job is to get information, not to give it."

"No good me telling you what you know already," Duncan grumbled. "Is it true the murder and Mr Thorne's disappearance are supposed to have something to do with each other?"

"The possibility is in my mind," Bobby admitted.

"Can't imagine how—seems a screwy idea to me," Duncan said; and then, with a slight but evident effort, he went on:

"Does that mean you've been hearing any of those idiotic stories that some fools tried to put about at the time?"

"You might care to give me your version," Bobby suggested. "I haven't heard anything specific, but there are one or two rather curious facts and inconsistencies I have noticed, and I am trying to find a general pattern they would fit into. There's more successful detective work done like that than by studying finger-prints and footmarks and cigarette ash left on the floor. I know there was strong feeling over the idea of joining up Hillings parish with one in Penton, and leaving Hillings to manage with a non-resident curate. The motive was supposed to be to get hold of the Hillings endowment for the benefit of Penton, where the money came from?"

"Yes, but it wasn't my father's idea," Duncan said. "He never even heard of it, much less started it, or even thought of it, till it was well under weigh. Mr Thorne got very worked up and bitter. The fact is, Hillings is about the richest sinecure in the whole country and Thorne had no idea of losing it."

"He couldn't be forced out, could he?" Bobby asked.

"Oh, no, parson's freehold and all that. But a lot of pressure could have been brought to bear. Might have been hard to resist. He was supposed to be busy with some awfully learned work about the early fathers, I think it was. That's what annoyed him so when he found Hagen was on the same tack. He gave Hagen lessons in Latin with the idea that Hagen could help him in research, and he didn't like it when he found Hagen was branching out on his own."

"I thought he helped him. Didn't Hagen say so?" Bobby asked. "Hadn't he been lending Hagen money to use buying books he needed?"

"I was rather surprised when I heard that," Duncan admitted. "I suppose he began to feel it wasn't quite the thing to be jealous of his own sexton. Quite decent of him. Hagen paid back half of it and he offered to pay the other half, but old Mrs Thorne told him to keep it for the time. Her daughter's a barrister and is using every legal trick she can think up to prevent the living being taken over. You can't wonder. I expect she really thinks her father may turn up again some day, safe and sound. Nothing to do with my father, and a dirty pack of lies that he was pulling strings. Of course," he added reluctantly, "some of the family on both sides—the Day side and the Bell side—have a lot to say in local matters."

"Do you mean it was actually suggested that Mr Thorne had been murdered and that Mr Day-Bell had something to do with it?"

"We never managed to get any proof that that was being said in so many words," Duncan answered. "Nods and winks and all that sort of thing you can't lay hold of. Too slippery slimy. At first my father wanted to refuse taking charge of Hillings in the interval before it was declared vacant, but it was put to him that that would look too much like running away."

"Do you think people took it seriously?" Bobby asked. "Or was it merely a tasty bit of scandal everybody liked and nobody believed? What was supposed to have happened? Mr Day-Bell wasn't in Hillings the night Mr Thorne disappeared, was he?"

"No, he wasn't; but that didn't bother the gossips one little bit. Thorne suffered from insomnia, and he often went for a long walk on the moor before bed. Anyone who knew that could have been waiting for him, I suppose. I expect I should have been the target for the gossips but for being in America at the time. It's an old story, and a damn silly one. I thought it had been forgotten, but it seems to have started again. Hagen told me. He heard it at the Hillings pub. He warned them there would be a libel action— and a damn good thrashing from me as well, most likely—if any of them got shooting off their mouth like that. Hagen's a good chap, and they all listen to what he says—a bit proud of him, too. The local rag once called him 'The Learned Sexton of Hillings'. That's what's said to have annoyed Mr Thorne so much."

"Well, an action for libel—slander in this case—would be better than direct action by way of fisticuffs," Bobby remarked. "That did happen, didn't it?"

Duncan stared as if at first he didn't understand the reference, and then he laughed, though rather wryly.

"Oh, you've heard about that, too?" he said. "Not much you haven't heard, is there?"

"There's a lot of talk going on," Bobby explained apologetically. "So there ought to be when it's murder. Often a great help. You and a young relative of Mr Thorne's, wasn't it?"

"Well, I wasn't going to put up with his saying I had seen the inside of a prison," Duncan explained. "So we had it out together, and then we shook hands. That's all. He wasn't such a bad chap really."

"Is there any truth about the prison story?" Bobby asked.

"No, there isn't," Duncan snapped. "What happened is that I got mixed up in a row in a London night club. They wanted to charge me three guineas, I think it was, for a bottle of rotten bad champagne. I told them to sue for it, and then the bouncer came along. Quite lively while it lasted, but some spoil sport rang up you chaps and—well, I spent the night in the cells and got an awful wigging from the beak next morning—twenty shillings and costs."

"You got off very lightly, in my opinion," said Bobby severely. "If you take the law into your own hands, you must expect to pay for it. I think you would be wise to remember that. I see you have a shot-gun there. You've a certificate for a revolver, too, haven't you? Is there any special reason why that was thought necessary?"

"Sheep-stealing," Duncan explained briefly. "I got one or two threatening letters—skull and cross-bones all complete and lots of red ink. Warning me not to interfere and what would happen to me if I did. The idea seemed to be that Canbar was fair game, as it was run by a woman and nothing to do with me. I had a good idea who the letters came from, and I put the fear of death into him. I suppose you would call that taking the law into my own hands? Anyhow, it worked. There's been no trouble since."

"Would you mind letting me have it?" Bobby asked. Duncan looked reluctant, hesitating. Bobby said: "I'm afraid it's necessary. Every pistol in the neighbourhood must be examined."

"To see which one was used?" Duncan asked sulkily. "I don't see why you should think so. Anyhow, I haven't got it here at the moment. I lent it to a friend."

"You mean you have the certificate and your friend has the gun? Rather more than highly irregular. Is your friend Miss Christabel?"

"Easy to guess that," grumbled Duncan. "I got wind a holdup at Canbar was being planned. Miss Merton pays out fifty or sixty pounds in cash every Friday. More if there's been much overtime. So I gave her the thing and told her to keep it handy and all she would have to do would be to show it and watch 'em run."

"I shall have to collect it," Bobby said. "When you ring up as soon as I've gone to tell Miss Merton all about it"—here Duncan's expression became a nice mixture of sulks, surprise and anger—"you might tell her I'm coming, and ask her to have it ready. There's one more question I must ask. Mr Pyle seems to have been making threats about getting both these farms—Canbar and Skeleton—inspected to see if they are being properly cultivated. Did you take that seriously?"

"Well, I suppose if you have a pull like the big newspaper barons, you can do a lot, and you never know what these inspector and committee chaps will be up to next. Anyone can always find fault with other people's work, and one or two dodges I've tried haven't turned out too well. I got so fed up with some of their meddling I did make rather a fool of myself."

"I can well believe it from what you've told me already," Bobby said acidly. "In what way this time?"

"I wrote them a letter beginning 'Dear Bureaucrats'. It did rather put their backs up. I suppose it was pretty insulting, come to think of it. I don't expect they would miss any chance of getting their own back if a bloke like Mr Pyle started a 'Better Farming' stunt in one of his papers. That's what he was hinting to Miss Merton. Well, he won't have the chance now, the little swine! I oughtn't to say that, I know, now he's dead the way he is, poor devil."

Bobby made no comment. He departed then, his mind full of disturbing and uncomfortable thoughts. He felt he had once again uncovered more than he had either expected or wished. At Canbar Farm he halted. He was clearly expected, for one of the men was on the look-out and asked him to go round to the side door to the office. There he found Christabel waiting for him. She said at once:

"I'm so sorry. It's Mr Day-Bell's revolver, isn't it? I can't find it anywhere. The cartridges are there still, but the thing itself isn't."

"You mean the cartridges it was loaded with when Mr Day-Bell gave it you?" Bobby asked, and when she nodded, he went on: "Where did you keep it?"

"In the bottom right-hand drawer of the desk," she explained. "Duncan said I must have it always handy so as to get it out any moment."

"When did you last see it? Do you remember?"

"I think it must have been one day when Mr Day-Bell was here—not Duncan, his father. I didn't like keeping the thing loaded because of perhaps it's going off by accident, and Duncan said I need only show it if I had to. So I asked Mr Day-Bell to take the cartridges out, and he did, and they are still there, but the thing itself has gone. I can't imagine what can possibly have become of it."

CHAPTER XXI
LIGHT IN THE RECTORY WINDOW

FROM CANBAR FARM Bobby went on to the cluster of cottages around the 'Green Man' beerhouse and the village general store and Post Office, all these together forming the centre of a village scattered with its two or three hundred inhabitants over a good many more hundred acres of land.

Bobby's arrival on his spluttering motor-cycle brought out to stare at him three or four men from their darts, their beer, or their gossip in the 'Green Man'; four or five women from their household duties that to judge from the appearance both of themselves and of their homes did not seem to be pursued very assiduously; and various children, some too young for school and some who ought to have been there but weren't.

The men regarded Bobby with a kind of sulky suspicion; one of the women said 'Police' in a not very welcoming voice, another said much more loudly, 'Snooping'; a third said in tolerant excuse, 'It's that murder'; and Bobby said:

"Could any of you tell me where Mr Chrines lives?"

A cottage was indicated and Bobby knocked. No answer. He knocked again. He was still being regarded with the same sort of rather hostile, sullen indifference as before. Apparently it was recognized that, while murder was different, all the same it was no concern of theirs, and, anyhow, on general principles visits from the police were not to be encouraged. A third time Bobby knocked. A woman called out:

"Most like he's in bed—fair upset he was."

"It must have been a terrible shock," Bobby agreed; and this time not so much knocked as banged at the door with an emphasis that seemed likely to knock it off its hinges and that now produced from within a muffled shout, coupling a demand to know who was there and a demand that whoever it was should go away. So Bobby called back "Police" and pushed the door open.

He entered a small room, not very tidy, not very clean, furnished with rickety and probably third- or fourth-hand chairs and tables, an old dresser and so on. The only unusual feature was provided by two enlarged photographs on the wall above a rusty fireplace. One of a young and very pretty woman, the other of an older man with a small pointed beard and carefully tended moustache, and a general overall resemblance to others Bobby had seen in Bloomsbury public-houses and Soho restaurants. Bobby noticed that in the photograph one hand was carefully held out so that it could not fail to be seen—and admired. It was a slender well-shaped hand of which the owner was obviously proud and one finger was adorned by a large signet ring. Shuffling footsteps descending the stairs that led directly from this room to that above suggested that Chrines had in fact been in bed till Bobby's summons roused him. He appeared; the tall, shambling young man Bobby remembered, with his odd little blob of a nose, his small tight mouth, his pale watery eyes behind large horn-rimmed spectacles. He was wearing a torn and dirty dressing-gown, his hands thrust deep into the pockets, and he looked pale, shrunken even, a little afraid, too, Bobby thought. He said sourly:

"I had a policeman here practically the whole of yesterday. Never stopped asking questions. I told them everything several times over. What's the idea, beginning all over again? I can't tell you any more. You've got no right to keep on at it all for nothing."

"I'm afraid," Bobby explained, "it is generally necessary in these cases to go over the same ground more than once. People often know more than they realize, and sometimes it is only gradually that small significant details come out to prove a great help. Especially when compared with what other people say. I think I saw you in the Hillings churchyard the other day."

"Well, what about it if you did?" Chrines demanded with that weak truculence Bobby was beginning to recognize as the other's chief characteristic. "I remember seeing someone. I didn't take any notice. There are always tourists staring and gaping, people who have probably never read a line of poetry in their lives. They seem to think the grave of a poet's love is just a penny peep-show."

"I am told a great many people visit it," Bobby agreed. "A romantic love-story, even for people who don't read poetry. Now this has happened, there will be more visitors than ever, most likely."

"Why?" demanded Chrines angrily. "What's it got to do with a man being shot and robbed by his own chauffeur? Look, if there's anything you want to know, just ask it, will you? and then please leave me in peace. It's all nothing to do with me. I just want to forget it. People like you can't realize what more sensitive people—people with nerves—suffer. What an ordeal it's all been to me. But I know you can't understand a poet's temperament," and for a moment Bobby was almost afraid this outburst in words was about to be followed by another outburst—tears.

But Bobby, always liable to retreat in dismay before a woman's tears, would have been more inclined, if necessary, to take Chrines by the scruff of his neck and put his head in a bucket of water. He said sharply:

"Pull yourself together, please. Are you quite sure it has nothing to do with you? I believe Mr Pyle came to see you a few days ago?"

"Well, why shouldn't he?" Chrines asked, his voice suddenly steadier. He looked at Bobby warily, slyly, hesitated, and went on: "He only came that once. We had mutual interests."

"It was in connection with those common interests that he came?" Bobby asked.

"I expect you know all about it," Chrines complained. "What's the good of asking? He knew I was a son of Stephen Asprey. I've no idea how he knew, but he did. I never tell anyone, never. People say it's a wise child that knows its own father. They ought to say it's a damn wise child that can prove it. How can you? So I never say anything." He moved a hand that Bobby saw, now he had taken it out of the pocket of his dressing-gown, was adorned by a large signet ring more or less resembling that on the hand of the figure in the enlarged photograph. "But I'm not going to be bullied into giving up the photographs of my own parents," he declared.

Bobby went across to look more closely at the woman's photograph. It was not a good photograph, nor had the enlargement been carried out very skilfully, but it did suggest a woman of character and intelligence, as well as of unusual beauty.

"Janet Merton?" he asked, turning to Chrines, who made no answer, unless a smirk is an answer, and Bobby decided that what the young man really needed was a good spanking.

A spoiled child, Bobby told himself; and spoiled children can be as dangerous and unpredictable as those who are lost and bewildered in their new environment. Chrines said:

"If that's all you want to know—"

"Oh, but it isn't," Bobby interrupted. "Sorry and all that, but I would like to know a little more about Pyle's visit to you. Was it in connection with a proposed biography of Stephen Asprey?"

"I should think I had the best right," Chrines said. "I've done a lot of preparatory work. Pyle had no business to come butting in. I have unique qualifications. Mine will be the definite biography of one of the greatest figures in English literature, even if for the moment the general public neglects his work. That often happens to the greatest genius. It did to Shakespeare."

"So I believe," Bobby agreed. "I think I remember Pepys thought the *Midsummer Night's Dream* the 'silliest fantastic play that ever he did see'."

"Pyle actually dared," Chrines went on, much encouraged by this sign of sympathy, "to try to buy certain family papers in my possession. As if I would ever dream of letting them be used for the sort of piffle a cheap, sensation-mongering paper like *Morning Daily* gives its readers. Impudence. To tell you the truth, I told him off good and proper, and, if you must know, in the end I kicked him out—literally. Literally kicked him out."

"The poor man seems to have had a rough time all round," Bobby remarked. "You kicked him out. The Duke of Blegborough threw him out of his car. Someone else threatened to shoot him, and now he has actually been shot."

"Who was that?" Chrines asked. "I mean, who threatened to shoot him? It wasn't Hagen, was it?"

"Has he a pistol?" Bobby countered, but Chrines shook his head.

"I don't know," he answered. "I think he has a shot-gun, that's all. He caught Pyle hanging about in the churchyard one night, didn't he? I've heard him say if he found anyone monkeying about in his churchyard he would pepper them good and proper. Souvenir hunters he meant, I think."

"I see," Bobby said. "Have you a pistol?"

"Me?" Chrines asked, and looked dismayed, and again a little frightened. "No. Certainly not. What should I want with a pistol?"

"We have received information," Bobby replied, watching him closely, "that following on some sort of scuffle or dispute in which you were mixed up, you stated you had procured a revolver and would use it if anyone tried to interfere with you again."

"That's what Duncan Day-Bell has been telling you, isn't it?" Chrines exclaimed angrily. "He came here trying to bully and bluster about those photographs. A pretty thing if you can't show your own family photographs. I told him off good and proper, and he went off with his tail between his legs. That's all. He tries to bully if he thinks he can get away with it, but stand up to him as I do and he soon climbs down."

"Did you ever have in your possession a pistol of any sort or kind?" Bobby asked.

"Never," Chrines answered emphatically. "Just a pack of lies. What should I want a pistol for? I can defend myself, I hope." He paused to give Bobby a look of brave defiance, much as if it were Duncan himself he was challenging. "I'll tell you something I heard this morning. The people here are saying there was a light showing in the rectory late last night. Do you see what that means?"

"I am afraid I don't," Bobby confessed.

"I thought you wouldn't," Chrines said, with more than a touch of patronage in his voice. "I didn't myself at first. Then I remembered about Mr Thorne. When he went out at night he always left a light burning to guide him home, and Mr Day-Bell did the same thing. Very sensible, too, if you haven't my rather unique sense of direction. But it shows Mr Day-Bell was out late that night, though he's never said so, has he?"

"Not that I know of," Bobby said when Chrines paused for a reply.

"Well, then," Chrines continued, looking very knowing, "I wonder if it's possible he did happen to see someone, only he doesn't want to say. I can't think why," and these last words were accompanied by such an air of 'I could if I would but I won't', that Bobby, in spite of the seriousness of it all, nearly smiled.

"I shall have to inquire into that," he said, and Chrines nodded approvingly. Speaking with more assurance, as if he felt he had now fully established himself in Bobby's confidence, he went on: "Naturally we all understand you've got to suspect everyone. But in my case there would be more sense to it if Mr Pyle had murdered me. He looked like murder all right when he got out his cheque-book and his fountain pen and I only laughed at him. You see, he wanted those family papers I have—wanted them the very worst possible way. He knew if he could get hold of them they would give the biography of my father he said he wanted to write—like his infernal impudence—a cachet it would never have in any other way. Why, he even began talking about using his influence to make sure that my next poems had a favourable reception from the critics. A full column he promised in the leading literary papers—Sundays and weeklies as well. Or getting his own *Daily Evening* to choose it for their book of the month," and here Chrines's voice trailed off into a kind of yearning, dream-like, far-off whisper, as again there swam before his eyes the vision of so great a 'might have been'. There were indeed tears in his voice, if not in his eyes, and Bobby experienced for him a touch of real respect, well deserved by such a show of stoic virtue as Bobby wondered Chrines had had the strength of mind to display. Surprising, he thought, and Chrines, recovering slightly, said:

"That was when we both got rather heated. I said my work didn't need that sort of string-pulling, and he said I was a fool, and I suppose I was by his standards and—well, I told you, the end was that out he went on his ear."

CHAPTER XXII
MIST ON THE MOOR

BUT AS Bobby rode away on his motor-cycle he began to wonder if possibly this feeling of respect for Chrines's artistic integrity was in fact fully deserved? Only his own word for it that such an offer had really been made and declined with so lofty a Roman virtue. Was it perhaps what Bobby himself had once called the lie imaginative, common with children and with communists and not unknown elsewhere; the lie, that is, telling what it is felt ought to be, and soon will be, and may therefore be quite properly described as already being—a mere transition from 'will be' to 'is'. And, doubts growing, had Mr Pyle really gone out 'on his ear'? With regrettable vulgarity, Bobby said aloud to the wind and to the moor:

"I don't believe that young man could throw out a sick cat."

Abruptly he brought his motor-cycle to a standstill. Two thoughts—arresting, even startling thoughts—had entered his mind almost simultaneously. The first, that these doubts might just possibly be pieces to fit into the jigsaw puzzle he was trying to put together; the second, that he had entirely forgotten his lunch—a thing that had hardly ever happened to him before.

So he alighted, sat down on a convenient bank, chose another with some speed when he found a nest of ants had staked a prior claim, produced the packet of sandwiches he had brought with him, and as he munched, meditated. But still he felt he could not quite be sure of the true significance of Chrines's story. It might mean much or nothing; and when he had come to the end of his sandwiches and rose to continue on his way, the only decision he had arrived at he expressed in the simple words:

"I shall have to ask McKie."

All the same, though his talk with Chrines might lack the strange significance he seemed to see hovering about it like a discarnate spirit seeking a body to inhabit, none the less there had emerged one statement it was necessary to follow up. If Chrines's story of the lamp burning in a rectory window did in fact carry with it the meaning that the elder Day-Bell was out on the moor on the murder night, then it was possible he had seen someone or something he had either not wished to speak of, or possibly that he had not thought worth mentioning. And while the most wearisome witness is the one who wanders off into a maze of irrelevant detail, including a full account of his or her own personal ailments, the most difficult is the one who only tells what he himself happens to think important.

So it was to the Hillings rectory that Bobby now directed his way. His approach was evidently seen—or heard, silence is no accessory of the motor-cycle—and before he had time to knock Mr Day-Bell opened the rectory door.

"I was half expecting you," he remarked as he led the way into the room Bobby had seen before. "Do you seem to be making any progress in this dreadful affair?"

"It's too early to say as yet," Bobby answered. "At present we are concentrating on trying to trace the weapon used."

"A difficult task," Mr Day-Bell suggested as he offered Bobby a chair and took another for himself. "Surely the murderer, if he is, as seems generally believed, this man who has disappeared, will have had ample opportunity to get rid of it. I hear he was seen taking the train to Bristol. He could easily throw it into the river there or somewhere like that, couldn't he?"

"There's that, of course," Bobby agreed, "but we can't take anything for granted, and Item Sims does seem to have a fairly strong alibi, though of course we are doing our best to find him. Till we do, I am trying to check up on every pistol we have heard of in the possession of anyone in the district. Your son, young Mr Day-Bell, had one, I think?"

"I believe he had at one time, but I'm not sure whether it is still in his hands," answered Mr Day-Bell and added: "You could ask him, of course."

"I have," Bobby said. "He states he lent it to Miss Christabel Merton, but she tells me she hasn't got it now and doesn't know what has become of it. She states that the last time she saw it was not long ago when she asked you to unload it for her."

"Oh, yes, I remember," Mr Day-Bell answered at once. "I thought it very sensible. But surely that was some considerable time ago."

"What did you do with it when you had taken out the cartridges?" Bobby asked.

"Well, I suppose I gave it back to Miss Merton. I don't remember precisely. But there's nothing else I can have done with it—I expect I put it down somewhere. I really don't know."

"You could have taken it away with you," Bobby suggested. "You might have thought you had better return it to your son?"

"Oh, no, I should remember if I had done that. Besides, if I had, he would have it, and you said you asked him."

"It seems, then," Bobby said, "that this revolver has been in the possession at different times of yourself, of your son, and of Miss Christabel, and that none of the three of you has now any knowledge of what has become of it. I am sure you will agree that that is a somewhat disconcerting situation, and I hope you will all make every effort to clear it up. I would like to stress how important that is. I am sure we can rely on your fullest co-operation."

"I must say," Mr Day-Bell protested, sitting very upright and speaking a little as if he were addressing some peccant parishioner, "I do not at all like the suggestion that seems to be implied. Do you really wish me to understand that because this pistol has been mislaid for the moment, you therefore suggest it was used in this unfortunate man's murder? I consider any such suggestion unreasonable in the extreme, most uncalled for."

"There is no need to suggest anything at present," Bobby replied quietly. "I can only stress again that it is most desirable in the interests of all concerned that it should be produced with the least possible delay. There is another matter I have to ask about. Information has reached us that you were out late walking on the moor on the night of the murder. Is that correct?"

Mr Day-Bell looked—and felt—still more indignant, still more taken aback.

"I don't understand that question," he said. "I must ask if I am to take it that you suspect me of any kind of complicity in this dreadful business?"

"I don't remember that I've said anything to suggest that you are," Bobby retorted, now somewhat impatiently. "In a case like this we require every scrap of information anyone can give us. I've asked a simple question. Were you out on the moor on the night of the murder? Or do you prefer not to say?"

"I was," Mr Day-Bell answered; and shut his lips tightly, as if nothing would induce him to let another word escape.

"Was it with the intention of visiting Mr Pyle's caravan?"

"I had that intention in my mind," Mr Day-Bell admitted. "On the way I decided not to, and I turned back."

"Was there any reason for that?" Bobby asked.

"It was getting late," Mr. Day-Bell answered, after hesitating for a moment or two. He gave the impression of a growing uneasiness, almost as if he were thinking up excuses or evasions from moment to moment. "Very late," he repeated. "I thought it would be better to wait till morning."

"For your talk?" Bobby asked, and went on: "I must really remind you that this is an inquiry into a case of murder, and therefore I am entitled to expect and to ask for your fullest cooperation. I am afraid I hardly feel at the moment that you are being entirely frank. Please remember, too, that every detail, even the most apparently insignificant, may turn out important. I ask you again, and please do answer frankly: Was there any other reason why you turned back?"

"Well," Mr Day-Bell answered slowly and not too willingly, "very likely I was mistaken, but I did think I saw someone else on the moor ahead of me, going towards the caravan. I think it struck me it might be another intending visitor. So I thought I had better put off my own visit. Besides, as I said, it was getting late. Mr Pyle had been very busy talking to different people. It seemed likely enough one of them wanted to see him again."

"Did you recognize the person you saw?"

"Well, actually," Day-Bell said, plainly growing with every question more and more troubled, "I thought there were two people, but one of them left the other and went off alone. I thought at the time that it was a woman. I'm not sure. It was growing dark and a mist was coming down from the moor. Her companion went on towards the caravan. I waited to see if he was actually going to it."

"And was he?" Bobby asked when again there seemed reluctance to continue.

"Oh, yes. Yes. When he got near he called out something and Mr Pyle came to the door of the caravan and asked who was there. I didn't hear the answer, but whoever it was went into the caravan. I went away then. I didn't think it was any good waiting any longer. It was plain I had been forestalled," he added, with a faint attempt at a smile.

"Did you recognize who it was?" Bobby asked.

"No, I can't say I did. No. But if you insist, my impression at the moment was that it was young Chrines. I didn't see his face; it was only the way he walked that made me think so. Very likely I was entirely wrong. Yes, something in the way he walked—a sort of shambling slouch—made me think of him. I certainly couldn't be sure. I don't think I ought to have mentioned his name. It was merely a passing impression at the time."

"Assuming your first impression was right," Bobby said, "it means Chrines was probably the last person to see Pyle alive. That has its importance. It is almost equally important if it turns out, as it certainly may, that it was not Chrines. So far as I know, there is no woman he would be likely to have with him. Of course, we must try to make sure of that. Anyhow, no such woman has come forward to say she was with him that night. In any case," he added severely, "we should have been informed of this immediately."

"I am only sorry I've told you now," retorted Day-Bell with spirit. "I don't feel I had any right to. It's throwing suspicion on a young man I can't believe had anything to do with it. I should never have said a word about it if you hadn't practically dragged it out of me in what I feel was a most unfair manner. I do most sincerely trust what I have said will not make you jump to any hasty conclusion about the young man?"

"We never jump to conclusions in the Force," Bobby told him, and, with certain memories still in his mind—vivid from days when he might have been a little less guarded than now in presenting evidence, he added: "If we did, it wouldn't take long for the Director of Prosecutions to jump on us. Will you tell me what it was you wanted to talk to Mr Pyle about?"

"An entirely private matter on which I prefer to say nothing. What I have already said is most unhappily liable to be wholly misunderstood."

"Was it," Bobby asked, "about Mr Pyle's threats to have the Canbar and Skeleton Farms inspected to see if they were being efficiently cultivated and whether, if not, their present occupants—or at least one of them—should be dispossessed?"

CHAPTER XXIII
LINED UP

FROM THE rectory, after this interview with Mr Day-Bell, an interview that had taken so strangely and so unexpectedly disturbing a direction, Bobby went on to see if he could find Hagen, for now he wished to talk to him.

To that last question he had put to Mr Day-Bell, Bobby had received no answer, nor had he tried to obtain one. He felt it needed none; he had seen it go home like the thrust of a dagger. Only too clearly had the threat to his son been the cause and reason for Mr Day-Bell's projected visit. But it was no part of Bobby's duty—or desire—to force any such admission. It must come without pressure if it came at all. Pressure, if it were to be used, must come only from prosecuting counsel in open court, and there, too, refusal to answer would be allowed.

Such considerations, however, do not prevent an investigator from drawing his own conclusions and expressing them in his reports. Nor indeed had Bobby's last question really gone unanswered. For the stricken look on Mr Day-Bell's face as he listened and was silent provided full proof to Bobby's mind that Mr Pyle's threat had been indeed the cause of the projected visit to the caravan.

Bobby had reached the churchyard by now. He leaned his motorcycle against the low wall surrounding it and on the wall sat down, feeling more worried and unhappy even than before, and feeling also the need to get his tangled thoughts more clear in his mind.

So many possibilities—ugly possibilities, possibilities he did not much care to contemplate—were jostling for expression and for precedence as he sat there, perpending.

One of them, too, not so much a possibility as a probability.

And all of them, he could not help being aware, inconsistent with that pattern in his mind to which hitherto he had thought all trails led. Did that mean, then—he had to face the question fairly—that this pattern he had seemed to see slowly weaving itself into a net to catch a cunning murderer was just a figment of his own too eager imagination?

For one thing, he had a strong impression that Mr Day-Bell's identification of one of the two shadowy figures he had seen, as young Chrines was very much of an afterthought, though now an afterthought that in Day-Bell's mind had no doubt transformed itself into a settled conviction.

Difficult, Bobby told himself, as he had had occasion to do before, to decide if the truth were being spoken when so often the speaker himself did not know. Were not the worst and most misleading of all falsehoods those that were told in the firm belief that they were true? so easy is it to build up an imaginary picture in the mind and then become certain it is factual.

The possibility had then to be considered that it was his son Mr Day-Bell had seen, and that he had turned back because he had not wished to seem to interfere. Or was it from some ob-

scure fear of what might be the outcome of such an interview between the impetuous and hot-headed young man and the man
who was threatening his own livelihood and that of the girl he
was plainly in love with? And then, when the tidings of the murder came, did this same more or less unconscious fear, again
more or less unconsciously, thrust the name of Duncan out of
his mind and substitute for it that of Chrines? If Day-Bell's mental processes had been like that, then an unacknowledged sense
of guilt might well account for the extreme emphasis laid on
Chrines's innocence and the transfer to Bobby of the anger—and
that anger had been strong—he had felt in his inner conscious-
ness against himself for having made such a substitution?

There was another factor to be considered, Bobby reflected,
as he sat pondering on the low churchyard wall. Chrines seemed
to live entirely alone—alone with his poetry, whether that were
good or bad or worse. No hint of gossip coupling his name with
that of any woman had ever been suggested. If, then, it were indeed Chrines who had paid that late visit to the caravan on the
night of the murder, who was this woman so suddenly appearing in his life and at such a moment?

It seemed unlikely in the extreme. At least, unless it were Mrs
Asprey who had made that footprint found near the scene of the
crime and who then had chanced to meet Chrines and spoken to
him? But she had never expressed any feeling of friendship for
the young man—had seemed, indeed, to resent his existence as
a living witness of her husband's infidelity; and she would surely
have been more likely to tell of any such meeting than to conceal
it? But Mrs Asprey was a strange woman, troubled in her mind
by long brooding on past memories, and Bobby felt strongly that
he had no idea of how she was likely or unlikely to behave.

If, however, it had been his son, Duncan, Day-Bell had seen,
or believed he saw, then Christabel Merton might well be the
woman seen, or thought to have been seen, in his company that
sad night of murder.

Yet another uncomfortable, disturbing thought, long at the
back of Bobby's mind, now managed to wriggle its unwelcome
way to the front.

The possibility must be considered that Mr Day-Bell had seen no one; that he had not turned back, but gone on; that it was to him the caravan door had been opened; that he might have had the missing revolver with him—and used it?

The threat of ruin so wantonly made to his son, threatening, too, as it would, his own position, might well have moved him to a deeply felt resentment—more deeply felt, perhaps, than he himself had realized; perhaps had not realized it at all till it had broken out in violent, unpremeditated form.

So Bobby mused, sitting there on the churchyard wall, ignoring the rain that was beginning to fall, balancing one theory, one possibility against another, and evermore, as he told himself, coming out by the same door as he had entered by. Nor did he think now, as he had thought at first, that the Duke of Blegborough had been cleared, now it could no longer be maintained that he was the last person to have seen Mr Pyle alive, and therefore automatically to be numbered among the suspects. He had certainly departed before the murder took place—Mr Day-Bell's story proved that—but his great Rolls-Royce would have enabled him to drive away, so establishing an alibi, and then to make a circuit that would have brought him back by lonely roads across the moor—unlikely anyone would have seen him at so late an hour—well before midnight, the hour at which Chrines, according to his story, had seen the distant blaze that had roused his curiosity and taken him out first thing next morning to discover what had caused it.

"And possibly," Bobby muttered half aloud, "if Day-Bell can be believed, well knowing what he would find."

So there they were, all these suspects, arraigned as it were before the tribunal of his mind, to answer as best they could the dreadful doubts they had aroused, each one of them with identity of time and place established in one way or another, each of them with motives it was conceivable might have driven them, even if half unconsciously, along the road to murder, motives more or less powerful as the case might be, but always existent and understandable.

The Duke of Blegborough.

He had certainly been on the spot at some time during the murder night, and though it seemed now that he had left before the murder happened, equally well he could have returned again. Motives he had beyond doubt. Dislike, even dread, at the prospect of the recovery of Asprey's letters with the vague accusations and insinuations they might well contain, and the consequent revival of an old, a horrible, and even yet perhaps not wholly forgotten scandal. Natural, too, that he should view with something more than repugnance even the faintest suggestion of the exhumation of the body of his dead wife. That would set every tongue wagging all round the world and back again, never to be forgotten, a theme for endless books by every writer avid for a subject likely to attract. And all this entirely irrespective of any question of either innocence or guilt. Indeed, Bobby felt, the measure of the Duke's entire innocence might well be also the measure of his anger and dismay; and who could tell how long brooding on such possibilities might not have worked upon his mind? One minor point also would have to be cleared up, though one that might have its own importance in all this strange and twisted story. Who had made that threat of blackmail which first had brought the Duke in such haste to Penton and to Hillings? But on that point Bobby had already formed an opinion he intended to put to the test as soon as possible.

Duncan Day-Bell.

Over him there had hung a threat of dispossession and of ruin. Even worse, the same threat had been aimed also at the woman with whom he was evidently in love. Here again, then, who could tell to what angry, fierce, and sudden action that hot-headed and impulsive young man might not have yielded?

Day-Bell, senior.

To him, too, much the same considerations applied. That he was a fond and proud parent had always been clear. The welfare of his son was dearer to him than his own. There were obvious personal considerations, too. Gossip, however irresponsible, had apparently already touched his name in connection with the still unexplained and mysterious disappearance of Mr Thorne, so conveniently clearing away opposition to a scheme which, whether he had initiated it or not, would have meant for him the practical certainty of soon succeeding to one of the richest livings in the country. And men, Bobby knew well, have killed for a smaller prize than that.

Samuel Chrines.

Of what his motive might have been, Bobby was less sure now than he had been before. Certainly it was both obvious and natural that the sudden appearance of a competitor, a rival, one so powerful and influential that the success, and possibly even the actual publication, of Chrines's own Asprey biography was threatened, should have had a highly disturbing effect. On it Chrines had clearly founded vivid hopes of fame and fortune; of making his way into the innermost literary circles; of, so to say, achieving a position at a blow. Then there had burst into this dream a figure so influential as that of the newspaper magnate, Pyle. And Chrines probably knew enough of the ways of publishers to be aware that if the choice lay between his book and one bearing Mr Pyle's name, decision would be automatic. Indeed, it would almost certainly be felt that there was no room for the two books, and his manuscript would be returned to him to lie neglected in some drawer till in due time it passed to its end in the dust-bin. A prospect so unbearable any means to avert it might to him have seem justified. Chrines had been living much alone, he was certainly of an unbalanced temperament, his account of his interview with the dead man had been highly imaginative. Impossible to say what had really passed between them. Equally impossible to be sure how Chrines might or might not have reacted. The anger of the weak can take strange and unexpected forms—from tears and lamentation to reckless violence. It seemed clear that Chrines could not be left out of consideration, even though that pattern to which Bobby had been working, in which Chrines had been cast for an essential part, seemed now less likely to prove a 'witness of truth'.

Mrs Asprey.

She, again, had been living alone too long with her memories and her thoughts. She had made it more than plain that she would do her utmost to prevent the opening of Janet Merton's grave, the recovery of her husband's letters, and their consequent publication. More bitter than death, utterly intolerable to her, this threatened proclamation to the world of her husband's infidelity not only of the body, but of the spirit. Many women have had to submit to the infidelity of their husbands, even to the extent of pretending that their faith was still secure. How much more intolerable to have that infidelity blazoned to the world, and for such treachery to go down to posterity as a glamorous, romantic tale of true love, one of the great love-stories of the world, a Lancelot and Guinevere, a Tristan and Isolde, an Abelard and Heloïse tale, to be wondered at and wept over from generation to generation. Was Mrs Asprey, that strange and brooding woman, of the stuff to submit to that? Bobby did not think so. But was she also of such a temper as might induce her to go to all extremities to stay so great a wrong to her dignity and self-respect? Again Bobby hardly thought so, and yet too much solitary brooding may well bring strange deeds to birth. Had not perhaps Mrs Asprey the strongest and most compelling motive of them all?

Well, there they were, lined up as it were before the tribunal of his questing mind; and among them, these inhabitants of Hillings to whom he had talked at one time or another, or to whom he had still to talk, whether in sharp, probing questions, or in apparently casual chat that nevertheless had always the one end in view—the unveiling of the truth—among them Bobby felt assured, with complete inner certainty, was to be found the murderer.

But to which of them the varying finger of accusation pointed the most clearly he was less sure with almost every moment that passed.

A heavy task, this unveiling of the truth, he told himself as he slipped off the wall on which he had been sitting all this time and began to walk towards Hagen's cottage on the other side of the churchyard.

CHAPTER XXIV
NOT FAR AWAY

ON HIS way across the churchyard Bobby stayed for a moment or two by the grave of Janet Merton. Strange it was, he thought, that this quiet spot of earth, this last resting-place that should have been so peaceful and so calm, had become the focal point of so much that was secret, dark, disturbing. Was it even, he asked himself, fancifully enough, a kind of judgment on one who, whether by the blind working of fate or by design, had so infringed upon and disturbed the life of another?

From such passing, fleeting thoughts he was roused by a sudden clap of distant thunder. The earlier splutter of rain had ceased but threatening clouds were piling up on the horizon and now, as a few heavy drops fell, Hagen appeared from behind his cottage. He was carrying his spade, and had apparently been working in his garden till this rapidly growing threat of an approaching storm had driven him to think of taking shelter. Seeing Bobby standing by the grave, he called out.

"Looks like a storm, sir, coming quick," he said. "We had better go indoors."

"Thank you; it does look black," Bobby answered. "In for it, I think," and as he spoke a vivid flash of lightning seemed to illumine Hagen's figure as he stood against the background of the cottage, followed almost immediately by a fresh and much nearer clap of thunder. "It seems to have come up all at once," he remarked as the roar of the thunder died away.

"The way of the moor, Mr Owen," Hagen said, coming nearer, "the way of the moor." Then he said: "Looks to me as if it might be drifting southerly." He went on: "A bad business all this. I've heard Mr Duncan's revolver is missing. It couldn't be what was used, could it?"

"No special reason to think so," Bobby answered. "It doesn't take long for things to get around here, does it? I came straight from Canbar to the rectory, and I wasn't there long."

"Oh, well, as far as that goes," Hagen said smilingly, "not much happens in Hillings that everyone else doesn't know about in two twos. If Mrs So-and-So's little Tommy has his face washed more than once in a day, everyone knows within an hour. What they call the grapevine. I had been thinking what was used was most likely the one I saw Mr Pyle's man busy with. Though it can't have been him did it, seemingly—Sims was his name, wasn't it?"

"Item Sims, known to his pals as 'Sticker' Sims," Bobby said. "It does seem a strong alibi, but there is the possibility of his having dodged back. That can't be overlooked till he's been found and questioned. I understand he struck you as being a trifle excited?"

"Well, sir, not much more than you would expect from a man being sacked at that time of night. I didn't pay much attention. It was more what he said sounded queer when you remembered it afterwards—about being left holding the bag and all that. In the 'Green Man' they all thought it was young Mr Chrines you were meaning. Disappointed they were to listen to them when you didn't march him off."

"Don't they like him?" Bobby asked.

"Well, I wouldn't say he was exactly popular, no more than I am, as far as that goes. Nobody ever is popular if he isn't the same as everyone else, unless he manages to be just the same, only much bigger—like Mr Churchill."

"There's nothing special they have against Chrines, is there?"

"No, nothing at all, any more than against me. It's only not being cut to pattern but not big enough to carry it off. None of them ever read anything except comic strips, and they don't know what I'm up to, always at my books, they say, and to them, books are a kind of magic. And Mr Chrines—well, with him it's rather like what it used to be in old times with the village idiot. You grin at him, you play tricks on him, the children throw stones at him, in a way you despise him, and at the same time you feel he carries with him a kind of tabu, an aura of the sacred, the numinous, and they had better be careful in case the unknown powers intervene. They know he writes poetry, and poetry means to them something rather silly but mysterious, too, and what's mysterious is best kept clear of, for who knows what's behind it all? It would be a relief if he wasn't there any more. So it would be if I wasn't, for that matter."

"Yes, I see," Bobby said. "Thank you. I was puzzled about his position, and you've made it much clearer. You would be ready to go into the witness-box if necessary, and swear it was a revolver you saw Sticker Sims with? I once had a case, years ago, when what was reported to me as a pistol turned out to be a gas-lighter made to look like one."

"Oh, yes, I could swear to that," Hagen answered at once. "No doubt at all. Army weapon I should say from its size. Not that I know much about firearms. I expect I'm about the only man in Hillings who has never fired so much as a shot-gun. I don't see how it could have been Sims used it, but it might be someone else knew Mr Pyle had a revolver with him on account of a caravan being generally a long way from police and that that someone thought how handy it might come in. Easy to get rid of, too. Throw it away on the moor or anywhere on the road to Penton where there's clumps of bracken so thick you would never get through them. Take a deal of searching, they would."

"It may have to be done," Bobby told him. "We don't spare either time or money or trouble when we are looking for a murderer."

"I can see that for myself," Hagen said slowly. He was leaning on his spade. He paused and then again spoke, still slowly and thoughtfully, almost as if the words came with difficulty: "Yes, I can see that," he repeated, "and I wouldn't much care to be him as you are seeking. Sleep ill at night, I think, he must, or maybe not at all. As far as that goes, it might well come as a relief to him when it's over, one way or the other. I wonder."

"How soon it's over will depend a lot on finding the murder weapon," Bobby remarked. "The moor seems the most likely spot to search first, I think. Major Rowley is putting a lot of faith in his small boys he has out there."

"The moor's a big place," Hagen said.

"There's one thing I wanted to ask you," Bobby went on. "You are in a good position to know what people are saying—I mean, what they say to each other, not what they say to us of the police and they know may be taken down on paper. Many people don't like that. It seems to frighten them somehow. If there is anyone in particular they talk about, it would be a help to know. It would help us to estimate the value of what they do tell us."

Hagen shook his head, and was silent for a little.

"No," he said finally. "Tongues are wagging. That's all I can say. But I don't hear all, not by a long way. You are wrong there, Mr Owen. None of them would ever say a word against Mr Day-Bell, or against Mr Duncan, as far as that goes, while I was there. But I am afraid that it's all started up again the old rubbish about it's being so handy for Mr Day-Bell that Mr Thorne disappeared just when Mr Day-Bell had bought Skeleton Farm—dirt cheap, he thought—and then found he had bought a mortgage as well that made it not cheap at all. Done down he was, as clergy often are when they start trying to be business-like which isn't their job at all. A facer that was for him, and but for him getting put in charge here, and being sure of the reversion to the new Penton-cum-Hillings living as was being talked about, it might have been the final end. Bankruptcy, and that's the finish for a clergyman."

"Was such a story really seriously believed," Bobby asked, "or was it merely talk for the sake of talking?"

"Hard to say," Hagen replied reflectively. "Not believed, of course, by sensible people—educated people. Major Rowley took care to let it be known Mr Day-Bell was certainly at home in bed in Penton all that night. But there was some talk that Hillings wasn't so far but a man could get up from his bed and get to Hillings and back again, and no one know, and what the police put out only meant they were hushing up what all the Days and all the Bells—and they're the big folk hereabouts—didn't want known, it being such a disgrace as they wouldn't ever have got over. It's not so much, Mr Owen," Hagen went on earnestly, "that people are malicious exactly, as that they do like to think badly of others because in comparison they can then think well of themselves."

"I had almost forgotten you were a philosopher, Mr Hagen," Bobby said smilingly.

"No, sir, that's not philosophy," Hagen told him, "that's psychology. Philosophy is not trying to understand people's mental processes: it's trying to get at what's going on around us and what real knowledge our minds bring us."

"To get at the real truth?" asked Bobby. "Well, that's a detective's job, too, though not by metaphysics. Just by putting together ordinary, everyday facts. Is it a fact, for instance, that

Mr Thorne always put a lamp in his window before he went out at night so as to be sure of finding his way back?"

"It's a point I brought out myself at the inquiry," Hagen said. He had still been leaning on his spade as he talked, but now he struck it deep into the ground and moved away a little, turning his eyes towards the overhanging moor as if to obtain of it a clearer, better view to question it more closely on its secrets. "I didn't think he ever forgot. It was the first thing I thought of when Mrs Upton—she was housekeeper at the rectory then— came running to tell me Mr Thorne hadn't been home all night. I asked her at once if he had put his lamp in the window as usual. Well, he hadn't. The lamp was cold and the curtains hadn't been drawn. He must have forgotten, and forgotten the very night he needed it most."

"Does Mr Day-Bell do the same thing?"

"Oh, yes," Hagen answered at once. "It was one of the first things I said when he came here, never to forget if he was called out at night or if he expected to be late getting home. Not that he ever goes for walks at night on the moor, as far as I know. I remember I said we didn't want another disappearance like Mr Thorne's."

"Then you still think Mr Thorne lost his way or met with an accident of some sort?"

"Well, sir," Hagen said, "what else is there for it?"

"There was a long, careful search, wasn't there?" Bobby asked in return. "Major Rowley doesn't strike me as a man likely to give up while there was any hope of recovering the body. I should have thought it could have been found without too much difficulty."

"Ah, sir," Hagen retorted, "you wouldn't say that if you knew the moor. There's bog up there where a man might soon sink in, and no trace left. There's deep pits, where the sandy subsoil has sunk and if a man fell in and hurt himself and couldn't move, and maybe the sandy sides caved in, there would be nothing to show. There's patches of brushwood, too, and parts no man has visited since creation." He turned his back to the moor and came again to his spade and took it up. "No, sir," he said, "I shall always believe that Mr Thorne's body lies not so far from where we stand. And I daresay it's all the same to him whether it's out there in bog or brushwood or sandy pit as if it were here in this churchyard, where he always said he wanted to lie at the end." With a sudden change of tone, Hagen said: "The storm is passing over, after all. But perhaps it may come again."

"So it may," Bobby agreed. "You never know. I had better be off while it's still fine. Make good use of your opportunities while you can. Philosophy or common sense or both? Well, so far as I can see at the moment, we've come to a dead end unless we can find the murder weapon. But we shall go on trying in the hope of getting fresh information somehow. Or it may be the murderer's nerve will crack if he feels the inquiry is being pressed hard and he gets to feel the strain intolerable."

"Coming forward to confess?" Hagen asked and almost smiled. "I can't think that's very likely to happen this time."

"Well, I don't know that I think it very likely myself," Bobby agreed. "But it does happen. Yes, it does happen. The burden becomes intolerable."

With that Bobby departed, and as he rode away on his motorcycle the last he saw of Hillings, as the dip in the road took it out of sight, was a glimpse of Hagen still standing by the Merton grave, still leaning on his spade, still deep in thought.

CHAPTER XXV
UNANSWERED QUESTION

THE FIRST thing Bobby did on his return to Penton was to write out as careful and complete a record as he could contrive of the various interviews he had had during the day and of the conclusions and inferences that he thought could legitimately be drawn from them. A long and tedious task.

That done, he had typed copies made and delivered to Major Rowley and Superintendent Evans for them to read and consider. With them, later on, he sat far into the night, deciding what steps should next be taken and what lines of inquiry it would be most profitable to follow up and to whom to allot them to be dealt with.

The Superintendent was quite clear about it all. Item Sims was his man. Criminal record, done a bunk, known to have been in possession of weapon of type made use of. 'That's good enough for me,' he said more than once, and Bobby made no attempt to controvert this, the plain, simple, common-sense view, since he knew well that nine times out of ten the simple, common-sense, down-to-earth view turns out to be the right one. But he did remind the other two, and with emphasis, that there were further, and more troubling, aspects of the case that should not be overlooked.

"The disappearance of Mr Thorne has never been explained," he pointed out. "Doesn't it seem likely that comes in somewhere? Two such strange affairs in one small town? And no connection? Not one of them growing out of the other? I can't think that probable."

Major Rowley, jealous for the reputation of Penton in all things, even in the providing of unsolved mysteries, inclined, too, on the whole to side with Evans—but not too openly—made a mild protest.

"Oh, I don't know," he said. "You wouldn't believe some of the things that go on here in Penton. I don't see myself why Thorne's disappearance and the murder of Mr Pyle should have anything to do with each other. Anyhow, don't you think one thing at a time is enough? Of course, there was all that mischievous nonsense you'll have heard of, about it all happening so conveniently for Mr Day-Bell. I can assure you with the utmost confidence that we satisfied ourselves Mr Day-Bell was at home in bed all night when Mr Thorne vanished."

Bobby thought, but did not say, that 'utmost confidence' is not enough, unless there is solid proof as well, and of that, as far as he knew, there was none. Nor did he forget that, by his own admission, the older Day-Bell had been near the scene of the crime not very long before it was committed. Nor indeed—and this was not to be forgotten—that a threat to his son might have moved him more profoundly, to a greater and a fiercer anger than one aimed solely at himself. Since, then, it was less personal he might have held it, too, more justifiable, and therefore found it also less easy to resist. But these were speculations that only flitted uneasily through Bobby's mind. Instead of giving them utterance, he turned to another aspect of this strange case and went on:

"I don't think either we ought to forget these papers buried with Janet Merton. Pyle seems to have stirred up some remarkably strong feeling by his talk of recovering them. Almost a mania with him, and in the end it brought him to his death."

"Well, that's what we've got to deal with," Evans put in. "I mean to say who killed him, not why."

"Oh, yes, quite so," Bobby agreed. "But the 'why' might lead us to the 'who'. There's clear evidence the papers were really placed in Janet Merton's coffin, and Hagen is very emphatic about it's being impossible the grave could have been opened without his knowing. I think we can accept that?"

The other two nodded assent.

"If they were ever there, that's where they are still," Major Rowley said.

"Vested interest," Evans said, with something like a chuckle; "that's what Hagen has in the Merton grave. Money to him, what with tourists and postcards and all. He keeps his eye on it."

"Hagen," Bobby went on, "seems to suggest that Thorne met with some kind of fatal accident perhaps during a ramble on the moor when he couldn't sleep. Something about it wouldn't have happened if Thorne hadn't for once failed to put a lighted lamp in his window to guide him home. Hagen appears convinced the body must still be there, probably not far off if only it could be found. But you told me a most thorough search was made and kept up for weeks?"

"That's right," said Evans. "Every inch gone over with a fine-tooth comb, so to say. Besides us, half Penton was out on the moor every week-end till the weather got too bad."

"All the same, it's possible Hagen is right about that, too," Rowley said. "There's bog on the moor and pot-holes and one thing and another. Yes, not far away, that's likely enough. But exactly where—that's different."

"The thing is," put in Evans, who for some time had been thinking quite a lot about his bed, "what's the best line to follow up?"

"Oh, all of them," declared Bobby at once. "One thing we have to go on is Mr Day-Bell's statement that he saw Chrines on the night of the murder near the caravan, in the company of a woman. I can't trace any woman likely to have been with Chrines. There's Mrs Asprey, of course, and there's that footprint might be hers. In fact, I don't see who else can have made it. No proof, but that's the snag all the time. I can't get hold of a single bit of really relevant, satisfactory evidence for any of the possibilities the whole case is thick with. And that goes for my own pet idea as well."

"You've never said what that is exactly," Rowley remarked, ill-temperedly for him, but then he, too, was growing increasingly 'bed-conscious'.

"I never like to put forward what are, after all, only nebulous ideas to the men I'm working with—not at least till I'm a lot clearer in my own mind than I am now," Bobby explained. "No good risking putting them on a wrong track when they might hit on the right one if left alone. Facts are different. The more more of us know more facts, the better chance of getting somewhere. With facts it's the interpretation that counts and their interplay between themselves—especially their interplay. It's a fact, for example, that Sticker Sims has taken himself off."

"Easy to interpret that," put in Evans, and, to himself, he thought, 'All he's just been saying—psychological stuff'.

"What I suggest," Bobby continued, "is for me to have another talk with Mrs Asprey. If it was actually a woman Day-Bell saw, she seems the only one for it, and if so, she may react. If she admits it, we can go on from there. If she denies it—well, we shall see. After that, the next thing will be to hear what Chrines has to say."

"Chrines?" asked Evans. "That's the London chap who moons about all day and half the night with his poetry. Last man likely to have anything to do with any sort of violence. I reckon he would faint at the sight of blood. Long-haired, lily-handed, that's him."

"You never know with poets, especially second-rate ones," Bobby told him. "Frustrated blokes because they can't get out what they feel in them. More than a touch of hysteria, too, in their make-up, same as women, and you know what hysterical women can work themselves up to."

"Yes, but," Evans reminded him in turn, "you can out a poet with a straight to the chin. Brings 'em round all right when they wake up. You can't with a woman," he added—regretfully.

"No," agreed Bobby; "outside the rules. Well, if you think so, I'll have talks with Mrs Asprey and Chrines to-morrow morning, and then I want to run up to town. I want to make a few more inquiries about Pyle's background and to see if I can pep up the search for Sticker Sims. I don't mean to let that get into a routine rut—it's always a danger you have to look out for. On your toes all the time, not routine, is what our job wants. Oh, I mustn't forget one thing I thought of. Do you think, Major, you could double the reward you offered your small boys you've let loose on the common, if they find the revolver used? And do you think it would be a good idea to stress that they should all remember to have a second look where they have looked before. A check up. Very important, I always tell our chaps, to check up on everything. First time is so apt to be hurried with you thinking what you're looking for is sure to be just round the next corner."

With that the conference broke up; and a little before ten next morning—not so early, Bobby had decided, that Mrs Asprey might be still invisible to callers, not so late that it was likely she would be out—he arrived at Two Mile End. Again he crossed that desolate patch where once a garden had flourished, again he found Mrs Asprey, grim, gaunt, and grey, waiting for him at the side door she used.

"Found out all about it yet?" she greeted him, half seriously, half mockingly. "Well, what do you want this time?" Without waiting for a reply, she turned back into the house. "Come in if you want to," she said over her shoulder, "and shut the door behind you. It's chilly this morning." She had turned to face him, and she did not herself sit down. She said: "If you think I'm going to tell you anything, you are badly mistaken."

"If there's anything you know or think you know that might help, don't you feel you ought to tell us?" Bobby asked. "Isn't that a general duty when it's murder?"

"Will hanging one man bring another back to life?" she asked in her turn. "Let sleeping dogs lie."

"Sleeping dogs sometimes wake and bite," Bobby retorted.

"No reason to suppose so this time," she said. She had lighted a cigarette for herself, but had not offered one to Bobby. He thought it a sign she was more troubled than her outward composure showed. "If only you would stop from meddling, everything would be all right," she complained.

He looked at her steadily, but did not reply. She threw away the cigarette she had only just lighted and immediately took another. She seemed to have forgotten his presence. The cigarette she had thrown away had fallen on the linoleum covering the floor and was smouldering. Bobby went to pick it up and put it in the old rusty iron grate. He returned to his seat. Mrs Asprey said nothing. He was not sure that she was even aware that he had moved. When now he spoke she started violently, and he had to repeat his words a second time when she looked at him blankly. He said again:

"A witness has come forward to say you were seen late that night near where Mr Pyle's caravan was parked."

"Who told you that?" she asked, but not as if she cared much. "One of the village people? I wouldn't trust too much to what they say if I were you. Liars all, and fully capable of putting you wrong on purpose. Few of them really like police poking about. Hagen? No, it wouldn't be him; he's a stickler for the truth. He thinks truth is important. I don't know why. He says it is what he is looking for in his books. Did you know truth was to be found in books? I didn't. That leaves no one but Day-Bell, that old dodderer. He ought to be stuffed and put in a glass case in a museum. I wanted to buy a plot of land in Hillings churchyard, next to Janet Merton's grave. Then I could be buried here, so she would always remember who was his true wife. He was deeply shocked. I don't know if I really meant it. Did he tell you that about seeing me near the caravan?"

"We never say more than from information received," Bobby answered. "Our information is also that there was a man in your company. Was it Mr Chrines?"

"Are you worrying about him now?" she asked. "He's a fool, a weakling, he's not a murderer. His stabs would only be from a pen in the back. Look somewhere else if you must. Me, for example? You asked me, didn't you? How many others have you asked?"

"Only you," Bobby answered calmly, and at that she at first looked considerably surprised and then laughed, but not quite naturally.

"Oh, well, perhaps you are right," she said. "I remember telling you I knew who it was. So I would if it was me, wouldn't I?"

"You haven't told me yet if it was Chrines with you," Bobby reminded her.

"He couldn't be if I wasn't there myself," she answered; but only after a pause, as if she had had to consider how to reply. "I'm not going to say anything more, so you needn't ask me. You've a way of talking and chatting as if you were making conversation at afternoon tea and all the time ferreting out what you want to know. Janet Merton lies quiet—or does she? Edward Pyle lies quiet—or will he? Let you be quiet as well—or can you?"

"No," said Bobby, "do not count on that." They were both standing now, facing each other, watchful, hostile indeed. "And Mr Thorne," he asked, "does he also lie quiet?" and at that she stiffened and was still, her dark, strange, smouldering eyes unmoving in their fixed gaze that never left his face.

"You ask too many questions," she said, almost whispering now, "though I told you I would answer no more. I think that you had better go."

"As you wish," Bobby said. "I had meant to ask about those letters and manuscripts your husband placed in Janet Merton's coffin. But if you are not willing to say more, I suppose it would not be much good. Only, please remember—a question that remains unanswered is sometimes answered all the more."

CHAPTER XXVI
FAMILY PAPERS

WHEN BOBBY had said this, he went away, leaving her still standing motionless and brooding, nor could he guess what thoughts of new things or of old were passing through her mind—memories perhaps of past triumphs and defeats that to-day could hardly be distinguished the one from the other.

In the road where he had left his car there was now another car waiting—a small sports car. In it sat Sandy McKie, waving a cheerful greeting as Bobby appeared.

"Oh, you," Bobby said, not too welcomingly.

"Me, all right," McKie agreed. "You might say how glad you are to see me."

"I always try to stick as closely as possible to the truth," Bobby retorted.

"Been having another heart-to-heart with the old girl?" McKie asked, ignoring this. "I guessed it might be that when I saw your car standing here. Get anything out of her?" He evidently expected no reply to this and he got none. He went on: "I was thinking of coming to join in, but I wasn't sure of my welcome."

"You might have been," Bobby growled.

"Do I seem to recognize a *double entendre*?" McKie inquired doubtfully, trying to look hurt. "Last time I tackled the old girl she got reaching for the broom—not that I would have minded that so much, but there was a slop-pail as well and I had on my very best reach-me-downs. Violent old party. Do you think she did it?"

"What I think," Bobby said tartly, "is that I've no time to waste listening to you asking questions you know perfectly well I shan't answer."

"No, I know," McKie agreed. "It's just a vague hope you might let something slip I could turn into a front-page scare headline. And let me tell you if we weren't such pals, and always ready to help each other, I should probably get up on my own hind legs, too, and turn over the hot bit in my pocket to my editor, same as is my professional duty, instead of to you, like the good little citizen from Golders Green I am, and no hope of lollipops in return from hidebound officials like Mr Bobby Owen, may his digestion soon be even as mine."

"Cut the back chat," Bobby told him. "If you've anything to tell me, let's have it. Is it Sticker Sims?"

"There's perspicacity for you," exclaimed McKie, and this time meaning it. "Always know it all before being told, don't you?" He produced from his pocket-book a dirty scrap of paper and handed it to Bobby. "Delivered by special messenger last night," he said. "Must be Sims. Can't be anyone else."

Bobby took the paper. There was neither date nor signature, and the writing was in block letters, crudely formed. The message ran:

"In confidence like, how about coming in on a deal with his Highness, you know what I mean, for what's his by rights and might save from unpleasantness what could land him where a gent like him wouldn't want to be, same being all on the square, fair price, fair deal, fair shares for a pal come in to fix it right, fair does all round. If he don't want, there's others. Ring up later."

"That's Sims sure enough," Bobby said.

"Does it mean he killed poor old Teddy Pyle?" McKie asked, rather doubtfully.

"Sounds to me more like blackmail," Bobby said thoughtfully. "There was a whiff of that earlier in the case, you remember. I don't know, though. I shouldn't have expected Sims to go in for blackmail. Nothing much he would draw the line at. Bad enough record in all conscience, but—blackmail. In gaol men will boast about every crime under the sun, exaggerate it. But men who would rob their mother on her death-bed, or sneak his last penny out of a blind man's tray, won't admit to blackmail if they can help. Nobody without his own little private scruple somewhere. There's a sort of emphasis, too, on fair deals all round. But then, how did he get hold of what he thinks the Duke of Blegborough will pay up for? Plainly that's who he means by 'his Highness'."

"Gone one up from Your Grace to His Highness," commented McKie. "Look, all us chaps feel rather badly about it. Pyle wasn't such a bad sort as proprietors go. Not that we common, garden, three-a-penny chaps ever saw much of him. He liked to sit above the turmoil and the strife and let go an occasional thunderbolt to show he was still there. Nobody ever took much notice. And quite reasonable if firmly tackled. Of course there's a lot to be said for bumping off a proprietor or two from time to time, but we don't like outsiders butting in. Why, when I told my boss I had something hot I meant to pass on to you blokes first, he said that was all right by him if it would help you get your man. That shows you—an editor turning down a bit of hot news."

"Did you get a ring?" Bobby asked.

"Oh, yes," McKie said. "It wasn't Sims. A woman's voice. My guess is Sims was there, telling her what to say. There were long pauses when I expect she was putting her hand over the receiver so I couldn't hear when she was talking to him. I told her I had to know more before I took it on, and they must ring me again when they were ready to tell me a bit more."

"Have they?" Bobby asked.

"No. I've got two of our brightest boys on the job. One to stall as long as possible if they come through, and one to ring the office to let your chaps know."

"When was all this?"

"Late last night, getting on for twelve. If it's Sims, he may have taken fright—cold feet?"

"Might be," Bobby agreed. "You haven't said anything to the Duke, have you?"

"Knocked him out of bed last night," McKie admitted. "I thought it better, in case Sims changed his mind and tried to do a deal direct. I don't think he quite liked it when I warned him not to try to handle it himself. If he didn't want the police in on his private affairs, us chaps were always ready to help him, and he could trust us implicitly—that is, when it was *Morning Daily*, though not always everyone else. Because there were one or two papers that did sometimes fail a little in tact and good taste."

"He didn't fall for that guff, did he?" Bobby asked incredulously.

"Well, you know," McKie said. "I rather think he did. It's not brains the poor fish wants, just experience. If I could have him to teach him the facts of life for a time, he would be fully up to standard—police standard, I mean, not newspaper standard. We've got one of our best men—the best I might say, after me," McKie interposed modestly—"to handle that end. Look. What is it Sims has got hold of he wants to sell? Are they the 'family papers' Chrines talked about and Pyle was trying to buy? If they are—well, are they the same that were supposed to be in Janet

Merton's coffin? If they are, how did Chrines get hold of them? What about Pyle getting them from him by some bit of funny work. Chrines finding out, trying to get them back, and in the row Pyle being shot?"

"It's a plausible theory," Bobby admitted. "There are difficulties in the way though and half a dozen others equally plausible."

"My editor told me," McKie said carelessly, but with a wary eye on Bobby to see how he took the suggestion, "to try to get a talk with Chrines—we thought he might talk more freely to us than to you with your handcuffs in your pocket. Or how about me going along with you and nothing published till passed?"

"You know very well I never carry handcuffs in my pocket," Bobby retorted.

McKie's suggestion was not very welcome, though it had been plain that it was coming. But he had no power to prevent McKie interviewing Chrines sooner or later and he had well-grounded fears that no warning he could give Chrines against talking to the Press would avail against McKie's powers of persuasion and cajolery. Far better for any such interview to take place while Bobby was present and able more or less to control the talk. Besides, McKie did deserve some recognition. He had brought a piece of information that might prove of great importance and that did appear more or less to fit into the private theory Bobby had in his mind and still hoped would in the end prove correct.

"Well, what do you say?" McKie asked, breaking in suddenly on Bobby's prolonged meditation. "Guff apart, us chaps can do a lot one way or the other, and I know a good deal already."

"Oh, tag along if you want to," Bobby said. "I never know whether you Press boys are the greatest nuisance ever or such a help we should have to invent you if you didn't exist."

"Give us the benefit of the doubt," McKie retorted, and then they started off without further palaver.

Soon therefore the two cars drew up by Chrines's cottage, and, under a battery of doubtful and suspicious eyes, their occupants alighted. This time Bobby's knock was soon answered by an unwashed, unshaven sleepy-eyed Chrines, who, though it was now beginning to draw near noon, had apparently not been long out of bed. He acknowledged Bobby's greeting with a surly scowl, looked doubtfully at McKie, muttered something half inaudible about why were they coming bothering him again, and went back into the cottage, where the remnants of an uninviting looking breakfast—or was it lunch?—stood on the table by the window. Bobby and McKie followed, and Chrines said over his shoulder:

"How anyone is expected to get any work done with these perpetual interruptions, I don't know. Not that I suppose that interests you at all. What's poetry to you, I wonder? Nothing probably. Never heard of Manley Hopkins, have you?"

"Never," promptly answered Bobby, not very truthfully, but anything to humour a witness, especially if it put that witness into a good temper, and gave him a sense of superiority than which nothing makes people more talkative. He went on: "Awfully sorry about bothering you, especially when you're busy, but one or two things have come to our attention we would like cleared up if possible. We have information that a woman was seen in your company shortly before Mr Pyle was killed. Who was it?"

"Who told you that?" demanded Chrines. "All nonsense. I'm always alone when I'm out late on the moor, and I often am. It is there in solitude, in the loneliness, in the darkness, in the beauty of the starlight night that inspiration seems to come to me most easily."

"Cripes," said McKie, but turned the word into something between a choke and a cough as he saw the outraged poet give him a furious glance.

"I can well understand that," said Bobby politely, making an effort, dexterously avoided, to tread on McKie's toe as a warning to him to be more careful. "Was it Mrs Asprey you met?"

"Well, it wouldn't be, would it?" Chrines retorted. "We aren't so friendly as all that. I'm a living reminder to her of what she wants to forget. I know nothing about her and don't want to."

Bobby looked at him doubtfully. He felt Chrines was lying, he noted that Chrines had given no direct denial, merely evading the question; he did not quite understand why. After a short pause, filled by McKie's offer of a cigarette to Chrines, its acceptance and lighting, he said:

"There's a footprint, a woman's, near the caravan. You'll have heard about that. Everyone has. It may have been any woman's. It may also have been Mrs Asprey's. It seems most likely it is hers."

"Well, if it is, I don't know anything about it," Chrines persisted sulkily. "She may be there all night and every night, for all I know. Get that? I've never seen her on the moor, I didn't see her that night, and I never have. Never. Neither that night nor any other."

"Don't protest too much," Bobby said. "Are you prepared to repeat all that in court? On oath?" Chrines did not answer, but he looked uncomfortable, for even to-day a difference is felt between the lie, common or garden variety, and the lie under oath, perjury. Bobby saw that momentary hesitation, that passing discomfort, and resumed, speaking slowly and gravely: "If you do, can you stand up to cross-examination by a Q.C.? Not everyone can, I think, for in cross-examination sometimes the truth comes out, or at least the lie is made plain and evident."

"Oh, well," Chrines muttered, sulkily, resentfully, evidently badly frightened by the picture Bobby had drawn, "if you must know—she was there all right. So was I. Why not? I promised I wouldn't tell anyone. I didn't want to. I didn't want to put you on her. She hasn't been even halfway decent to me, but still—well, she was my father's wife, wasn't she? and I suppose it's natural for her to feel sore at me."

"Did you ask her not to say she had seen you?"

"Well, she couldn't, could she? without letting out she was there, too."

"How long were you with her?"

"Only a minute or two. You don't think we sat down for a comfy chat, do you?"

"We shall have to ask you to make a formal statement to Major Rowley," Bobby said. "I should suggest it would be best for you to go to Penton and call on him there. There's no need to attract more attention than necessary."

"I don't see what for," Chrines grumbled. "All right, if you think I ought to."

"There's one other point I must bring up," Bobby went on. "It may be important. You have in your possession what you described to me as 'family papers' and you said that Mr Pyle was pressing you to let him have them."

"He tried everything to get them from me. As if I would part with them. Not likely—not to him, anyhow."

"Are they still in your possession?"

"Of course they are. What do you mean?"

"Have you any objection to looking to make sure? We have information that papers of the same kind are being offered for sale."

Chrines sat staring, suddenly afraid—more than afraid—for to Bobby it seemed that all at once panic possessed him, panic that showed in his stricken face, in his wild, staring eyes. With a kind of muffled yell he jumped to his feet and scrambled, stumbled, staggered his way up the steep, narrow stairs that led from this room to the room above.

CHAPTER XXVII
WEAPON FOUND

IN COMPLETE bewilderment, Bobby, like McKie, could only sit and stare, wondering why so sudden and so complete a loss of self-control. McKie said:

"Well, that touched him on the raw, didn't it?"

Bobby said nothing. He was on his feet, listening to the noises going on in the room above. Now they ceased. He made a motion towards ascending the stairs to join Chrines above and then changed his mind. McKie said:

"Well, why?"

The silence overhead was broken by an outburst of shouting. The only word distinguishable seemed to be 'Gone'. Then Chrines came tumbling down those steep bedroom stairs—literally tumbling, for at their foot he only just saved himself from going sprawling on his face.

"They've gone," he screamed, his voice high and shrill; "they aren't there, they've gone! Oh, my God, what—what—was it you?" he cried; "was it?" He made a short, sudden rush towards Bobby and then stopped. "Was it?" he repeated, and then suddenly sat down and burst into tears. "What shall I do?" he sobbed. "I'll kill myself."

"Oh, for goodness sake, man, pull yourself together," Bobby exclaimed impatiently. "What is it that's gone? Papers? Letters? What?"

"You get out, get out of my house," Chrines shouted at him. "I'll throw you out if you don't," he threatened weakly. "You've no right—have you got them?"

"Where did you keep them?" Bobby asked. "I suppose you're sure they've been taken? You've not simply mislaid them?"

"They were in a box under the flooring under my bed," Chrines answered. "No one could possibly have known, no one could possibly have found them there. Now they've gone. I'll kill myself."

"Don't be a bigger fool than you can help," Bobby said unsympathetically. "Pull yourself together," he repeated, "and tell us what's really happened."

"Oh, you can talk, can't you? It's all you," Chrines retorted. "Now it's all over. I'll kill myself," he threatened again, and once more began to sob.

"I suppose there may be getting some sense out of you presently," Bobby said, as much to himself as to Chrines.

He went up the stairs then to the bedroom above, wretched and squalid. The bed, on it a tumbled heap of not too clean blankets and sheets, had been pulled out of place. Where it had stood, the cheap, unswept linoleum covering the floor had been turned up, a portion of the boarding had been lifted, so revealing an empty space beneath. Near by, lying on its side, was a tin deed box, fitted with a cheap lock any expert thief could have opened in less than a minute with the aid of a hairpin. It was empty. Bobby picked it up carefully. There might, he supposed, be 'dabs' on it, though that he did not think likely. He looked round with some distaste. Traditional, a poet in a garret; but need the garret be so ill-cared for? Meticulous for rhyme, rhythm, scansion, why not for material surroundings as well? He shrugged his shoulders and supposed he would never understand the artistic temperament; but, then, he wasn't an artist.

He descended the stairs to the room below. McKie was alone now, busy scribbling in his note-book. He said:

"Chrines made a sudden bolt for it. The last I saw he was pelting off towards the moor in top gear. Last thing he said was that he was going to kill himself. You don't think he will, do you?"

"Nothing less likely, I should say," Bobby answered, but a little uneasily all the same.

"These hysterical blokes, you never know," McKie said. "What was in these family papers of his to upset him so?"

"Your guess is as good as mine," Bobby said.

"Oh, for the Lord's sake, quit trying to be a blasted clam," protested McKie. "It can't be Pyle's murder, can it? I mean, implicating him in some way. It must be Sims got them. Only then, why should the Duke be expected to buy what's to do with Chrines? He can't be the Duke's by-blow, can he?"

"You never know, do you?" Bobby said. "I shouldn't put that into print, though, if I were you. Anyhow, ask the Duke first. Oh, and remember, nothing published till we've seen it. I'm having this deed-box tested for 'dabs'. If it was Sims there won't be any. Could you hang on a bit longer, in case Chrines comes back? I want to get to Penton to ask Rowley to send some of his best chaps out—his finger-print expert if he's got one."

"It'll be all right if I get the O.K. from Rowley, won't it?" McKie asked innocently, knowing well he could get past Rowley what Bobby would never allow, and yet that Bobby could not very well seem to slight Rowley's competence. "You needn't worry," he added, understanding instinctively that Bobby had realized what had been in his mind, "I can do an A. 1. exclusive innocent as new-born babes, and as hair-raising as new-born triplets to Papa."

Bobby said he hoped so, nodded farewell, and went out to his car. Every inhabitant of every cottage near was there, all alight with curiosity, all a-bubble with excitement, all telling each other all about it and none of them listening. When Bobby appeared they became at once as it were one huge incarnate stare, all their existence in their eyes as before it had been in their tongues. Bobby said briefly:

"There's been a burglary. Things of great value to Mr Chrines have been taken. He should be back shortly. I am sending out officers from Penton to make further inquiries."

"Was it him did it?" someone called.

"Did what?" Bobby asked sharply. "Robbed himself, do you mean?"

"It's him as killed Mr Pyle you're looking for, ain't it?" the voice retorted. "What's this bloke bunked off for?"

"You had better all of you mind what you say," Bobby warned them. "You can easily get yourselves into bad trouble if you aren't careful. At the moment we're looking for the burglar. I only hope he won't turn out to be a local man."

This last suggestion he threw out, not because he in any way thought it likely, but since he could in no wise stop them from talking, in the hope that he might turn their talk into new channels, and so relieve Chrines from some of the pressure of neighbourly curiosity.

But tongues were buzzing again almost before he drove off, and then he changed his mind. He had intended to drive straight back to Penton, but now he decided to visit Hagen first. He was still a little uneasy about Chrines's intentions and there was no urgency over following up the theft of what Chrines had called his 'family papers'. Who had taken them was, to Bobby's mind, quite clear, though the object of the theft and the nature of the 'family papers' was much less so. Now it was in his mind that it might be useful to hear what Hagen thought of it all and to ask if he, who knew Chrines better than most, thought there was really any risk of Chrines's carrying out his threat of suicide. Nor was Bobby altogether unaware that the longer McKie was kept waiting for the promised arrival of the West Mercian men, the longer he would be kept, as Bobby put it to himself, 'out of mischief'.

This time Hagen did not make an immediate appearance as hitherto had been his habit when he heard cars approaching. It was not, indeed, till Bobby had knocked a second time that Hagen came to the door.

With only the barest word of greeting he ushered Bobby into the small front room, where he had evidently been busy writing. On the table by the window manuscript was lying, the ink still wet on the last page. He pushed a chair forward for Bobby and occupied himself gathering these various pages together, taking care apparently to be sure they were all in correct order. Bobby could see that on the page at the top of the little pile was written in large carefully formed letters: 'Apologia'. With some care, Hagen put the MSS in a drawer of the table, carefully locking it.

"It is not yet ready to be seen," he said apologetically.

"When it is," Bobby asked "would it be for specialists or for just ordinary folk?"

"Oh, I suppose in a way for both," Hagen answered. "But I do rather anticipate that it will be widely read, and I expect long remembered. I'm a little afraid, though, that if I make it public—I expect I shall have to—it may overshadow my work in other directions."

"That would be a pity," Bobby said. "A great pity," he repeated, and he saw Hagen looking at him intently, as if wondering why he thought so. "I heard," Bobby went on, "you were corresponding with a learned Jesuit on the Continent?"

"We've exchanged a few letters," Hagen admitted modestly. "He knows only a word or two of English and I know no Spanish at all, so we have to write to each other in Latin—the best of all languages for our purpose. English is the language of drama and of poetry, not of metaphysics."

"I never thought of it like that," Bobby said.

"Though it may be," Hagen went on, "that what I am trying to work out has as much to do with poetry as with philosophy as a theory of knowledge. The relation of the eternal to the temporal, as Plato called it. The treatise I am working on, though perhaps I shall never complete it, is an attempt to co-ordinate all forms of knowledge by showing that knowledge goes beyond itself, as physics seems to be doing to-day." He began to walk up and down the room as though the pressure on his mind was too great to allow him to be still. He resumed: "There's the knowledge that we get in daily life, there's the knowledge that grows as it were by feeding on itself in thinking, there's the knowledge that is given us in the visions of the mystics, in drugs, as well. For I think these, too, lift the curtain that hides from us other forms of truth. Have you ever thought that the rats and pink elephants seen in delirium tremens may have an objective reality—not as material elephants or rats, but as existents translated into such forms as he who sees them can understand? Primitive peoples may have been nearer to the truth than we are in thinking that the madman stood in some special relation to the unknown powers."

"I'm afraid all that is beyond me," Bobby said. "Even at Oxford I was always inclined to fade away when Plato and people like him came up. Couldn't see what it was all about."

"Yes, I know many people feel like that," Hagen said. "Only somehow I wanted to tell you what I was trying to do. I thought it important. I still do—more important than anything else in the world. I was trying to break into realms of thought where no one yet has ever trodden. Well, now I think I never shall, never be able to get my treatise finished. My kind Jesuit friend is warning me against speculations, that may lead me and others dangerously astray, he says, and imperil my own soul. Am I a kind of Faust? He seems to hint it. Perhaps my soul is in greater peril already than he ever dreams. Who was it said Philosophy might turn Procuress to the Lords of Hell?" Abruptly Hagen sat down. The strange fever of the mind that had seemed before to possess him passed and was over. He said: "I'm sorry. I wanted to impress you, I think. Show off. Swank. Not merely the learned sexton, and so wonderful he actually knows Latin. But you didn't come just to listen to me. I'm sorry I got so carried away."

"In point of fact," Bobby said, "I came about Chrines and his 'family papers', as he calls them, that Pyle was trying to get him to part with. They've been stolen, and when Chrines found out he went completely off his head—raved, wept. Finally he rushed out of the house shouting that he was going to kill himself. You know him better than most. Do you think there's any real fear he may commit suicide?"

"I certainly shouldn't have thought so," Hagen said after a long pause. "No. But I don't know. Hard to tell. I think he might try, but I fancy he might make sure first that he wouldn't succeed. Do you know where he went?"

"He was heading for the moor, fast as he could go," Bobby answered. "I hope there's no chance of what happened to Mr Thorne happening to him."

Hagen did not reply at first. He put out his hand to the drawer in which he had placed the MSS he had been busy with when Bobby arrived. He pulled at it, and when it did not open he seemed to remember he had locked it, and he took his hand away.

"There's a map of the moor I have somewhere," he said. "I must get it. The boy must be found. Not that there's any fear of what happened to Mr Thorne happening to him. If the cycle of events does repeat itself, certainly not so exactly as that. I know the moor as well as anyone, and I'll go and look for him this afternoon."

"That will be a great help," Bobby said. "I'm going back to Penton now, and I'll ask Major Rowley if he can spare any of his men to help in the search. I am wondering what these 'family papers' really contained. Chrines never talked about them, did he?"

"Certainly not to me," Hagen answered. "Nor to anyone else, as far as I know. I did gather he depended on them to prove his claim to be a son of Stephen Asprey and Janet Merton, but I don't know, and I never asked. He used to hint sometimes that they would make the biography of Stephen Asprey he was writing as famous as Boswell's *Johnson*. If he really thought that, and then he lost them—that might be what upset him so."

"It might be that," Bobby agreed. "Yes, it might be something like that. Anyhow, I'm relieved to know you don't think Chrines is of the suicide type. It was rather worrying me. A poor way out, don't you think? Just running away from it all."

"Or running to meet it?" Hagen suggested. "When death is sure, when you know your order of discharge has been signed and dated, why not? If death is waited with resignation—good. If it is greeted so to say on the doorstep, with a free man's proud welcome, surely that is better?" Abruptly Hagen changed the subject without waiting for any reply. "Did you know the revolver used has been found?" he asked.

"No, indeed," Bobby exclaimed. "That is important. Are you sure? If it is true, it should bring us a good deal nearer a solution."

"It was those kids Major Rowley promised a reward to," Hagen explained. "Some of them left their bicycles here. For me to look after, I suppose. Two or three of them came running back an hour or two ago, and one of them was carrying a revolver. I told them to take it to the police. I told them to be careful with it, in case it went off. They were much too excited to listen, and I only hope they haven't managed to kill themselves or anyone else. You think it ought to help?"

"Now it only needs the decisive proof I think I know where to look for," Bobby said slowly. "Of one thing I am sure: I shall never be nearer than I am now."

CHAPTER XXVIII
NEW INFORMATION

THOUGH A little relieved by Hagen's confirmation of his own belief that Chrines was in no way likely to carry out his threat to kill himself, Bobby, driving back to Penton, was not entirely at ease. He was inclined to think that in the present mental condition of that young man there was no rash or foolish action of which he was not capable.

He tried, as he often did, to think himself into the other fellow's skin, but this time found it difficult—impossible, indeed. Too great a dissimilarity, he supposed, between their two temperaments. Far apart as the east is from the west, as a better poet than Chrines has put it, were he and Chrines apart in disposition.

All the same, as he drove on an idea came into his mind, and when he reached Two Mile End he stopped his car and once more went round to that side door Mrs Asprey used. There, for proof that his guess had been good, a motor-cycle stood leaning against the wall of the house, and Bobby, who noticed and memorized car and motor-cycle numbers almost automatically, knew it at once for that of the machine he had seen Chrines using. He knocked, and, somewhat to his surprise, Mrs Asprey opened the door almost immediately. With more civility than she was always inclined to show, she invited him in, bustled to find him a chair, and instead of the broom and slop-pail with which on other occasions she had seemed inclined to welcome visitors, produced a box of cigarettes, and offered him a light.

"Very kind of you," Bobby said, warily accepting this show of unexpected hospitality and wondering what it meant. "I suppose you've heard of this latest development?"

"What is that?" she asked cautiously.

"Hasn't Mr Chrines told you?" Bobby countered. The roar of a motor engine became audible. "There he goes, doesn't he?" he added. "He might have waited a minute or two. He can hardly be in such a hurry as all that."

Mrs Asprey looked both disconcerted and angry; and not until the sound of the engine had died away and Bobby was still sitting there, instead of rushing off in pursuit, as she had at first expected, did she turn on him to say with undiminished anger:

"How did you know?" she demanded. "Can't you leave the poor boy alone? He is nearly crazy, distracted with the way you keep on at him, nagging and threatening and bullying."

"He has nothing to fear unless he is guilty, as I think he may be," Bobby answered gravely. "He would be well advised to tell us all he knows, and I think that is much."

"Nonsense! he's just an irresponsible child," Mrs Asprey retorted. "It's a disgrace the way you trapped him into saying I was there—bawling at him till he hardly knew where he was, catching him out in trifles, and pretending that showed he was lying, and you were going to arrest him then and there. No wonder the poor boy broke down."

"The poor boy seems to have given you a rather highly coloured account of our talk," Bobby remarked drily.

"Well, don't try that with me," Mrs Asprey warned him, and he assured her—both smilingly and truthfully—that nothing could be farther from his thought and intention. "Not that I mind your knowing," she interrupted these assurances. "It's only the way you wormed it out of the child. If you want to know, I've been there every night since Mr Pyle came, watching to see what he and that man of his—the man who shot him, I mean, before he ran off—were going to do. It didn't take me long to guess he was meaning to open the grave himself, if he couldn't get permission. I suppose he thought he was so important he could do things like that. I was there, though they didn't see me, when Hagen chased them away. Pyle didn't know then what a careful watch Hagen kept. But even if he did manage somehow to get Hagen out of the way, he wouldn't me. I was making sure of that." She paused, and when she spoke again, it was with a low, steady flame of determination in voice and manner alike. "His letters are mine," she said. "Stephen's letters, and no one shall have them but me." Again she paused, and still when she spoke it was as if every fibre of her being was concentrated into what she said. "Neither God nor devil nor man," she said, and while she was speaking, Bobby was almost persuaded that so great a force of will, so fierce an energy, must somehow, some-time, someway, achieve its purpose. Was there indeed anything from which, to do so, it would shrink? Then, she said—an anti-climax, he felt: "No, nor you either," and with that sank back in her chair as though exhausted.

Bobby allowed two or three minutes to elapse to give her time to recover herself, so emotionally shaken did she seem, before he said:

"I can assume, then, that he told you of the loss of what he calls his family papers?"

"Assume what you like," she answered in a voice now grown tired and faint.

"He didn't tell you what they were?"

"If he had done," she retorted, with a flash of her former energy, "I shouldn't tell you. I don't repeat what has been said to me in confidence."

"It's a point that interests me a good deal," Bobby explained. "I mean why they were so important as to cause their loss to be such a shock. If he panicked as he did, it was because of their loss, not because of anything I said. He strikes me as a very unbalanced young man, and he may easily do something to make things still worse. If he tries to recover his papers himself, he may find he's running bigger risks than he knows. Did he seem to suspect anyone?"

"He mentioned that man Mr Pyle brought with him. Sticker he called him."

"Did he, though," Bobby exclaimed. "That may be important."

"Why?" Mrs Asprey asked; and when Bobby did not answer, went on suspiciously: "How did you know he was here?"

"Oh, I just thought he might come to you," Bobby explained. "He wants someone to hold his hand all the time—mothering. The mother complex," and now Mrs Asprey was really angry, not as she had been before, with the stark, strange wrath of the tragic heroine, prepared for all, since all was at stake, but angry with the anger of an offended virago, with a broom-and-slop-pail anger.

"I . . . you . . . he . . ." she stuttered, so near to choking she could hardly get the words out. "Mothering him . . . me . . . mothering . . . me . . . him . . . that . . ." and now words failed her, and she lapsed into a bewildered, astonished, protesting surprise.

"I'm so sorry," Bobby said, getting somewhat hurriedly to his feet, startled by the violence of the storm he had aroused and a little afraid that next thing would be the appearance on the scene of a broom-and-slop-pail complex. "It was only an idea I had he might come to you, make a clean breast of having let it out he saw you, and be comforted—the way kiddies run to Mother to tell her all about it. I didn't mean to upset you."

"I'll mother him," she stormed, "next time I see him, if I ever do. You as well if you come poking round here any more."

"Oh, I say," protested Bobby, more than a little alarmed at this threat; and then, in the hope of averting her wrath, or at any rate changing its channel, he added: "A revolver has been found on the moor. Did you know?"

"Are you going to pretend that poor child used it?" she demanded. "Don't be silly. You keep talking and talking, as if what Stephen put in Janet Merton's coffin had anything to do with him. It hasn't. He's not her son. He knows he isn't. He likes to pretend. That's all. He may be Stephen's son, but not hers. His mother was a Mrs Chrines. I remember her quite well. Her husband kept a public-house near where we were living then. I knew all about it. I always did. Her husband didn't care. He was doing the same sort of thing. Stephen was infatuated. He always was at first. With all of them in turn. Then he tired and came back to me. But before he tired he generally wrote a sonnet—to her nose or her hair or something. Very bad most of them, and often the same one when he couldn't work the new love's name in. Mrs Chrines's was Gladys, but he wrote her the usual routine sonnet, all the same. That boy showed it me. He had a few letters, too, notes rather. Promises to see her soon and excuses for not coming. It all amounted to less than nothing, and so I told him."

"I see," Bobby said, without pointing out that now she had given him all the information he had asked for previously and that then she had indignantly refused to supply. But he had still to ask himself if Chrines had told her everything. Probably not, he thought, for in what Mrs Asprey had said there seemed nothing to induce the panic into which Chrines had been thrown by the discovery of his loss. "Well, thank you very much," Bobby said finally. "I won't trouble you any longer."

He went away then, leaving her looking more subdued, more thoughtful, more troubled, or, at least, less self-confident, than always before she had seemed to be.

These talks, with Hagen and with Mrs Asprey, had delayed him so much that it was late before Bobby got back to Penton. Neither Major Rowley nor his second in command, Superintendent Evans, was there, however, both being still engaged in following up the discovery of the revolver on the moor of which Bobby had heard from Hagen, and other less important aspects of the case. So till their return Bobby busied himself drawing up a full report of his day's activities and of some deductions, but not all, that he thought could properly be drawn from them. Facts he never attempted to hold back for even the shortest time, but his opinions he liked to keep to himself till he had evidence to support them. This task he had only just completed when McKie appeared to show Bobby the story he had written for *Morning Daily* of recent happenings.

It was a masterpiece of 'I could if I would but I won't', leaving the reader—unless he were unusually 'newspaper resistant'— convinced that *Morning Daily* knew it all, and was only waiting for dilatory official action to catch up for everything to be told in succeeding 'exclusives'. But there was nothing that could reasonably be objected to, even if Bobby did rather wince at the implied picture of dim-witted police slowly blundering on in the wake of, and under the guidance of, *Morning Daily*.

"Got a good conceit of yourself, haven't you?" Bobby growled, handing it back.

"It is important," McKie pronounced solemnly, "that the implicit faith of readers in the omniscience, benevolence, and wisdom of *Morning Daily* should never be diminished but, on the contrary, continually increased."

"Oh, stow it!" retorted Bobby, "and don't try to infect innocent-minded policemen with your horrible journalistic cynicism. By the way, did you see Chrines when he got back?"

"No, first thing I knew was when I heard him starting off on his motor-bike. I didn't know he had one. Any idea where he was likely to be going?"

"I wish I had," Bobby answered. "You never know what sort of fool trick he won't be playing next. As soon as Rowley gets back I'm going to ask him to have Chrines picked up as soon as possible."

"Are you, though?" McKie said, surprised. "You really think you've got enough to go on? Well, that's all right by me. I don't mind who you pinch—that 'exclusive' of mine covers every possible candidate." He got up to go, and then seemed to remember. "I had nearly forgotten," he said. "You wanted to know if poor old Ted Pyle had taken a gun with him to guard against the perils of voyaging in a solitary caravan. So I set my spies to work. Always ready to help—that's me. They report that Pyle borrowed a gun from one of our subs—probably he had it for protection against some poor devil like me whose best ever story he had cut to hell—and then had sent the thing back through the post. Sticker Sims had undertaken to clean it, and then found it wouldn't work. Safety-catch stuck fast at off."

Bobby stared at him, as completely taken aback, as utterly surprised as ever he had been in all his long experience.

"If I had known that before," he said slowly and then, more slowly still: "I ought to have known that before."

"What's biting you?" McKie demanded; but Bobby made no answer.

So lost in thought he was, indeed, he hardly heard McKie repeat the question. Nor when McKie, who knew these moods of complete abstraction, gave it up and took himself off, did Bobby notice his departure, beyond a vague wave of the hand and a muttered:

"You'll know some day."

But presently Bobby gathered his papers together and went to see if he could find Major Rowley, who in fact had just returned and who was looking flushed and excited.

"Case practically closed," he told Bobby. "The revolver those kids found is the one belonging to young Day-Bell, and it was the one used in the murder."

CHAPTER XXIX
BEATEN UP

BY THE last train leaving Penton for London that night, Bobby travelled to town. He had the compartment to himself, and his thoughts were so busy with the conclusions that he had so little desired to reach, but that it seemed were now being forced upon him, that when he reached the London terminus he nearly forgot to alight.

There was much, he felt, that needed his personal attention; and it was still early next morning when he started out, his first task to prepare the papers he had brought with him for the conference it would be necessary to hold, since for the action he contemplated, authority superior to his own would be required—and unless he could put his case very clearly and convincingly, that authority might not be granted. Then there were urgent instructions to be issued for every possible effort to be made to find and 'bring in' both Sticker Sims, and young Sam Chrines.

"The 'Sticker'," Bobby remarked to the Chief Inspector to whom he was talking, "is no meat for a youngster like Chrines, who is a mere baby in practical matters. If Sticker hears that Chrines is making inquiries about him, he may easily take alarm."

"More than likely," agreed the Chief Inspector. "There are times when fools rush in—"

"Where police fear to tread," Bobby completed his sentence for him, but not as had been intended.

"Well, I wouldn't say that altogether," protested the Chief Inspector, more than a little offended by the use of the word 'fear'.

"I should have said 'angels'," Bobby explained. "Quotation—'where angels fear to tread'."

"Oh, I see," said the Inspector, but now more than a little puzzled by the use of the word 'angels', for, proud of his men as he was, he wasn't sure that he could describe all of them as angels'—at any rate, not all of those under the rank of Chief Inspector.

"I wish," Bobby went on, "we could keep an eye on Mr McKie, but I don't think that can be done. Got to remember the power of the Press when it gets cross. I must ring McKie, though, and get old Tom Long's address."

"Old—who?" asked the Chief Inspector, trying to remember any criminal of that name.

"Professor of poetry at some University or another," Bobby explained. "McKie told me about him. He is the great authority on Stephen Asprey's work. He may be able to help. Heard anything from the Home Office?"

"They wrote Pyle," replied the other, consulting a note he had by him, "that 'up to the present no adequate reason seemed to have been presented demonstrating that an order for exhumation should be made available, but that the decision arrived at was tentative and remained open for reconsideration if more substantial grounds for the issue of the order heretofore referred to should at any future date be brought to their attention'."

"What a mort of words," commented Bobby, "for saying 'no, but have another go if you want to'. What it means is that with a little more pressure and persistence Pyle would get his order all right. I shall have to pay them a visit and see what I can do in the 'more substantial' line. And I think we had better send a good man down to Blegborough to see if anything has been happening there and if Sims has put in an appearance. If I can manage it, I'll pay Blegborough a visit myself later on. You might remember to see there's a fast car available for me if necessary. You know there've been approaches to the Duke that rather smell of blackmail? I should call him the dark horse in all this. I've got a fairly clear idea in my mind of all the others, but not of him."

"It's about his wife and this Asprey bloke, and did he do her in out of jealousy, isn't it?" the Chief Inspector asked.

Bobby nodded. He said:

"Any man—duke or dustman, innocent or guilty—faced with the prospect of a story like that being dug up after all this time, might react very violently. No telling. I think some would."

"Smearing his wife, too," the Chief Inspector commented, "and her dead as well. No good asking for an injunction either. Only make more talk. Sort of caught every way." After a short pause, he added: "Might think there was only one way out."

That ended their talk. The Chief Inspector went off to see that the measures Bobby had suggested were put into effect, and Bobby rang up the *Morning Daily* office to ask if he could be put through to McKie. Fortunately McKie was available, and soon Bobby heard his voice.

"Always come running to Papa when you're up against it, don't you?" it was saying. "What does little Tommy want now?"

"Less cheek, for one thing," Bobby retorted. "When you were talking to Sam Chrines, do you remember saying anything about 'Sticker' Sims? It's possible Chrines may be trying to find Sims to get back those papers of his. If he is, it might mean trouble."

"So it might," agreed McKie, and now his voice sounded a little uneasy. "Especially if 'Sticker' got it into his head Chrines was working for you. His sort don't hold with amateurs interfering—don't like it, offends their sense of fair play. I do remember warning Chrines to keep clear of Sims and laying it on a bit thick about Black Tom's café in Soho, and how if you went in you were lucky to get out with your life—read 'wallet' for 'life' and perfectly true, whether extracted by cosh or by girl. Had I better ring Black Tom and tell him if Chrines turns up asking questions to get a Nannie to take him back to you?"

"I think perhaps the Nannie had better be me," Bobby said. "I'll go round there at once."

He rang off then, made a note in his diary, caught a 'bus going Soho way, and was soon at Black Tom's café. Incidentally Black Tom was not a coloured man, but an Irishman of a cautious and pacific temperament, who always liked to stay in the background and to leave to other people any fighting that might be necessary. His real name was Tom Black, and, since he was of the dark type of Irishman, it had soon got itself transposed into Black Tom. Whereon, Mr Black, who had no colour prejudice so long as the money was right, changed the name of his establishment to 'The Negro Boy', though as Black Tom's it was generally known.

Bobby's entrance produced the usual atmosphere of uneasy tension that was so oddly apt to result among Black Tom's customers from the appearance of a policeman—especially one of rank. Even those whose consciences were—for the moment—comparatively tranquil began to drink up their coffee or their soft drink, for it was, of course, not yet the permitted hour, and to decide to carry on their often confidential talk elsewhere. Bobby ordered a cup of coffee and a bun he had no intention of consuming—especially not the coffee—by way of paying his footing, assured Black Tom in answer to that gentleman's solicitous inquiry that his health remained good, begged him not to be disappointed by this information, and explained that he wanted to get into touch with a youngster whose mother was anxious about him; and how Bobby wished Mrs Asprey could have heard that observation. The young man in question, Bobby went on to explain, had come up to London from Penton, and it was feared he might have got into bad company.

Mr Black listened very attentively, didn't believe it, wondered what was behind it and then said:

"Now, could it be it's the poor lad I took in last night after closing time, just as we were going to bed, keeping early hours here as we do? If you'll step upstairs you can see for yourself if it's like to be him you're asking about. I've had the doc. in to see him. No bones broke and as well as ever in a day or two, but mighty lucky for him there was a bloke like me ready to do what I could out of Christian charity, same as a good Christian should," for Mr Black was still a more or less devout member of the Church into which he had been born, and fully intended to go to confession as soon as his bank balance permitted, obtain full absolution, no matter how severe a penance a stiff-minded priest might impose, and so retire to his native island, there to live with a tranquil mind, his future secure both in this world and the next, of whose existence he never doubted for a moment or of the validity of the rules governing their acceptance or rejection. "Might have been dead by morning," Mr Black added, "if left lying there all night, same as could have easy happened but for me," and then he smirked and looked at Bobby, hoping—optimistically—for a word or two of commendation.

"Did Sticker Sims do the beating up himself, or did he ask you to fix it for him?" Bobby asked, and not too amiably.

"Now, Mr Owen," protested the other, hurt and disappointed, "you oughtn't to say a thing like that, and me that out of Christian charity—"

"Cut the Christian charity line," Bobby ordered. "You've got about as much of that in you as a bottle of poison has of good health, and remember, this is a murder investigation—beatings up when it's men like Sticker Sims easily lead to murder, and if you get mixed up in that sort of thing we shall soon be finding out more about you than we know at present—and that's plenty."

"Mr Owen, sir," exclaimed Black, really disturbed now, "murder's a thing I don't hold by, and never will. If it's killing, I always tell the boys, keep away from here or count me in with the busies. Murder's a thing you can't ever hardly get absolution for, not unless you've owned up, and where would you be then?"

The reply being obvious, Bobby did not attempt to supply it. Instead he said:

"Well, you've been warned. Come along. Where is he?"

Obediently Black led the way upstairs into a room even more squalid and ill-cared for than the one at Hillings, and there, on a tumble-down bed, Bobby saw a battered, bandaged, bruised Chrines, dozing uneasily.

"I'll send an ambulance for him immediately," Bobby said. "You'll probably hear more about this when we can get a statement from him."

"The poor lad!" Mr Black said, sympathy fairly oozing from him. "I'm doubting if he'll be able to say much. Or want to. When I asked him what had happened he just had the strength to whisper as it was a fight about a girl he had picked up, but for the good God's sake not to say a word, or disgraced he would be and disinherited for ever more, clean ruined and cast out, he said, if his family ever heard."

"Got it all worked out, haven't you?" Bobby growled. "Are those his clothes over there? Don't make a mistake and give them to a second-hand dealer instead of to the ambulance men. What was in his pockets?"

"Not a thing on him," Black declared. "Plucked like a turkey at Christmas when ready for the oven. Who is going to pay me for all the trouble I've took, and the doctor as well, and the brandy I gave him liberal and—"

"Take it out of what Sims gave you to fix it for him," Bobby suggested. "Leave you plenty, besides what you found in his pockets. They would be empty all right though—after you had been through them," and Mr Black looked at him reproachfully.

"You're a hard, unbelieving man, Mr Owen," he sighed.

CHAPTER XXX
VITAL CLUE

BOBBY LEFT the Tom Black café, sadly sure that no responsibility for what had happened would ever be brought home to that careful and cautious 'back-room' operator, little consoled by the wishful thought that some day he was bound to slip up, but also a good deal relieved that Chrines had escaped with nothing worse than a bad beating up and the loss of all the contents of his pockets.

The arrangements for Chrines's removal to a hospital, and for a more thorough examination of his injuries to be made there, were soon completed, and Bobby went on to call on Professor Long—'old Tom Long' to Mr McKie—said to have read all the verse ever published in the British Isles and to know most of it by heart, and said also to be the worst golfer in the whole wide world. Both statements were probably exaggerated, since it seems that in golf at least there is always beneath the deepest depth a deeper still.

Ushered into the study of the professor, previously warned of his visit, Bobby saw a spacious book-lined room with a large table by the window piled high with books and manuscripts; the manuscripts all neatly arranged in heaps, often labelled, the books with many slips of paper protruding from their pages, presumably for convenience of reference. Running across the room from one booklined wall to the other was a clear stretch of carpet that looked very much as if on it golf strokes were often practised—a presumption heightened by two clubs—a driver and a putter—lying thereon. At first Bobby thought the room unoccupied, but then there emerged from beneath the table by the window a little thin man with enormous spectacles perched on a nose so enormous that one was hardly aware that he had any other features at all. He was holding a golf-ball he had apparently been engaged in retrieving, gave it an affectionate polish with a large red hand, and held it up for Bobby to observe that a long stretch of strong elastic depended from it.

"My own invention," he said proudly.

"Indeed," said Bobby, polite, but puzzled.

"My own invention," the professor repeated. "You attach a suitable piece of elastic to the ball, the other end of the elastic you fasten to the floor. You can then practise drive or putt with complete safety to other objects," and his glance wandered rather apprehensively round the room, as if to assure himself that nothing this time had been broken. "Unfortunately the elastic does not invariably hold. Are you a golfer, Mr Owen?"

"Well, really, I don't find I have much time for outdoor games," Bobby admitted.

"A pity," pronounced Mr Long. "Golf provides innumerable, ever-changing problems. Practice in solving them would surely aid you in solving others that no doubt present themselves to you from time to time."

"They do," murmured Bobby. "But of a different character, perhaps."

"A problem of whatever character remains a problem," pronounced the professor, and without giving Bobby time either to agree or dissent, went on: "I find it a great relief, when dealing with the sources of some difficult passage, to try a few practice strokes in the room here. It is what I was doing just now, only the elastic broke. But you haven't come to talk about golf, have you?" and Bobby thought that as the professor said this there sounded in his voice a lingering hope that possibly that might turn out to be the real object of Bobby's visit. "About the Pyle murder, isn't it? I am immensely intrigued to hear from McKie that you think I might be able to help. I can't imagine in what way. But McKie tells me you and he often work together in cases of exceptional difficulty."

"It's what he would say," growled Bobby, not at all pleased by this description of their very occasional association.

"McKie," observed Mr Long, "is a most interesting companion—though probably the worst golfer in existence. You should see the divots he leaves behind him and tries to pretend other people are responsible for."

"He would," commented Bobby, and then produced the copy of Chrines's last book of verse with which he had taken the precaution to provide himself. "I am told I may be sure you've read this?"

"Certainly," answered Mr Long. "I imagine no verse is published here that doesn't come to me." He waved a hand round the book-lined room. "The best are here," he said. "The 'also rans' are in the attic upstairs. Chrines is there. I am having new shelves put in next week. But the *Saturday Supplement* was unduly severe on him in its review of that last book of his. Not mine, though I got the credit for it. *Saturday Supplement* reviews are not signed, you know [Bobby didn't], and it's not supposed to be the thing either to confirm or deny. 'No comment', as the politicians say. There are distinct gleams of talent here and there in all Chrines's stuff, and there is one superb sonnet that ought to live—that *will* live. 'Lament for Life', it is called, and it begins: 'The winter comes with days of wrath'. A fine introduction to the thundering lines that follow. Yes, such a magnificent thing would alone justify Chrines's whole existence—if he had written it. Unfortunately he didn't."

"Didn't write it?" Bobby asked, puzzled. "Isn't it in this book of his?"

"Oh, yes, it's there all right," agreed Mr Long. "But he didn't write it; he pinched it. Did you know he was an illegitimate son of Stephen Asprey's?"

"I knew he made the claim," Bobby answered, "and that Janet Merton was his mother."

"He invented that bit," the professor explained. "You know about Stephen Asprey having his last poems and letters buried with Janet Merton? A great pity. It ought to be put right.

Chrines thought it would be a good idea—more romantic, better publicity value—if he claimed her for his mother. He tries hard to make himself believe it. In fact, he is the product of one of Asprey's affairs—a Gladys Chrines it was, the wife of an innkeeper who doesn't seem to have minded much so long as she stayed to help him run the inn. I understand his birth certificate shows Mr Chrines as his father."

"Legally, he is so," Bobby answered. "A child born to a married woman is assumed to be that of her husband unless there is irrefutable evidence to the contrary. May I ask how you come to know this particular sonnet is the work of Asprey himself, and not of Chrines?"

"Well, there's the quality of the thing. Not conclusive, you say. It might be a sudden inspiration. You remember the man who produced one immortal line—'a rose-red city, half as old as time' and never wrote another word worth remembering? It might have been something like that. The Muses have their passing favourites they pick up and forget almost simultaneously. But this time I happen to know. Asprey showed it me himself when we met at some literary dinner or another. Critics had been saying for some time that his best work was behind him, and he asked me if I thought that showed any falling off. I didn't, and I said so. Almost the last time I saw him. It was immediately after his first meeting with Janet Merton, and I always think it was in the glow and excitement of that meeting—she must have been a remarkable woman—that he regained his poetic vision. It didn't last. I don't think he ever wrote anything else worth anything, and I believe he knew it, and that's why he wanted his later work buried, so that no one should ever know how it had fallen off. I don't know anything about the letters, of course. His genius may suddenly have turned to them. It may be that in them it found its last, its true, expression. I would give a lot to have a chance to read them."

"Have you ever mentioned this before?" Bobby asked.

"No. You mean I should have. I know. My duty. An impudent fraud. Literary treason. Unforgivable. I ought to have denounced it at once. Well, I didn't, and I don't mean to. The smoking flax I shall not quench. The young man has gleams of talent—very faint, very small. They may die out altogether as he gets older. Very possible. They may develop, and Lord knows there isn't so much poetic talent in the country just now that we can afford to throw any away. Besides—" He paused and looked at Bobby with his head a little to one side. "Besides, I have no incontestable proof to offer, only my own memory. Anything that can by any possibility be disputed, and that you say in public, you must be prepared to prove up to the hilt. You can't imagine," he assured Bobby earnestly, "how difficult it is to produce absolutely fool-proof evidence no one can possibly pick a hole in."

"I suppose it must be very difficult indeed," Bobby admitted meekly. "How do you think the sonnet got into Chrines's hands if it was only written after the first meeting with Janet Merton? After, that is, the connection with Mrs Chrines had been broken off?"

"Well, that is a puzzle," admitted the professor. "That's what I should at once be asked to explain if I said in public that it was Asprey's work, and not Chrines's. Land me in a libel action, perhaps. All the same I'm perfectly certain the sonnet in Chrines's book is the one Asprey showed me. I wrote it down from memory as soon as I got home. But it's in my own handwriting, of course, so that's no good as proof. I had no idea any other copy was in existence. Asprey," he went on, "would fall in love in the most casual way. He would be thrown into ecstasies of devotion by a glimpse of a gloved hand on a railway carriage door, and then at once be all agog to follow in the next train going the same way. Or else to sit down and write a poem about it—'To an Unknown's Glove', perhaps. Work it off that way. No, I can't imagine how young Chrines got hold of it. The 'Lament for Life', I mean. I suppose he must have found a copy lying about somewhere. If it's true he was beginning to write Asprey's biography and was trying to get hold of any papers of his, he may have come across a copy in that way. If that is what happened, he would know it had never been published and—well, 'conveyed the wise it call'."

"Shortened to 'Won it' to-day," Bobby remarked.

"I prefer the older expression," said the professor seriously. "'Won it' is a little vulgar, don't you think? Of course, more concise, and this is an age of speed; and then it does avoid the rather crude 'Picking and stealing'."

"Yes, there's that," Bobby agreed. "Personally, I prefer 'picking and stealing'. Professional prejudice, perhaps. Thank you very much for what you've told me. I mustn't detain you any longer. It has been most interesting."

"I am only sorry," Mr Long said apologetically, "that I have not been able to give you more assistance."

"Your assistance has been most valuable," Bobby assured him. "You've given me a vital clue. Taken with what I knew or suspected before, I think it should enable me to make an arrest almost immediately."

CHAPTER XXXI
INCREDIBLE

IT WAS much later in the day, after Bobby had got back from a prolonged visit to the Home Office—at the moment, in fact, when he was beginning to think of going home—that he received the unwelcome information that Mr McKie of the *Morning Daily* was below and wanting to see him.

"Oh, all right," Bobby said resignedly. "Fetch him along. I wonder what he's up to now?"

He soon knew, for as soon as McKie entered the room, he said:

"Did you know Item Sims has disappeared?"

"My dear, good man," Bobby protested. "Did you know Queen Anne was dead?"

"Yes, but," McKie said, "now it's his pals, not you chaps, who don't know what's happened and want to find him."

"Do they expect him to broadcast his movements," Bobby asked, "when he knows how badly we want him? 'Silence is best' is his motto just now."

"Did you know Chrines got himself badly beaten up last night?" McKie asked, disregarding this.

"Is that the latest news hot from the Press?" Bobby demanded. "I found him in Black Tom's café early this morning, and now he's in hospital. Sims, of course, but not in person. Most likely he was busy fixing an alibi. Explains why his pals have lost him for the time."

"I could tell you the names of the two who did the job, as far as that goes," McKie said. "The point is, Sims didn't turn up to pay them as he had promised."

"Oh, he will," replied Bobby. "Nothing in that. Got prevented somehow—or drunk. They'll get their money all right. Gangsters don't bilk each other unless it's very much worth while. They know what would happen next dark night if they tried it on."

"It's not only them," persisted McKie. "It's his wife as well: wife pro forma, of course, but they've stuck together for twenty or thirty years—very happily except when fighting, and it's not always been Item who went to hospital afterwards. But they trust each other utterly, and I don't believe anything would make either of them let the other down."

"I've heard that before," Bobby admitted. "Like lost dogs when the other's away. Not the sort of thing you can put before a jury. But I expect it will count when all's added up. What about it?"

"She's really worried, afraid, I think," McKie explained. "First she got drunk and said a lot, and now she's cold sober and saying nothing. When drunk she seems to have been telling her friends that no one would get away with anything, even if dukes and princes and such like—justice she would have one way or another."

"Last thing I should have expected her to want, either for herself or her pro-forma hubby," Bobby interrupted. "Though of course no one ever squeals louder than the crook when he gets done down himself."

"Oh, listen, can't you?" McKie snapped. "I've got a hunch there really is something wrong. Mrs Item Sims doesn't work herself up the way she is doing at present for nothing. She's an old hand. Another thing. Sims was last seen in Blegborough."

"Are you sure? How do you know?" Bobby asked, beginning now to be more impressed.

"I told you I worked an assignment for one of our chaps to hang about there and keep his eyes open, in case anything broke. Can't afford to neglect chances. But then some jackass in the office—that's the trouble with *Morning Daily*: never know who is really responsible for anything—got him back. Luckily there's a local bloke on tap—*The Blegborough Express-Mail*—and he reports a man answering Sims's description was in Blegborough day before yesterday, had drinks in one or two pubs, asked the way to Blegborough Castle, appeared nervous, was last seen on his way there, and nothing known of him since. There it is. Wife worried about him and pals worried about their pay. Papers were stolen from Chrines—probably by Sims—and their loss put Chrines into such a sweat he panicked. Threats of blackmail made, and the Duke very upset, and may think the honour of his house and of his dead wife, and his own safety, all involved. Well, what does all that add up to?"

"To something quite incredible," Bobby answered, "so we may take it that the addition is wrong."

"Where?" asked McKie.

"Oh, well," Bobby said.

"Nothing's incredible," pronounced McKie.

"No, it isn't, is it?" Bobby agreed. "Not when it happens."

"Well, then," said McKie and waited.

"I was looking forward to carpet slippers and a quiet evening at home," Bobby said resignedly. "Now I suppose I shall have to go chasing off to the other end of England, all in the pursuit of the incredible."

"Give you a lift if you like," offered McKie. "I've got my little Sports Super outside."

"You know very well," Bobby said severely, "that it would be as much as my life is worth to be seen in a car with you. The whole collective knife of all the rest of the British Press would be in my back up to the hilt for evermore. Talk not of jealousy till thou hast seen a bunch of newspaper scallywags all chasing after the same exclusive. All the same, due credit will be given as and when and where deserved."

McKie grinned, accepted this as proof that his services were properly appreciated, and departed in a haste that convinced Bobby he would be in Blegborough as soon as a sports car capable of a hundred miles an hour, and a generous disregard of speed limits, could get him there. Bobby himself had various arrangements to make, colleagues to warn of his proposed journey and so on, so that it was late before he could make a start, and much later still before he arrived at Blegborough Castle.

There was no glimmer of light to be seen, no sign anywhere of waking life. His knocks remained unanswered. It was nearly eleven, and very possible, he supposed, that duke, butler, and housekeeper—the entire household, as he knew—were all sound asleep. He gave it up and drove back to the little town itself, where, in the one small hotel the place boasted, he found McKie sitting alone in the smoking-room, melancholy before bread, pickles, and processed cheese.

"All you'll get here," McKie told him. "Service with a scowl. All respectable people should be in bed by eleven. And nothing whatever to drink except—water," and this last word he brought out with difficulty, as if not quite sure that such a thing really existed.

"Too bad, too bad," Bobby said, and added smugly: "I got my wife to put me up sandwiches—ham and beef. And a thermos flask. All now consumed," he added, as he saw McKie was about to speak.

"Trust you for that," McKie grunted. "Been to the Castle?"

"No answer," Bobby said. "All in bed and sound asleep—presumably. And you?"

"Told His Grace was not at home by the stiffest old mummy outside the British Museum," McKie answered. "He might be back to-morrow, and then again he mightn't. It would be advisable, in the mummy's opinion, to write and ask for an appointment, and when I started to let him see I had a ten-bob note in my hand, the mummy didn't seem to know what it was. It ought to have been shekels, I suppose, or whatever mummies used when alive."

"A healthy corrective to journalistic cynicism," Bobby told him; and retired to bed, leaving McKie indignantly protesting that there was no trace of cynicism in his innocent and child-like mind.

Next morning Bobby drove again to the Castle. He had no better luck. The aged butler, so unfairly described as a 'mummy', a little tottery perhaps, more than a little deaf, but dignified, bland, and alert as ever, repeated that unhappily His Grace was not at home. Nor had His Grace said when he was likely to return. Nor had he, the butler, received any instructions to answer questions about His Grace's probable movements. When, however, Bobby showed his official card and asked if he could be permitted to leave a note for His Grace's perusal on his return, no objection was raised, and Bobby was shown into a plainly furnished sitting-room. There he wrote a note, wording it with some care, to the general effect that he was engaged on an inquiry into the recent murder near Penton of Mr Edward Pyle, of *The Morning Daily*, and that there were some matters of detail on which it was thought His Grace might be able to give useful information. Could therefore Major Rowley, head of the West Mercian police force, be informed as soon as possible when it would be convenient for His Grace to allow himself to be seen? Bobby added that of course the most complete confidence was felt in the willingness of the Duke to co-operate, and Bobby flattered himself that in these last sentences he had made it sufficiently, though politely, clear that if complete co-operation was not received, complete compulsion would take its place. In all this, too, Bobby was very careful to make no reference to Sims. Sims could come later.

Satisfied with his literary efforts, Bobby departed, rang up from the first call-box he came to, as he had promised the waiting McKie he would, to report no success, and as he was returning to his car saw trudging determinedly up the road towards the Castle a tall, angular woman in a worn, ill-fitting, check tweed coat and skirt, with about her no air of the country at all, but rather a complete aroma of the back streets of Soho. He crossed over to the other side of the car so as to wait directly in her path, and as she came nearer he could tell that she had immediately recognized him, though his memory of her was less certain. Probably she had never come under his direct notice, as equally probably he had come under hers, for though Bobby knew most crooks with small exception, all crooks knew him with no exception at all. She seemed to hesitate for a moment, but then came defiantly on. When she was nearer, Bobby lifted his hat and said politely:

"Mrs Item Sims, isn't it?"

"Well, suppose it is?" she said, and added truculently: "And don't you come none of your fancy airs with me, Mr Owen. Won't go down."

"No, no, of course not," Bobby agreed. "Bit uneasy about what's happened to Mr Sims, I hear?"

"I ain't looking to you for help," she retorted.

"Why not?" he asked. "I am making a few inquiries myself. Care to tell me anything?" She made no reply, but only stared at him with a kind of angry suspicion. He resumed: "I've just been trying to see the Duke. No luck, though I think it's very likely he's there all the time. Is that what you've come for, to have a chat with the Duke?"

"Nothing to do with you if I have," she retorted.

"Well, you know, madam," Bobby said, "I wouldn't be too sure of that. Strange what a lot of things have to do with you, or you with them, when it's murder. But if you do find Mr Sims, tell him from me there's nothing for him to worry about if—but only if—he can make his alibi stand up. We know he got on the train for Bristol, but he may have got off again. If he shows proof he spent the night at Bristol, he's clear. But, then, can he? If he did take a little cash with him when he left Mr Pyle's caravan—rather in a hurry, apparently—well, it would be hard to prove, and we shan't worry too much about it. Tell him that from me, will you? And now shall I give you a lift back to the Castle? It's all of two long dusty miles. Not all the way up to the door, of course, or you might be taken for a friend of mine, and I'm sure you wouldn't like that. Just up to the entrance to the drive."

She hesitated for a moment, and then snapped a 'No'.

"Don't trust the likes of you," she announced. "Never know with you blokes."

"Oh, surely," Bobby protested, trying to look hurt.

"It's not so much you," she admitted grudgingly. "It's that tongue of yours."

"An unruly member," Bobby agreed. "I never fear the Greeks so much as when they offer lifts, is that it?"

"I ain't having any," she repeated, "if that's what you mean. And I tell you straight, if there's harm come to Sims from that there Duke, or any other ruddy lordship, I'll have his innards out and fry 'em for supper."

"Dear me, what a very unpleasant meal!" commented Bobby, climbing back into his car.

But though he had spoken lightly enough, he remained sitting there for some time, watching the tall, angular figure in its worn ill-fitting 'tailor-made', trudging determinedly along the road towards Blegborough Castle. Even when he drove on his way he was still looking thoughtful, still thinking he would not much care to be in the shoes of any who injured Item.

"Loyal to him, if to nothing else," he reflected.

CHAPTER XXXII
MORE TROUBLE BREWING

FROM BLEGBOROUGH, Bobby drove on to Penton, meaning to acquaint Major Rowley with recent developments and to inform him of future plans in which his help would be needed. Firstly, however, before listening to him, the Major had news of his own he was anxious Bobby should hear.

"'Phone call," he said. "I don't know whether to take it seriously. From one of those newspaper men. Still hanging about, some of them. This is a Mr McKie. I think you mentioned him once or twice."

"I expect I did," Bobby admitted. "He's the sort of chap whose name you have to keep on mentioning. What's he got to say this time?"

"He's got hold of some fantastic story about London gangsters preparing to beat up the Duke of Blegborough in his own Castle or some nonsense like that. Tipped off by his contacts, he says. Has he any contacts?"

"Who? McKie? Plenty," Bobby answered. "Crime reporters of national newspapers know a lot. No red tape to tie them up, and if they turn in a good story, no quibbling over expense sheets."

"But why on earth should London gangsters want to beat up the Duke of Blegborough?" demanded Rowley, thoroughly shocked. "Talk about democracy—" he said, and lapsed into a bewildered silence.

"Put it like this," Bobby said. "Item Sims stole papers from young Chrines, since badly beaten up himself. There seems to be some connection between the papers stolen from Chrines and those Stephen Asprey placed in Janet Merton's coffin before her burial. Copies, duplicates, or what? They may revive, if they become public, an old scandal affecting the good name of the Duke's late wife. Sims may have tried to sell them to the Duke. It appears Sims was last seen or heard of in Blegborough. If he did try to make a sale, what happened? Mrs Sims wants to know, for one. I saw her this morning on her way to the Castle and expressing an intention to possess herself of the Duke's 'innards' for culinary purposes. I was on my way back from the Castle when I met her. They told me there that the Duke was away, but I don't very much believe it. It may be true, of course."

"But all that is incredible, quite incredible," protested Rowley.

"So it is," agreed Bobby, "but it may happen all the same, and it's not quite clear what can be done about it. I don't think the Duke will be co-operative. It may be he won't dare. The initiative is always with the criminal. Most unfair, like a cricket captain who always wins the toss. Have you done anything?"

"Thank Heaven," Rowley said, "it's not our direct responsibility. I've been on the line to Bristol. McKie had rung them before us. They weren't much inclined to take him seriously."

"A mistake," interposed Bobby. "Always take the Press seriously—a strange, unpredictable force. Roaring emptily like a bull of Bashan or hurling thunderbolts from high Olympus. You never know which. Have they done anything?"

"They got on to the Inspector at Blegborough to ask if any suspicious characters had been seen there. He said none at all, not even any strangers, except one woman, and one woman wasn't likely to cause trouble."

"Did he really say that?" Bobby asked in an awe-struck voice.

"Well, of course, he meant in the beating-up way," Rowley explained.

"Even then," Bobby said. "Even then. An innocence beyond conception. The Inspector's, not the woman's. Did it never occur to him that she might have friends waiting not far off? If they've a car—and gangsters always have—and they are in reach of a 'phone call—and they will be—they could be on the spot soon enough and the Blegborough Inspector know nothing about it. The Castle is a good distance from the town you know. And Mrs Sims doesn't look on when it's scrapping. In a ladylike fashion, she's handy with a broken beer-bottle, I'm told. I really think it would be wise to put a bit of pressure on Blegborough, even if it's only to keep their eyes wide open."

"The Castle is used as an agricultural college or something of the sort, isn't it?" Rowley said. "Plenty of students and so on about. I don't see what could happen."

"Oh, plenty," Bobby assured him. "Even a duke can be beaten up—or worse—in comparative silence. There's night, too, when I suppose the agricultural college or whatever it is sinks to slumber. I wonder if anything has happened to Sims. You know, I've always felt the Duke was very much of a dark horse. You can't always trust these shy, shrinking, apologetic chaps. Break loose at times. Yes, I think Blegborough had better have a little pressure applied. I'll see what they can do from the Yard. Straight from the Yard's mouth, so to speak. Meanwhile I want to explain what in my idea should be our next move. I want to know how it strikes you."

He entered into full details of what he now proposed, and Rowley listened in silence, offered one or two suggestions of his own, undertook to give every possible support, and agreed that complete secrecy must be observed.

"If you're right," Rowley said, a little doubtfully still, "it will certainly be better to let no rumour of what we suspect get about. And even yet, you know," he added in a burst of candour, "I can hardly believe it."

"I may be wrong," Bobby admitted, though he did not think so. "I know I'm taking a big risk. My name will be mud for evermore if I am."

Rowley said he hoped not, but inwardly was by no means sure it wouldn't happen. During their talk he had mentioned in passing that Mrs Asprey herself was in the town, doing some shopping. In answer to a question from Bobby, he added that on these occasions she almost invariably lunched at a small café off the High Street, much favoured by other ladies visiting Penton on similar errands. Light refreshments only, Bobby was informed, but all the same, though a little sadly, for he had breakfasted early, thither he now made his way, and presently equally shocked, surprised, and delighted the little waitress who had served him by asking for a second sardine salad after somewhat swiftly disposing of the first. That also having been got rid of, he wondered whether he dared say 'same again', or whether that would seem too utterly devastating, when Mrs Asprey appeared. She did not notice him; and not till she had been served with an egg mayonnaise, and he with the cup of coffee he had asked for in place of the contemplated third sardine salad, did he move over to her table, where she greeted him with a blank stare of mingled surprise and disapproval.

"Good gracious!" she exclaimed. "Are you always everywhere?"

"Oh, no," he protested. "Not at all. Not even always welcome when I am," he added sadly.

"How did you know I was here?" she demanded suspiciously.

"But you weren't," he pointed out. "Not when I got here. I had nearly finished lunch—an excellent salad, though perhaps leaning rather more to the dainty than to the substantial—when I saw you come in. I thought you might like to know that young Chrines has got what he deserved."

"What do you mean?" she demanded.

"Oh, he's got himself badly knocked about, that's all. He's in hospital now. He'll get over it with a little good nursing, though I don't know where he'll get that. They won't keep him in hospital—no beds to spare for strays. I must say he was a sight when we found him in a low-class café in London. Serve him right."

"Oh, indeed," she said, visibly bristling. "Serve the poor boy right? Well, let me tell you that if everyone got what served them right—" She did not complete the sentence, but the glare with which she accompanied it made her meaning clear.

"What he really wants is someone to look after him—a lonely sort of boy," Bobby observed. "A wife or sister or something. Not a wife—somebody older, more experienced. Not a job anyone is likely to take on. Only an utter fool would think of it, and jolly few could tackle it, even if they wanted to. Too much sense, most people. I'm no judge myself, but I've been told he really has some talent." He took from his pocket the volume of Chrines's poems he had shown Professor Long. "Have you seen this?" he asked. When she shook her head he opened it at the page on which was printed the sonnet the professor had declared to be the work, not of Chrines, but of Stephen Asprey. "Will you read this?" he asked.

She glanced at it, read it, looked up at him.

"Stephen wrote that," she said. "I remember it quite well. It wasn't among his papers after his death. I never knew what had become of it."

"Thank you, that's what I wanted to know," Bobby said, getting to his feet.

"What do you mean?" she asked, more suspiciously than ever. "What's it got to do with you who wrote it?"

"You've confirmed the last bit of evidence I needed," he told her. "I think now I shall be able to make an immediate arrest."

With that he went away, leaving her sitting there, silent and troubled, and he knew that she knew that the end was near, and he knew, too, that she was afraid.

But now, with this fresh confirmatory evidence he had obtained, he returned to London. Official wheels turn slowly, and he wanted, if possible, to get them moving more quickly. There were final arrangements to be made, too, precautions to be taken against any leakage of what was intended, as well as many other details that needed his supervision and attention.

Then once more, towards evening, McKie made his appearance, and Bobby put aside what he was busy with to receive him, for he was more uneasy than he had admitted, even to himself, over the reported disappearance of Item Sims at Blegborough, and the subsequent arrival there of the *soi-disant* Mrs Sims.

"Heard anything fresh?" Bobby asked, offering the ritual cigarette as McKie was shown into his room.

"Not a thing," McKie answered gloomily. "Everything shut down tight, and I don't like it. All my contacts gone dumb. Won't even have a drink. Unheard of. Scared stiff. That's what it is. Scared stiff," he repeated.

"About Sims or about the Duke?" Bobby asked.

"Over Mrs Sims, I think," McKie replied. "As far as I can make out, there's nothing really known; not even in the best-informed circles of crookdom, but the whole lot of them feel that if Mrs Sims cuts loose there'll be the worst kind of trouble. They don't want it, because of course they're all for a quiet life. Before everyone went deaf and dumb, I was tipped off that she had been seen with two of the most dangerous men out of gaol—or in it, for that matter. I didn't get names. Even then the fellow who was talking wasn't going to say too much. But what it all seems to come to is that they think there's been an attempt to do what they call business with the Duke and that it's gone wrong. Well, how wrong?"

"Yes, there's that, isn't there?" Bobby said.

"Well, if it's that way," McKie asked, "what's Mrs Sims going to do? Perfectly reckless, if you ask me."

"Or me," Bobby said.

"The devoted wife?" McKie said. "Is that it? What's it mean? Love? Between him and her? What a word to use when it's two like them!"

"Do you know a better?" Bobby asked.

"Give it up," McKie said. "It beats me." He said this as one who could hardly believe that such a thing was possible. "All the same," he said abruptly. "I've a hunch there's something funny going on."

"So have I," said Bobby.

"What are you going to do about it?" demanded McKie.

"Nothing we can do," Bobby answered, "except what we've done already—send out a warning that we believe there's trouble brewing at Blegborough Castle and wouldn't it be as well to give instructions for it to be watched? I don't think it's being taken very seriously. Probably a feeling that round a duke there's still left a bit of the divinity that once did hedge a king about."

"Well, of course, a duke is still news," admitted McKie.

"The modern way of saying the same thing," Bobby suggested.

"I'll go down there to-night," McKie decided; and when Bobby nodded approval; "What about you?" he asked.

But Bobby shook his head.

"I can't interfere," he said. "Nothing substantial to go on. Also I've got certain last-minute arrangements to see to. I'm returning to Penton to-morrow. I think I'll go to Blegborough on the way—out of the way rather. There really are a few points I should like to ask about—good enough to serve for an excuse, anyhow."

"I'll go down there to-night," McKie decided. He made for the door and then paused. "I don't really suppose for one minute," he announced, "that anything has happened to the Duke, and I'm sure I hope not, but if it has—what a story, eh? What a story! Exclusive, too. Watch the *Morning Daily*, my boy, just watch it."

CHAPTER XXXIII
McKIE'S MISADVENTURE

BOBBY WAS anxious to make as early a start as possible next morning, and was in fact on the point of driving away when a constable appeared with a message just received by 'phone. It came from Blegborough, and was to the effect that a suspicious character had been seen in the grounds of Blegborough Castle, had made use of offensive and insulting language, had refused to give any account of himself, and would be charged with being found on enclosed premises for a presumed unlawful purpose. The suspect claimed, however, that he could be identified by Deputy Commander Bobby Owen of the Metropolitan Police.

"Well, I could certainly identify plenty of crooks," Bobby remarked, puzzled, "but it's not often any of them want me to do it," and then a faint glimmer of a wild surmise crept into his mind. "It just couldn't be," he said aloud. Then to the constable who had brought the message he said: "Tell them I'm on my way to Penton in connection with the Edward Pyle murder, and I'll branch off to call on them and have a look at their suspect."

"Very good, sir," said the constable, saluted and departed; and Bobby drove off.

He would have to cover nearly another hundred miles to take in Blegborough on his way to Penton, but that could not be helped. Fortunately there was comparatively little traffic on the road he was following, and not too many built-up areas, so he was able to keep up an average speed of not far short of a mile a minute.

At Blegborough he was expected, and when he drew up before the police station, the Inspector in charge—Inspector Brown—came out to greet him.

"Glad to see you, Mr Owen, sir," he said. "The suspect is creating all the time. Most obstreperous. I'm not sure he oughtn't to be medically examined."

"Can I see him?" Bobby asked. "He's here still, is he? Not been brought into court yet?"

"No," answered the Inspector. "In view of his repeated asseverations that he could be identified by you, I thought it would be advisable to wait your arrival."

"Very sensible, very sensible indeed," Bobby approved—with relief.

He followed Inspector Brown into the building and into the Inspector's office, where the suspect and a large and, at the moment, rather flushed-looking constable were waiting. The suspect and Bobby looked at each other. Bobby said nothing, just gasped. The suspect said nothing, just scowled. The constable said:

"The language used as per previous reports has remained continuously offensive and insulting."

"What are you grinning at?" demanded the suspect furiously.

"Who? Me?" asked Bobby. "I'm not," he declared indignantly, for even if his face had become one vast, ever-increasing smile, a smile is not a grin. He turned to Inspector Brown, who was beginning to look a little uncomfortable. He said: "This gentleman is Mr Alexander McKie, a very important and influential journalist, a highly placed member of the staff of *Morning Daily*, and all its offshoots, dependencies, and subsidiaries, here and elsewhere. You'll be lucky if *Morning Daily* doesn't pillory you from one end of the country to the other. Gestapo methods." The Inspector had turned a little pale now. "Probably get people marching up and down Whitehall, shouting 'Brown Must Go'." The Inspector stopped turning pale and became a sickly green instead. "Hadn't you better shake hands and say no more about it?"

"Yes, sir; certainly, sir," said the Inspector hurriedly. "The report said 'Acting suspicious, re private entrance, Blegborough Castle'. Why didn't the gentleman say who he was, instead of all the things he did?"

"Did he say things?" asked Bobby sympathetically. "I shouldn't wonder. It's his trade. Did you?" he asked McKie.

"Certainly not," McKie answered. "I merely gave in studiously moderate terms an accurate analysis of the I.Q. of these ornaments of the police and a careful consideration of the means and methods by which they had escaped being where they belong—in the nearest home for the mentally deficient."

"There you are, Mr Owen," said Inspector Brown moodily. "I.Q. I.Q.-ing all the time. My men didn't like it. You can't wonder."

"Why on earth couldn't you tell them who you were and be done with all this nonsense?" demanded Bobby, turning suddenly on McKie.

"Oh, be your age!" McKie exclaimed impatiently. "Do you think I wanted all Fleet Street laughing its silly head off over me getting run in by country bumpkins? Never hear the last of it. And all of them spotting at once I must be on something good, and rushing down here, the whole boiling, to find out what it was. For the Lord's sake, let's get out of here and I'll tell you all about it. Have you a car outside? The sooner we get there, the better."

"Get where?" Bobby asked.

"The Castle, of course," McKie snapped. "There's something going on, and I want to know what, if you don't. I've been trying to tell these beauties, but they wouldn't listen."

"Suspicious action re private entrance to Castle, that was the report," said the Inspector plaintively.

Ignoring the Inspector, McKie took Bobby by the arm and hustled him out to the waiting car. They got in, but it was McKie who grabbed the wheel and started the car. Bobby said, rather indignantly: "Here, hold on." McKie didn't seem to hear. Bobby said: "What's all this about the private entrance to the Castle?"

"I was looking through the keyhole," McKie explained. "I couldn't get any answer, but I was sure there was something wrong. So I took a peek through the keyhole, and then that fat oaf of a policeman grabbed me. Thought I was trying to pick the lock."

"Well, I wouldn't put it past you," observed Bobby, still slightly ruffled by the way in which McKie had plumped himself down in the driving-seat. "Not if you thought there was a good news story on the other side."

McKie said, dexterously avoiding a placidly grazing cow by the wayside:

"But I did see what looked like a leg."

"A leg?" repeated Bobby. "Requiring to be medically examined, the inspector thought," he murmured. "Hi, don't take corners like that. What on earth—a leg, did you say?"

"A leg," repeated McKie firmly. "A man's leg, and the man was lying on the floor. Why should anyone be lying on the floor at that time of night unless he was either drunk or dead?"

"Didn't you tell them at Blegborough?"

"I tried. No good. They wouldn't listen."

"You ought to have told them who you were, and got through to me," Bobby said, frowning. "Most likely it doesn't mean anything—a shadow, trick of light, anything. But it may. It may. I suppose the truth is you were thinking about your blessed exclusives, as you call them."

"Man," said McKie, turning to him, "man, there's nothing under Heaven to compare with bringing in a good genuine exclusive."

By now they were driving up the long and stately avenue that led to what once had been a castle and was now an Agricultural Training College where girls and boys alike were taught to reap and sow and plough and be a farmer's boy. McKie stopped the car before the door that had been the scene of his lamentable misadventure. Both men jumped out; but once again their summons remained unanswered, and that solid door unopened and firm as if past days of sudden sieges and unexpected forays had returned. A voice from behind them said:

"It ain't no good, knocking. No answer. The postman couldn't get one, nor the milkman neither, though it's pay day, nor no one. Dunno what's up; they're generally around long afore this. Goings on, if you ask me, and a woman no one hadn't ever seen before in these parts as was hanging around yesterday and wouldn't say what she wanted."

"Do you work here?" Bobby asked.

"Gardener," the other answered. "For the Agricultural Board when it took over now all the nobs has been put down, as is only right, it being Social Justice."

"The lock wouldn't be any trouble," Bobby said, considering. "But there are sure to be bolts as well." He turned to the gardener. "Is there any other door, do you know?" he asked.

"Not to this part," the gardener answered. "That's where His Nibs lives—rent free. Privilege, that is. The workers have to pay rent, not like him. There's the doors connecting with the College part, but all fastened up. And the College closed for the day on account of the Agricultural Show."

"Isn't there a caretaker?" Bobby asked.

"He mayn't be there," the gardener suggested hopefully. "Nigh dinner hour, too, so he'll be off duty."

"I'm afraid if he is he'll have to come on duty again," Bobby retorted; and the gardener looked quite shocked, and would probably have pointed out that that wasn't social justice, only for Bobby having hurried off, McKie following, to the north side of the building, where he had noticed a signboard showing the way to the College entrance.

Fortunately the College caretaker soon appeared and proved to be rather less preoccupied with 'social justice' than had been his gardening colleague. He, too, was of opinion that there had been 'goings-on'. Odd-looking strangers had been noticed, loitering about in a highly suspicious manner, unusual and indeed inexplicable noises had been heard, repeated knocking had produced no answer. But as for gaining admission from the College portion of the building to that small part reserved for the use of the Duke, that was very different. For his part, the caretaker didn't see how it could be done. All connecting doors had been carefully sealed, some even bricked up, and it would take another squad of workmen to open them again.

"It ought to be done, though," declared the caretaker, considering the problem. "I'm none too easy in my own mind, and wasn't before you came. Old Mr Hopkins—him as was butler in the old days my dad's told me about, when I asked him—when it was open house here, and the gentry coming and going, and everyone jolly and friendly, same as they aren't now and a helping hand for all." He paused, lost in the memory of those past glories of which his father had told him. He resumed: "Mr Hopkins—eighty if he's a day—is always up and about first thing. It might be he's ill. Food poisoning. Never heard of it before all this rationing came in, but now it's everywhere."

"Just so," said Bobby, trying to bring him back to the point; "but about these connecting doors?"

"Well," the caretaker answered, "there is one in the cellars that looks to me as if the workmen forgot it when they did up the rest. It's locked, but it's not fastened up tight like the others. Leastways, it doesn't look it."

"You might let us see it, will you?" Bobby asked; and then, when the man hesitated, he added: "I am a police officer. From London. I will take all responsibility."

"Don't do any more damage than you can help," the caretaker said, yielding. "Very particular the College gentlemen are about damage, except when it's them students. They can rip around all they like and nothing said."

Grumbling thus—evidently the perennial feud between caretakers and students was raging here in full force—he led the way down some stone steps into the almost endless cellars that underlay this huge old rambling building. Bobby, by the light of an electric torch, examined the lock of the door the caretaker showed them. It did not look too difficult. He produced a small gadget he generally carried with him. It was not the first time Bobby had had to pick a lock, and if he was not as skilful as are professionals like Item Sims, still this was a fairly easy job. In two or three minutes he had the door open and was flashing his torch into a dark, damp emptiness, a welter of passages and cellars, where it seemed lost souls might wander for evermore and living creatures never find their way to the upper air. The deathly silence was broken only by a faint skurry of rats and mice and the rustling sound of disturbed spiders, beetles, and so forth. These faint sounds died away and Bobby said:

"There ought to be an exit somewhere on the Duke's side."

Orienting himself as best he could, he took the direction both he and McKie thought the most promising. They came presently to a flight of stone steps, similar to that by which they had previously descended. The door at the top was open. They went through it into another long passage that led them to the hall, where, rather to the relief both of Bobby and McKie, no corpse was to be seen.

"Your leg must have walked away," Bobby told McKie. "Natural thing for a leg to do, I suppose," and then at the top of his voice, he shouted: "Anyone at home?" and heard his voice go rumbling away into those vast, ancestral silences. Once more he shouted at the full force of his lungs: "Is anyone here?" and again there was no reply.

CHAPTER XXXIV
ORGY

Bobby stood waiting, still hoping there might come some response to that loud shouting of his. But McKie said:

"We had better see what's up."

Bobby nodded in assent, gave another glance up the stairway, for he had thought for a moment he had heard something stirring there. McKie touched him on the arm.

"Look," he said, "look at that door," and he indicated one beneath which a tiny stream of liquid had seeped to become a small pool. McKie went across to it, stooped, dipped his finger in it, smelt, and came back to Bobby. "Brandy," he said wonderingly. "Brandy."

Before Bobby could reply, the door opened and there appeared, somewhat unsteadily, the Duke himself, unkempt, unwashed, bleary-eyed. Clinging to the door-post for support. He said, slurring his words a little:

"It's polishman, jolly ole po-policeman." He beamed upon them foolishly. "All fren's together," he said.

Bobby was silent. So was McKie—a thing that did not often happen. But then neither he nor Bobby could find words to utter. The Duke turned and went back into the room. Bobby and McKie followed. The Duke sat down on the nearest chair, supporting his head on his hands. His smile had vanished now. He was saying in a kind of monologue:

"My head, my head, oh, my head, my poor head!"

The room was brightly lighted by overhead electric lamps. The windows were closely shuttered, the curtains drawn. The air was heavy with the fumes of alcohol. There were bottles and glasses on the table and on the floor. Those on the floor were mostly broken, and from them had spread that trickle of brandy which had reached the door and seeped beneath it. In a capacious arm-chair sprawled Item Sims, or rather he had been, but now was making spasmodic and ineffectual efforts to rise. On a couch Mrs Sims was lying full length. Her eyes were wide open and her face was wreathed in a seraphic smile. She said:

"Besh time ever. Good ole bloke, good ole me, good ole Ity, good ole everyone," and then she closed her eyes, but continued to smile even more happily than before.

By this time Item—or 'good ole Ity'—had managed to get to his feet.

"It's all ri', Mish Owen, sir," he announced. "You've nothin' on me. Fren's all roun', same as the bloke said."

He pointed to the Duke to make it plain who was the 'bloke' referred to, and then fell flat on his face and was violently and noisily sick.

Mrs Sims opened her eyes and said once more; "Good ole bloke, good ole me, good ole Mish Owen, good ole everyone," and then she crossed her hands on her breast and began to croon softly to herself.

The Duke, wagging an admonitory finger at the still silent Bobby, the still speechless McKie, said:

"I know what you've come for. Family papers. There aren't any. Not now. See!"

He pointed to the grate, filled with a pile of ash. The 'family papers' had been burnt with great thoroughness. First soaked with brandy, Bobby thought, and then, when they had burnt out, more liquid—wine, perhaps—had been poured upon them and the whole mass stirred together.

"That's the end of them," Bobby said slowly. To the Duke he said: "What were they?"

"Don't know, ole boy," the Duke told him. "Never read 'em. Best burnt. Cost me two fifty. Go away, please. My God, my head!" and he lifted both hands to it as if in an effort to hold it still.

"Paid willing as between fren's, value received," said Mrs Sims, interrupting her crooning for a moment and then resuming it.

McKie came across to the Duke. He had a brandy flask in his hand.

"Hair of the dog that bit you," he suggested. He offered his flask to the Duke. "Here, that's enough," he said, withdrawing it when the Duke seemed inclined to finish at one gulp all the flask held. "Feel better?" he asked.

"Yes, thank you, thanks awfully," the Duke said. He got out a handkerchief and wiped his face and hands. He pointed to the prostrate and groaning Sims. "Is he all right?" he asked anxiously.

"He'll be better when he's had a bucket or two of water thrown over him," McKie said.

Bobby said:

"If you feel up to it, hadn't you better tell us what's been happening?"

"Certainly, certainly," agreed the Duke. "All very extraordinary, but all over now. Family papers burnt. I've an act of indemnity, covering all charges of false imprisonment. My friend, Mr Sims, I do hope he'll soon be better, very decent sort really, has my cheque for two hundred and fifty. Most satisfactory all round."

"I suppose these family papers, as you call them," Bobby said, "are those stolen by Sims from young Chrines?"

"Are they?" said the Duke, whom the hair of the dog that bit him seemed to have restored to an almost normal condition. "I don't know. Asked no questions. Why should I? Very decent sort of chap."

"Who? Sims?" asked Bobby. "I've heard him called many other things, but never that before."

"Mr Sims came to see me," the Duke went on. "Ordinary business transaction. He had something to sell. Did I want to buy? Would I like to have them? Family papers. Rooms full of them upstairs. Why not more? He put the price high. Good business man. Always quote your top price first. I said: 'Too much'. I said: 'Not buying any pigs in pokes. Family papers handed over first. And two hundred only, and not a penny more.' He said, 'O.K.' and he would go fetch 'em. I said suppose he forgot to come back and got a better offer from someone else. We argued it out—my poker v. his knife. My poker won—there's an awful lot of sound logic in a poker. So I put him for safe keeps in the old wine-cellar and warned him there he was stopping till I got my family papers."

"In the wine-cellar?" Bobby repeated, slightly dazed.

"In your wine-cellar?" echoed McKie, almost envious.

"That's where the joke was on me," the Duke explained. "I thought it was empty. Sold most of it when the old dad died to help pay death duties and sent the rest to London. Somehow a small case of brandy—Napoleon brandy at that—and bottles of champagne, pre-first war, were overlooked in a corner. Sims found them."

"He would," said McKie. "Trust him. Or me either if I had the chance."

"Next thing," the Duke went on, "was Mrs Sims, worrying about her husband, as a good wife should."

"That's me," said Mrs Sims, still crooning happily to herself on her couch. "Sims is a rat, but Sims is my man."

"I told her," the Duke resumed, "no family papers, no husband; I knew she wouldn't dare go to the police."

"Police?" said Mrs Sims. "Police? Not me. I never could abide busies. Poison."

"But two hundred waiting for the family papers," the Duke added.

"Business deal," said Mrs Sims. "Not blackmail, and busies keep out."

"Family papers there," said the Duke, again nodding towards the ashes in the grate. "Cheque two hundred for them and fifty extra for bill of indemnity against false imprisonment, in Mr Sims's pocket, and everything friendly all round. Sims very cheerful in his cellar, though. Didn't deserve that extra fifty, didn't want to leave cellar. I told him to bring up what was left and we would all have a drink together to show there was no ill feeling."

"Of course not," said Mrs Sims indignantly. "What for should there be?"

"Those family papers," the Duke said. "On my mind. Very much. I didn't know what was in them. I didn't want to know. I didn't want anyone to know. Now no one ever will." He paused and spoke slowly and deliberately. "Not that it mattered. Nothing in them of the least consequence. But better burnt. Thank God."

"Were Stephen Asprey's last poems with them?" Bobby asked.

"I don't know," the Duke said. "I didn't look. I didn't care either. All I cared for was ending a nightmare I thought would drive me mad. Now it's lifted for ever. I feel released. Released. Relaxed. Safe at last from all the hints and gossip that are hell, hell, hell! So I had a drink with Sims. The nightmare all gone. Nothing to keep me awake at night. I went on drinking, we went on drinking, all of us."

"Besh party ever," said Mrs Sims, and that seraphic smile of hers returned—stronger even than before.

"That's all," the Duke said. "Nothing like it since I got sent down. An orgy, they called it then, I remember. That's all," he repeated, and rose suddenly to his feet, shaking again as he did so his admonitory finger at Bobby and at McKie. "Never," he said, "never, whatever you do, no matter how released you feel, never mix brandy and champagne."

"I won't," Bobby promised.

"Chaps like us don't get the chance," said McKie sadly.

"Well, you have the chance now," said the Duke, indicating the bottles on the table. "I don't think they can all be empty."

"Can't they?" said Mrs Sims. "That's all you know, ducks. Ha, ha."

"I don't think there's anything more for me to do here," said Bobby. He turned to McKie. "Coming?" he asked.

McKie shook his head.

"I'll stay around a bit," he answered. "You might tell them at Blegborough to send my car along, will you?"

"You aren't going to try to make one of your blessed exclusives out of all this, are you?" Bobby asked, alarmed.

"They wouldn't print it if I did," McKie said with resignation.

"I'll ask them to try to get hold of a doctor as well," Bobby promised. "I think one had better see Sims."

"He's all right," said Mrs Sims. "He's a rat and always was, but he's all right and you can't touch him. Alibi—and not faked either. Not like them two Bristol tickets to get you so as you would think there was two to pick up. Genuine all through."

She paused to contemplate this unusual fact with considerable surprise and then went on: "With an old pal in Bristol the night the newspaper bloke was done in and same the night the young chap walked into trouble in London. Learn him to go round asking questions. No one should go round asking questions. Asking for trouble, that is. If family papers got pinched— where did young chap get 'em? Tell me that. He won't raise no bother. Knows better. Happy ending all round."

The door opened. An elderly woman stood there. She had a hearing aid in one ear, she held an old-fashioned ear-trumpet to the other. She did not speak at first. She let a severe and disapproving glance travel round the room, and beneath it all visibly quailed. Even Mrs Sims felt it. She rose hastily from her couch.

"We'll be off," she said.

"Oh, Mrs Hopkins," said the Duke. "Er—how is Hopkins?"

"As well as could be hoped," said Mrs Hopkins, "when picked up by me drunk in the hall, as never happened before, and him serving here respectable nigh on seventy years, man and boy, which little did I ever think to live to see the day and trying to excuse himself, as being as good as told he had to," and saying this she surveyed the Duke with a cold, unwavering, accusatory stare.

"I must be going too," Bobby said, a little afraid that that disapproving eye might next be turned upon him, and as he went he heard a voice more icy now than all the polar regions put together.

"Would it be quite convenient, your Grace, if I began now to clear up the—MESS?"

CHAPTER XXXV
THE LAST DISCOVERY

FROM BLEGBOROUGH Bobby drove on to Penton at all speed possible. There was much yet to be seen to, many arrangements to be made before nightfall, much that required his supervision. Precautions had to be taken, too, to prevent any leakage of information; and Bobby was by no means sorry that McKie was safely occupied at Blegborough, well out of the way, for once or twice it had seemed to him that McKie had a better idea of the lone line of thought Bobby had followed than had anyone else. Certainly, it had come to Major Rowley as a profound shock when Bobby first explained to him his suspicions and his intentions. Even Superintendent Evans had been less astonished.

"I've had my doubts all along," Evans had said. "It didn't seem natural like, if you see what I mean."

By nightfall all was ready; and the little cavalcade started off—Bobby, Rowley, Evans, two doctors, two hospital attendants, two Penton constables, stolid and unmoved, for to them all this was just part of their job. Of all the little party, Bobby was in fact the most nervous. He was very conscious that if his careful theorizing, by virtue of which, with no clear fact to be marshalled in support, he had managed to extract the necessary consent from a reluctant Home Office, proved to be ill-founded, then his prestige and authority would be too badly shaken for him to hope to be permitted in the future the kind of independent action to which he always felt he owed so much of his success.

The cars—there were four in all, the one containing the two Penton constables conveying also a good deal of paraphernalia of one sort and another—started at slightly different times and left the town by different routes, so as to avoid attracting attention. At the place arranged on the Hillings road they all met. From it they drove on together, for now the hour was late and they were little likely to be seen. At Hillings church they halted and all alighted. There was nothing to indicate that their arrival had been noticed. Even Hagen's cottage showed no light. In silence Bobby left the others to make their required preparations while he walked on alone to the rectory. He returned soon with an angry, protesting, frightened Mr Day-Bell.

"There were reasons why it was thought better that information about what was intended should be kept back for the time," Bobby explained. Not to much effect. "I am sure the Home Office—"

"Home Office indeed," Mr Day-Bell broke in with an indignant snort. "This is sheer Erastianism. The Established Church has its rights."

Bobby did not attempt to argue the point, especially as he was not quite sure at the moment what Erastianism really was. Also because he had heard in the distance what sounded very like another car coming—and coming fast. A dire suspicion entered his mind. Major Rowley came up to him and said:

"Mrs Asprey's here. She was here when we got here. She says she's staying on. What can we do?"

"If she insists, I don't see that we can do anything," Bobby answered.

Mrs Asprey had followed Major Rowley. She heard these last words. She said:

"You had better not try. The moor is free to all—common land. I've been here every night. Watching. That man"—she pointed a finger at Bobby—"I knew what he wanted to do."

"Do you know why?" Bobby asked.

Without answering, she went back to stand near the Janet Merton grave. The cars in which the party had arrived were now so arranged, the head lamps so directed, that the grave had become as it were an oasis of light in the midst of the surrounding darkness. In this illumined circle men were busily coming and going. Rowley, Evans, and the two doctors were standing watching. Rowley said to Bobby:

"There's a car coming; I can hear it plainly."

"Ten to one it's McKie," Bobby said. "We had better hurry."

"Can't we warn him off?" Rowley said. "A churchyard isn't public property."

"As well try to warn off a hungry tiger from its food," Bobby said. "Besides, what would be the good? He could see all he wanted looking over the churchyard wall."

The car they had been listening to was quite near now. It came at such speed that it was within inches of the wall when McKie brought it to a standstill. He jumped out and hurried towards them. No one took any notice. The two Penton constables had produced spades and picks and had already taken down the headstone. Now the door of Hagen's cottage opened, and he himself came out. He was carrying a powerful hurricane lamp in one hand and he had shovel and pick on his shoulder. He was wearing his working clothes. He came to the grave, and the two constables paused in their work to look at him. He waved them away. He said:

"This is for me, not you."

The two constables looked at Bobby, waiting for orders. Bobby said:

"If he wishes it, he has the better right."

The two men stepped aside. They were more than willing to be spared the gruesome task before them. Hagen put down the hurricane lamp at the edge of the grave and began to work with the silent, swift efficiency born of long practice. In silence he worked and in silence the others watched. Even McKie, who had now joined them, was silent. The only sounds to be heard were those made by pick and shovel as slowly the excavation progressed. It was knee deep now, then deeper still, and still Hagen worked on, steadily, expertly, without pause or rest or speech. It was work he had done before. Abruptly he stopped. He climbed out of the open grave. He said softly, but so clearly all heard him well in that midnight silence broken by no other sound:

"I see a man's hand, and I think it is greeting me."

When he had said this he went aside a little and lay down.

Bobby switched on his electric torch and directed its beam into the open grave, already well lighted by the hurricane lamp on its verge.

Major Rowley said in a kind of strangled whisper:

"Look. Look."

No need to tell them to look. They were all looking. There, thrusting through the dry, disturbed, loosened earth, was what once had been a human hand, was indeed still so recognizable. On a sudden one of the constables gave a loud cry. One of the doctors began to run. The other followed him. They had heard a strange, gurgling sound. The first doctor called out:

"He has cut his throat, cut it to the bone."

Bobby said:

"Do what you can." To the two constables, he said: "Carry on. It will be the body of Henry Thorne, the clergyman who disappeared so long ago, but it must be properly identified. Be careful. Disturb it as little as possible. The coffin must be opened, too. We must make sure whether there is a casket there and, if so, if there's anything in it. Probably not, but we must be certain." He went across to the two doctors, only to be told what he had been sure of from the start. Death had been almost instantaneous. He stood for a moment looking down at the body of one who might, he felt, in other circumstances have been of some service to man in his effort to understand himself and his environment. "Waste," he said aloud. "A high endeavour and an ill ending." He went back to Rowley and said to him: "Hagen may have left a letter or statement of some kind. I expect he has. He saw what was coming, and there was no escape. Don't you think it might be as well to see if there is anything like that?"

Rowley nodded assent. Leaving Evans in charge of what had still to be done, he and Bobby went across to the dead man's cottage.

CHAPTER XXXVI
APOLOGIA

WHAT HAD been chiefly in Bobby's mind when he made this suggestion to Major Rowley was his memory of the MSS he had seen Hagen put away the last time they had talked together. It had been headed, he remembered: 'Apologia'. It was still there in the kitchen table drawer where Hagen had placed it. Bobby took it out, glanced at it, and began to read it aloud, while Rowley listened and took notes. It started:

'Ever since I began to try to think for myself—and that is many years ago—I have kept commonplace books. Twenty-seven of them in all, and all full, though the new one I bought recently has no entry in it yet, and now it may be that it never will have, for I think it likely that the end I have watched, as rabbit watches snake, is now close upon me.

'There have been times when I pleased myself by playing with the notion that these records of my thought, uninterrupted since the day when I started to put down my ideas in writing, might be considered worthy of publication. Or rather, extracts from them, for in all they must contain several million words. When and if, that is, I had succeeded in making clear my belief that there are objective links in all vision, whether drug-inspired, or coming by way of prayer and fasting, or spontaneous in moments of thought and wonder and deep emotion, or even in the dreams that come to us sometimes in sleep. In all these varieties of experience we are translated, knowing another circle of being that should be higher but may be lower, but that in either case has as clear an objective reality, existing independently, in its own right, as the material world we know, that in which we live and move and have our being, and whose identity continues through the changing conditions of time and accident all creatures, having what we call life, experience from day to day. The axiom that we never step into the same river twice is merely a bald truism. What is important is the sameness which permits the same river always to be there.

'It follows, then, I think, unless my reasoning is sadly at fault, that it should be possible, conditions being fully understood, for all intelligences, no matter dressed in what appearance, whether of our human flesh or otherwise, to move freely from one sphere of being to another, and then to return with full knowledge and understanding, able to report on these other spheres in absolute truth and being, and so make plain to all what is our complete environment in sober factual reality.

'Now, what a quest is there, and yet I gather from the chatter I hear from time to time that there are those who vex themselves with plans for what they call "space travel", and are concerned to be the first to reach the moon, though they reach it and return no different from what they were when they set out, with no greater knowledge or understanding of themselves, but only of another piece of matter in transient form. My quest is other.

'This thesis I believed or hoped I might be able to sustain by such convincing argument, once I had made my reasoning clear, as to give to metaphysics a new vitality, a new significance. But I doubt if any but myself could even begin to put together a coherent scheme out of these necessarily disjointed jottings of mine in my commonplace books, or to follow what I know must seem to others the confused and wandering thread of my thought. So many false starts, so much apparently sound logic that so often ended in blind alleys of contradiction.

'Nor does it now seem likely that I shall be allowed the time to essay a task that possibly I myself should never have been able to bring to completion. It may be that in the great final plan the role assigned to me was that of path-finder and to that I have been called on to sacrifice myself.

'Indeed, there have been times, as my good Jesuit friend warned me recently, when it seemed even to me that I was trying to force an entry into realms of being and experience for which no human being is yet ready.

'However that may be, all that I have ever mused on, all the fruit of my long meditations, is recorded in that great pile of my commonplace books. But this that I am writing now will appear in none. None will read it while I live, and if I live through these next few days, it will be burned. What makes it necessary, I wonder, that I should put it down in writing on paper? Can it be that in some strange way, by thus repeating in words what was done in deed, I shall rid myself of the burden of that deed?

'I had always known that there were some who wished to recover the letters and papers the poet, Stephen Asprey, had placed in Janet Merton's grave. But the possibility seemed remote in the extreme, since I knew that the freeholder of the grave would never consent to such an act of what she called desecration. Yet at that time I, too, felt it unfortunate, indeed wrong, that the last poems of a man like Stephen Asprey, and his letters, which there was good reason to believe were of outstanding literary value, should be lost by reason of a moment of profound emotion.

'It seemed a waste; and I have always been forced by poverty to be so economical that waste to me has always been abhorrent.

'But then there came a time when I was obliged to realize that the movement to recover these MSS was becoming much stronger and, if carried out—as it seemed it well might be—then the way I had chosen to conceal Mr Thorne's body, which till then had seemed so safe, would prove my destruction.

'If it had been hidden elsewhere, and afterwards I thought of so many places where it would have been equally safe, then the grave could be opened and no suspicions roused. That the casket was empty would have been taken merely as confirmation of what had been already suggested more than once—that the story of its containing the poems and letters was merely a bit of the characteristic play-acting Asprey so often indulged in. Humbug. And not the least suspicion would ever have rested on me or on young Chrines.

'For it was with him that it began which now I think is near its end. The combination of what Chrines wanted, of Mr Thorne's angry jealousy, of Mr Pyle's sudden intrusion, wove together the threads of the web in which I am taken.

'Soon after Chrines's first arrival in Hillings he told me he was a son of Stephen Asprey and of Janet Merton. The dates made it hard to accept that she was his mother, but he had letters that did support his claim that Asprey was his father. Chrines said he intended to write a life of his father and had come to Hillings because he felt that writing it on the scene of Asprey's last passionate love affair would be an inspiration—and give it actuality and attract general attention.

'Soon he began to hint that he would be willing to pay well for the recovery of the Asprey poems and letters. He kept saying it was what his father himself would have wished once he had got over the shock of Janet's death.

'I saw no great harm in all that, but, harmless or not, I felt I did not wish to be mixed up in it.

'I did not know then how fate was loading the dice against me.

'Earlier, when Mr Thorne first became aware of my craving for knowledge—it was a passion like that of the lover for his mistress—he was kind, encouraging, helpful in every way. He helped me with my Latin. He lent me books. He had a good library. He even had what I must call a wholly superficial, routine knowledge of metaphysics. I think at first it amused him to tell his friends of his sexton's efforts to aspire to scholarship. Then that changed. Slowly, but it changed. I think it started when once or twice I had occasion to correct his Latin in translations he was endeavouring to make from Cicero. Then I wrote to *The Herbert Quarterly*, criticizing an article they had published. The editor suggested my putting my criticism into another article. I did so and it was published. I showed it to Mr Thorne, expecting him to be almost as pleased as I was. I did not know then that contributions he had offered to the same journal had been promptly returned. I began to find it difficult to get him to lend me the books I needed for my studies. I found I was being cut off from my sources. Some of the books I needed so badly I could obtain by or through the Penton Library. But not all, and not those I needed most. These I had to buy to have them by me, though I had no money, and though I knew they were there on the rectory shelves, unused.

'Well, that made me think again of the money Chrines had hinted he would pay for the recovery of the Asprey papers, and of those books I needed so badly but had no money to buy. The next time he came with his hints I told him that I would see what I could do. But he must not ask how, and he must pay beforehand in one-pound notes.

'He agreed.

'In some way Mr Thorne must have become suspicious, and I think now that he had begun to watch me.

'When the next dark night came I opened the grave. It did not take me long. I took the papers from the casket, and then I put it back in the coffin, and as I did so I heard Mr Thorne say:

'"So that's it, is it?"

'I climbed out of the grave. He said he would report it to the police. He talked about how disgraceful my conduct was. Then he said he would show me more mercy than I deserved. I must sign a full confession for him to have and keep. I must promise to give up my absurd pretensions to learning. I must devote myself entirely for the future to my proper work. He said that it was plain my attempts to become a scholar, and the encouragement given me so generously, had gone to my head and I had to be taught my place.

'I listened. I never said a word. I listened while he talked and talked. I stood there and listened, leaning on the pick-axe I had been using. I think that I was so silent made him still more angry and all he said became still more bitter. When he had finished, I lifted the pick-axe and drove at him. The sharp point took him on the side of the head. I don't expect he ever knew what had happened.

'I remember standing there looking at him as he lay, and wondering if I had done it or if the deed had got itself done through me?

'I pushed the body into the open grave so that it lay on the coffin. I filled in the earth and made all as it had been before. I returned home and made myself a cup of cocoa before going to bed. I remember how well and soundly I slept, though that did not last.

'I told Chrines it would be our opportunity to secure the papers he wanted as soon as the search for Mr Thorne died down. If they were ever missed, I said, then it would be thought that Mr Thorne had taken them and that that accounted for their disappearance. That satisfied him. He might have been suspicious of some connection if I had handed him the papers immediately after Mr Thorne vanished.

'I took other precautions, such as telling everyone what a good friend I had lost and how he had lent me money to buy books. I was afraid it might come out I had been spending more money than I could well account for, on rare and expensive books. I even put a part of what was left of the money Chrines had given me in a drawer at the rectory, and let it be understood that it was some Mr Thorne had lent me and I had just repaid.

'Not the slightest suspicion ever attached itself to me.

'It seemed that I was perfectly safe and that Mr Thorne's disappearance would become one of the great unsolved and unsolvable mysteries one hears of from time to time. I was sorry, of course, for what had happened, but I could not blame myself unduly.

'I had been tried beyond endurance. What I had done had been forced upon me.

'He had wished to kill my mind and I had killed his body. A lesser evil and one committed in self-defence.

'But deeds are seeds that bear in themselves their own growth and fruit.

'I had soon to realize that by my action I had made myself the prisoner of a grave.

'For now I did not dare to be away from it for long.

'Of course, there still stood between me and it Miss Christabel's determination and her power as freeholder to forbid any such desecration of her aunt's grave. I knew I could rely on that. I knew that nothing would ever shake her resolve. But then later I had to realize that with all the renewed interest being taken in those buried letters and poems, permission might be secured to override her rights. Or such influences be brought to bear as she would not have the power to resist. Or even that attempts might be made by unscrupulous parties to open the grave and obtain them in defiance of all law and right.

'I had to remain ever watchful and afraid. Fortunately my vigilance aroused no suspicion. It was attributed to my need for the money I obtained from visiting tourists who guessed so little what the grave they gaped at, and sentimentalized over, really hid.

'The crisis came when Mr Pyle arrived, explaining that he, too, intended to write Stephen Asprey's life. What, I wonder, made him decide on him? Are there not so many others he could have chosen? Or was it only the necessary outcome of what I had done, as from the sowing of dragon's teeth, death must ensue? He hinted—it was hardly a hint—that he would pay a large sum—much larger than that Chrines had given me—for help in recovering the buried papers. He said I need know nothing about it. All I had to do was to stay sound asleep one night. I made it equally plain that nothing of the sort would even be considered by me. My stubborn, determined refusal would have surprised him less if he had known the reason. But in his turn he made it plain that he was determined to have the grave opened and would use all his influence to get permission. And if not—well, he didn't say, but when I caught him and his man, Sims, by its side at night, reconnoitering, I knew.

'That is why in the end I had to kill him.

'It was my life or his, and I felt it had to be his, since mine was so much more valuable. All he wanted was the kudos of writing a popular biography. What I wanted was to change, extend, the whole field of human knowledge.

'The opportunity soon came. I knew it would. I was prepared. I knew Mr Day-Bell had a revolver belonging to his son he had taken from Miss Christabel and put away and forgotten. I had no trouble getting hold of it, and then there was Sims, late at night, borrowing my bicycle. He said Mr Pyle wanted him to do his dirty work and he wasn't going to. He said if he did, Mr Owen would be on him at once. And he didn't like monkeying with the dead. "Monkeying with the dead." That made it clear once more what Mr Pyle intended—and soon. It had become urgent. And Sims to put the police off. I felt certain he had stolen money and would keep out of the way for a time. I went across to the caravan and I shot Mr Pyle and set the caravan on fire. I gather now Mr Day-Bell saw me, but did not recognize me. It was misty on the moor that night, and perhaps he thought it was his son.

'I was sorry, of course, but Pyle had brought it on himself.

'Before this, Mr Owen—the man from Scotland Yard Sims seemed so afraid of—had been to talk to me. He said he wanted to be sure the grave had not been disturbed, as the Duke of Blegborough was making inquiries. Mr Owen asked a great many questions I had no difficulty in answering, though my words often bore a hidden meaning he did not suspect. Chatty and pleasant enough, he seemed. Not of any high intelligence, of course. Any abstract thought would probably be far beyond him. A practical intelligence, I judged, but with a quick, probing quality about it. I felt at times as if he were trying to insinuate himself into my mind. Not with much success.

'After there had happened what had to be, he came again. I had not expected that. I had thought that the Penton people would be the ones to deal with it. He came to me several times, still asking his questions, interminably chatting, as if at random, interminably returning to what he called the case. I answered more warily now. I began to feel it had not been wise to say so much earlier on that had had hidden undertones I did not think he could possibly appreciate. I began to be afraid that something I had said had made him deeply suspicious. I can't imagine what, but I am increasingly aware of the possibility that he suspects—or knows.

'So again I am taking precautions.

'And he again is continuing those chatty talks that often seem to have so little relevance, but that you feel may slowly, drop by drop, be distilling forth the truth.

'He came again and left me feeling certain that he knows, and that he knows where proof is waiting—waiting as patiently as only the dead can wait.

'The odd thing is that often it comes to me that he wishes he did not know and that the truth was other than it irrevocably remains. Even that he is sorry about it all. Perhaps he has penetrated more deeply into my mind than I dreamed was possible. Somehow we have come to respect one another, even I might say to like and to understand one another. Not that that will stay him from doing what he holds to be his duty—or me from doing what remains for me to do.'

CHAPTER XXXVII
CONCLUSION

LATER ON Bobby had to return to Penton to appear as a witness at the two inquests, though he was careful to say as little as possible, nor indeed was he pressed to be more explicit. The notoriety given to the little town had not been appreciated. The sooner a decent veil was drawn over recent happenings the better, was the general opinion.

In the first inquest—that on the body of Mr Thorne—the verdict was inescapable—'Wilful Murder'—the earlier suggestion 'Guilty but Insane' having been rejected by the Coroner as unacceptable. The verdict in the second inquest, however, could be, and was, 'Suicide during temporary insanity', and that met with general approval. The emphasis thus laid in both cases on insanity as the cause of what had happened was due partly to this feeling that the less said about it all, the better; partly to a vague but general feeling of compassion; but chiefly perhaps to the fact that certain portions of the 'Apologia' had been read in court.

"Don't make sense to me," the foreman had declared while the verdict was being considered, "and I don't reckon it did to him or to anyone else either," and there had come a general murmur of assent from the other members of the jury.

Major Rowley, too, was of much the same opinion, and said so to Bobby later on.

"All that stuff," he complained, "about circles of existence all round us, only we don't know it; and pink elephants and rats being real; and did he do it or did it get itself done through him? Well, I ask you. Off his head all right. Clean mad."

"Not so much madness as vanity," Bobby said. "He came to think so much of himself and his own work that he lost all sense of proportion. A sort of madness, I suppose. I don't think I've ever had a case where vanity wasn't somewhere at the bottom of it all."

"I suppose there's that," Rowley conceded. "But you know I don't even yet quite follow how you arrived at it all. Is there anything in what Hagen said about feeling he had let something slip which had made you suspect him?"

"Well, yes," Bobby answered. "A queerly ironical twist. I thought Hagen must be lying when he told me he had seen Sims cleaning a revolver. I knew Sims had a superstitious fear of all firearms because he had been told that the cards showed he would die from a shot he would fire himself. So he had sworn he would never touch a gun of any sort. Used a knife instead. So I thought Hagen was lying and if so—well, why? That made me feel he had to be watched and yet all the time what he had said was true. Except that Sims hadn't been cleaning the gun—he had been fixing the safety-catch, to make sure that the thing couldn't be fired or the prophecy come true.

"That's what started me off wondering about Hagen. My first idea was that he was behind the anonymous letters the Duke had been getting. But that seemed to link up with the Asprey papers, and did they in their turn link up with Mr Thorne's unexplained disappearance? Long before I found out Hagen had spoken the truth about Sims I was beginning to take notice of other small points and to wonder if they didn't add up to something pretty serious. Perhaps they didn't, but also perhaps they did.

"I remembered I had heard Mr Day-Bell say in a joking sort of way that he was growing quite jealous of Hagen. Embarrassing, he said, to have a sexton who was a better Latinist than you were yourself. I wondered if the vanished Mr Thorne had felt the same and if that had led to ill-feeling and possibly to a quarrel. From young Day-Bell I got confirmation that there had been such jealousy and ill-feeling, if nothing more. He told me, too, of his surprise at hearing that Mr Thorne had been lending Hagen money and that some of it had been repaid immediately before his disappearance. I couldn't for the life of me see at the time what was the significance of that, but I felt I had better keep it tucked away in my mind. Oddities seemed to be accumulating, and oddities need accounting for.

"One oddity that struck me as very odd indeed was Hagen's apparently fixed determination to stay at Hillings and to refuse all offers of a change, even those that appeared likely to give him what one would have expected him to want more than anything else—the opportunity that is, to consort on equal terms with people interested in all that most interested him and ready to help him. He compared his craving for knowledge, you remember, to the craving of a passionate lover for the beloved one's presence. He didn't act like that, and I wondered why. Was there some reason no one had any idea of?

"Then, once I had begun to feel like that, I noticed that many of his answers could bear a double meaning. He assured me, and so earnestly I couldn't help but feel he was speaking the truth, that by no possibility could the grave have been opened without his knowledge. Well, had it been opened with his knowledge? I even felt that he had talked a little oddly the first time I saw him about the dead lying still in their quiet graves, and it came to me after a time that he might have some reason for fearing that was not always true. It worried me a bit.

"I felt the oddities were mounting up in a rather odd way.

"I began to notice, too, that even quite little things were beginning to point the same way. I took pains to let Hagen know that the recovery of the revolver used in the murder was important and might provide the necessary evidence. Also I said that I expected it would be found by some of the small boys you had put on the job. Next morning it was found—found by small boys, as I had told Hagen I thought might happen. And again I didn't find it quite natural that Hagen, instead of taking charge of the revolver himself, should simply have told the boys to be careful and to take it to the police. It almost suggested he had no wish to handle it himself. Trifles light as air, of course, and hardly even any sort of confirmation. But I noticed them all the same.

"Then there was Chrines. Was he here wholly and solely for local colour? He claimed to possess important family papers, as he called them. He also claimed and tried to persuade himself that he was a son of Asprey and of Janet Merton. Was he hoping the letters, if he could get hold of them, might support that claim? Another complication was that suggestions were apparently reaching the Duke that the Asprey papers, said to have been buried with Janet Merton, had come into some third party's hands. The whole case seemed in one way or another to be mixed up with those buried poems and letters.

"The final, and what I felt was the conclusive, piece of evidence came when I found that a sonnet Chrines had included with his own poems as his own work was identified both by Professor Long and by Mrs Asprey as having been written by Stephen Asprey himself, one of his very last poems, and one that therefore should have been with the other last poems in the Merton grave. That was the one solid fact, as apart from theory and inference, I was able to produce, and but for it I don't believe I should ever have got the necessary authority for the opening. By that time, though, putting all I knew together, I had quite convinced myself that in the Janet Merton grave Mr Thorne's body lay hidden. That I felt was the secret of his disappearance."

"Well, it turned out that way in the end," Rowley admitted, but still as if he didn't quite know why.

"I should have found myself in jolly hot water if it hadn't," Bobby admitted in his turn. "But by that time I had to know. I simply had to make sure. By the way, do you know if it is true that Mrs Asprey collected young Chrines from the hospital and went off with him?"

"She told me she was giving up Two Mile End," Rowley answered, "and going back to Bristol. Apparently she was intending to look after young Chrines till he was better. She said she was a sort of step-mother in a way, and mothering was what he wanted. Oh, and I was to tell you it was all your doing, the way you bullied her into it. I don't know what she meant."

"I'm sure I don't," Bobby protested indignantly. "Bullying Mrs Asprey, indeed! Sorry for anyone who tried. All I did was to tell her Chrines was a young ass who needed someone to look after him—as far as that goes, she'll be all the better, too, for someone to look after."

"Probably that's what she meant," Rowley remarked thoughtfully. "Do you know, there was something she said made me think that she had believed at first Chrines was guilty?"

"I had that idea myself once or twice," Bobby said. "She told me she knew who it was but she wasn't going to say. And then she made a rather feeble attempt to make me believe she meant Christabel Merton. I rather imagine that at first her suspicions gave her an odd sort of respect for him and made her feel she had misjudged him, as a mere weakling, and then, when she found that was all wrong, she felt she ought to try to make up to him for having again misjudged him. Muddled thinking, but I imagine it was more or less like that. Not thinking so much as feeling."

"Women don't think, they feel," Rowley pronounced. "Another thing she said, just as she was going, was that if you ever came snooping Bristol way and wanted a cup of tea, you could come and see her. I took her up pretty smartly about 'snooping', but she went off without listening."

"She would," agreed Bobby. "Very good of her to suggest a cup of tea—if, that is, she didn't mean a broom-and-slop-pail tea. Have you any idea what happened to all those commonplace books of Hagen's?"

"Gone to the incinerator," Rowley answered. "First thing the executor did. A cousin of his—landlord of the 'Bull and Bell' here. He said they were no use to anyone or any good and best got rid of."

THE END

FIND THE LADY

Originally published in the Evening Standard,
21 December, 1950

THE SMALL writing-room of the Hotel Nimini, Bloomsbury, was full of bustling, living men, and one who was dead.

All were very busy, each with his own special job, except the dead man, slumped in his chair, and Sergeant Bobby Owen, standing with his back to the blazing fire.

The doctor said:

"Death must have been pretty nearly instantaneous. Stabbed to the heart. Pity you haven't got the knife."

The Inspector said:

"Ah, that would have been evidence, that would."

The fingerprint expert said:

"As fine a set of dabs as you could ask for. A woman's. The table must have been fresh polished to take 'em like that."

The hotel manager said:

"Every morning, first thing. That's routine. Room dusted. Furniture polished. Fire made up for the morning. Routine. You can't run a hotel without routine."

The Inspector said:

"It wasn't robbery. Wallet stuffed with notes. Gold watch."

One of his assistants said:

"There's been a woman. If it was not robbery, then it was jealousy."

Sergeant Bobby Owen turned round and began to warm his hands at the fire.

The police photographer said:

"Isn't it hot enough in here, for you, Sarge? Suffocating, if you ask me."

The doctor said:

"I wish I could keep a fire like that in my surgery. Can't get delivery. I've allowed for the temperature of the room, Inspector, in my estimate of the time of death. Ten o'clock at the earliest and probably a little later."

The hotel manager said:

"Our cellar's nearly empty. I don't know what Jake was thinking of, a fire like that. Trustworthy, careful man. Jake. Must have thought he was stoking the furnace."

Sergeant Bobby Owen said, over his shoulder:

"It's 11 o'clock now."

The Inspector said:

"There's a clock in the room we can all see for ourselves, Owen, thank you. I thought I asked you to make a plan of the room. Don't stand there all day doing nothing."

Bobby Owen said:

"Sorry, sir. I was only thinking."

The Inspector said:

"Dreaming, you mean."

The hotel manager said:

"A thing like this does a hotel no good. Frightens people. Old and valued client, though a bit too friendly sometimes with the staff—the female staff."

The Inspector said:

"Hell, there's the set-up."

He sat down at the table and began to write. Bobby Owen left the fire and went to the door. It opened on a long passage which a woman was busy scrubbing. She was in a bad temper because she foresaw very clearly that with all this traipsing to and fro she would probably have to do her work all over again, as already she had had to do in part. When Bobby opened the door she scowled at him as if she held him personally and solely responsible.

Bobby said:

"You are quite certain that the lady you told us about is the only person who went into the writing-room while you were working here?"

The charwoman said:

"How many more times do you want to be told? All alone the poor gentleman was, as I'll take my dying oath, and then she come along like as there wasn't a minute to spare, as well I remember, seeing she kicked my pail and splashed a lot of soapy water over what I had just dried, and only God's mercy it wasn't pail and all, but never took no notice or apologized or nothing, and then I heard 'em talking, which I suppose I ought to have been listening at the keyhole and been able to tell you all they said. But such isn't my way, even though they was talking pretty loud, so it wouldn't have been no keyhole required if I had wanted, which I didn't. Not my way, it isn't."

Bobby said:

"I'm sure it isn't."

The charwoman said:

"Not as any keyhole was needed, if I had wanted. Fair shouting at each other they was, the two of them."

Bobby said:

"You told the Inspector you couldn't describe the lady, didn't you?"

The charwoman said:

"Same as I couldn't, not giving her so much as a look, but grabbing hold of the pail, for fear of it upsetting. That's how guests is. Always in the way. Now staff, you don't ever need to notice, them having their work to do, same as you, so they gets out of your way and you gets out of theirs.

"But guests ain't like that. Always where they can muck up the work the most. Staff's different. Staff steps careful, minding pails and such, and not stepping where it's still wet and soapy before dried. But not guests. Gives your pail a kick and never notices or apologize nor nothing, but back again from in that there room on the run and gone before you could say Jack Robinson, which ain't in no way surprising, seeing what she had been and done."

One of the other C.I.D. men put his head out of the room. He said:

"The old man's in a paddy, Sarge, you slipping off like that. Wants you at once."

Bobby said he was sorry and went back into the room. The Inspector was looking very cross. He said:

"What the devil's the matter with you this morning, Owen? How much longer am I to be kept waiting for that plan?" Bobby said again he was sorry. But he said it in an absent-minded, perfunctory manner, and the Inspector was in no way appeased. To the hotel manager, Bobby said:

"Has the charwoman outside been here long?"

The hotel manager said:

"Who? Her? No. Why? A day or two. You don't think she had anything to do with it, do you?"

The Inspector said, and only the general rule that sergeants should not be rebuked before constables prevented him from saying a whole lot more:

"For the Lord's sake, Owen."

Bobby did not seem even to be aware of the Inspector's muffled wrath. He said, still to the hotel manager:

"Got a new under-porter, too, haven't you?"

The hotel manager said:

"New kitchen-porter? Why? How did you know?"

The fingerprint man said exultingly:

"Got another prize set of dabs. That's proof that is. Open and shut in quick time."

Bobby said:

"Nothing to do but find the lady?"

The fingerprint man said:

"That's right."

Bobby said:

"Inspector, may I have five minutes before I start on the plan? I think I can be back with the murderer in that time, only I'm afraid if I'm not quick, there's a risk of important evidence being destroyed."

The Inspector didn't say anything because he was for the moment incapable of speech. But for the fact that it was morning, he would certainly have suspected drink.

The doctor chuckled. He said:

"Quick work—five minutes. May I stop and see the lady— when produced?"

The Inspector, recovering slightly, said, with almost complete self-possession:

"Very good, Sergeant Owen, very good indeed. Five minutes? Five minutes then. Mind, not a second more. And if you aren't back in that time, murderer and all, then I think I shall have to ask the Super if he can spare time for a chat with you—five minutes, not one half second more."

Bobby said:

"Yes, sir, thank you, sir, very much indeed. It shouldn't really take that long, only I want to be on the safe side."

It was in less than three that he was back. He was carrying a bucket of coal. A small, nearly bald man, his face very dirty, in very dirty working clothes, was with him. A little mouse of a man he seemed; and yet he held his head high and somehow he was clothed as with a strange and distant dignity.

Without waiting for Bobby to speak, he said—while all stared and gaped—and his voice was calm and perfectly steady:

"That's right. I did it. Though how you knew so soon I can't think, and even where I had the knife hid."

Bobby lifted the coal bucket. He said:

"In here. That's why I wanted to hurry. I was afraid the knife would go into the furnace with the next lot of coal."

The Inspector said—in gasps:

"But—but I mean to say—well, how did you guess?"

Bobby said:

"Well, sir, I heard stoking up the furnace mentioned and, of course, it was obvious that would be a very satisfactory final way of disposing of the weapon."

The little mouse of a man said:

"That's how I had it worked out. Another minute or two and the coal in that bucket, and the knife with it, would all have gone into the furnace together. What about your evidence then?"

Bobby said:

"The bucket was near the furnace, all in line for the next stoking."

The little man said:

"Another five minutes and I would have gone to lunch and I wouldn't have come back. Well, you were too quick for me and maybe this way's best."

The Inspector said:

"But there's only been a woman in here and no one else. That's what the charwoman outside swore and stuck to it."

Bobby said:

"She was only thinking of the people staying in the hotel—the guests. She told me you never noticed staff.

"What put me on to the truth in the first place was the fire. If the fire was made up first thing to last all morning, as the hotel manager said, why at 11 o'clock was it blazing the way it was? It ought to have been beginning to die down. Had fresh coal been added? To provide an excuse for entering the room without attracting attention?

"Then, too, the manager happened to say he was getting short of coal, so was it likely a man like Jake he called careful and trustworthy—I took Jake to be the head porter— would be so wasteful? I asked if the charwoman was new and so unlikely to notice any change in routine, and that someone else was doing what the man, Jake, generally did.

"Well, she was, and so I asked if there was a new under-porter, and anyhow there was a new kitchen-porter. It all seemed to fit."

The fingerprint man said:

"Best set of dabs ever—and all for nothing."

The little mouse-like man said:

"That's right. Got it all worked out. No one noticed me. Why should they? He didn't—him in the chair there. He just looked up and went on writing and I put the coal on and then I came back by where he was sitting and writing, and I put the knife in him. and I don't reckon he knew a thing till he was dead.

"You see, that was my wife you were looking for, my wife he took from me and then he ditched her. He took my wife from me, so I took his life from him. Fair enough?"